Rosamund grinned at Will like the urchin she felt herself to be.

The play as always unfolded before her, laying out its riches as if onto a magic carpet, transporting her to a world far from her own. At the end, she applauded wildly, her eyes dazed with wonder.

"You enjoyed it." Will stated the obvious with a pleased smile. He couldn't take his eyes off Rosamund's radiant countenance and her light-filled green eyes. The page's costume she wore excited him with a sense of the forbidden. It revealed the lines and contours of her body in a way that thrilled him. She was so small and shapely, her hips and buttocks curving in a soft swell in the trunk hose, her bosom a mere hint below the doublet.

"What are you looking at?" Rosamund had never seen that hungry, lustful look on a man's face before. It made her feel hot, her skin tight and prickly, but it excited her, too, gave her a feeling of power even as her body stirred beneath it.

"You." Will shook his head as if he could thus dispel his disturbing fantasy. "Sweet heaven, Rosamund, if I'd known what those clothes would do. . . ."

"Rich in period detail."
—*Booklist*

"A truly fantastic novel."
—**The Romance Readers Connection**

"Terrific."
—Genre Go Round Reviews

All the Queen's Play

ALSO BY JANE FEATHER

Rushed to the Altar
A Husband's Wicked Ways
To Wed a Wicked Prince
A Wicked Gentleman
Almost a Lady
Almost a Bride
The Wedding Game
The Bride Hunt
The Bachelor List

"Holiday Gamble" in the *Snowy Night with a Stranger*
anthology

JANE FEATHER

ALL THE QUEEN'S PLAYERS

POCKET BOOKS

New York   London   Toronto   Sydney

Pocket Books
A Division of Simon & Schuster, Inc.
1230 Avenue of the Americas
New York, NY 10020

This book is a work of fiction. Names, characters, places, and incidents either are products of the author's imagination or are used fictitiously. Any resemblance to actual events or locales or persons, living or dead, is entirely coincidental.

Copyright © 2010 by Jane Feather

First Pocket Books paperback edition February 2011

POCKET BOOKS and colophon are registered trademarks of Simon & Schuster, Inc.

For information about special discounts for bulk purchases, please contact Simon & Schuster Special Sales at 1-866-506-1949 or business@simonandschuster.com.

The Simon & Schuster Speakers Bureau can bring authors to your live event. For more information or to book an event contact the Simon & Schuster Speakers Bureau at 1-866-248-3049 or visit our website at www.simonspeakers.com.

Manufactured in the United States of America

Cover design by Lisa Litwack
Cover illustration by Larry Rostant

10 9 8 7 6 5 4 3 2 1

ISBN 978-1-4516-1302-5
ISBN 978-1-4391-6898-1 (ebook)

ALL THE
QUEEN'S PLAYERS

Prologue

THEY HAD COME to her the previous evening. Amyas Paulet, her jailer and Puritan tormentor, and dear, loyal Shrewsbury, who had looked as if it were his own impending death he had come to announce.

It was Shrewsbury who had spoken, tears running down his cheeks. Her death warrant, signed by the queen, had been received. She was to die in the Great Hall at eight o'clock the following morning. Little enough time for her final preparations, the letters to be written, the disposition of her personal possessions, her final confession. But the death warrant had come as no surprise for all the unseemly haste of its execution.

And so here she was, at the appointed time, in the Great Hall. It was a bitterly cold morning, still dark outside. Within, sconced candles threw shadows against the walls. Her visitors of the previous evening stood behind the newly erected scaffold at the far end. Other members of the household, together with the sheriff and his men, her ladies, with the exception of the two who attended close beside her on this, her last walk, stood against the walls, some with downcast eyes as she approached the scaffold.

Mary became aware of her little Skye terrier pressing

into the voluminous folds of her black velvet skirts. She paused for an instant, her gaze roaming the hall, lingering on the faces of those who had come to witness her death. Her eyes stopped, rested on the face of a woman, younger than her other ladies. She raised a hand and the young woman stepped forward and came over to her. She curtsied low.

"Rosamund, will you take my dog?" Mary asked softly. "I fear he may become distressed if he remains too close to me."

"Of course, madam." Rosamund bent and picked up the little creature, caressing his rough head. She stepped back into place again, and the Queen of Scots continued to the scaffold.

Mary mounted the five steps. A disrobing stool stood beside the block, a kneeling cushion in front of it. She averted her eyes from the bloodstained butcher's ax. Presumably all they could find at such short notice, she reflected. Royal castles did not, in general, include a headsman's ax among their furnishings. Fleetingly she wondered if they had remembered to sharpen it after its last use on some luckless animal.

But there was no time now for further thought. Her ladies and executioners were moving to disrobe her. She removed her cross and the Agnus Dei from around her neck, giving them to her attendants as she blessed them both with a prayer and the sign of the cross.

Her executioners knelt for forgiveness and she smiled, saying clearly, "I forgive you for you are about to end my troubles." Her ladies fastened a Corpus Christi cloth over her face, a veil that she herself had embroidered.

Rosamund Walsingham held the little terrier against her breast, turning its eyes away from the scaffold. Her own remained riveted as the executioners and the two women removed Mary Stuart's black gown, two petticoats, and her corset, until she stood only in her petticoat and chemise. Both garments were scarlet, the color of martyrdom. Rosamund knew she must be sure to include that detail in her report to Sir Francis. There were official witnesses of this execution, but Sir Francis Walsingham would, as always, demand from her a personal, unofficial, and totally accurate description of even the most minute and seemingly irrelevant detail.

Mary Stuart smiled faintly as they undressed her and made some soft comment to the executioners that Rosamund could not hear. Her attendants helped the queen to kneel, and Mary placed her head upon the block, her hands gripping the wood on either side.

One of the executioners moved her hands, and Rosamund shuddered at the significance. Had they been left there, they would have been struck off with the head. Mary Stuart stretched out her arms behind her and offered her final prayers in loud, clear tones.

The little dog whimpered against Rosamund's breast as her arms tightened convulsively with the first stroke of the ax. In horror, she saw that the ax had missed its target and had struck the back of the victim's head. Mary's lips moved soundlessly. The ax fell again.

Rosamund closed her eyes when the executioner sawed at the last remaining tendon that held the woman's head still affixed to her neck. And then he lifted the head free, declaiming, "God save the Queen."

A collective gasp of shock ran around the gathering as the veil that had been fastened to her hair came free in the man's hand, and with it the long auburn tresses of a wig. Mary Stuart's own hair was short and gray. The head fell to the straw, and the face was that of an old woman, barely recognizable as the tall, elegant, auburn-haired beauty of before.

It was over at last. Rosamund, soothing the terrier with soft words and a gentle hand, joined the mass exodus from the Great Hall as the sheriff and his men prepared to take the body abovestairs to where the surgeons waited to embalm it.

Her legs started to tremble and at the head of the stairs she sat down on the wide stone ledge of a mullioned window and gazed out at the Northamptonshire countryside. How responsible had *she*, Rosamund Walsingham, been for Mary's execution? She had borne some part in it . . . had had no choice but to do so. She just hadn't realized how her participation in that secret world ruled by her fearsome cousin Francis could be used, twisted to suit his purposes. She should have known, of course. Her brother Thomas had dropped enough hints, but his little sister had thought herself impregnable, safe behind the fortress walls of her own self-will. But she should have remembered what was said about those who touched pitch.

Her hands were clammy and she felt her heart begin to race. She tried to remember what Kit Marlowe had told her of the actor's trick of breathing to overcome stage fright. Or maybe it had been Ned Alleyn? It would make better sense, he was after all an actor. Kit lived and breathed the stage, but he had never trodden the boards. His passion lay in playmaking.

This dark, dank imprisonment seemed to have lasted an eternity. What she would give for another tantalizing glimpse of the wonderful boisterous, roistering, down and dirty wildness of the players' lives.

She thought of Will, and that one glorious afternoon

they'd spent with the players. Perhaps by now Will, if he was not performing some service for Sir Francis, was back in their midst, drinking with the players, applauding in the pits, eagerly showing his own attempts at playmaking to Kit, or Thomas Watson, or Tom Kyd. And when he was not among the players and playmakers, he would be at court playing his lute, reciting his verses, singing his love songs. Will was a courtier who knew he must make himself pleasant to those who mattered. He had perfected the skills, observed the manners and techniques of those older and more experienced than he in the art of influence peddling so necessary to survival in Elizabeth's court. And yet Rosamund would never forget the mischievous glint in his eye, the wicked spontaneous suggestions that led them both into paths that should not have been trodden.

That night in the buttery at Chartley seemed to have happened to two other people in another life. Even her arrival at Fotheringay seemed a thing of distant memory. And only a few months later, it had brought her to this day of Mary's death.

The little terrier wriggled in her arms and licked her chin. She carried him to the inner apartments where Mary and her ladies had been housed. The Queen of Scots' bedchamber door was open and servants were stripping the bed of its hangings. Already the sense of death, of finality, lay heavy over the chamber, and the little dog whined.

Twelve months ago Rosamund Walsingham had barely given the Queen of Scots a second thought, and now she wept for her, cradling the terrier against her breast, her tears falling thickly on his head.

But her servitude here would soon be over, Rosamund thought. The queen did not easily forgive the offenses of those she considered she had favored, but maybe her

Chapter One

Scadbury Park, Chiselhurst, Kent, May 1586

THE LEMONY LIGHT of the early-spring sun seemed to accentuate the delicate new greenery of the apple trees and the soft blush of pink on the creamy white flowers. The blossom was so delicate, so fragile, so impossible to capture to her satisfaction, that Rosamund Walsingham, from her perch high in the crotch of an apple tree, muttered an imprecation under her breath, wiped the slate clean of chalk, and began anew. Chalk was not a good medium for such dainty work, but paper was a luxury as Thomas was always telling her. His usual refrain of not being made of money, so oft repeated, had become a mantra. Not that it prevented him from dressing as richly as he chose, or from riding a handsome gelding with the finest leather saddle and silver harness, she reflected, her nose wrinkling as she studied the blossom anew.

And in all fairness, her brother kept her short of nothing important, and he only limited the supply of paper, which merely meant that she couldn't afford to make mistakes. Once she'd captured something to her satisfaction with chalk on slate, then she could transfer it to paper with the sharpest, finest quill she could find. It wasn't perfect, but she could manage.

Absently she brushed back behind her ear a stray lock of chestnut hair that was tickling her nose and leaned against the trunk of the tree at her back surveying the slate with a critical frown. It was almost perfect, and it would be easier to capture the impression of the blossom trembling a little against the leaf when she had the fine nib of a quill pen at her disposal.

Voices drifted into the orchard from below her hidden perch. Rosamund listened, her head cocked. It seemed her brother Thomas was back from his travels. He never sent warning of his returns from his frequent absences, so that was not in the least strange. And neither was it strange that he would bring a visitor with him. The voice was not one she recognized. Thomas had many visitors when he was down at Scadbury, some of them friends, others rather harder to define. The latter moved around in the shadows, it always seemed to Rosamund. They rarely acknowledged her with so much as a glance or a nod, and never spoke at all. They came and went at odd times of day and spent their time enshrined with Thomas in the study. Rosamund had learned to disregard them and was quite happy to keep to herself at such times.

She peered through the pale greenery as the voices came closer. Something about being hidden up here, looking down at the two men as they strolled the alley arm in arm between the fruit trees, brought her a little thrill. She was about to announce herself when they stopped on the path and turned to face each other, their conversation suddenly ceased.

Rosamund watched, fascinated as they kissed, murmuring softly, their hands stroking, moving over each other with increasing fervor. And now she wished she were anywhere but hidden in the apple tree. Her moment to declare herself was gone. Now she could only pray that Thomas would never find out that she had been a witness to this, whatever it was. Her brother was easygoing for the most part, carelessly affectionate to his younger sister when he was in her vicinity, but in general he paid her little attention, and that suited them both. He did, however, have a fearsome temper when aroused, and Rosamund had no desire to be on the receiving end of what she knew would be a terrifying rage if she was discovered.

So, trapped, she watched. They moved off the path, still holding each other, and the stranger leaned up against a tree, Thomas pressed against him. And then they slid slowly down the trunk and out of sight in the lush grass of the orchard. Rosamund could not see, but she could hear, and she'd heard enough stable talk in her rough and ready growing to have an idea what was happening between them, although the logistics of the act had never been clear to her. When her brother gave a howl that sounded as if he were in pain, she clamped her hand over her mouth. She could hear moans mingled with little cries, then silence.

After a minute that seemed to last an eternity, she heard them whispering, laughing softly, and the grass rustled. Their voices rose and fell barely above a whisper, so she could make out little of their words, but they sounded happy, in tune with each other. And then Thomas said in his normal tone, "Ah, Kit, if it's coin you need during the long vacation, then you must speak with my cousin. He is always looking for men such as yourself."

Rosamund could see Thomas again now as he stood up and leaned down, laughing, to hold out a hand to the brown-haired stranger who went by the name of Kit. The stranger rose, lacing his trunks, then brushing the dust of the ground from them. He was dressed poorly, his

shirt darned, his black trunks shiny with grease, his dark
cloak threadbare. He seemed a strange companion for her
always elegant brother. But then Thomas frequently kept
strange company.

Rosamund was excruciatingly uncomfortable in her
apple tree. Her bladder ached, her back itched as if ants
had dropped down her neck, and she longed to stretch her
cramped legs. But she held herself still, barely breathing,
lest something make them look up through the delicate
screen of leaves and blossom. But they were too taken up
with themselves to give thought to their surroundings,
and finally they moved away down the alley towards the
sweep of lawn that led up to the half-timbered, slate-roofed
house.

She dropped her slate and chalk to the ground, then
swung herself down from one of the curved branches to
drop beside them. She dived into the trees to relieve herself in the thick grass at the side of the orchard, then she
straightened her skirt and petticoat, picked up her chalk
and slate, and made her own way up to the house.

She entered through a side door and walked down the
narrow, stone-flagged passageway that led from the servants'
quarters at the back of the house to the front hall. As she
emerged into the sunlit hall, she caught a movement out of
the corner of her eye. A shadowy, black-clad figure sidled into
the gloom on the far side of the central staircase. It would be
Frizer, of course. Ingram Frizer, her brother's . . . her brother's what? She was hard-pressed to think of what role Ingram
Frizer played in Thomas's life, but it was certainly ever-
present. Thomas rarely came to Scadbury without Frizer
clinging to his coattails, hugging the shadows in brooding
silence. He seemed more a servant than a friend, but more
a confidant than a servant. Their manner towards each

other seemed to imply shared secrets. Somehow though Rosamund couldn't imagine that Thomas and Frizer would have the kind of congress her brother had been having in the orchard with the stranger.

Where was the stranger? *Who* was the stranger? If Thomas didn't want his little sister to meet his visitors, he ensured that she didn't, but this particular visitor Rosamund was determined to meet. She hurried up the curved oak staircase towards her own bedchamber thinking of various casual ways to effect an introduction.

As luck would have it, she was halfway down the corridor that led to her bedchamber when Thomas emerged from his bedchamber, accompanied by the stranger. He stopped as he saw his sister coming towards him.

"Rosamund, where have you been hiding?" His voice was cheerful, no indication of an underlying motive to the awkward question.

"I was walking in the fields, sketching a little," she offered as she curtsied. "I am glad to see you home and well, Brother." Her eyes darted as she spoke to the figure standing beside him. It was the stranger from the orchard, but he was transformed. The threadbare, grimy garments were replaced with a winged doublet of emerald velvet slashed over a lining of cream silk, his trunks were the same velvet, and his shirt was adorned with a collar of Thomas's favorite cobweb lace. Thomas's generosity extended even to his wardrobe it seemed. The two men were much of a size, and of similar coloring.

Thomas was looking at her quizzically and she realized that she was staring. "Kit, let me make you known to my little sister, Rosamund," Thomas said. "I fear she has never seen your like before, judging by her ill-mannered stare."

"Forgive me, sir," Rosamund said with a quick curtsy,

stammering a little as she tried to extricate herself. "I didn't intend any discourtesy."

"I perceived none," the man responded. "Indeed, such scrutiny could be seen as a compliment, if I choose to take it as such." He smiled. "Christopher Marlowe at your service, Mistress Walsingham."

The smile transformed him as much as the clothes. The rather arrogant cast of his angular features, a certain suspicious wariness in the brown eyes, disappeared. "I trust it was a compliment."

"Indeed it was, Master Marlowe." Rosamund had recovered herself and responded with a smile of her own and another curtsy.

"I swear, Rosamund, you grow into a flirtatious minx," Thomas declared. "It's past time we found you a husband, else you'll be sporting a swollen belly the next time I come back."

"Not with the fare available in Chiselhurst, Brother."

Thomas frowned at her. "You must learn to put a guard on your tongue, miss. Not everyone appreciates a coarse wit in a woman."

Rosamund blinked in confusion. Thomas had never shielded her from his own coarse humor, indeed had always invited her to respond in kind, and since he was the only member of her family since earliest childhood to pay any consistent attention to her, she had never found anything in the least objectionable in the way he spoke to her, or considered the possibility that her own responses might be frowned upon as unbecoming.

Master Marlowe came to her rescue. He clapped his friend on the shoulder, saying, "I for one appreciate an honest tongue in a woman, Thomas. The world is not a pretty place. Why should anyone, man or woman, have to pretend that it is?"

"If they want to find a husband, Kit." Thomas walked off towards the galleried landing. He turned at the end to look back at them. "We will dine at four, Rosamund. Join us, I have matters to discuss. Do you come now, Kit?"

"Aye." He moved off after his host, his stride lengthening.

Rosamund turned aside to her own chamber feeling rather bruised. It was unlike Thomas to turn on her without just cause. That had been more their mother's forte whenever her youngest surviving daughter had ever intruded upon her consciousness. She hadn't known what to do with Rosamund, who had so unaccountably survived childbirth and early childhood, while most of her other babies had either been stillborn or had simply withered away within months. The tiny stones in the village graveyard made a pathetic line alongside one pathway.

But Dorothy Walsingham had been dead for several years now, and her last years had been so marked with ill health that as far as Rosamund was concerned, her mother might just as well already have been in her grave. She had learned to rely on Thomas for the lessons of life, and he had generally obliged in a haphazard fashion, sometimes answering her questions, sometimes telling her the answers weren't fit for a maiden's ears. Their elder brother Edmund was never at Scadbury, even after he inherited. He preferred London, and his succession of mistresses . . . whores, Thomas called them, who according to Thomas had rendered him poxed and senseless for the most part.

In truth it had been so long since she had last seen Edmund that Rosamund couldn't summon up a clear picture of the present head of the family. She closed the door of her bedchamber behind her and took her slate to the scratched deal table beneath the window. Here she kept her precious supply of paper, quills, and ink. She set the slate down and gazed critically at her chalked sketch in the light from the mullioned window. It still seemed good to her, and she could see how to create just the right impression of fragility, the delicacy of the little tremors the blossoms made against the pale green foliage.

Excitement coursed through her and she forgot her brother's puzzling and hurtful criticism, forgot the scene in the orchard, forgot Christopher Marlowe, as she sat down on the stool and smoothed out a sheet of paper. She tested the tip of a quill and sharpened it quickly, impatient with a task that had to be completed before she could begin. Then she dipped the quill in the standish and began to draw.

It took two hours to complete, and she leaned back away from the desk and gazed at her drawing. Such a small, delicate object was difficult to render with accuracy, much more difficult than a person, or a scene, but she thought she had succeeded. The sound of voices below her open window brought her out of her reverie, and she leaned over the table to peer down to the terrace below.

Thomas was sitting on the low parapet of the terrace and Ingram Frizer was standing beside him, a sheaf of papers in his hands. Frizer always reminded Rosamund of some malevolent creature of the undergrowth. His skin had an unhealthy greenish cast, always with a slightly greasy sheen, his lank, dirty fair hair hung to his shoulders in rats' tails, and his clothes looked and smelled moldy as if they'd just emerged from a crypt. His voice had a squeak to it, which reminded her again of a nighttime predator, but his eyes were what chilled her. Opaque, hard, tiny pinpricks of an indeterminate color, but a massive malice.

He was presenting papers to Thomas, who was sitting at his ease, one crossed leg swinging casually, as he read. "You're a fine man of business, Frizer," he said with one of his infectious, booming laughs. "You'll make me a fortune yet, my friend."

"As long as there are fools in the world," the other responded with a dour nod. "'Tis no crime to take advantage of such."

"Well, some might not agree." Thomas handed back the paper he held. "But I've too many debts of my own to fret over such niceties. See that they're executed. You can be on your road to London within the half hour."

Frizer looked askance. "You'll be rid of me then?"

"Aye . . . about your business." Thomas stood up. "What's to do, man?"

"What's the stranger doing here then?" Frizer jerked his head towards the house behind him.

"None of your business, my friend. He's a man of words, a playmaker, a poet . . . and soon he'll be joining our little fellowship. Leave him be." Rosamund could hear a hint of threat in her brother's voice. It would seem that Thomas recognized the need to keep Frizer in check.

She moved away from the window back to her drawing. What did that mean? What was this fellowship? The little clock on her mantel chimed three o'clock, and she put the question aside for the moment, turning her attention to the armoire. Dinner at four in the company of her brother and his friend merited a certain degree of effort. Most days she dined in the kitchen with the servants, it was more cheerful than the solitary meals that would otherwise be her fate, but it required no change of dress from her usual simple country gowns.

She examined the meager contents of the armoire with a somewhat disconsolate frown. It would have to be her Sunday gown.

Chapter Two

"THAT'S ONE FELLOW I wouldn't want to meet in an alley on a dark night," Kit Marlowe observed, draining his wine cup as the study door closed on the departing Ingram Frizer. "What is he to you, Thomas? No ordinary ruffian, I'll wager."

"A man of many parts . . . Master Ingram, as some call him," Thomas answered, taking up a flask at his elbow and leaning forward to refill Kit's cup before attending to his own. "I grant you, not a man of the most salubrious appearance. But he's very good at certain types of business, the kind that a man such as myself must needs embrace if he's to keep decent clothes on his back and a good horse to ride . . . not to mention good wine in his cup." He held up his cup with an appreciative smile. "More than treachery comes out of France, my friend."

"Oh, I grant you that," Kit said, then drained his cup again and held it out for a refill. "Is this business to do with Master Secretary?"

Thomas smiled. "Frizer runs errands for Sir Francis from time to time, but I employ him on other matters concerning my personal finances. He is a maker and a breaker of deals *par excellence,* and he keeps us both solvent."

Kit's eyes narrowed, but he let the subject drop.

Thomas turned his chair at a light tap at the door. "Come in."

Rosamund stepped into the room. Her eyes darted in swift assessment to her brother's guest, lounging at his ease in the corner of the deep window seat. A ray of sunshine caught a reddish glint in his brown hair brushed back from a wide forehead. He had a neat mustache but only the faintest outline of a beard, unlike her brother's trimmed but luxuriant growth.

She dropped a curtsy, aware as she bowed her head that the same ray of sun would illuminate the deeper russet tints in the smooth, rich fall of her own hair. "Am I too early? Shall I go away again?"

"No, no. Take a cup of wine." Thomas waved her casually to a stool by the table. "I have some news for you anyway."

Rosamund took the cup he handed her and sat down, arranging the skirts of her green silk gown so that the hem revealed her dainty satin slippers and her trim ankles. She was proud of her slender ankles and feet, although she rarely had anyone to admire them. Not that she thought she had an audience here. Thomas was certainly indifferent to his sister's appearance in general, and after what she'd seen and heard in the orchard, she rather thought that Master Marlowe was probably uninterested in such feminine details. Nevertheless, she wasn't one to pass up a rare opportunity to show them off.

"Are you come from London, Master Marlowe?" she inquired politely.

"No, from Cambridge. I met your brother there some weeks ago and he was kind enough to invite me to visit him."

"Are you at the university, sir?"

"At Corpus Christi. I have taken my BA and hope to be admitted for an MA shortly."

"Master Marlowe is a poet and a playmaker, when not at scholarship," Thomas said, picking up the now empty wine flask. "He has more interest in the theatre than in the Church, for which, alas, he is destined." His tone was ironic and he cast a quick complicit glance at his guest, who shook his head with a grimace of distaste.

Marlowe said only, "Is there wine in that flask, Thomas? I've a powerful thirst."

"When have you not?" Thomas held out the flask to his sister. "Take it to the buttery and fill it from the cask marked Aquitaine, Rosamund. And tell Mistress Riley that we're sharp set, and if it pleases her to feed us at some point before sundown, we'll be eternally in her debt."

Rosamund took the flask and left the study. She had no intention of delivering her brother's caustic comment to the cook. Mistress Riley was likely to throw a saucepan at her head and storm out of the kitchen, leaving Rosamund to deal with a half-prepared dinner, and she was no cook at the best of times.

The kitchen was hot and steamy, fat spitting in all directions from the pig roasting on the spit over the fire, cauldrons seething and bubbling as if they were in hell's furnace. The pot boy turned the spit, his eyes glazed as if mesmerized by the hissing flames. The stone floor was sticky underfoot and Rosamund trod as carefully as she could, conscious of her delicate footwear and the hem of her green silk gown. She went into the buttery to fill the flask. Mistress Riley was throwing dough onto the deal table, kneading it vigorously with her fists before turning and throwing it again. She glanced at Rosamund when she emerged from the buttery. "You can tell Master Walsingham his dinner'll be on the table in ten minutes."

Rosamund contented herself with a nod and hurried

out of the kitchen, accidentally treading on a cat's tail in her haste. The cat let loose a howl of outrage that immediately set the dogs barking in the kitchen yard, and Rosamund fled, perspiration gathering on her forehead.

She paused outside the study to wipe her brow with her sleeve and cool her heated cheeks before going in. She took a hasty gulp of the wine in the flask, then opened the door. Her brother and Marlowe were standing together at the window looking out over the park. Her brother had his arm draped casually over his friend's shoulders and they seemed unaware of Rosamund's return.

"Dinner will be on the table in ten minutes," she said, her voice pitched a little louder than necessary. She sounded awkward to her own ears and felt herself flush. But if the men noticed they said nothing, merely turned away from the window and returned to their seats.

She poured the wine and served them, then drank rather deeply of her own. A current of tension, or something, was in the room that she couldn't identify. But it seemed more exciting than menacing. "You wanted to talk to me about something, Thomas?"

"Yes." He cleared his throat. "You're bidden to London."

"To London?" She could hardly believe her ears. "Why? By whom? What for?"

"It seems that your existence has come to the attention of our august cousin, Sir Francis Walsingham," Thomas told her with the same ironical tinge to his voice as before. "He wishes to see you."

Rosamund frowned. "But he's the queen's secretary of state. What could he want with me?"

"Sweet sister, there's no knowing what his excellency the secretary wants with any of us until it pleases him to inform us," Thomas stated, tossing back his wine. "I daresay he wishes to look you over, see if you might make an advantageous connection."

"But that's for Edmund to decide." Rosamund looked askance. She had seen little enough of her oldest brother in her lifetime, but he was the head of the family, and if she was to be given in marriage for the family's benefit, then it was up to him to make the decision and the choice.

"Edmund has no interest in you, girl. He has eyes only for his latest whore." Thomas laughed and with a coarse oath stood up. "Let's dine. My belly's cleaving to my backbone."

The dining parlor was as simply furnished as the rest of the house, a plain pine table, stools, and a massive oak sideboard. It was so rarely used that it smelled musty to Rosamund, and she flung open the windows in the deep bay, letting in the scents of the early roses from the bed below.

A servant entered with the joint of pork, which he set in the middle of the board together with a jug of gravy, a loaf of wheaten bread, and a bowl of buttered greens. Marlowe lifted the empty flask and looked plaintively at his host. "We have need, mine host."

Thomas nodded. "Fill it up, Jethro."

The servant took the flask and left. Rosamund sat down and reached for a manchet of bread. Thomas was already cutting into the joint with his dagger, an implement not available to his sister, who had to make do with a small knife beside her pewter trencher. Marlowe had his own knife, but he cut the thinnest of slivers from the meat and took but a spoonful of greens. His eyes were on the door, his hand circling his empty wine cup, and he only returned his attention to the room when Jethro returned with the recharged flask. He filled his cup to the brim and drank greedily.

Rosamund forked a piece of meat into her mouth and

chewed reflectively, her mind busy with her brother's news. Her cousin Francis was an important man, the queen's trusted councilor, a man of considerable influence. It had never occurred to her that he would take an interest in such an unimportant relative as herself. She knew that Thomas had dealings with him, but Thomas was a man, it made all the difference.

She knew what her future looked like. She had no overly romanticized notions of a woman's marital lot in life. If she was lucky, she might find a considerate husband. Maybe even a man with whom she could give and receive affection and companionship, but that would be the luck of the draw. Someone, presumably Edmund, would choose a husband for her, a match that would benefit the family in some fashion, and she would do as she was told. It was what women did. If Edmund hadn't been so occupied with his own interests, he would probably have disposed of her long since. Seventeen was almost old to be still unwed. Thomas had clearly never given the matter a second thought, so she'd been left in undisturbed tedium in the Kentish quiet.

If she wished to, she could probably show herself to her cousin in such a light that he would wash his hands of her. He was only going to look her over, after all. But she had never been to London and the prospect thrilled her. If she pleased Sir Francis, then he might allow her to stay, at least for a while. She might even attend the court. Of course, if he married her off to some dull country squire, she'd be no better off than she was now, worse off with a swollen belly every year. And when would she have time to draw? She had seen her mother waste away, lose all interest in anything outside the needs of her family and household, until in the last few years she had had no interest in those either.

But before that happened, Rosamund could enjoy the excitement of London, there was no knowing whom she might meet, or what opportunities she might encounter.

She didn't realize she was crumbling the bread between her fingers, while stabbing ineffectually at her meat with her fork, until Marlowe said, "I was under the impression the pig was already killed, Mistress Rosamund."

She looked up, startled. "Oh, forgive me. I was thinking about something else."

"That seemed obvious." He refilled his cup again.

She gave him a faint smile, noticing that while he was drinking deep, he was eating almost nothing. His eyes had a sheen to them, a brightness that was almost febrile, and his cheekbones were touched with red. He would have a hard morning, she thought, turning to her brother.

"When are we to go to London, Thomas?"

"A week, I should think." He helped himself to more meat. "How long will it take for you to get ready?"

"Less than half an hour," she said a shade tartly. "My wardrobe is small."

"And out of fashion, judging by that gown." He frowned across the table at her. "Is that the best you could do?"

Rosamund swallowed the surge of resentment and declared flatly, "Yes."

"Good God, then you'd best do something about it. You can't be seen looking like a pauper."

"I need money for that," Rosamund informed him, setting her fork aside.

Thomas groaned and reached for the wine again. "All right. But I've little enough to spare. What's it cost these days to fashion a gown?"

"I don't know, Brother. Probably what your doublet cost."

"This?" He ran a hand down the rich crimson velvet of his gold-buttoned doublet edged in jet. "Don't be ridiculous, Rosamund. This cost me twenty crowns. I can't spare that."

"Then how am I to manage?"

He glowered at her. "I'll see what I have and we'll discuss it tomorrow. In the meantime, see if Mistress Riley has one of her syllabubs for us."

Contented with her half victory, Rosamund went to the kitchen. When she returned with the bowl of syllabub, Thomas nodded his thanks as she set it on the table. Immediately he dug into the frothy cream with his spoon, gesturing to his guest to do the same. Marlowe shook his head and instead refilled his wine cup.

Thomas frowned. "If you're to make your mark on Master Secretary, you'll need a clear head, Kit. This immoderate drinking will sour your belly, yellow your eyes, and set hammers ringing in your head. I warn you, my cousin is a man of moderation and likes to have about him men who practice the same."

Marlowe laughed, leaning back in his chair, lovingly stroking the bowl of his wine cup. "Then mayhap I'm not for his service." His tone was one of indifference, and Rosamund, dipping her own spoon in the syllabub, could see the clouds gathering behind her brother's eyes.

"You'd do well to consider your words," Thomas stated. "Unless you're minded to live and die an impoverished curate in some wilderness parish."

"Oh, Tom, Tom, ye of little faith." Marlowe laughed again, then tipped the contents of his cup down his throat. "I'll mind my tongue and my manners when needs must. Here . . ." He pushed his cup across the table. "Fill it to the brim, friend. Your august relation is not here, unless he's hiding behind the wainscot."

Thomas picked up the empty flask and upended it. "We'll have no more." His tone was sullen but definite, and Marlowe's eyes narrowed, his flush deepened. He stood up, kicking back his chair. "Then I'll find it for myself." He grabbed up the flask and then with a flourish bowed at Rosamund. "Mistress Rosamund, direct me, if you please, to the buttery."

Rosamund looked at her brother. He was not himself particularly abstemious, and his light eyes were as blood-shot as his friend's. A telltale muscle twitched in his cheek, and she knew he was close to one of his fearsome explosions of rage, always worst when he'd been drinking. He was staring at Marlowe, who returned the stare with a derisive laugh.

"Is it a brawl you want, Tom?" Marlowe tossed the pewter flagon into the empty grate, where it bounced and rolled with a clatter. "Come on then, I'll best you yet." He put up his fists and Thomas sprang forward. Rosamund fled.

Safely beyond the closed door, she stopped to listen. There was a thud, another one, a yell that she thought came from Thomas, then suddenly laughter, boisterous, uproarious gales of laughter. Softly she lifted the latch and opened the door a crack. She peered into the room. The two men were holding each other, swaying together. It was impossible to tell whether they were locked in combat or in an embrace of affection. They were laughing, but the laughter had an edge of danger to it, of passion unresolved.

Whatever this was, she had no place in it. Rosamund closed the door silently and went up to her own room. She felt uncertain, uneasy, lost in some way, as if her understanding of the world was mistaken.

But then what understanding of the world could she, a sequestered, sheltered girl of seventeen, expect to have?

* * *

Morning brought a renewal of Rosamund's usual optimism. She remembered first that she was to go to London, and that the journey meant new clothes, or some at least. Only after she'd savored that prospect did the memory of the previous evening's discomfort start to niggle again. Had Thomas and Kit Marlowe mended their friendship? Despite the laughter and the strange warring embrace she had witnessed, they had definitely been angry with each other. Drunk, of course, both of them, otherwise such a small matter would not have provoked such a scene. But drunken rages in her experience were the most fearsome kind.

She dressed, thrust her bare feet into a pair of woven sandals, and went downstairs in search of breakfast. The door to the dining parlor was ajar and she smelled spilt wine as she passed. She paused and looked in. No one had been in since the previous evening judging by the dishes still on the table and the wine cups lying carelessly on their sides. A bottle of brandy, only a quarter full, was on the sideboard. It hadn't been in the room when she'd left, so presumably Thomas and Master Marlowe had made up their quarrel over the brandy bottle.

How had they met, those two? she wondered as she made her way to the kitchen in search of breakfast. On the surface they seemed completely unalike. Thomas was an elegant courtier, Kit Marlowe an impoverished student with aspirations to be a playmaker.

In the kitchen she dodged cats and two of the dogs, who should have been in the yard, but were snapping at each other over a bone in the corner. She cut herself a slice of wheaten bread, buttered it liberally from the crock in the pantry, and went out into the kitchen garden.

Mistress Riley's son, Jem, was flying around the garden in pursuit of two hysterical chickens, who, somehow aware of the fate that awaited them, managed to fly up onto the henhouse roof, where they sat, cackling and squawking as they ruffled their feathers.

"They keep goin' up there," Jem wailed, tugging at his jerkin. "How can I catch 'em up there, mistress?"

"Obviously with difficulty," a voice declared from behind Rosamund. She turned around. Master Marlowe, his doublet hanging open over a wine-stained shirt, stood bleary-eyed by the sundial. "Fetch a ladder, boy." He rolled up the sleeves of his fine lawn shirt, now much the worse for wear.

Jem brought a ladder and set it up against the henhouse and Marlowe climbed up. He swore a series of oaths as the chickens danced back from his grasping hand. He hauled himself farther up onto the roof and lunged, catching one of the birds with both hands. Still standing on the ladder, he wrung its neck with a viciously efficient twist of his hands and dropped it to the ground before lunging for its squawking sister, who met the same speedy fate.

He climbed down, wiping his hands on his britches, while Jem gathered up the birds and scampered to the kitchen with them.

"I get the impression you've done that before," Rosamund said with some awe.

"Many times," he agreed with a short laugh. "A family of nine children consumes chickens aplenty, and a cobbler's wages can afford little of anything else for the pot."

"Where are you from?"

"Canterbury." He wiped the back of his hand over his eyes as if to clear his vision. "I've an urgent need of ale, Mistress Rosamund."

"I'll fetch it for you." She turned back to the house. He

followed her into the scullery, where she drew a foaming tankard from the keg. He drank it down in one and asked for a refill. She drew him another. "The hair of the dog they call it, I believe."

"Aye," he agreed. "And if ever a dog needed another hair, it's this one."

"You drank deep with my brother last night."

"Aye. My besetting sin, but when the wine's on my tongue, I'm in present paradise and future hell holds no sway."

"Will you break your fast?" She made a move back to the kitchen.

"I've no appetite." He followed her through the kitchen and into the main house. "Is there a quiet room where I can work undisturbed?"

"The study." She showed him to the room where he'd been sitting with Thomas. "No one will disturb you here."

"And there's my satchel." He set down his tankard and picked up the leather satchel that he'd brought with him the previous day and left on the window seat. He unbuckled it and drew out a sheaf of parchment. "Is there quill and ink?"

Rosamund gestured to the oak desk against the far wall. "I filled the inkwell myself only yesterday." She perched on the window seat, watching curiously as he set out his parchments and drew a stool over with his foot.

"Is it a play?" she ventured. "May I see a little?"

For answer, he held out a sheet of parchment. She hurried to take it from him and stood beside him silently reading. After a minute she looked up, puzzled. "But it doesn't rhyme."

Forsake thy king and do but join with me
And we will triumph over all the world.

"How can you have a play that doesn't rhyme? There is no poetry."

Marlowe regarded her for a moment. "So they will say, I'm sure. But that is how I hear the lines. They have a rhythm of their own and the rhyme is of no importance. It is still verse to my ears."

Rosamund took the sheets and returned to the window seat. She read under her breath so that she could hear the rhythm, and after a few lines realized that indeed they read like poetry. "It's true." She sat with the parchment in her lap. "After a while you don't notice the lack of rhyme. Has Thomas read this?"

"Thomas, my dear Thomas, is pleased to approve," Marlowe said with a sardonic twitch of his lips. "And where is he on this fine morning?"

"Still abed, I expect. If you sat late drinking."

"I detect a note of sharpness, Mistress Rosamund." He dipped his quill in ink and added something to the paper. "You do not approve of the gift of Bacchus?"

"It's not for me to approve or disapprove."

"No, that is probably true." He continued with his writing.

"What is the play about?"

"The only thing men wish for, the thing they strive for, the thing they will die for." He looked at her then, half smiling. "Can you tell me what that is?"

Rosamund could think of only one thing, the obvious one, the one thing that everyone was taught was all that mattered in the world. "The love of God." But even as she said it, she knew it was wrong and was not surprised when he shook his head impatiently.

"That is all very well, and in the name of that love men will commit atrocities the world over, so you could be excused for thinking that, but, no, Mistress Rosamund, that is not what my play is about. It is about power. The love of power. The fight for power. Men will increase their power in God's name, they will torture heretics in God's name, but the things that they do in that name make them frightful and thus terrible in their power. And it is that that they love."

Rosamund nodded, although she was uncertain that she fully understood. She gave him back the papers. "I won't disturb you further."

"So here you are, Kit." Thomas came in just as she was moving to the door. He was in a dressing robe, loosely tied so that she could see the white flash of his belly when he moved. She averted her eyes instinctively and ducked from the room. Thomas didn't seem to have noticed her, his eyes were only for Kit. He went over to him and bent to kiss him, the last thing Rosamund saw before she hurried away.

Chapter Three

THEY JOURNEYED TO London, the three of them, a week later. Rosamund was by this time so accustomed to Kit Marlowe that she barely noticed the occasional exchange of complicit smiles, the murmured words, the brushing touches between him and her brother. Her thoughts were concentrated on the pleasures of her two new gowns and the rather alarming prospect of the coming presentation to Sir Francis Walsingham.

Although it was but a three-hour ride to London, they set off on horseback soon after sunrise. Rosamund was surprised to find a lump in her throat as they rode down the driveway. She had never left her home before, and even Mistress Riley had in her gruff fashion shown some emotion, pressing upon her a package of her favorite spice cakes. She nibbled one now, savoring the taste of the childhood she was leaving behind.

Jethro kept up the rear of the little party, riding a pack mule whose leather panniers contained Rosamund's necessities as well as the new gowns and two new pairs of slippers. Thomas had bidden her pack for a fortnight's stay in case Master Secretary could not see her immediately, and the prospect of two whole weeks in London filled her with anticipation.

Despite the early hour the roads were crowded with

carts heading for market. Once in a while a herd of cows milled across the narrow lanes as they were driven from meadow to milking shed, and for nearly a mile a flock of sheep slowed traffic to barely a walk. Thomas and Kit seemed oblivious of the delay, deeply engaged in theatre talk, and Rosamund listened avidly, noting the names of Burbage and Ned Alleyn and a man called Watson, another Thomas it appeared. They were all men of the theatre, actors and managers and playmakers, apparently well-known to her brother.

"We shall go to the play, maybe this afternoon, if these godforsaken sheep ever leave the path," Thomas announced. "You shall meet Watson, and Tom Kyd too, if he's about. His plays have a following, but without a patron he must needs live on the charity and friendship of others."

"A fate that will befall more than Kyd," Marlowe said, reaching sideways to pluck a hawthorn blossom from the hedgerow so close beside him the branches snagged his horse's flank.

"The service pays if you've a mind to it and Master Secretary is minded to employ you," Thomas said.

"I doubt I have a turn for spying." Kit inhaled the scent of the blossom before letting it fall to the ground.

"Oh, the skills are not hard to develop, my friend, particularly when necessity rules."

"We shall see."

Rosamund was all ears as she rode just behind the men. What was this service Thomas talked of? And what did it have to do with spying? She gathered it had everything to do with the queen's secretary of state and presumably Thomas's work for his cousin. She wanted to ask her questions, but there was something excluding about the way the men rode side by side, heads together, that she felt awkward drawing attention to herself and instead turned her meandering thoughts to the possibility of going to the theatre with them. She decided not to broach that subject either until they had reached London. Thomas would be more approachable with a tankard to hand and a good pasty in his belly.

Meanwhile it was lovely to be riding on such a beautiful morning. She settled into the easy rhythm of her palfrey, a neat roan mare who was her pride and joy. Jenny had been born and bred in the Scadbury stables, which were well-known for miles around for the quality of their horseflesh. Rosamund had appropriated her as a colt and had broken her to bridle herself. Cleverly she had ensured that whenever a buyer for a Scadbury horse came to the stables, the roan mare was never there. Neither of her brothers had seemed to notice her gradual acquisition of the animal, and now it was generally accepted that Jenny was Rosamund's saddle horse without anyone really questioning how it had happened.

It was a soft May morning, the air balmy, the sun warm but far from fierce. The scents of hawthorn filled the air and the hedgerows were massed with primroses, harebells, ragged robin, and the delicate, lacy flowers of cow parsley. A knife grinder had set up the tools of his trade on the village green of a hamlet they rode through. He called out his services to the women pouring out of cottages with pots that needed soldering and knives for the grindstone. Close by a man sat in the stocks, a troop of children dancing around him, jeering as they threw rotten eggs and last year's maggoty windfalls at him. He cursed them vigorously but it only made them laugh and throw harder.

"At least we don't see the stakes in every town," Thomas observed soberly, watching the man's misery with a degree of compassion. "I heard tell that when Bloody Mary was queen, there was a stake in every hamlet. Heretics must have been in abundance," he added with a cynical twist of his lip.

"There's burnings aplenty even so," Kit responded.

"They burned a woman for a witch in Chiselhurst some weeks ago," Rosamund put in. "She claimed she had holy marks upon her. They said she was a heretical witch and burned her in the town square."

Kit glanced back at her. "Do you remember what I said about power, Mistress Rosamund? Men burn the flesh of others in the name of God, and by so doing enhance their own earthly powers."

"Have a care how you speak, Kit," Thomas warned, his eyes flashing. "And don't teach my sister your atheistical heresies. I'll not have it."

Kit Marlowe merely shrugged and urged his horse forward, singing a bawdy song in a low but clear voice. Thomas scowled but let him go. Rosamund held her peace.

They rode through Greenwich, past the palace where the royal standard fluttered to indicate that the queen was in residence. Rosamund hung back for a more lingering look at the gleaming building set in its lush green parkland, the river, packed with craft, flowing at its edge. The royal barge was moored at the pier and strains of music rose in the air from a company of musicians playing in the prow.

"Her majesty must be intending to take to the river," Thomas observed. "They would not otherwise be playing."

"Can we stay awhile to see her?" Rosamund asked.

"No, there's no time. Doubtless you'll see her in London. She is often abroad," he responded carelessly.

Rosamund swallowed her disappointment. A mile farther on they drew rein at a ferry crossing. "We'll cross the river here," Thomas said. "It's less crowded than the crossings closer to the city and the horses will be calmer." He dismounted, leading his horse to the bank. Rosamund and Marlowe followed suit, watching as the ferry was poled from the opposite side of the river.

Farmers' wives, ragged children, peddlers with their baskets, crowded onto the ferry as it nudged the bank. Thomas used his whip with abandon, slashing right and left to clear a path for himself and his companions with their mounts. For the most part people gave way with relative good nature, with only the occasional curse and gobbet of spit at his feet to indicate resentment of his lofty assumption of priority.

Rosamund stayed close to Jenny as the flat craft was poled back towards the spires of the city, which were now showing clearly against the midmorning sky. The mare was restless and nervous in such close quarters. It was an ill-smelling crowd to boot, and Rosamund found the smell of warm horseflesh infinitely preferable to that of her fellow humans. Despite the discomfort she was excited. She had rarely left Scadbury and had never been to London.

"We'll lodge at the Four Swans in the liberty of Shoreditch," Thomas said as they led the horses onto the far bank. "It's a goodly inn, well thought of among theatre folk. It keeps a fair table, and it's easy distance from the playhouses. The Theatre and the Curtain are hard by. And unlike most of the inns there it does not let rooms for whoring."

He glanced back at Rosamund as she mounted Jenny with the aid of a tree stump positioned for that purpose. "Listen well, Rosamund, in the liberty you'll not stray from my side, is it understood?"

"What is that . . . the liberty?" Rosamund answered his question, which was purely rhetorical, with her own.

"There are several of them ringing the City of London itself," he explained. "A liberty is a part of London but not under the city's jurisdiction." He touched his heels to his horse's flanks, encouraging the animal to break into a trot. "The city officers hold no sway there, so there is little enough enforcement. It makes all manner of pleasures available without the supervision of the city officers . . . no place for a woman of your kind to go abroad."

If Rosamund needed further explanation it was provided by her own eyes as they rode into the narrow, crowded streets of the city. Women lounged on every corner and in every doorway, their necklines low enough to expose their nipples. Doors stood open to gaming houses, where she glimpsed men and women throwing dice, their exuberant shouts or vile curses on each throw filling her ears. A man leading a mangy and emaciated dancing bear was surrounded by a crowd of ragged urchins, poking the wretched animal with sticks in an effort to get it to dance. She averted her eyes when they passed the bull-baiting pit, the snarling and bleeding dogs throwing themselves at the staked animal amid the jeers and cheers of the spectators.

By the time they reached the Four Swans Inn her head was beginning to ache from the raucous noise of the streets and the vile stench from the open sewers. The inn was a handsome building, galleried on four sides around a cobbled courtyard. Sleeping rooms opened off the gallery; the tavern rooms beneath opened directly onto the courtyard. Thomas had chosen their lodging with care. Apart from its proximity to the theatres, Seething Lane, where Master Secretary had his house and his offices, was but a short ride.

Rosamund was shown to a small corner chamber while her brother and Marlowe occupied a larger apartment next door. "There'll be dinner served in the ordinary, sir, unless you'd like a private parlor," the landlord said, handing over the keys.

Thomas regarded Rosamund doubtfully. He was not flush with funds, and for himself and Kit the ordinary would have done well enough, but his sister couldn't really partake of the common meal in the common taproom with all comers. "A private parlor," he said with a grimace, hoping that their sojourn in the Four Swans would not last above a day or two.

They sat down to rabbit stew, and Rosamund began to feel better almost immediately. She sipped a little wine and waited until her brother had quaffed his first cup of burgundy before saying, "Are we to go to the theatre this afternoon?"

"Not you, sweetheart," Thomas declared, reaching for a manchet of bread. "'Tis no place for a gently bred maid. You'll stay here in seclusion and first thing tomorrow morning we will pay a visit to Seething Lane. If nothing more important occurs, mayhap our cousin will be pleased to see you then."

"Why is it no place for me?" Rosamund speared a turnip on the tip of her knife and let the gravy drip onto her manchet before eating it.

Thomas and Kit Marlowe exchanged a glance. "Because of the stews that surround it," Kit said, pushing aside his barely touched bowl of food and reaching again for the flagon of wine. "I take it that your brother would keep you safe from such dens of iniquity."

"No respectable woman would be seen at the theatre," Thomas stated.

"But I've heard it said the queen herself enjoys the play."

"Not in the theatre. They are performed for her in the

palace by her own company, the Queen's Servants. The players are chosen by the Earl of Leicester, selected from all the acting troupes in the country. It is very different from the common theatre. You are not to go and that is all there is to it."

Rosamund held her tongue. She knew there was no point arguing with her brother when he spoke in that tone, but if their stay in London was to be extended, by hook or by crook she would see a play.

At the end of a tedious afternoon and evening spent alone in her chamber, she was ardently hoping that nothing would prevent Sir Francis Walsingham from seeing her on the morrow and not keep her kicking her heels any longer. Scadbury for all its familiar tedium was better than this. She could not go out unaccompanied, despite the enticement of the bustle in the yard below. She had only her slate and chalk to occupy her, but her customary concentration deserted her with all the noise and bustle around her, and after a while she gave up trying to sketch the scene in the courtyard below her window and instead just sat on the deep sill and watched it. Her brother and his friend left for the theatre soon after dinner and had not returned by the time she took herself to bed.

She slept fitfully, unused, after the country quiet of Scadbury, to the continuous racket from below that went on well into the night. She awoke at dawn to the sound of kegs being rolled across the cobbled yard amid shouted instructions. Doors banged, iron-shod hooves rang on the cobbles, footsteps raced along the gallery outside her door. With a groan she sat up, shivering in the chill of early morning. Her head pounded and her eyes were as tired as if she hadn't closed them all night. Resolutely she lay down again, closing her eyes, willing herself to relax.

Miraculously she dozed off despite the noise, and when Thomas knocked on her door an hour later, she awoke much more refreshed. He put his head around the door. "'Tis past time you were up, slugabed. If you want to break your fast before we ride, you must hurry. Master Secretary expects me before eight o'clock and he is a man who keeps careful time."

Rosamund sat up. "Is there water to be had? I would wash my face before meeting our august cousin."

"I'll send someone up with a jug. Do you need help with your gown?"

"Maybe with the lacing." She pushed aside the coverlet and swung her legs over the side of the high bed. The air was still chill and goose bumps popped on her bare arms.

"I'll tell the girl to help you when she brings the water." Thomas left and she stood up, stretching. She went to the window, peering down at the scene below. It seemed as chaotic now as it had the previous evening. Unlike yesterday, the day was overcast and a draft was coming from below the ill-fitting mullioned window. She shivered in her thin linen shift, her bare feet cold on the wooden floor.

A timid knock at the door brought a young girl with a jug of water into the room. "'Tis not hot, mistress," she apologized, setting the jug on the dresser. "Cook needs all the kettles on the range for boiling tripe."

"No matter." Rosamund, hoping that tripe would not make an appearance at the breakfast table, poured water into the basin. She splashed her face and washed her hands, examining her wavering reflection in the polished tin mirror. She looked well enough, she thought, and her russet hair, freshly washed before the journey, still had a burnished luster to it. It was a good color for her new apple-green velvet gown.

She pulled on her new cotton stockings, tying the ribbon garters above the knee, then stepped into the canvas farthingale, fastening the tapes at her back. With the help of the young maid she eased the velvet gown over her head. "How tight shall I lace, mistress?" The maid took the laces at the back of the boned bodice and tugged.

"Not too tight." Rosamund was unaccustomed to the restrictive garment; such fashionable necessities were not needed with the simple country gowns she normally wore.

"You've such a small waist anyway," the girl said admiringly as she pulled on the laces. "You scarcely need the bones."

Rosamund smiled at the compliment and slipped into her new heeled shoes of green leather. She tried to see her full reflection in the wavery mirror. It was impossible to get the whole effect, but it felt right, even though the unaccustomed heels made her feel a little unsteady. She brushed her hair and then left it loose over her shoulders. The style suited her well and denoted her virginal state. Of course, once she'd lost that in the marriage bed, she'd have to confine the long, luxuriant locks, but not today.

With a word of thanks to her tiring maid she made her way to the private parlor, where she found Thomas alone, slicing into a sirloin. Candles were lit to combat the gloomy outdoors. He looked her over with a critical eye, then nodded. "I have something for you . . . something of our mother's." He reached into the inside pocket of his slashed black velvet doublet and laid a delicate silver fillet on the table, where it winked in the candlelight.

"Oh, how pretty," Rosamund exclaimed, lifting the dainty piece. She had nothing of her mother's and had often wondered what had happened to the various bits and pieces of jewelry that Dorothy had owned. She fastened the fillet around her forehead and felt instantly elegant and sophisticated.

"It looks well on you," Thomas observed, waving the point of his knife to a stool at the table. "Break your fast."

Rosamund took a manchet of bread and accepted the slice of sirloin that her brother cut for her. She buttered the bread lavishly, sipped the small beer in her tankard, and ate. "Where's Master Marlowe?" she mumbled through a mouthful of bread and meat.

"Still abed." Thomas shrugged and was clearly displeased. He poured ale for himself.

"Are we to go without him?"

Her question was answered by the opening of the door. Kit Marlowe, bleary-eyed, waxen complexioned, came in and slumped at the table with a groan. "Ale," he croaked.

Thomas said nothing, merely filled a tankard from the copper jug on the table and pushed it across to him.

Kit drank deeply, then, somehow instantly refreshed, sat up straight at the board, regarding Rosamund with a curious eye. "You look neat and tidy, Mistress Rosamund. In honor of your cousin, I assume."

"You'd do well to smarten yourself up as well in honor of Master Secretary," Thomas grunted. "Look at you. Anyone would think you were still drunk."

"Calumny." Kit waved the comment aside with a careless flick of his hand. "Nothing that a touch of water and a comb won't set right." He brushed at his doublet, another one borrowed from Thomas.

Thomas drained his own tankard and pushed his stool back from the table. "I'm going to order the horses. Be in the stable yard in fifteen minutes." The door clicked shut decisively on his departure.

"I have displeased your brother, I fear," Kit mused,

refilling his tankard. "But, alas, he is right. I cannot afford to make a poor impression on Master Secretary. Poverty and playmaking are natural bedfellows, and if I'm not to starve in a garret, then I must needs take more lucrative employment." He stood up as he spoke, tossing back the contents of his tankard. Fascinated, Rosamund watched the way his throat worked as he swallowed in one gulp without taking a single breath.

"I shall go and make myself respectable," he declared, and departed the parlor.

Rosamund went to fetch her cloak and gloves. On impulse she slipped her slate and chalk into the deep pocket of her cloak. She had a premonition that she would be spending a large part of this day in antechambers, particularly if Sir Francis had no time to see her today. As she made her way to the yard below, she drew the hood of her cloak carefully over the rich fall of her hair, setting it back a little on her head so that the dainty silver fillet was visible.

Her gloves were of soft green leather to match her shoes. Thomas had grumbled at the expense, but he was far too much of a dandy himself to deny the need for symmetry of color. There was no knowing whom his sister might encounter in the corridors of Seething Lane, and she must be a credit to her name and her august relative.

Thomas looked much more cheerful when Kit Marlowe appeared in the yard, spruced up, his linen clean, his hair tidy beneath a tall velvet hat, crowned with a black plume, his doublet and trunks brushed, his stockings straight, his shoes gleaming. He gave Thomas a mocking bow, his heavy-lidded brown eyes ironic.

Rosamund mounted Jenny hastily. There was provocation in that look and it made her uncomfortable. Thomas grinned and buffeted Kit on the shoulder before swinging onto his own gelding and trotting out of the Four Swans' yard and into the street beyond.

Rosamund followed, her nose wrinkling at the stench from the open sewer running down the center of the lane. The stench was easily accounted for by the careless men untrussing alongside, letting loose odiferous streams into the reeking channel. She edged Jenny to one side of the alley, as far as possible from the danger of splashes, just managing to avoid a three-legged dog who darted beneath the mare's belly, making her stumble on the slimy cobbles.

A dark, forbidding building reared up at the end of the street and a crowd stood at the barred gates, shouting for admittance. A man appeared on the other side of the gates. He opened a small gate within the larger one and the crowd surged forward, but only one at a time could get through the gate, and before he would permit them entrance, he extended a filthy hand for a copper coin, which he dropped into a leather pouch at his waist, before waving them in.

"What is that place?" Rosamund drew alongside her brother.

He broke off his conversation with Kit to look. "Oh, it's Bedlam," he answered with a careless shrug.

"The madhouse? But why are they all paying money to enter?"

"Oh, they wish to see the madmen, they have all kinds in there. It gives good entertainment. . . . Keep up beside me, now. The streets are rough around here."

Rosamund needed no further admonishment and kept Jenny neck and neck with her brother's gelding until they had passed the madhouse and the street widened a little with an archery butt set up in a small green space to one side. Two youths were practicing with their bows, and it seemed an incongruously peaceful, almost countrified activity compared with the bubbling, barely suppressed violence of the lanes behind them.

This street, called Bishopsgate, was much wider than the lanes that surrounded it, and it still maintained some of the characteristics of the original old Roman road, although the paving was no less slimy and the kennel no more fragrant. Gardens stretched on either side, and she could hear from behind the unruly hedges giggles and murmurs and occasionally an uglier sound of flesh on flesh. It was not hard to guess what was going on behind the hedges, prostitutes at their work even at this early hour.

Thomas turned his horse once more off the broader thoroughfare and into the narrower streets leading to the river. He drew up at the door of a substantial house on Seething Lane and dismounted. The door opened directly onto the street and he banged the brass knocker vigorously. It was opened by a dour manservant dressed in unrelieved black, who said, "Master Walsingham?"

"The very same," Thomas agreed. "I bring my sister Mistress Rosamund Walsingham to see her cousin Sir Francis at his bidding. And also a gentleman whom I venture to believe Master Secretary will be pleased to interview."

The manservant stepped aside, calling something over his shoulder. A young man came out at a run and took the horses as Thomas and his companions were ushered into the house.

It was dark, gloomy, and chill in the hall and Rosamund blinked until her eyes had grown accustomed to the dimness. The air smelled stale and dusty, as if windows were never opened. The wood paneling was dark, as were the oak boards beneath her feet. She glanced over her shoulder at Kit, who for a moment seemed to have lost his arrogant self-possession. He looked uncertain, ill at ease.

She wondered how much was at stake for him with this interview. He needed money, she knew. Was his need truly desperate? Dressed as he was in her brother's finery, he didn't look like an impoverished student, poet, and play-maker. But she guessed that the queen's secretary of state was unlikely to be deceived by appearances.

Thomas clicked his finger at her, shaking her out of her reverie, and she followed the two men, who were in turn following the manservant down a long corridor. They were ushered into a small, paneled inner chamber, furnished with a long bench that she guessed was there for the comfort of petitioners awaiting the favor of an interview with Master Secretary, and a bare pine table in the window embrasure.

The manservant disappeared and they waited for a moment in an awkward silence. Kit began to hum one of his bawdy songs and Thomas leaned against the table drumming his fingers on the surface. Rosamund went to look at one of the two gloomy oil paintings that adorned the paneling. It was a particularly unpleasant rendering of the flaying of Marsyas, not that there could ever be a pleasant rendering of such a subject, she reminded herself when, after a moment's horrified fascination, she turned away.

The manservant returned. "Master Secretary will see you now, Master Walsingham, with your guest. Mistress Rosamund is to remain here."

Rosamund sighed. She'd expected nothing else. At least she'd brought her drawing materials.

Thomas and Kit Marlowe followed the manservant.

Chapter Four

A DARK-VISAGED MAN rose from the chair behind the vast desk and regarded his visitors without expression for a few moments. His mouth was concealed by a lush mustache that curled at its ends, and his long, sharp chin was accentuated by a neat black beard. He wore a tight black cap over short-cropped graying hair, and his doublet and hose were both of purple velvet so dark as to seem black in the dimness of the room, which was lit by a brace of wax candles on the desk throwing their illumination almost exclusively onto the documents laid out beside the quill and inkstand.

Sir Francis Walsingham fingered the great seal of state that hung around his neck, resting against his belly, as he considered his visitors in a silence that seemed to Kit to have taken on a life of its own. After a moment Sir Francis spoke directly to Marlowe, appearing to ignore Thomas. "So, you I take it are the disaffected Cambridge scholar, Master Marlowe."

Kit looked faintly alarmed. "Disaffected, sir? I would not lay claim to such."

"Maybe you wouldn't, but I know what I know." Sir Francis turned his gaze onto his cousin. "You have discussed matters in depth with Master Marlowe, I trust, Thomas?"

"I have explained the nature of the business, sir."

Thomas's eyes sent an urgent message to Kit, who somewhat belatedly bowed to the formidable Master Secretary.

Master Secretary nodded and sat down again. "So, I am assured by my cousin here that you are ready to commit yourself to the service of your queen and country."

Kit was taken aback. He was willing to be employed occasionally but he didn't think he had ever expressed himself to Thomas in such definite terms as making a commitment. "I am committed to my studies at the university," he said. "I am hoping to be admitted to an MA. There is no reason why I should not be. My BA was well earned in a timely fashion."

"Yes, yes, I know all that. But I also know that you hold some questionable views for a scholar destined for the Church . . . hmm?" Sir Francis's gaze was bright with sharp intelligence.

"It is true that in the interests of scholarly discourse, sir, I have on occasion ventured provocative opinions," Kit responded, well aware that an accusation of atheism would finish his academic career. "But such opinions are offered in the interests of enlightenment."

"Are they indeed?" Sir Francis did not look impressed by the argument. "But a reputation you have garnered for, as you say, provocative opinions will prove useful in the service."

"I do not follow you, sir."

"No? Well, let me be clearer. The service is interested in those who would return a Catholic to the throne of England. Scots Mary to be precise. Both France and Spain strive devoutly for that end. They will not . . . *must* not succeed. Their minions are at work plotting across France and Spain and even here in our own land. We will root them out to the very last twig. Do you understand me, Master Marlowe?"

"You are very clear, sir." Kit wished he could sit down. The morning's ale sat sourly in his belly, and a poor and short night's rest did not help his sense of well-being. But he had not been invited to sit, so he stood, concentrating on his interrogator with fierce attention. Sir Francis wielded immense power, and he had a fearsome intellect. Sloppy concentration could result in a signature that would bind Kit to a lifetime's contract without his being fully aware of its ramifications.

"You have earned a reputation for holding doubtful views on the Church," Master Secretary continued. "Those views could gain you the confidence of others who look for the doubtful to convert to their own heresies. You will gain those confidences if you invite them. Your doubts will ensure your acceptance among those groups of Catholics eager for converts among the doubtful members of the Protestant church. We need their names, knowledge of their intentions, and . . ." Here he paused, stroking his beard. "And we need to sow seeds, instigate, implant ideas, plots. Plots that will encourage our enemies to walk into our traps."

Kit shifted his feet. "I see." He did see and he did not like what he saw. This was going too fast for him and he could feel Thomas's impatience like a heat wave behind him. "But I still say, Master Secretary, that I am a scholar, soon to be admitted to my MA."

"You may take an absence from Corpus Christi occasionally without it drawing too much attention, Master Marlowe. And such absences on the queen's service could be . . ." Walsingham's hard black eyes bored into him. "Shall we say lucrative. I do not expect my agents to work for nothing. I understand you are also something of a poet, with aspirations to be a playmaker. You must know well that such pursuits will not put bread upon the table."

88 JANE FEATHER

"Maybe not, but—"

The secretary of state rose again abruptly to his feet, and his voice was glacial. "Let us come to points, Master Marlowe. You are in no position to argue the matter. Your atheistical, nay, heretical views are known to the service. Turn them to our profit, or suffer for them. Believe me, I have no scruples about dealing decisively with enemies of the queen, and those who hold your views are indeed enemies of the throne." He pushed a paper across his desk towards Kit. "Sign, Master Marlowe, or accept the consequences."

Kit felt Thomas at his back now, his body warm against his, his hand on his elbow in a fierce grip. And he knew that he had no choice. Francis Walsingham was rumored to turn the thumbscrews himself if he felt such methods would bring him the information he needed. It was said he would condemn a man to the rack, to the tender mercies of Richard Topcliffe, the queen's torturer in the Tower, without a second thought if he believed it was warranted. And Kit at this moment felt the full force of Sir Francis Walsingham's power like a bright light.

Silently he reached for the quill and signed the document committing him to the service of the queen. As he did so, he felt Thomas relax behind him, his hand falling from Kit's elbow.

"Good." Sir Francis took the signed document. "Remember this, Master Marlowe. Knowledge is never too dear and I will pay whatever price is demanded of me in its acquisition. You will do the same. Thomas will apprise you of your first errand for us. When that is completed, you shall receive payment. I bid you good morning, Master Marlowe."

Kit bowed and stepped back to the door. Thomas said,

"You wished to see my sister, Sir Francis. She is in the ante-chamber and awaits your pleasure."

The secretary frowned as if trying to remember, then he nodded. "Ah, yes. So I did. Bring her in, Thomas. Let me look at her."

Thomas bowed and followed Kit from the room. He opened his mouth to speak, but before he could utter a word, Kit drove his fist into his belly with all the impact of a sledgehammer. Thomas doubled over groaning, cough-ing, his eyes streaming, unable to speak.

"You told him of my views, my doubts . . . you betrayed me," Kit stated in a venomous whisper. He was white with anger, his entire slender frame seemed to quiver with his rage as he raised a fist and drove it once again into Thomas's belly, spitting the words out as he stood over his convulsed lover. "You trapped me. You're naught but a trai-torous dog reeking of the slum kennels."

With a contemptuous kick to Thomas's shin he stalked away, out of the house, and the crash of the front door seemed to shake the house itself. Thomas in agony leaned against the wall, struggling for breath, fighting nausea. He knew well enough that Kit had a volatile temper, easily aroused to violence, particularly if the drink was in him, but somehow it had never occurred to Thomas that the man with whom he had shared so much passion could turn on him with such savagery, without even giving him a chance to defend himself.

Rosamund from the antechamber heard the thump, the gasping choke, the violent crash of the front door, and darted to the door of the antechamber, opening it cau-tiously, peering into the corridor. *"Thomas."* She ran to her brother, slumped against the wall. "What happened? Where's Master Marlowe?"

It was many minutes before Thomas could speak, and Rosamund stood anxiously beside him, wondering what she should do, afraid that someone would enter the corridor and find her brother in this condition, but the corridor remained eerily empty.

"Gone," Thomas gasped at last. "God rot him . . . the ungrateful bastard. He can burn in hellfire for all I care." He allowed his sister to help him straighten up against the wall, where he stood taking shallow breaths until the nauseating pain in his belly lessened and he could breathe more easily.

Finally Thomas pushed himself off the wall and staggered into the antechamber, dropping onto the bench, leaning his head against the wall at his back, waiting for his vision to clear and his breathing to become normal.

Rosamund gazed helplessly at him. "What happened?"

Thomas didn't answer and after another minute he said curtly, "Master Secretary wants to see you."

"Now?"

Her brother groaned. "Ten minutes ago." Painfully he heaved himself to his feet. "Come along."

Rosamund gathered up her slate and chalk and followed Thomas back into the corridor. Outside the secretary's office, Thomas knocked and went in, his sister on his heels.

Sir Francis Walsingham looked up from his papers. "What kept you?"

"A minor matter, sir." Thomas still looked ill, and his voice had a slight croak, but if Walsingham noticed, he said nothing. "May I present my sister, sir? Mistress Rosamund Walsingham." Thomas drew her forward.

Rosamund realized she was still holding her drawing materials and could not make a respectable obeisance unless she put them down. Awkwardly she put them on the edge of the desk before sinking into her curtsy, head bent, skirts sweeping around her. She rose slowly and stood, hands clasped against her skirt in front of her, her green eyes steadily meeting Master Secretary's black gaze.

He examined her in silence for a long minute, then reached for the slate, turning it to face him. When he saw the chalked sketch, he looked up in surprise. "This is your work?"

"Yes, sir. Forgive me . . . I didn't know where to put it," she stammered.

He waved a dismissive hand and returned his gaze to the slate. His black brows met in a deep frown. "It is a remarkable likeness. You have captured the features admirably. But I must question my servant's devotion to his duties if he's willing to take time to sit for his portrait."

"Oh, but he didn't, sir," Rosamund said hastily. "He never came back after he took Thomas and Master Marlowe to see you."

"So this is from memory then?" He sounded incredulous.

"Yes, sir."

"You spent maybe three minutes in his company and retained enough of his image to reproduce it so accurately?" He sounded as if he was accusing her of lying.

"Rosamund has an excellent memory, Sir Francis." Thomas spoke up for her. "She has no small talent for drawing and frequently sketches from memory."

Sir Francis stroked his beard, still gazing at the slate. "A useful talent . . . yes, a most useful talent." He looked up at her again, subjecting her to an intense and most uncomfortable scrutiny before pronouncing, "You might be quite useful after all."

Rosamund frowned and greatly daring asked, "How, Sir Francis?"

"You'll know when you need to." He pushed the slate back to her across the desk and turned to Thomas. "Is she schooled in court conduct?"

"Up to a point, I believe," Thomas replied cautiously. "I do not know how much my mother would have taught her . . . she was weak and ill in her last years."

Rosamund wondered why the secretary had not asked the question of her directly, but it seemed as if both men had forgotten her presence even as they discussed her. She wasn't at all sure she knew anything very much about court conduct. She knew how to curtsy, she knew she must always give precedence to those of higher rank, but she knew nothing of any of the more arcane practices.

"She had better stay here and Lady Walsingham will see to her training. Bring her tomorrow, Thomas." It seemed as if that was the end of the conversation. Sir Francis moved a candle closer to the document he had been studying when they entered and resumed his reading.

Rosamund, once again surprised at her daring, cleared her throat. "Forgive me, Master Secretary, but am I to go to court, then?"

He looked up again, annoyed at the interruption. "You may assume that, yes. Now I have much to do."

Thomas took his sister's arm and hurried her to the door, too quickly for her to do more than offer the semblance of a curtsy. Once on the other side of the closed door he said, "You'll have to learn to accept dismissal without argument, little sister."

"I merely wished for clarification," she protested. Her eyes sparkled. "But truly, Thomas, I am to go to court." The prospect gleamed jewel bright, filled with novelty, opportunity, excitement. There would be new people, new clothes, a world filled with an endless round of activity, of dancing and music, interesting conversation, of hunting and picnics. She had heard the queen most particularly enjoyed picnics and excursions on the river. And most dazzling of all, there would be plays.

"So it would seem." Her brother laughed a little at her obvious excitement. He was beginning to recover, his color slowly returning to its usual ruddiness. "I don't wish to dampen your enthusiasm, little sister, but I should warn you, there's more to court than pomp and circumstance. The rules are rigid and I doubt you'll enjoy the confinement. You've led too free a life up to now, so don't get too excited."

Rosamund's eyes narrowed. She didn't really believe him, but she saw an opportunity. "If that is to be my fate, Brother, it seems only just that I should enjoy my last day of freedom."

"What do you mean, miss?"

"Why, that I would go to the theatre. Just once. No one need ever know. I have no reputation to damage at this juncture, no one knows who I am. I can pull my hood over my eyes and I promise I will stay close beside you all afternoon." She put a hand on his arm. "*Please,* Thomas." Then she added in a musing tone, "Besides, once I am ensconced at court, I might well be useful to you too. There's no knowing whose ear I will have, or what favors I might be able to perform."

"Why you manipulative little—" Thomas cut himself off before he uttered a word that should never be applied to a sister. But he could not help admiring her maneuvering and he was not such a stickler for propriety himself that he could see too much harm in indulging her just this once. After tomorrow she would no longer be his responsibility, she would be in the hands of the queen's secretary of state, and she was right, there was no knowing how useful she might be to her family in the rarefied atmosphere of the court.

"Oh, very well. But now I'm parched. The King's Head is close, we'll go there. The horses can remain here." He didn't add that as the King's Head was the closest tavern to Seething Lane, Kit, in high dudgeon, would inevitably have found his way there, and if Thomas was prepared to forgive the violent and unprovoked attack, then they would patch up their quarrel over a flagon of burgundy. The quarrel must be patched, however resentful and angry he still felt, because he had Kit's orders from Sir Francis and the secretary would not countenance a failure of his new recruit to perform his assigned errand.

Rosamund glowed. Her victory had seemed almost too easy, but her brother was preoccupied by whatever had happened with Kit and less likely to examine the issue closely. She followed him out of the house, an exit accomplished without the assistance of the manservant, and along Seething Lane to Tower Street. The King's Head was a respectable-looking tavern on the corner, the sign freshly painted, creaking in the breeze.

Thomas opened the door and ushered his sister into the narrow, flagged passage. Immediately on the left was the taproom and he pushed open the door, looking anxiously around. He felt a surge of relief at the sight of Kit hunched morosely over a tankard in a drinking booth in the far corner. Bitterly angry though he still was at Kit's treatment, he could not afford to let the wound fester.

"Come, Rosamund." He pushed her ahead of him with a hand in the small of her back. The taproom was quiet at this hour of the morning, only the landlord at the counter, desultorily polishing pewter tankards on a filthy rag. The newly thrown sawdust underfoot was still clean and un-clotted by spilled beer and spittle.

Kit looked up as they entered. His eyes were bloodshot. He said nothing until Rosamund was sitting on the stool opposite and Thomas had called for a flagon of burgundy and a cup of sherry wine for the lady.

"So, my traitorous friend," Kit said, pushing his tankard towards the flagon. "The least you can do is give me wine."

Thomas controlled the urge to give Kit his own back. "Did you ever talk with a man called Nicholas Faunt?" Carefully he poured the burgundy into two tankards. "At Cambridge?"

Kit frowned. It seemed a strange question in that it had nothing that he could see to do with the disastrous events of the morning. "I recall one such," he said at last. "A man of intellect, of good propositions. I found him in the Eagle one evening. A good drinker, generous too." He drank deeply. "What of him?"

"He spends time at the university looking for prospects for Master Secretary," Thomas said. "He listens to the debates, to the idle and not so idle chatter in the taverns frequented by the students. He hears things. And when he thinks he has heard something that might make a man susceptible to an . . ." Thomas paused, taking a gulp of bur-gundy. "Susceptible to an offer from Master Secretary, then he reports back, and I, or someone like me, is sent to pull in the net."

Thomas faced Kit across the table. "Believe me, Kit, I have told Walsingham nothing about you. I was told to go to Cambridge and bring you in. I did so. That is the extent of my involvement. No more and no less."

Rosamund listened, fascinated, trying to make some sense of this. At least she understood now what had first brought her brother and Kit together, a contrivance of Master Secretary's. And it was clear that this morning her brother and Kit had had a falling out, a violent one at that. But what was this talk of treachery? She asked no questions, however, in case she annoyed Thomas and he reneged on his promise to take her to the theatre. She sipped her sherry and listened.

"I like him not, our Master Secretary," Kit muttered into his tankard. "I would not trust him any farther than I could throw him."

"Oh, you may trust him, right enough," Thomas stated. "He is a most conscientious spymaster. You may trust him to execute his work for the queen to his last groat. His pockets are not overly deep but he expends every penny on the service, maintaining his own army of eyes and ears across the Continent. Her Majesty's interests are all that concern him. And she likes him not for it. Her Moor, she calls him, and it is meant unkindly. She cares not for his dark visage." Thomas leaned back in his chair, wincing at the stretch in his bruised belly.

Kit caught the wince and shifted uncomfortably on the bench. He extended a hand across the narrow table and lightly touched Thomas's, an apology in his eyes. Thomas offered a glimmer of a resigned smile. Kit was Kit, and in truth he had good reason to be resentful, although he could have waited to launch such a violent assault until he had all the facts.

"And yet he continues to use his own money to serve her?" Rosamund was still fascinated by Sir Francis.

Thomas shrugged. "Aye. He told me once that her majesty had said to him that if she could manage without him, she'd do so more than willingly. But the queen is no fool.

She knows which side her bread is buttered, and she knows Francis for her most loyal and honest servant." He raised a hand, gesturing for a refilled flagon. "And one of the cleverest men in the realm."

Rosamund nodded. "I wonder what work he wants of me."

Kit looked at her with interest. "He's taking you into his service, Mistress Rosamund."

"He didn't say how, but he said I could be useful to him. I'm to go to court, so perhaps he has a use for me there." She couldn't contain the excitement in her voice. "Tomorrow I am to go to his lady wife for instruction in courtly matters."

"You will be missed at Scadbury," Kit said with a smile. "I was counting on you to read my play, Mistress Rosamund."

Her eyes glowed. "The play about power?"

"That one. My *Tamburlaine*."

"Is it finished?" Thomas asked sharply.

Kit shook his head. "Not quite, but near enough. How I'm to finish it if I'm to be running errands for Master Secretary, I don't know." His voice had a sour edge.

"You'll have time enough between errands," Thomas said. "Sir Francis employs many errand boys and they can't all be at work at the same time. He'll make sure you have time enough to complete your MA even as he uses you. You'll be well situated among the religious doubters at Corpus and other colleges to turn a few into the paths of righteousness as identified by her majesty's master spy." Thomas's tone was ironic and Kit still looked sour.

"When are we to go to the theatre?" Rosamund decided it was time to turn the conversation into an avenue that had less scope for antagonism. "What time does it start?"

"Aha," Kit exclaimed. "So you are to come with us. The stern brother has relented."

"She'll not be identified." Thomas sounded defensive. "No one knows who she is."

"And if there's an affray?"

Thomas laid a hand briefly on his sword hilt. "The apprentices have been quiet enough these last weeks. But if there is a hint of rioting, then she will have my protection."

"An affray?" Rosamund leaned forward on the table. "Why would there be fighting at the theatre?"

Thomas gave another of his careless shrugs. "It pleases some of the louts among the apprentices to start a ruckus, particularly when drunk. Their lives, whatever the trade they're apprenticed to, are hard and tedious and their masters give them little enough opportunity for liberty. When they get it, they make the most of it. The atmosphere of the theatre seems to encourage wild antics and there's always danger the mayor's officers will close the theatres if the rioting grows out of hand."

"But I thought in the liberty the city officers had no authority," Rosamund pointed out.

"Oh, 'tis all confusion." Her brother pushed back his stool. "No one knows for sure whose authority reigns over an apprentice from London causing a ruckus in a theatre in the liberty. . . . Come, I would eat." He walked to the door, pausing there to look back to where Kit still sat at the table gazing into his tankard. "Do you come, Kit?"

Marlowe seemed to shake himself awake. "I come." He stood up, but his eyes were far away. "I had some lines there, good ones." He strode past Thomas and out into the street where he stood, his arms raised to the heavens as he declaimed:

I hold the Fates bound fast in iron chains
And with my hand turn Fortune's wheel about,
And sooner shall the sun fall from his sphere
Than Tamburlaine be slain or overcome.

He laughed exultantly. "What think you of that, Thomas?"

Thomas was looking at him with naked admiration, and again Rosamund recognized the passion that underlay that admiration. "It is fine, Kit, very fine." Thomas flung an arm around his friend's shoulders. "I would hear more."

"And so you shall, my dear, so you shall." Kit laughed again. It seemed he had completely overcome his earlier dark mood and he almost danced down the street, his arm through Thomas's, as he burst into a bawdy song at the top of his strong baritone voice.

Rosamund hurried in their wake back to the house on Seething Lane. It seemed as if her brother had forgotten about her, so absorbed was he in Kit Marlowe, adding his own couplets to the song whenever Kit paused for breath. She listened in wide-eyed fascination to the words of the songs that Kit sang, sliding effortlessly from one to the other. She wasn't sure if he'd made them up himself, but rather thought he must have done. His talents as a wordsmith, it seemed, were not confined exclusively to the magnificent heights of his playmaking.

Chapter Five

ROSAMUND GAZED UP at the flag waving in the late-afternoon breeze. It was atop the building called simply the Theatre. A man stood in the entrance to the building blowing a clarion call on a trumpet, and a group of actors in wigs and stage paint held placards proclaiming Burbage's men were to act *The Danish Prince* by Thomas Kyd. A raucous, jostling crowd was gathered outside in the muddy lane, vendors moving among them selling pies, sweetmeats, and fruit.

"What is this *Danish Prince* about?"

"'Tis another of Tom Kyd's playmaking. A grand tragedy with poison and swordplay, and even a ghost or two," Thomas told her, grinning.

"Are all the plays by Master Kyd?"

"No, not all, but Burbage, who owns the Theatre, has a fondness for his work. Yesterday they showed his *Spanish Tragedy*. Ned Alleyn, his chief actor, is particularly suited to the parts. He is particularly accomplished at fencing and will have plenty of opportunity for cut and parry in this play."

"Come now, Mistress Rosamund," Kit cried. "Encloak yourself tightly." He pulled her hood up over her head, drawing the string tight beneath her chin. His eyes glittered with amusement and mischief and he tweaked her nose playfully as he pulled the hood low over her forehead. "No man must see more than your eyes in this den of iniquity, if you're to be a great lady of the court. Is that not so, Thomas?"

Thomas grunted. In truth he was beginning to regret his indolent agreement to this outing. If their cousin, Master Secretary, were to know of it, Thomas would never hear the end of it. But it was done now, and here they were among the swirling, noisy throng of theatre patrons eager to push their way into the pit. He took hold of Rosamund's hand, fastening it in the crook of his elbow, and moved forward, his free hand on his sword hilt as he pushed his way through the throng, ignoring the curses and blasphemies hurled at him.

The pungent stench of humanity reminded Rosamund of rotting flesh and she held her breath, keeping her head down, almost butting her way through the crowd, but then they were in the theatre itself and she lifted her head, forgetting about her hood, which fell back from her head as she gazed around. The pit was below the stage and was already filling with jeering, laughing flocks of people. There was a gallery above, overlooking the stage, and she assumed Thomas would direct them there, but instead he prodded her forward and up the steps to the stage. A row of stools was positioned on either side of the stage. They were to sit right there almost in the middle of the performance.

Rosamund could barely believe it as she took the stool beside Thomas. They were well away from the throng, up here, insulated from prying eyes, but she made no protest when Thomas pulled her hood up again. "It matters not if the players see you, but I don't know who's in the gallery," he murmured into her ear.

Rosamund nodded her acceptance and sat, hands

clasped tightly in her lap, her eyes darting from side to side.
She might have to be covered, but she wasn't going to miss
a single detail.

There was a disturbance in the pit below, then a figure
jumped up onto the stage, not deigning to use the steps. He
turned to face the pit, his hand on his sword. A ground-
swell of irritation grew into a roar, and four young men
with the flat caps and blue garments of apprentices surged
forward, fists raised. Two of them held clubs.

"Young fool," Thomas muttered. "Get backstage before
there's a riot," he yelled at the man, who glanced at him,
then threw him a cheeky grin.

"My apologies, sir, but I'll not turn tail. They were after
my purse."

Thomas glanced at Kit, who was already standing, his
eyes bright with the promise of action. Thomas sighed,
recognizing the inevitable. Kit loved a fight and would
never turn from one, indeed often enough went in search
of them, finding offense on occasion where it did not exist.
He had no weapon except his fists against the cudgel-
wielding apprentices, so those better supplied had little
option but to fight at his side.

Thomas drew his sword and stepped up beside the
young man. Without waiting for assistance Kit jumped
down into the pit, fists at the ready. There was a surge
forward and the four men and Kit were engulfed. Thomas
leaped into the melee. Rosamund could see nothing, but
her eyes were on the young man on the stage, who for a
moment looked irritated as it seemed his fight had been
taken over, then with a war whoop he jumped back into
the pit, flourishing his sword, plunging into the fracas.

Suddenly the crowd fell back, revealing the four apprentices crumpled on the sawdust of the pit. Men bent over

them hauling them to their feet, helping them limp from the theatre. Kit Marlowe jumped back on the stage, wiping a bloody fist on his britches. Thomas came up beside him, sheathing his sword. Blood was on the edge. The young man, flushed and laughing, sweat dampening his curly hair, jumped onto the stage, wiping his sword with a white handkerchief that instantly reddened.

"Nothing like a melee to give a man a thirst. Where's ale?" Kit rubbed his fist into the palm of his free hand.

Thomas glanced at the young man, who Rosamund now saw was richly dressed in a crimson-slashed doublet and emerald green trunk hose. His hair fell in luxuriant brown curls to his well-padded shoulders, and he still held his sword as if waiting for the opportunity to use it again.

Thomas looked irritated, and Rosamund reflected that after his quarrel with Kit that morning he was probably growing tired of sudden squabbles.

"You almost caused an affray with the apprentices, Master Creighton. The officers of the lord mayor are always on the watch for a 'prentice riot. Burbage can ill afford for his theatre to be closed." Thomas's irritation was clear in his voice.

Kit chuckled. "Come, man, you sound as prim and priggish as a schoolmaster."

The young man grinned and sheathed his sword. With a mock bow he said, "In penance, sir, I shall fetch sufficient ale to quench the thirst of an army."

"Good man." Kit threw an arm around his shoulder. "Hurry, I'm as dry as a nun's tit."

Thomas glowered as the man left the stage, and Kit, with a knowing chuckle that seemed to annoy his lover even more, took his seat on the stage stool again.

"Who is that?" Rosamund asked, anxious to diffuse the

tension before her brother decided he'd had enough of this outing and stormed off, dragging her with him.

"A young cub with a lot to learn . . . Will Creighton." Her brother's brow cleared as he took his seat. "He has aspirations to be a playmaker, thinks himself something of a poet, and even more a lover. There's not a junior lady of the court he hasn't attempted a flirtation with."

"He's very handsome," Rosamund said.

Thomas turned to look at her. "Keep away from idle flirtation at court, miss. It will do you more harm than good, and that one has no money, no prospects. It's not an alliance that the family will countenance, so keep well away."

Rosamund said nothing, merely lowered her eyes to her lap. When William Creighton returned within five minutes bearing a foaming pitcher and two tankards that he presented to Kit with another mock bow, she raised her eyes and smiled. He looked at her curiously and, without returning the smile, offered a half bow before taking a stool on the opposite side of the stage.

Rosamund wondered if her smile had been a little forward. But then for the next two hours she forgot all such concerns. She was enraptured. The play laid a carpet of verse and action before her. She had no thought for Will Creighton, no thought for the groundlings in the pit, no thought for Kit Marlowe or Thomas on either side of her. She absorbed the musical verse of Thomas Kyd, felt shivers as the ghost paced the battlements, gazed openmouthed at the dance of the rapiers, as Hamlet the Prince of Denmark fought his battles, felt the slow exhalations of the dying as they lay crumpled on the stage. The roar of applause rising from the crowd below brought her back to the real world and she sat blinking, dazed, trying to recapture a sense of who and what she was outside the magic of the playmaker's art.

Her brother was on his feet applauding and she jumped up beside him, her hands stinging from the force of her appreciation. Kit Marlowe's acknowledgment was less enthusiastic, she thought, glancing sideways at him. He clapped, but in a muted way, and he was frowning as if not quite pleased with the afternoon's entertainment.

"Was it not wonderful?" she exclaimed, her eyes shining as she looked at Thomas.

But he wasn't listening to her, indeed, seemed to have forgotten her existence altogether. He was moving rapidly backstage, his arms outstretched to encompass any of the players he encountered. Kit followed him, still with that expression of qualified rapture. Rosamund looked around. Suddenly she was alone on the stage and the groundlings were surging towards the doors amidst a cacophony of laughter, curses, blasphemies.

With a decisive toss of her head she let her hood fall back and followed in her brother's footsteps. She found herself in the tiring-room and shrank back into a corner as she realized this was no place for a woman. The players were wiping the white paint from their faces, stripping themselves of their costumes, those who had played the female parts stepping out of farthingales, unrolling stockings, tossing wigs to the tables. The hubbub filled her ears and she had difficulty disentangling the threads of the conversation.

There was talk of the low takings, of the imminence of closure because of the affrays, of jocular arguments on the manner of swordplay. Whether it had been sufficiently skillful, acrobatic, whether Ned Alleyn should return for more tutoring at the fencing school next door to the theatre.

Ned Alleyn laughed off the criticism as he wiped his

face clean and donned his street clothes. "I'll challenge any one of you to handle the rapier on that stage against me."

"A challenge I'll take up with pleasure," Kit Marlowe said, stepping forward. He was not known to this group and Thomas Walsingham said swiftly, "Ah, my friend is of choleric temperament. He will fight before he will kiss. Let us go drink, my friends. My purse is at your disposal."

"No . . . no, Thomas." Kit laid a hand on his friend's arm. "Let us see if our player prince here will meet my challenge. But you must needs lend me your rapier."

Ned Alleyn regarded him with narrowed eyes. "Are you drunk, sir?"

Kit laughed. "Not nearly enough to make this anything more than a pleasant exchange. You issued a challenge, I accept it."

The actor shrugged and took up his rapier. "Then let us get to it."

Resigned, Thomas unsheathed his weapon and handed it to Kit. "I assume you're versed in the art," he said softly.

Kit merely laughed and stroked the hilt of the sword. "Come, Master Alleyn, onstage."

The company followed the two back onto the stage, standing at the rear as the two laughing combatants took their stances at the front. Rosamund stood at the back, still unnoticed, still, she assumed, forgotten by her brother. She caught sight of Will Creighton standing, equally ignored, to the far side of the stage.

The long, thin rapiers were hard to maneuver with any delicacy, but Rosamund saw clearly that Kit Marlowe had somewhere learned the art. He was perhaps not quite as accomplished as Ned Alleyn, but he gave him a good match and they ended with laughter and mutual congratulations.

"We must drink," Kit declared, flinging an arm around

his erstwhile opponent. "A flagon of sherry wine or burgundy? Which would you prefer . . . my dear friend Thomas will supply it." He beamed at Thomas, who acceded with a small nod.

Rosamund thought she should make her presence felt once more and stepped forward, laying a hand on her brother's forearm. He started, then looked at her. "God in heaven, are you still here?"

"Where else should I be, Brother?" Her tone was tart.

He shook his head as if dispelling cobwebs, then said, "Nowhere, of course. But what the devil am I to do with you now?"

"Why should you do anything? I will stay at your side. No one will notice me . . . they haven't thus far, after all."

If Thomas was aware of the subtle dig, he gave no sign. Kit was loudly demanding his company to the tavern and the players were all moving together towards the street door.

Rosamund could read his dilemma as if it were an open book and she waited for the decision she knew he would make. Thomas was too engaged in present company. He had drunk his share of ale and wasn't prepared to let Kit Marlowe spend the evening in that company without himself.

"Come." He strode off after the departing players, and Rosamund gathered her cloak around her and followed quickly. Will Creighton joined the tail of the procession, chatting with a young apprentice who had played one of the female parts. He seemed familiar with the players, Rosamund reflected. He certainly behaved with the confidence of one accepted by the troupe.

They went out in a crowd, jostling and jesting, onto Bishopsgate, and made their way to the Black Cock tavern.

It was busy with theatre-goers, all in high spirits. Voices were raised in greeting as the players entered the taproom, and Ned Alleyn doffed his hat with an elaborate flourishing bow in acknowledgment. Her brother seemed well-known to the groups of drinkers, Rosamund observed. They called him by name and he responded with a laughing word or two. A small man emerged from the shadowy corners of the taproom, shabbily dressed in a greasy doublet and worn hose, but his eyes were bright with intelligence and he greeted Walsingham like a long-lost friend.

"Ah, Tom . . . Tom Kyd, the playmaker," Thomas declared, flinging an arm around Kyd's shoulders. "We have much enjoyed your words this afternoon, my friend, but see here, I would have you meet a potential rival, my friend from Cambridge, Kit Marlowe. He has a play in the making."

Tom Kyd regarded Kit with a wary suspicion. "'Tis a hard life and pays but little. Let me see your words."

Kit reached into his doublet and produced a sheaf of closely written pages. "See what you will."

Kyd examined the first page. "This is no play," he declared, "'tis the obscenities of Ovid unless I'm much mistaken." He continued to read even as Kit stood watching him with a grin on his face and a gleam of malice in his eyes. "'Tis a most excellent translation, sir," Kyd said after a few moments. "For all its obscene content. But you should have a care who reads this. Obscenity and heresy go hand in hand these days and receive much the same treatment. They both go to the fire."

Kit laughed and took back his pages. "It is a work of scholarship for all that. But I mark your warning, sir, and it shall be read only by those of an open mind. Thomas, here, is much taken with it." Kit turned his grin onto Walsingham, who stood beside him. "Are you not, Thomas?"

"It is indeed a work of scholarship," Thomas said. "But best kept for the eyes of those who would appreciate it. Come, let us go to the back room, where we may drink in private. Do you accompany us, Master Kyd?"

"Most willingly." The party moved into a room at the back and Rosamund followed, keeping close to her brother, who seemed to choose to ignore her presence. At least he showed no inclination to introduce her. She guessed that either she was cramping his style somewhat, or he had the notion that if no one acknowledged her, it would be as good as if she weren't there at all. Either way, she could do nothing about it. He took sufficient notice of her, however, to provide her with a cup of canary wine, while the rest drank flagon after flagon of good burgundy, and she sat on a stool in the corner content to listen to the conversation, aware even through her absorption of Will Creighton, wine cup in hand, leaning against the wall alongside the door.

He seemed totally absorbed in the company, his sharp-eyed gaze roaming over the group, resting attentively on whoever was speaking. It seemed to Rosamund that he was absorbing every word, every gesture, with a hunger that she understood. He wanted to be a part of this world as much as she did. And it would be a lot easier for him, she reflected wryly, than it would be for her female self.

After a while she noticed the pages that Kit had read from earlier discarded upon the table. One sheet was blank on the back, and almost without thinking she took up a quill lying nearby and began to draw the scene in front of her as she listened to the lively discussion.

Kit Marlowe was having a heated argument with Kyd about the mechanics of blank verse. He was far from tactful in his comments on the play he had just heard, and finally Kyd, goaded, demanded that he prove himself by reciting some part of his play *Tamburlaine*.

Kit jumped onto the table in the middle of the room, the company gathered around, tankards at their lips, cheering him on, as he launched into verse:

> *Villain, art thou the son of Tamburlaine*
> *And fear'st to die, or with a curtle-axe*
> *To hew thy flesh and make a gaping wound?*
> *Hast thou beheld a peal of ordnance strike*
> *A ring of pikes, mingled with shot and horse,*
> *Whose shattered limbs, being tossed as high as heaven,*
> *Hang in the air as thick as sunny motes,*
> *And cans't thou, coward, stand in fear of death?*

He raised his tankard and drained it, his face unnaturally flushed, his eyes heavy-lidded. "So, thus speaks a man who cares only for power and ambition to his son, who sees the folly in such obsession."

"It sounds a bloody play," Ned Alleyn observed, stroking the hilt of his sword. "Is there a part in it for me? We have need of new plays. Tom Kyd here cannot keep up with the demand." He gave the other man a not-too-playful buffet in the shoulder. "*The Spanish Tragedy* and this young Prince of Denmark are fine enough, but the audience grows restless after the second or third showing."

"I do what I can," Kyd grumbled, holding out his tankard for a refill.

Kit jumped down from the table and called for more wine. Someone else called for venison pie, and Rosamund finally cast aside her cloak. It was hot in the small, crammed room, and no one gave a damn who she was or why she was there. She was also hungry and the prospect of venison pie set her mouth watering.

"Ah, friends, I thought I would find you here. Ned . . . Thomas . . . Kyd, what an afternoon that was. A majestic performance." The exuberant tones came from a new arrival, an elegantly dressed gentleman with fine cobweb lace at his throat and wrists, the hilt of his rapier glittering with diamonds, his gloves edged with pearls.

Rosamund instinctively took a step backwards into the shadow of her corner. This gentleman might well be one who should not see her in this company. Her brother had risen to embrace him, then gestured to Kit. "Kit, you must make the acquaintance of Witty Tom, another Tom, I fear, but we manage to keep ourselves apart." He laughed, clearly pleased with himself. "Tom Watson, here is Kit Marlowe, a playmaker, translator of Ovid's obscenities, poet, wordsmith. Kit, here is Witty Tom, poet extraordinaire, a composer of the pastoral verse, the most elegant translator from the Latin. And a veritable madman when the mood takes him."

Thomas Watson bowed with a flourish of his feather-adorned hat. Kit followed suit, saying, "An honor, indeed, sir, if you are the author of the *Passionate Century of Love*."

"The very same," Watson said with a pleased smile. "You are acquainted with my verse?"

"Intimately," Kit said. "Thomas, call for more wine. Master Watson has a thirst." Kit tucked his arm into Tom Watson's and drew him to a seat on the far edge of the bench at the table in the center of the room.

Rosamund thought her brother looked less than happy at this development, but he signaled to the innkeeper for more wine to be served with the venison pie. The pie was brought in, steaming beneath its golden crust, and the company moved to the table, jostling for places on the benches.

"Why, this is a fine sketch indeed." Ned Alleyn, about to take his place, caught up Rosamund's discarded drawing, holding it up to the lamplight. "It seems we have an artist in our midst." He held it high for the others to see.

"'Tis me to the life, I swear it. And there 'tis you, Tom Kyd, all besplattered and besmirched with last night's dinner." Laughter rose around the board, and Tom Kyd protested even as he brushed ineffectually at the vivid pattern of grease spots on his doublet.

"Whose work is this?"

Rosamund, sitting next to her brother, blushed crimson. Thomas gave her a startled glance, then said, "Oh, my little sister has some talent in that direction. But 'tis hardly courteous, Rosamund, to draw a man without his knowledge." He frowned at her.

"On the contrary, Thomas. The best and most truthful likenesses are caught when the subject is unaware." Thomas Watson smiled at Rosamund as he examined her sketch. "You are indeed skilled with a pen, Mistress Rosamund. A faithful rendering of the scenes from the play would be of much help to the actors, to remind them of the staging in past performances."

He turned to Burbage, who was already delving into the pie. "What think you, Burbage? How many arguments would be saved if you had in front of you a faithful rendering of the staging of last month's *Spanish Tragedy,* or some such?"

"You have a point there, Tom, a point indeed." Burbage nodded to Rosamund, the first time he had acknowledged her. "You must bring your sister whenever you come, Thomas. If she's willing, she can sketch as the play unfolds."

"Unfortunately that won't be possible," Thomas said, passing his sister a spoon and trencher. "My sister is destined for court and there'll be no more theatre outings of this kind."

Rosamund's pleasure in the compliments faded at this; however she held her tongue and the rest of the company lost interest in the subject in favor of venison.

Will Creighton, who had not been invited to the board, set down his wine cup and turned to leave, but Ned Alleyn called out cheerfully, "Come eat, Master Will. Thomas here has loaned his purse and I daresay he'll welcome you at the board."

"As long as he doesn't stir up any more foolish trouble," Thomas declared, slicing again into the pie crust with his dagger. "Burbage has troubles enough without that."

Will bowed towards Thomas, saying, "I venture to suggest, sir, that if a group of ruffians attempted to slice your purse from your belt, you'd give them a fight for it."

Thomas hesitated, then a reluctant smile tugged at the corners of his mouth. "Well, I daresay I would. And you gave Master Marlowe here a welcome opportunity to put up his fists. Come, take a place on the bench."

Will thanked him with a smile and swung a leg over the bench beside Rosamund, who moved up obligingly. "My thanks, Mistress Walsingham . . . it is Mistress Walsingham, I do have it right?" He raised an interrogative eyebrow.

"You do," Rosamund said. "But should we meet at court, I would prefer it if you didn't mention my presence here."

Will accepted a tankard and a slice of pie before saying, "I am entirely at your service, Mistress Walsingham." He glanced sideways at her, his bright blue eyes full of laughter. "Your brother must be a most complaisant guardian to accompany you into this den of iniquity."

Rosamund couldn't help an answering smile. "He's not exactly my guardian, that position is taken by my elder brother, who, alas, has little interest in it. Thomas perforce takes on the role when the mood suits him."

"And when it doesn't, he leaves you to your own devices. That must be very convenient." Will drank deep from his tankard, regarding her over the lip with the same laughing eyes.

"It is," she agreed with a chuckle. "Most convenient except when he remembers convention again."

"Well, it's to be assumed it won't be convenient for him to watch over you too closely at court," Will observed, watching her closely, eyebrows raised.

"I understand that life at court is sufficiently rigid and constrained to do his work for him," Rosamund responded lightly, helping herself to another manchet of bread.

"Superficially, yes," Will agreed, his eyes still on her, reading her expression. "But it is not beyond the average courtier's powers to find ways around that if they so choose."

"And do you so choose, Master Creighton?" Rosamund felt as if she were walking on dagger points. She'd never conducted such a devious conversation before and it made her feel wicked and sophisticated. An invitation to mischief was in every word, and she could hardly wait to accept it.

"It depends on the incentive, Mistress Walsingham." His gaze held hers for a moment, then with a quick grin he raised his tankard to his lips.

Chapter Six

CHEVALIER ARNAUD DE Vaugiras stood naked over the woman on the bed, looking down at her with a half smile. "I must say, *ma chère* Agathe, your late husband certainly taught you well when it comes to satisfying a man."

The woman moved languidly on the silk coverlet, her ivory skin a startling contrast to the crimson beneath her. "Leinster was a savage, Arnaud. A barbarian of the first water." She shuddered delicately. "I could not begin to tell you the things he made me do."

He laughed. "You have no need to tell me, *ma chère*. You demonstrate them so beautifully. And neither do you need to waste your breath in protestation. I know what you like, and presumably so did Leinster."

Agathe tugged at her hands, bound to the pillars of the poster bed. "Let me loose, Arnaud." He bent and untied her and she sat up, rubbing her wrists. "He knew nothing about me. I was thirteen when I was married to him, a mere child. An innocent girl."

Arnaud chuckled. "And you will tell me he depraved you with his debauched tastes in the bedchamber." He went to a sideboard and poured wine from the silver flagon into two silver cups.

"It is easy enough to corrupt an innocent child who is totally within your power," Agathe declared, taking the cup he offered her. But her eyes, a deepest blue, narrowed with sensual memory.

He shook his head, a cynical twist to his thin, well-shaped mouth. "I doubt you were ever an innocent, *ma chère.* You are barely twenty now."

She sipped wine and made no attempt to dispute the statement. Leinster had certainly taught her how to please him, but he had also taught her to acknowledge what pleased her. She had not mourned his death on the hunting field, but she had missed much of the sensual excitement of their marriage . . . until she met Arnaud. And then she had realized how lacking in finesse Leinster had been. Arnaud was an adventurer, suave and sophisticated, rich enough to indulge his whims, a well-connected courtier welcomed in every set, envied by many, respected by even more. Agathe adored him, could refuse him nothing, but she knew that she didn't really know him and suspected no one ever had or ever would.

Sometimes she toyed with the idea of marrying him, but never seriously. The life of a rich widow suited her well, and she knew that marriage to Arnaud would give him total control over her person and her considerable wealth, a control that he would exercise to the full. No, she loved being in his bed, his body drove her to the edge and beyond of ecstasy. She could never get enough of him, whatever his mood. Sometimes his lovemaking could be almost gentle, but always there was the hint of violence beneath the artful caresses, and for as long as she had that and her independence, then she had everything she could want.

Now her gaze was speculative as she regarded her lover. "Something made you more than ordinarily fierce tonight, *mon cher* Arnaud. Who angered you?"

A shadow passed across his eyes. "Why would you think that?"

For answer Agathe rubbed her wrists again. "You bound me tightly, *mon cher*. And I know that look in your eyes by now. Something, or someone, aroused your wrath most powerfully this evening."

The chevalier turned away and she gazed hungrily at the lean, muscled strength of him, the ripple of muscles in his back and buttocks. He was an athlete, a horseman, a swordsman, and it showed in every move he made.

He picked up a night robe from a stool and shrugged into it. "I saw an old enemy this afternoon," he said almost casually. "I didn't care for the memories." He refilled his wine cup.

Agathe slid off the bed, drawing the crimson silk coverlet around her shoulders. She trod the waxed oak boards to stand beside him. "Who was it? Do I know him? It was a man, yes?"

He gave a short laugh. "Yes, *ma chère*, you need have no fear. No woman has ever bested me."

"And this man did?" She was fascinated, unable to believe that anyone could get the better of the Chevalier de Vaugiras. "How? Where?"

"Oh, in Paris some time ago." He shrugged. "I prefer not to think of it." Reflectively a fingertip touched the thin, white line beneath his chin.

Agathe reached up and traced the line with her own fingertip. "He did this, yes? I always wondered how you acquired the scar."

He slapped her hand away, turning on her, his hands moving to her shoulders. With a swift movement he pulled the coverlet from her and bore her backwards to the bed. She fell onto the white sheet, fear and excitement warring in her eyes. She never knew when this mood took him quite how the bout would end and she reveled in every twist and turn.

The morning after the theatre, Rosamund found herself once more in the antechamber of Sir Francis Walsingham's office on Seething Lane. She wore the second of her new gowns, a tawny damask over a cream underskirt. The green kid slippers and gloves went as well with this gown as the other, as Thomas had been pleased to point out. The remainder of her possessions were in the leather panniers in the corner of the room. Thomas, much the worse for wear after the previous evening, was slumped on the bench awaiting the secretary's summons.

Before it came, however, a booming voice lifted in teasing mockery came from the corridor outside the antechamber. "Ah, Mortlake, you've the look of the graveyard about you, a green and wasted air. What debauchery have you been about?"

The manservant who had shown them in answered huffily. "I've no inclination to debauchery as well you know, Master Watson. I leave such diversions to my betters. Are you to see Sir Francis? Should I announce you?"

"No, don't trouble. I'll just put my head around the door."

"Indeed, Master Watson, but there are others with appointments who await his excellency's attention." The servant's voice was stiff.

"Ah, then let us see who it is. I shall be the judge of whether they warrant taking precedence." The door of the antechamber was flung wide and the poet Tom Watson loomed in the doorway, a tall, big-shouldered man with a jocular expression and a wicked gleam in his eye. He looked none the worse for the previous evening's drinking, and his handsome brown velvet doublet edged in gold lace would have graced any royal court.

"Oh, 'tis no one but our friend Walsingham," he said, chuckling. "And here is the little maid from last even. A veritable artist indeed. I'm delighted to renew our acquaintance, Mistress Rosamund." He bowed to Rosamund, his eyes atwinkle.

Rosamund curtsied, careful with the sweep of her gown, the grace of her bent knee, the fluid rise as she raised her head. His smile was so infectious she found herself returning it.

"I'd ask you to keep silence over my sister's presence at the theatre yesterday," Thomas said rather stiffly.

"Certainly, if you wish it." Watson straddled a chair with an air of one who had nothing pressing to do. "Did you enjoy the play, Mistress Rosamund?"

"Very much so, sir. I hope when I am at court to see many such plays."

"Aha, so you are to grace our divine majesty's court . . . excellent, excellent. I trust we shall further our acquaintance there." He swung himself off the chair. "And now, Thomas, grant me a few minutes with our lord and master before you go in. I have an urgent message for his ears, but I'll not be long about it."

"Go to." Tom waved a weary hand towards the door. "We will wait."

"My eternal gratitude." Watson swept them another elaborate bow and left the antechamber.

"Is Master Watson also in Sir Francis's service?" Rosamund inquired.

"There are many of us," her brother returned vaguely.

"Is he always so cheerful? He seems to have suffered no ill effects from last night's burgundy."

"Watson never shows it," her brother responded with a wince. "And unless something rouses his temper, he's as cheerful as a flea on a monkey."

"Oh, rather like Master Marlowe." Rosamund watched her brother's reaction.

Thomas frowned but he made no response, merely slumped back against the wall, closing his eyes against the fierce pounding in his temples.

Rosamund took up her slate and chalk and, remembering the talk last evening, began a sketch of the theatre, and the final scene of *The Danish Prince*. Fallen bodies, rapiers cast aside, cups of poisoned wine, the scene was rich in detail and she wished she could do it justice with paper and pen.

"Sir Francis will see you now, Master Walsingham." The manservant had opened the door so quietly they had neither of them heard him enter.

Thomas stood up, smoothing down his doublet, adjusting the lace at his sleeve. He looked Rosamund over, then nodded. She was enviably bright-eyed and pink-cheeked. "Come."

She followed him into the paneled office where the secretary was seated as before behind his great desk. He looked up as they came in, and he too subjected Rosamund to a close scrutiny. "You choose your colors wisely," he observed. "Or did someone else have the ordering of your clothes?"

"No, sir. I chose them."

"Good. That bodes well. And have you any further sketches to show me?"

"I left my slate in the antechamber, sir."

"Then fetch it."

She curtsied and hurried next door. She couldn't hide

what she had been sketching, but neither could she pretend she had invented the scene on the slate. He would know that she had attended the theatre, and it would reflect badly on Thomas. She held it against her skirts, hoping the material would smudge the chalk sufficiently to make it unrecognizable.

"Here, sir." She curtsied as she laid the slate on the desk. The lines were blurred a little, but it was still recognizable for what it was.

The secretary took it up and frowned at it. He rose and walked over to the window where he held it up to the light. "Where was this?"

She threw an anguished glance at her brother before saying, "At the Theatre, sir. It was a play about the Prince of Denmark by Master Kyd."

Thomas exhaled on something like a groan. Sir Francis turned on him. "You took her to the *theatre*?" He sounded scandalized.

"He didn't wish to, Sir Francis, but I begged him." Rosamund spoke in a rush. "And in truth no one saw me, no one knew who I was." There was no need to mention the rest of the day's entertainment, thank God.

"I'm talking to your brother, not to you," Sir Francis said sharply. "What in God's name were you thinking, Thomas?"

"In truth, sir, no one saw her. I can guarantee it."

Only Will Creighton and Thomas Watson, Rosamund thought.

Sir Francis glowered at him for a moment before saying, "You had better be right." He returned his frowning attention to the slate. "Rosamund, I would have you draw this with ink on paper," he said curtly after a minute. "This afternoon, after Lady Walsingham has taken charge of you.

If you're to be any use to me, I need to see how accurately you can render a scene in something more permanent."

Rosamund curtsied again, flooded with relief. She had no idea how her sketching could be useful to Master Secretary, but if it compensated for indulging in a dubious outing, then she could only be grateful.

Sir Francis reached for a small bell at the far side of his desk and jangled it. When the manservant appeared instantly, he said, "Ask my lady wife if she would be good enough to come to me."

The man bowed and vanished, closing the door silently. Sir Francis said to Thomas, "Have you given Master Marlowe his instructions?"

Thomas too seemed relieved that the dangerous subject had been put to bed. He responded with alacrity, "Yes, sir. He leaves for the Low Countries with the packet tomorrow."

"Good. Send that man of yours, Frizer, with him. He'll need supervision. I'd send Robin Poley, but he's still at work nosing out renegade priests in the Fleet."

"He's been in that filthy prison for six months," Thomas said.

"Aye, and it's long enough. We don't want him catching some pestilence. I'll arrange for his release next week."

"Has he made any turns?"

"Possibly two. He has a silken tongue does our Robin when it comes to convincing a frightened Catholic priest of the wisdom of turning coat. No one can paint the torments of Master Topcliffe's dungeons and a bloody end at Tyburn better than Robin." Walsingham's smile was dour. "We'll have some useful spies in the ranks of the heretical."

Rosamund listened, absorbing every word, although the full meaning was lost to her. While it was rather mortifying to be so utterly ignored by the two men, at the same time her apparent invisibility gave her some fascinating information. Presumably they thought her of such little account that they could talk openly in front of her and she either wouldn't hear or would fail to understand a word. Well, they were wrong on both scores. And what she couldn't piece together now, she would learn to understand later.

"Oh, so here is the dear child." A warm, friendly voice spoke from the door and Lady Ursula Walsingham sailed into the room, her gown of purple embroidered damask over a wide Spanish farthingale barely fitting through the door. "Come, Rosamund, let me look at you."

Rosamund made yet another careful curtsy. But this time she didn't rise until Lady Walsingham took her hand and drew her up.

"Charming, quite charming," Lady Walsingham declared, tipping Rosamund's chin on a forefinger. "We shall make you a beauty, my dear. The envy of all her majesty's ladies."

"I'd advise against that, my dear wife," Sir Francis said drily. "The last thing any ingenue wants among that basket of cats is to draw attention to herself."

"Oh, nonsense." Ursula's smile was serene. "Anyway, I shall ensure that the dear child is well equipped to deal with them. Come along now, my dear. We must leave the gentlemen to their work. Bid your brother farewell. He will come to visit soon enough."

Rosamund murmured her acquiescence, accepted her brother's farewell kiss, curtsied to both men, and turned to follow the lady from the room.

"Provide her with paper and ink, as much as she needs, madam. I have set her a task for this afternoon."

Ursula looked back at her husband with a slightly

hesitant frown. "You know best, of course, sir, but is it really necessary so soon? May she not settle in first?"

"Oh, I think you'll find that Mistress Rosamund will take to the task with alacrity," Sir Francis said aridly. "I doubt she'll find it a hardship. Quite the contrary." He gestured to the slate on his desk. "Don't forget this, Rosamund. I look forward to seeing the fruits of your labor at dinner."

Rosamund hastily picked up her slate, dropped a curtsy, and followed Lady Walsingham from the room.

"Now, my dear, I'll show you to your chamber first. I trust it will please you, it overlooks the garden at the back and is quite quiet."

Rosamund followed the wide damask skirt down the corridor and through a door at the end that opened onto a square hall. A carved staircase rose from the rear to a galleried landing. This part of the house was very different from Master Secretary's lair. It was light and open, the diamond-paned windows gleaming, the paneling polished to a deep, rich glow. The rush-strewn flagstones beneath her feet were clean and fragrant, a hint of lavender rising from the rushes.

"You will always find me in my parlor, my dear." Ursula led the way across the hall to where a door stood half-open. She pushed it open, showing Rosamund a charming parlor, with a deep bay window overlooking the street. A fire burned in the grate, although it was already May, and a bowl of roses stood in the center of a small, round table beside a chair and a tambour frame. "My door is always open, so you must feel free to find me here should you have questions or needs."

"Thank you, madam." Rosamund was painfully conscious of the neatness of this house compared with the grubby, careless state of Scádbury since her mother's death. In fact, even before her mother's death, order had slowly disappeared from the household. How would she order her own household, should she ever find herself in charge of one? She'd had no real training in the domestic arts. But first she had to learn the courtly arts. It all seemed rather overwhelming to a girl who loved her solitude and whose only real interest lay in pen and paper.

"Let us go abovestairs. It will be so pleasant to have a young woman in the house again," Ursula was saying as she preceded Rosamund up the stairs. "Ever since our own dear Frances married Sir Philip, I have felt the lack of companionship, I confess. Of course Sir Philip Sidney is a most wonderful man, a great soldier and such a poet . . . I could never have wished for a better, more congenial match for dear Frances. But I do miss her. And I fear she is lonely these days with Sir Philip governor of Flushing and fighting the Spaniards in the Low Countries.

"Here we are." Ursula opened a door. "Such a trial for women, these never-ending wars. . . . So what do you think, my dear? Will you be happy here?"

Rosamund stepped into the room. It was a small, round chamber at the corner of the house, with windows following the curved wall. A carved bed hung with turquoise velvet and a huge oak chest at its foot dominated the space. There was a simple dresser with jug and basin, and a linen press for her gowns. A low chair and small table were set by the grate. But what took her eye immediately was the deep, cushioned window seat that followed the curve of the windows, so that she thought it was like a cabin in the prow of a ship.

"It's lovely, madam," she said with utter sincerity. "I have never had such a delightful apartment." She went to the window, putting one knee on the cushioned seat as she leaned forward to open the window. A sliver of water, shining in the sun, caught her eye at the end of the long garden. "Is that the river, madam?"

"Yes, Frances used to love this chamber because of the river. In the winter, of course, when the trees are bare, you can see it clearly."

"Was this then your daughter's chamber?" Rosamund looked back at the woman who stood at her shoulder.

"Yes, I thought it suitable," Lady Walsingham said. She went to a heavy rope hanging from the ceiling beside the door and pulled it vigorously. "You must meet Henny, who will attend you."

The bell was answered so quickly Rosamund thought the young girl who appeared must have been waiting just outside. "Yes, madam." She looked very young, no more than twelve, Rosamund thought, but she had merry eyes and a pleasing plumpness that seemed to imply a person who enjoyed the good things of life.

"Henny, this is Mistress Rosamund, she is to be your new mistress during her stay here."

"Mistress Rosamund." Henny curtsied, her curly hair springing loose from the cap that was supposed to confine it.

Rosamund smiled at her, unsure how to respond, never having had a personal maid before.

"Now Henny will unpack your belongings, while I show you the rest of the house," her hostess said. "And then we shall have a light noon meal. Sir Francis does not care to dine before five o'clock. It interrupts his work. He returns to work after dinner, of course, but I have finally managed to persuade him of the benefit of taking an hour or two to dine each day." She sounded resigned as she led the way around the galleried landing. "He works so very hard, I barely see him."

They were walking now down a gallery that ran off the landing. Portraits adorned the walls. "Your ancestors for the most part," Ursula said. She stopped in front of a painting. "That is Sir Francis's stepfather, in whose house my husband grew up. He was connected to the Boleyns and the family thus claims connection there with her majesty." She glanced at Rosamund. "You too, of course, can claim that connection."

"It seems very loose, madam." Rosamund stepped back to observe the portrait more closely. With no blood connection there she could not expect to see any likeness to her own family of Walsinghams.

Ursula smiled. "It matters not, my dear. In the world of the court the most tenuous links are proclaimed if they can be put to good use. As you will no doubt learn."

Rosamund spent the afternoon in her chamber, amply supplied with paper, three new quills, and a full inkpot, re-creating the final scene of the play in sharp black ink. She closed her eyes trying to recapture Ned Alleyn's face as he lay dying in front of her, his hand slipping from his rapier as it lay bloodied beside him. Then she sketched in less detail the faces of the audience sitting on stage stools on the far side of the stage. Will Creighton was one of them, but she found when she'd finished that somehow, contrary to her intentions, quite precise details had crept into the sketch of his face and form as he leaned forward, his eyes intent on the action. Just how had that happened?

She sat back and looked critically at the drawing. She had not even been aware of her pen strokes as she re-created this accurate likeness. The luxuriant, glossy dark curls were perfectly arranged, shaping his square-jawed face, his mouth had just the right curve to it, the straight nose was exactly right, and his eyes seemed to look out from the paper with all the bright intensity of reality.

Her hand had clearly had a mind of its own with the result that Master Creighton stood out from the surrounding, vaguely outlined audience like a sore thumb. Sir Francis would notice and probably remark upon it. If he was acquainted with Master Creighton, which would not be unlikely, such an accurate portrait would certainly make him question Thomas's assertion that no one from court had seen her in such dubious company. With a curious reluctance she crumpled the paper and tossed it into the wastebasket before reaching for another sheet.

The afternoon passed so rapidly that Henny's knock on the door just before five startled her. "Begging your pardon, Mistress Walsingham, but my lady requests your presence in the great parlor before dinner."

"Is it that time already?" Rosamund jumped up, carrying her drawing over to the window to examine it closely in the light. In general it pleased her, but she wasn't entirely sure she'd captured the shadows at the rear of the stage satisfactorily. But that could be worked upon.

She went to the dresser where Henny had already unpacked her comb and brushes and tidied her hair, fixing the silver fillet around her forehead, letting her hair fall loosely to her shoulders. She washed her hands in the basin that Henny had filled from the jug and smoothed her tawny damask skirts over the stiffened canvas frame that supported them.

"Will I show you the way to the great parlor, mistress?" Henny opened the door for her.

"Yes, if you please, Henny. I don't believe Lady

Walsingham showed me that chamber." Rosamund picked up her drawing again. Sir Francis had said he wanted to see it at dinner. She was unaccountably nervous as she followed Henny down the stairs and across the hall.

The girl stopped outside a pair of double doors. "In here, mistress."

Rosamund nodded her thanks and lifted the latch. She curtsied in the door before moving forward into the room. Ursula greeted her with a smile. "Come in, Rosamund. We are a little more formal this evening as we have a guest."

It was a much larger apartment than Ursula's parlor, or the room where they had eaten earlier. Wood-paneled with a few rugs scattered across the oak floorboards, it was as fragrant and polished as every other chamber in the mansion on Seething Lane.

"Rosamund, this is Master Phelippes. He works with Sir Francis and is dining with us this afternoon." Ursula, smiling, introduced Rosamund to a short, thin gentleman, his face much pockmarked, with thinning yellow hair and a neat yellow beard. He was slightly hunchbacked as if he'd spent many hours crouching over a desk. A pair of spectacles hung on a chain around his neck and she noticed that his fingers were ink-stained.

"Mistress Walsingham." He gave her a nod of a bow. "Sir Francis was telling me of your skill at depiction. I look forward to seeing an example."

"Were you able to complete the drawing of the theatrical scene, as I asked, Rosamund?" Sir Francis, standing beside the empty grate, regarded her over a goblet of wine.

For answer, Rosamund handed him the sketch and then stepped aside, waiting anxiously for his reaction.

"Good," he pronounced after a few minutes. "You have Ned Alleyn to the life, and Richard Burbage too, here with the pike. You have considerable talent, although I would prefer it applied to more conventional subjects." He handed the drawing to Master Phelippes. "Ignore the subject matter, Phelippes, but see if you agree with me on the skill."

His guest donned his spectacles and nodded over the drawing for quite some minutes. He refrained from comment on the subject, merely saying, "A talent to be put to good use, I trust, Master Secretary."

Walsingham nodded. "I have some ideas. Shall we dine?"

Thomas Walsingham sprawled in a chair in the Four Swans, cradling a tankard of ale, watching Kit fitting his scant possessions in a leather saddlebag. "Did Phelippes explain anything to you of the message you carry?"

Kit scowled over a creased shirt as he rolled it tight. "Merely that it was in cipher. He took my boot and kept me shoeless for an hour while some cobbler secreted the message into the heel." He stamped his foot. "And it's as uncomfortable as the devil. It feels like a stone."

"Well, you'll be rid of it when you reach Ghent," Thomas said. "But I think you need a sword, my friend."

"And where am I to come by such a weapon?" Kit's scowl deepened. "I don't have a gentleman's purse."

Thomas laughed. "Frizer is bringing you one. You may think him an unsavory creature, but he knows this work well and you can trust him while you're on this mission. Of course, I wouldn't recommend trusting him if you aren't working with him. He needs a vested interest to be trustworthy."

Kit grunted. "You comfort me." He crammed the shirt into the bag and fastened the straps. "Why am I chosen for this task, Thomas?"

"Because you are available," his friend responded simply. "And in need. You will be paid on your return, remember."

"And how am I to pay for my passage?"

"Frizer will take care of all that . . . passage, lodging, all the necessities." Thomas got up from his chair and went to refill his tankard. He paused at the window to look down into the yard. "Ah, and see, here he comes. Sidling around the wall as usual. Frizer never cares to be noticed. If you'd take a word of friendly advice, Kit, you'll watch how he does it. It's a useful trick to learn in this business."

Kit said nothing, merely flung himself onto the bed and took up his own tankard, draining it in one swallow. "Will you be at Scadbury when I return?"

"Probably, unless my cousin has work for me also. He has mentioned Paris. I may well be sent there to cozy up to Morgan. He works in close secret for Scots Mary and is in secret correspondence with her. It may be that he is the means to finish her."

"Finish her . . . in what way?" Kit's eyes sharpened.

"You know of the Bond of Association?"

Kit shook his head, reaching for the flagon of ale.

"Well, 'tis decreed that if a plot conspires to treason, to do harm to the true queen, then all involved shall be executed for treason, including the one who should benefit from the treason, even if said person was unaware of the conspiracy."

Kit sat up. "That's abominable. How can one who is innocent and unaware be condemned for the fault of another?"

Thomas's smile was ironic. "My cousin considers it an invaluable tool in his work, which, my dear Kit, is simply to ensure the queen's continued reign and the safety of this our beloved realm from the threat of invasion. Spain

Chapter Seven

MARY STUART EDGED her chair closer to the meager fire. Despite the season, her apartments in this outbuilding of Chartley Hall were always damp and chilly. She coughed into a lace-trimmed handkerchief, and as so often, one cough triggered a violent spasm that left her gasping for breath, her eyes streaming. Her little Skye terrier lying at her feet lifted his head, regarding her with big brown eyes.

"Madam, why do you not take to your bed? You are ill and weak." One of her ladies came forward anxiously, bending to wrap a lap rug around her knees and adjust the shawl over the queen's shoulders.

"I would be right enough if I were permitted to take the air." Mary shivered in the shawl, then resolutely took up her needlework. Embroidery was her most beloved occupation, but in this grim, drafty prison she found less and less pleasure in it. She sighed, remembering the old days at Shrewsbury Castle when George Talbot had been her guardian and she and his wife, Bess, had passed so many happy hours at their embroidery. The tapestries they had worked on together were some of her most precious achievements.

She looked around the gloomy chamber with a sigh. It was so damp and chill that if it weren't for the curtains and tapestries, it would be uninhabitable. Her ladies huddled around the fire and she felt a stab of guilt. She knew it would be right to release them from their duty to her, but she could not manage without them. She needed their companionship, and their nursing.

At the beginning of her long years of imprisonment she had had her own court in exile and enjoyed all the trappings of royalty. Those days were long gone and the comforts of her first confinement at Shrewsbury replaced by one increasingly grim prison after another. Over those interminable eighteen years the ladies who had accompanied her into exile had gradually disappeared. Some had died, others had returned to their own lives and families. They had been difficult to replace and now her personal attendants numbered only five ladies of the bedchamber, who were served by four maidservants.

Illness had rescued her from the horror of Tutbury Castle, high on its windy hill where every needle draft through the ill-fitting windows and walls of her prison had given her an ague so fierce the physician had despaired of her life.

She should have died. That would have saved her cousin Elizabeth some trouble, she reflected with grim humor. It was worth hanging on to life, such as it was, simply to thwart the queen of England.

She heard the outer door to her prison opening and recognized instantly the hard tread of her present and most pernicious jailer, Sir Amyas Paulet. The door opened and he stood there, not even baring his head. The little dog growled softly but didn't move.

"I am glad to see you out of your bed, madam. Your health is improving, it would seem."

"Not really." She selected another silk from her basket. "But I find it lifts my spirits to be occupied. Of course, that probably annoys you, Sir Amyas. Since you spare no efforts to keep my spirits in the trough of despair." She looked briefly at him, loathing the sight of him, the neat ginger mustache and little beard, the thin lines of disapproval on either side of the downturned mouth, and the hard eyes of the fanatical Protestant.

He ignored this, glancing over his shoulder to click his fingers at two men who stood in the door. They moved swiftly to Mary's chair of state set beneath the cloth of state that she herself had embroidered at the beginning of her imprisonment with her chosen motto: *In my end is my beginning.*

Under Mary's shocked gaze they dismantled the cloth of state and removed it, together with the chair.

"What are they doing?" Mary's chief attendant faced Paulet in white-faced fury. "By whose order is this done?"

"That is no business of yours, my lady."

He turned to leave but Mary's voice arrested him. She spoke quietly, wearily. "What is the meaning of this, sir?"

He turned back to her. "Madam, you know its meaning. You are no longer possessed of royal status, thus you are not entitled to the accoutrements of royalty. In future you must consider yourself a subject of Her Majesty Queen Elizabeth." With a bow he turned on his heel and left.

Mary stared into the fire, hearing only distantly her ladies' outraged protestations. She knew what it meant. By stripping her of her royal status she was rendered subject to the ordinary rule of law like any other subject of the realm. Would her cousin dare to subject her to a trial, dare to order her death? Cold fingers of fear crept up her neck. She had never envisaged this. She had been certain that Elizabeth would honor their kinship, and, so passionately wedded to the divine rights of her own royal lineage, that she would never lightly cast aside those of another queen.

But she had been wrong. Elizabeth had perhaps succumbed to the persuasions of her councilors, or men such as Paulet, who saw in Mary an implacable and most dangerous threat to the throne. Her lips thinned. And she would be so, if she were given the chance. The stakes were even higher now. She must gain her freedom, ascend the throne of England, if only to save her own life. And in the doing she would return this poor realm to the only religion of salvation.

She set aside her embroidery and went to a locked chest standing against the damp wall. A film of mold was growing on the wood where it pressed against the wall. She took a tiny key from within her bodice and unlocked the chest, taking out a packet of letters. They had been delivered to her by a young man, Robin Poley, who had first come into her service when she was at Tutbury and had had the freedom to ride out over Hanbury Hill. Poley had humbly worked with her horses as far as the world knew, but the truth was quite other. He brought letters from her agent Thomas Morgan, in Paris, who recommended the messenger as a loyal servant, one who could be trusted. Ever since, Poley had somehow managed to appear at irregular intervals, following her finally here to Chartley, bearing letters from Morgan describing the efforts being made by her French cousin the Duc de Guise, and the Spanish king, Philip, to order a combined French and Spanish invasion in her name.

It was in the interests of both France and Spain to have a fellow Catholic on the throne of England, to bring that renegade country back into the Catholic fold, where it would cease to pose a military threat. Mary's smile was a touch cynical as she reflected that they would expect to rule England through her, but they would find that she was not quite the weak and malleable woman they believed her to be. She would rule in more than name, just as she had ruled Scotland, leading her own army in battle on several occasions.

Mary sat down by the fire and opened the packet. The letters gave her heart as always. She was not forgotten in this northern wasteland. But it was time she issued her own call to arms, gave some indication that she appreciated their efforts and was willing to do her part to encourage the Catholic gentry in Scotland, who fretted under the yoke of Protestant England. Even though her own son, James, supported by Elizabeth, was on the Scottish throne, ruling as a Protestant king, Scottish Catholics still considered Mary their queen, and they would rally to her cause.

"Charlotte, would you send Barbara to me?"

"Yes, madam. Is there anything *I* can do for you?"

"Yes, could you bring me parchment and pen?"

Charlotte fetched an inlaid ivory standish containing the required articles, and Mary after a moment's thought began her letter to Scotland. She used the code she always used in her clandestine correspondence and, when she had finished, sanded and sealed the letter, using not the royal seal but a simple imprint from her rosary that hung at her waist. It would identify it as authentic for her supporters, but no one else would understand the significance. Or so she hoped and prayed.

She handed it to the maid Barbara, who stood waiting for instruction. "Take this and look out for the man Poley. He will make his appearance at some point in the next weeks to do me service. He will be in the village, or in the stables, anywhere he won't be easily noticed. Give him this."

Barbara took the letter and tucked it into her bosom. "I will, madam."

Mary sat down again, leaning her head against the hard

wooden back of her chair. Her prison, always grim, was now denuded. Her cousin had taken the last vestige of royalty from her. But she could not take away her God. She touched the Agnus Dei on her breast and closed her eyes.

Sir Francis Walsingham made his way through the long corridors of Whitehall Palace. His brow was furrowed, his step hasty, and he carried a sheaf of papers under his arm. Servants and courtiers dodged aside as he progressed, apparently blind to his surroundings, until he reached the antechamber to the queen's privy chamber. The two pikemen at the door raised their weapons and banged them down resoundingly on the stone-flagged floor.

The door opened and a young woman stepped into the corridor. She curtsied. "Her majesty will see you at once, Sir Francis." She stepped aside for him and glided away, leaving him to enter the royal presence alone.

Francis bowed deeply, took three further steps, and bowed again. "Your majesty is good to see me."

"Nonsense, Francis. I could hardly refuse to see my secretary of state." The queen set aside her quill and rose from the desk. She was magnificently dressed as always, her gown of crimson velvet edged with pearls, a massive diamond pendant reaching the sharp vee of her stomacher, and her gold and sapphire pomander hanging from her jeweled girdle. She was fifty-three and her once vibrant red hair, faded now, was concealed beneath a jeweled hood.

"So what have you to say to me? Your message implied some urgency."

Her tone was sharp, her dislike of her secretary never far from the surface. Francis was accustomed to it and rarely let it deflect him from any course of action he deemed in his sovereign's best interest.

"Not so urgent, madam, that I would interrupt anything more important," he said with a faint questioning inflection. When she waved impatient dismissal of this, he continued, "I would beg a personal boon, madam."

Elizabeth looked at him with interest. "Indeed, that is unlike you, Francis. You hector me constantly on what I should be doing to protect the realm and further my own interests, but I do not recall your ever asking me a personal favor."

"I beg to contradict your majesty. I do not believe I ever *hector*."

The queen shook her head impatiently and took a seat. "I will call it what I wish."

Francis bowed. "As your majesty wishes."

"So, what is this boon?" She waved a hand towards a chair and gratefully he took it. The queen was capable of standing for hours and had kept many a diplomat and statesman on his feet almost to the point of collapse.

"I have a young cousin, madam. Rosamund Walsingham. She is orphaned and in the guardianship of her eldest brother, Edmund, who is . . ." He paused, carefully putting the sheaf of papers onto his lap. "Who is quite unsuited to the task. Her elder brother Thomas has done his best, but, as you know, Thomas works in your service and cannot be always in attendance on his sister."

"Thomas works for *you*." It was a crisp correction. In certain moods it pleased her majesty to deny knowledge of or interest in her secretary of state's secret service. In other moods she would question Francis closely on every detail, and some of his agents, those engaged in the more respectable end of the service, were actually servants of the crown, paid by Sir Thomas Heneage, the treasurer of the Queen's Chamber, on presentation of a warrant signed by Sir Francis. The less reputable were paid off the books, frequently out of Walsingham's own purse and dealt with by Master Phelippes on a mission-by-mission basis. Most of the time, Elizabeth chose to ignore their contribution.

"Quite so, madam." Francis bowed his head in acknowledgment, although he knew the queen had talked several times with Thomas about aspects of some of his missions. "And as such cannot undertake full guardianship of his sister."

"How old is the girl?"

"Seventeen, madam."

"And of what person . . . what character?"

"A pleasing enough countenance, I would say." Francis chose his words carefully. "But I doubt she would stand out too much in a crowd." The queen could quickly become jealous if one of the ladies of the court seemed to outshine her, and she was particularly sensitive to this in the more youthful ladies of her retinue.

"And her character?" The queen played with her jeweled fan in her lap, opening and closing it with rapid, little movements.

"As far as I know, madam, exemplary."

"And you ask my patronage for her?"

"I would beg your majesty to take her into your service as a most junior lady of the bedchamber."

"Is she able to provision herself? As you know, the ladies in my service receive only one court dress a year. She must be able to make shift for herself otherwise."

Francis hid his inner sigh. He knew well the queen's parsimony, a frugality that did not apply to her own wardrobe. "I will undertake to provide her with all necessities. When she has acquired a little court polish, I will find a suitable match for her."

"If I take to the girl, I will find her a match myself," her majesty declared, standing up. "You need not trouble yourself. Bring her to me." She walked towards a door in the far wall, which Francis, rising swiftly to his feet, knew led into her bedchamber. "Is that all, Master Secretary?"

"There were one or two other matters, madam." Francis gathered his papers close to his chest and followed her.

Elizabeth walked into the vast chamber. Virginals stood against the far wall, a fire burned in the grate. Even in summer the stone walls of the ancient palace held a chill. "Tell me," she commanded, sitting down at the instrument.

"Madam, I would urge you once more to act more decisively against your cousin." Francis laid his papers on the top of the instrument. "I have letters here from Mary to Thomas Morgan in Paris, asking him how much support she can expect from the French king. How big an army of invasion will he guarantee."

Elizabeth's mouth thinned. "I have told you, Master Secretary, that I will do no more against my cousin. I have removed her chair of state, but I do not believe that that in itself can uncrown a queen, for all that Sir Amyas believes it can. Those letters you have can show me nothing worse than I have seen countless times before. My cousin is well guarded, her imprisonment not as pleasant as hitherto, and I am convinced Amyas Paulet will let nothing slip past him." She ran her fingers over the keys. "I am tired of your gloomy prophecies, sir."

Francis selected a paper from the sheaf. "If your majesty would only read this, you would see how necessary it is to act now. For the love of God, madam, let not the cure of your diseased state hang any longer on deliberation. We must act to root out the danger twig by twig."

"Oh, the devil take your twig by twig." Elizabeth sprang

to her feet. "I am master of this realm, and I will make the decisions necessary to its health." She hurled her fan at him and he sidestepped just in time.

Francis bent to retrieve the fan and handed it back with a bow. It wasn't the first missile she'd hurled at his head in their long association.

The queen glared, then said more moderately, "That was ill-mannered of me, but you do test my patience, Francis."

"If I may say so, madam, you test mine."

She took a turn about the room, her skirts moving stiffly with her stride, then she stopped and turned to face him. "What do you want of me?"

"Merely that you agree to the Bond of Association in regards to your cousin Mary Stuart."

Elizabeth sighed. "I cannot like it, Francis. I have never believed in reflective guilt. To punish an innocent for the crimes of others. It is not right."

"Madam, Mary Stuart is not an innocent. She is working ceaselessly to have you removed from the throne. She is in continuous correspondence with the Duc de Guise, her cousin in France, to raise an army of invasion, her agents work in Spain to raise support for such an army there. She is *not* guiltless, madam. You must see that."

Elizabeth's face suddenly looked old beneath the rouge and white powder. She gazed at her secretary of state for a long minute, almost as if she didn't see him, then said, "I have heard you out. I will hear no more today. You are dismissed."

"Madam." Francis bowed and moved backwards to the door. He hesitated for a moment as he reached behind him for the latch. "And my cousin . . . ?"

"Yes, you may bring her to me." The queen returned to

her instrument and began to play as her secretary of state left the royal apartments.

Francis made his way back along the long series of corridors, his brow deeply furrowed, his head down as if he were watching his feet. He turned a corner and came to an abrupt halt as he found his way blocked by a group of courtiers deep in conversation. He glared at them irritably as they moved aside for him. One of them, a tall, elegant gentleman with an olive tint to his complexion, bowed deeply and broke away from the group to walk beside the secretary as he continued on his way.

"I have a message from Thomas Morgan in Paris, Sir Francis." The man spoke softly, his head lowered towards his companion's ear. Master Secretary continued walking, almost as if he didn't realize he was being spoken to. "I understand the Duc de Guise is close to amassing a considerable force in readiness for an attempt to rescue the Queen of Scots."

"Do you indeed, chevalier." Sir Francis raised his eyes to cast a brief glance at Arnaud de Vaugiras. "I have received similar intelligence. But my sources have not as yet discovered the details of how this rescue is to be accomplished. Where they intend to land, for instance, would be most useful."

"If I can discover that information, sir, I will inform you immediately." The chevalier bowed, his eyes giving nothing away.

"The queen will be deeply in your debt, chevalier." Sir Francis nodded and turned a corner. He continued on his way out of the palace, so lost in thought that he barely noticed the bows and greetings proffered as he passed. Something about the chevalier made him uneasy. Nothing concrete, just an instinct, and Master Secretary had learned to trust his instincts.

Nothing in the chevalier's circumstances justified this unease. The man was wealthy, had had an English mother although he was brought up at the French court. As was often done, he had been sent as a youth to the English court to finish his education and had since then moved seamlessly between the two courts. Elizabeth favored him. He was handsome, not too young and not too old, and had just the right deferentially flirtatious touch that always pleased her in a courtier.

Several months ago he had offered his services to Sir Francis, maintaining that he had a close relationship with Thomas Morgan, the Queen of Scots' chief agent in Paris. The chevalier was a devout Protestant with Huguenot relatives, some of whom had been killed in the great Paris massacre of St. Bartholomew's eve on that dreadful August day in 1572. The chevalier was therefore a passionate enemy of the Catholic Church and the Scots Queen in particular.

Sir Francis could find no evidence to dispute this history. But it all seemed too perfect a fit. He preferred to have something to hold over the men he recruited. Loyalty was best achieved through fear and coercion in Master Secretary's experience, and not through personal conviction. So far the tidbits of information the chevalier had brought him had been fairly insignificant, but they had been accurate. Yet Walsingham remained chary of using the man in a more devious role. There was just something about him . . .

He resolved to set Ingram Frizer onto him. If anyone could ferret out murky details, old rumors, deeply buried secrets, it was Frizer. If there was anything to justify the secretary's instinctive unease, Frizer would find it.

Rosamund waited impatiently for her instruction in proper court conduct to begin, but the days passed in the mansion on Seething Lane with no mention of it from Lady Walsingham. Rosamund longed to bring up the subject herself, to give vent to the host of anxious and excited questions about this new life that awaited her, most of all about when it was to begin, but something about Ursula's quiet serenity was inhibiting, and she felt it would be a grave discourtesy to try to hasten the matter. It might appear as if she were rejecting the kindness and hospitality that made her feel so welcome, and such a discourtesy was not to be thought of.

The days slid one into another as she sat with Ursula in her parlor, sketching while Ursula worked on her embroidery or her household accounts. Then Rosamund realized that she had been missing the point all along. All she had to do was listen to Lady Walsingham to gain insight into the world she was to enter. Nothing further had been said about her court presentation, but in a roundabout, chatty fashion her hostess discoursed on rituals and expected conduct at court.

"The queen's ladies are most conscious of their status," she said one afternoon. "Such a fuss they do make about who has precedent, who sits where, who does what task. I remember one poor child who made the mistake of picking up her majesty's fan when she dropped it. Such personal duties, of course, are the province of the ladies of the privy chamber. As I'm sure you know, they are the most important ladies of rank among the queen's attendants."

"What happened to her, madam?" Rosamund nibbled the end of her quill.

"Oh, she was ostracized for weeks. No one would speak to her, she was forced to sit on the outskirts of any gathering, and excluded from any of the activities. By the time she was returned to favor she was a shadow of her former self, a mere wraith." Ursula shook her head. "It is wise, my dear, in the early days at court to watch carefully, listen, and observe before you venture to act or speak."

Rosamund nodded and continued to listen avidly, ask questions, and absorb the answers. Slowly the picture began to take shape, and at times it seemed utterly terrifying, but then Ursula would talk of the dancing, the music, the excursions on the river when the court would take to the barges for the day and there would be music and games, and picnics on the riverbank. These were the images that Rosamund hung on to, that she hugged to herself at night before sleep. She who had met so few people in her life outside her family and the villagers and tenants around Scadbury was about to meet a whole new world of people, men and women. There was no knowing how her life would change, who or what would be the instrument of change. And then she would be overcome with impatience, and she would toss and turn through the warm night, desperate for the beginning of her life.

One gloriously sunny morning, she entered Ursula's parlor just as Sir Francis was leaving his wife. "Good morrow, Rosamund."

She curtsied. "Good morrow, sir."

"Come to me in my office in half an hour. I have something to discuss with you." He gave her a nod and walked away, heading for the door that led into the office side of the mansion.

Rosamund felt a surge of excitement. Was it to begin at last? "Do you know why Sir Francis wishes to see me, madam?"

Ursula looked up from her tambour frame and said placidly, "No, dear, he didn't tell me. Would you sketch me a rose from that bowl, I find it easier to set my stitches correctly when I have one of your drawings to work from. They are most accurate."

"With pleasure, madam." Rosamund selected a rose from the bowl and sat down at the small table that had been set up specially for her in the window. After half an hour she laid the completed drawing on the table beside Lady Walsingham's chair. "I must go to Sir Francis, madam."

"Yes, my dear. Oh, this is remarkably good." Ursula smiled at the drawing. "I shall copy that tiny blemish on the petal."

Rosamund dropped a curtsy and hurried away, anxious not to be late. She entered the long corridor behind the door that was always kept firmly closed and made her way to the door at the far end. Ahead of her a door on the right of the corridor opened and a man came out.

"Master Marlowe." She quickened her step as she walked towards him. "You are back from your travels then?"

Kit grinned. He was looking mightily pleased with himself. As he tossed a small leather pouch from hand to hand, it clinked merrily. "Aye, Mistress Rosamund, back safe and sound, and Master Phelippes has been pleased to pay me for my trouble."

"I'm glad. Have you seen my brother since your return?"

"He's with Master Secretary at this moment. He and I came together but I was sent to collect my payment from Master Phelippes while Thomas remained in close confabulation with our master. But what of you, Mistress Rosamund? How have you passed the weeks since our last meeting?"

"Here. With Lady Walsingham. She has been most kind, but . . ." She paused, afraid to sound ungracious.

"But what?" asked Kit, leaning against the wall, hands thrust into the pockets of his britches. His eyes gleamed in the dim corridor and his teeth flashed in a white smile.

She sighed. "Oh, I have no wish to be ungrateful, but in truth, Master Marlowe, sometimes the days drag on forever. It is so peaceful and nothing happens. Nothing at all. And I never see the outdoors except for a stroll around the garden. I have time and materials aplenty for my drawing, but even that palls sometimes when it is all there is to do."

She tossed her head, reminding Kit of a colt tossing its mane in its eagerness to gallop. "I need something to happen, this new life to start, Master Marlowe." Her voice had an almost despairing urgency and she clapped her closed fists together, the knuckles knocking with her impatience.

Kit grinned. "Why, I can see that well enough. What can we do to hasten it?"

"Nothing, of course," she said with a note of resignation, adding somewhat wistfully, "But I should dearly love to visit the theatre again."

Then she said hastily, "But I must present myself to Sir Francis at once. I bid you good morrow, Master Marlowe." She bobbed a curtsy and hurried towards the door at the end of the corridor. She knocked and Sir Francis's voice bade her enter.

Thomas was sitting at his ease in a chair in a corner of the room. The secretary was at his desk examining a document through a magnifying glass. He set it down as Rosamund entered and curtsied. "See, here is your brother, Rosamund."

Thomas uncurled himself from his chair and kissed his sister. "You are looking well, my dear. Prettier by the day."

"Thank you, Brother. I trust you are well." He looked rather pale she thought.

He grimaced. "I will be soon enough when my belly settles after a damnable crossing."

"Crossing?" She had no idea what he was talking about.

"The Channel. La Manche as the French call it. I have been in Paris."

"Such a discussion is not germane to the business in hand, Thomas. You may indulge in idle personal talk when we have completed our business."

"My apologies, Sir Francis." Thomas's bow was ironic and he returned to his seat, leaving Rosamund still standing.

Sir Francis came straight to the point. "The queen has graciously agreed to see Rosamund, but the girl will need a court dress. An expensive proposition as you realize, Thomas."

Thomas sat bolt upright, his expression wary. "I know it, sir."

"Yes, I daresay your own court dress cost a pretty penny."

"I would not disgrace the family name by appearing in less than the requisite finery, sir."

"No, I'm sure you would not." Francis, who rarely wore anything other than a black gown and close-fitting cap in the queen's presence, gave him a sardonic twist of his lips. "So, how much can you contribute to Rosamund's gown?"

Thomas flushed. "Little enough, I fear. There are debts outstanding . . . the estate is managed by Edmund, he takes everything he can out of it. I myself sail close to the Fleet prison on occasion. I have no personal fortune."

Rosamund shifted from foot to foot. She was beginning to feel uncomfortable. Neither of these men wanted to underwrite her court dress and she had listened enough to Lady Walsingham to know that her presentation, even if perfect, would be fraught with potential problems. She must make an impeccable impression or spend fruitless hours trying to establish a position among the queen's ladies.

Impetuously she spoke up. "Thomas, surely it is as important for me as for you to appear to good advantage at court. If you would not show yourself in anything other than correct dress, you cannot expect me to do so. Would you have me appear at a disadvantage among the queen's other ladies? People would assume either that my family are as poor as church mice, or that they don't know what's required to show all due respect at court. It would reflect badly on you," she added as a final shaft.

Thomas flushed with annoyance. In all honesty he couldn't deny the truth of her statement, a knowledge that merely added spur to his irritation. "You are impertinent, miss," he stated sharply. "You'll hold your tongue, if you know what's good for you."

Sir Francis smiled grimly. "If Rosamund pleases her majesty on her presentation, then mayhap the queen will be pleased to provide one gown for ceremonial occasions. Ordinarily the gift is not made until after a year of service, but I will see if I can persuade her majesty to advance her generosity."

Rosamund was wearing the green velvet this morning. She had alternated her two gowns throughout the month she had been in Seething Lane, and it had to be said they no longer had the sheen of a recent purchase. She could not possibly be presented to the queen as she was. "Perhaps I should return to Scadbury if proper provision cannot be made," she declared, hearing how tart she sounded but unable to disguise it.

"Indeed you will not." Francis looked at her in clear annoyance. "I need you here. I have work for you to do."

Impasse it seemed. Rosamund took a deep breath. "Am

I to be paid for this work, sir? As Master Marlowe has been, and I presume Thomas. If so," she continued before either of them could recover from their astonishment, "then perhaps you could advance me the necessary funds for a court dress." She stopped, shocked at her daring.

"You are ill-schooled, miss," Master Secretary declared in icy tones. "You do not know your place."

Rosamund merely curtsied.

Thomas said hastily, "I will have the schooling of her, Sir Francis. I swear she will never again utter such insolence."

The secretary glanced at him. "No, leave her here with me and wait in the antechamber."

Thomas left instantly and Rosamund heard the door closing behind him as a death knell. She waited through a long silence while Walsingham picked up his magnifying glass again and resumed his examination of the document in front of him.

She didn't dare move. The silence was oppressive and the room became hot. Perspiration trickled down her spine and itched beneath her breasts. She longed to mop her brow. And then he spoke without looking at her.

"I do not tolerate insolence from those in my service. You will remember that in future. Just as you will remember that I am your benefactor, and what I give with one hand, I can take away with the other. When I no longer need you, you will return to Scadbury unless you have managed to take advantage of the opportunity I am giving you to form a respectable alliance."

He fell silent again, returning his attention to the document on his desk as if something fresh had caught his eye. Rosamund shuffled her feet, unsure whether she had been dismissed with this silence.

After a few minutes, again without looking up, he said,

"You may go. I have no further need of you today. Send Thomas back to me."

Rosamund curtsied deeply and fled with as much dignity as she could muster. Thomas was standing in the corridor, his face dark with anger. Kit Marlowe stood beside him, cleaning his fingernails with the tip of his dagger.

"Are you run quite mad, you wretched baggage?" Thomas demanded in an undertone, grabbing her arm. "I have a mind to beat you to within an inch of your miserable life. How dare you put us all in jeopardy—"

She tried to twist out of his hold, saying urgently, "He wants to see you again, Thomas. Right away."

Thomas glared at her, then with a muttered imprecation almost threw her from him and stalked back into Master Secretary's office.

"Well, you certainly seem to have irritated your brother, Mistress Rosamund," Kit said with a half smile. "What's to do now?"

Rosamund grimaced at the closed door. "I don't think I can risk being here when Thomas comes out again." She glanced at Kit, a gleam of mischief in her green eyes as a wave of recklessness surged through her. Everyone was so angry with her already, what had she got to lose? "Sir Francis says he has no further need of me today. Take me to the theatre, Kit."

He whistled softly. "You would drag me into this imbroglio, would you?"

"*Please.*"

Chapter Eight

IN A NARROW house colloquially known as the Little Rose on Rose Alley in Bankside, Will Creighton with one final thrust gave a great cry of exultation and fell onto the soft body of the woman beneath him. He lay panting, his face buried in her ample breasts, until she gave him a tentative push. "You've had your half hour, Master Will. You know how Master Henslowe keeps a close watch on the clock. He'll fine me if I keep a customer over his time."

Will groaned but rolled sideways, falling onto his back on the faded coverlet. One hand rested on the woman's stomach as he blinked blearily at the beamed ceiling above. Philip Henslowe's brothels were cleaner than most and his women were regularly checked for the pox, but he kept a tight rein on his girls, and a close eye on his clientele. The girls put up with the cut he took from their earnings because he kept them safe for the most part, unless they were willing to indulge in rough sport, then he would charge the client a pretty penny for it and the girl would get something extra for her pain.

Will turned his head to smile at the girl lying beside him. "I wish I could afford to take you out of here, Lily. But I could never meet Henslowe's price."

She leaned on an elbow, stroking his mouth with a fingertip. "I know. But I could meet you private sometimes."

Her eyes looked a question even though she knew the answer.

Will sat up, shaking his head. "Don't be foolish, Lily. If Henslowe found out you were entertaining privately, he'd make sure no man would ever want to look at you again. I wouldn't be responsible for that."

The girl made no reply, instead climbing from the bed and going over to the cheap dresser underneath the window. Will was right. Philip Henslowe was a ruthless master and she'd seen what he did to women who cheated him. Scalding water, branding irons, sharp knives were all in his arsenal. But sometimes she thought Will, who professed such ardor for her, ought to be powerful enough, queen's courtier as he was, to take her far enough away out of Henslowe's reach. But either his ardor was not as strong as he maintained, or he had not the courage to brave the brothel king's fury. Whichever it was, the result was the same. If she couldn't meet a savior, she was doomed to the life of a brothel whore.

She spent a few minutes at the washbasin with a cloth, freshening herself for her next customer, then pulled down her skimpy shift and dropped her tawdry gown over her head. Will watched her with a mixture of hunger and compassion. He had been her regular customer for almost six months now, and she knew well how to please him. He was fond of her in his own way. She was young, still with the freshness of a girl, firm-fleshed and supple, her skin clear. He wondered how long it would take for that bloom to wither, the ripe flesh to lose its firmness. Once she no longer drew customers, Henslowe would cast her out and she'd be selling herself in the stews, behind the hedgerows and in the alleys.

It was a melancholy thought and Will wondered if it

would make a poem, maybe a ballad. He could compose a doleful ditty about failing beauty and set it to music. The ladies of the court, particularly the younger ones, tended to gaze with soulful eyes on a courtier plucking sorrowfully on a lute.

He got off the bed and laced his britches, straightened his stockings, and looked for his shoes. In the importunity of lust he'd cast them off in such haste they were at opposite ends of the chamber. Silently Lily fetched them for him, then went to the door, waiting while he fastened the buckles.

As he came to the door, Will reached awkwardly into the slit in his doublet that gave access to his purse and fingered a penny. He would have to pay Henslowe himself directly for Lily's services, but he wanted to give her something for herself. The trouble was, he had little enough to spare. But a penny would be an insult, a suitable douceur for a whore from the stews, and his fingers closed over a shilling.

He took out the shilling and pressed it into her hand, bending to kiss her cheek as he murmured, "I'll be back soon."

Lily managed a small smile, her fingers closing over the coin, identifying it by touch. It wasn't a gold noble, but neither was it a copper penny. A silver shilling would add to her hidden cache of coins beneath the loose floorboard under the bed, and one day she might have enough to buy her freedom.

She opened the door, and with a quick wave Will took the narrow stairs down to the hall. Philip Henslowe appeared as if conjured from the air as Will came off the bottom step.

"You enjoyed your afternoon, I trust, sir? Lily looked after you? I'll keep her fresh for you for next time."

Henslowe leered. "Blood runs hot in a young fellow like yourself."

Will didn't answer. He handed the whoremaster his silver penny and went out into the warm afternoon as Henslowe said to his back, "We're always here, Master Creighton. A service for all tastes. When Lily no longer suits, I'm sure I can find a girl, someone fresher perhaps, who will."

Will's orgasm-induced euphoria faded as he stood on the slimy cobbles of Rose Alley with Henslowe's grimy insinuations in his ears. Habituating brothels was a tawdry business even when the harlot was as sweet and appealing as Lily. But a man had his needs when all was said and he had no realistic hope of finding a mistress at court. Oh, the young ladies there were more than willing to flirt, sometimes even to exchange a kiss, but they had too much to lose to go any further down the paths of passion with a youthful courtier who had looks to recommend him but little else in the currency of wealth and influence on which the court operated. Besides, Will had no desire to find himself fighting a duel on Finsbury Fields over some maiden's lost virtue.

He could hear the roaring of the crowd from the bear garden at the end of the alley and set off in that direction. At the end of the alley he paused to watch workmen scurrying over a building they were erecting. Philip Henslowe had fingers in many pies and this was his latest venture, a new theatre to be called the Rose. It was said in the world of players and playmakers that the popularity of the theatres of Shoreditch would not last much longer. They were too far from the city center and the other amusements, the bear garden and bull-baiting ring in particular. Henslowe had bought a share in the bear pit and was constructing his theatre a few yards from it in what had been a rose garden. Already he was trying to lure players away from Burbage's ventures in Shoreditch, and he was searching for new plays.

Will himself was working on a play about Odysseus' return to Ithaca and the archery contest with Penelope's suitors. It had a grand feel to it, romance and passion, bravery and skill in equal parts. Of course it would have to be licensed by the queen's Master of the Revels before he could hope to see it performed. But it was another good reason to maintain cordial relations with Henslowe, a man who could soon be in a position to buy new works by an untried playmaker.

His feet had found their way to the bear garden. He hesitated, wondering if he could afford the penny entrance fee after his afternoon's pleasuring. Later he intended to attend a play at the Curtain and he would need coin for that. It was one of Achelley's works, with the player John Lodge. Will had not yet seen Lodge on the stage, but he had heard enough about the player's inimitable skill to make him anxious not to miss the opportunity.

Even as he hesitated, he caught sight of two people in lively discussion at the gates to the garden. He recognized them immediately. The newcomer Kit Marlowe and the same girl he'd seen with Marlowe and Thomas Walsingham at the Theatre, Mistress Rosamund Walsingham.

He hurried over to them, greeting them with a sweep of his hat and a bow. "Well met, Master Marlowe, Mistress Walsingham. Are you going to the baiting?"

"That is a matter for discussion, sir," Marlowe said rather glumly. "I am in the mood, but the lady here is reluctant."

"I cannot endure the cruelty," Rosamund stated. "And

the smell of blood makes me vomit. You will not wish to be by my side in such a circumstance I assure you, Master Marlowe." Even as she spoke, a great shout went up from the crowd and folk started surging back through the gates.

"It seems the problem has found its own solution," Will said. "The entertainment seems to be concluded. Either the bear or the dogs must have succumbed sooner than usual."

Kit looked disappointed, but the crowd for the most part seemed in affable mood, laughing, squabbling, tripping over each other. The bloody nature of the entertainment must have come up to expectations, he reflected, even if it was somewhat curtailed.

"Well, so much for that," he said. "Now for the theatre. Do you join us, Master Creighton?"

Will responded swiftly, "Indeed, I should like to. I was going myself in the hopes of seeing John Lodge at the Curtain." He smiled at Rosamund. "You have no objections to my company, I trust, Mistress Walsingham."

"Not in the least, Master Creighton. On condition, of course, that you forget you ever saw me this afternoon." She returned the smile, her eyes slightly narrowed against the sun that made her hair glow rich and russet.

He bowed again. "That goes without saying, madam."

They began to move with the crowd towards the riverbank and the skiffs that ferried folk across the river.

"We should take a skiff across," Will said as they reached the river. "It'll take an hour to walk across the bridge with this crowd." He turned towards the place on the bank where a flotilla of skiffs touted for custom. Kit put two fingers to his lips and whistled. Three of the little ferryboats turned instantly in response, and with a volley of curses the ferrymen jostled with each other, one pushing another away with his oar. The victor brought his boat to the wooden quay and Kit jumped in, holding out a hand to Rosamund, who took it and jumped lightly into the stern.

The ferryman pulled strongly to the opposite bank. London Bridge rose on their right and Rosamund's gaze fixed in fascination on the row of blackened, eyeless heads on pikes that adorned the structure. She could count over fifty on this side of the bridge alone. The realm had many enemies.

They stepped out onto the water steps on the far side of the river and Kit reached into his pocket to pay the waterman. Will made some murmur of protestation but didn't press the matter when Kit waved him down, tossing the coin to the ferryman.

"I'm hungry," Rosamund announced as her stomach growled suddenly. She had broken her fast very early that morning.

"There's an eating house close to the Curtain Theatre," Will said. "They have a good ordinary."

Kit was rarely hungry, but always thirsty he agreed readily enough and they made their way to a tavern next door to the theatre where the flag flew jauntily, the trumpet sounded its clarion call, and the groundlings already gathered at the doors.

They ate at the communal table, digging into the pots of veal stew and braised leeks as they circulated, ladling the fragrant contents onto bread trenchers. Flagons of burgundy were passed around and a great round of cheese. Rosamund kept her head down, anxious not to draw attention to herself. Even though her brother was not here, she felt an obligation to conceal her identity as far as possible. Kit seemed unconcerned and, as usual, filled his cup many times over while the food cooled on his trencher.

Will devoted his attention to Rosamund, making sure

she had everything she wanted and that her wine cup was full. He was very curious as to why she was on such an unconventional outing with only the playmaker's escort. "Where is your brother this afternoon?" he asked, cutting into the round of cheese as it passed him.

Rosamund grimaced. "He was deep in conversation with our cousin Sir Francis when we left."

"Ah, of course, you are cousin to the secretary of state." Will nodded and offered her a piece of cheese on the point of his dagger. "An august relative, I congratulate you."

Rosamund took the cheese and gave him her impish smile. "It's hardly a matter for congratulation, Master Will, since I had little to do with it."

He inclined his head in smiling acknowledgment. "Nevertheless you are too modest. Most people at court take credit for their august relatives regardless of what they did to deserve them."

"I daresay I will learn such ways eventually." Rosamund reached for her wine cup.

"When are you to be presented?" He concealed his great interest in the answer. Apart from finding her increasingly attractive, both in her free and easy manner and in her appearance, he was interested in all things Walsingham. He was hoping to augment his meager income with some work for Master Secretary, and cultivating the secretary's young cousin could only do him good.

Rosamund frowned. "I don't know as yet. There is the matter of a court dress to be settled first." As she sipped her wine, she became aware that she had drunk more than usual and her tongue seemed to be running rather loosely. Instinct told her it would not be wise to share that particular quarrel with this near stranger or indeed with anyone associated with the court. The story of her impoverishment and the meanness of her relatives could run like wildfire along the gossip channels and would do her no good at all.

She was saved from further indiscretion when Kit pushed himself back on the long bench and rose to his feet. "Come, 'tis time for entertainment."

The performance was as magical for Rosamund as the last one. The play was different, more amusing, and as she laughed at the comical antics of one of the players, she found herself inching closer to Will Creighton, who seemed to be sharing her delight and her amusement in equal parts. He laid a companionable hand on her arm at one point when they both lost themselves in peals of laughter and she made no attempt to shake it off or move away.

As they emerged into the gathering dusk, still chuckling at the finale of the play, Will was hailed by a group of young men coming down from the gallery by the outside stairs. Hastily Rosamund took a step back so that she was behind Kit. She adjusted her hood, drawing it tightly over her forehead. Will glanced over his shoulder, then gave her a quick conspiratorial wink and hurried away to join his friends.

Kit turned to face her with a comical frown. "Let's hope our friend is discreet. Now we had better hurry back and face whatever music is to be played."

He waited at the door to the mansion on Seething Lane until Mortlake let her in, then with a bow stepped back into the street. "I wish you luck, Mistress Walsingham. If you need my assistance again, pray call upon me."

Rosamund couldn't help a little grin, despite her trepidation. She made her way to Ursula's parlor and was amazed when she was greeted with a serene smile and asked if she had enjoyed her outing. "Master Marlowe is a close friend of your brother's I understand. There can be no objection to your having such an escort with your brother's permission." Ursula set another stitch.

Rosamund smiled her assent. The issue of Thomas's permission was best left to go by default. He wouldn't do anything to harm his sister's chances with Sir Francis by denying it had been given, however furious he might be with her. She gave an exaggerated yawn. "I would seek my bed, madam, if you will excuse me. The day has been rather tiring."

"Of course, my dear. And in the morning, we must discuss your wardrobe."

Rosamund's eyes widened in surprise. She curtsied. "Oh . . . but of course, madam. I am at your disposal." She curtsied hastily again and beat a retreat.

"Now, Rosamund dear, let me see how this works." Lady Walsingham held up a gown of rose velvet embroidered with seed pearls in a delicate flower pattern. "Help me with the train, Henny, 'tis very heavy." Henny rushed to hold up the long train.

"What do you think, Rosamund?"

Rosamund clasped her hands together in delight. "It's beautiful, madam." When Ursula had told her at breakfast on the day after her excursion with Kit that she intended to have two court dresses fashioned for her out of two gowns that she no longer wore, Rosamund had done her best to sound thrilled and grateful, but the thought of wearing Lady Walsingham's castoffs had depressed her. She had let none of that show, however, during a morning of measuring and discussions about ribbons and pieces of lace, and gold thread. Now, three days later, looking at the finished article, she forgot all her reservations. "Should I try it on?"

"Yes . . . yes . . . but you must have a Spanish farthingale. You will need to practice wearing it, there is a knack to handling the width it gives the skirts. Take off your dress and petticoat."

Rosamund obediently divested herself of the well-worn tawny velvet, reflecting that it needed cleaning and some time in the linen press with fresh lavender in the folds. She stepped out of the stiffened canvas frame and stood in her linen shift and wool stockings.

Lady Walsingham fussed as Henny fastened the boned farthingale at Rosamund's waist. "It must sit just so. If 'tis not straight, the gown will not move correctly. There . . ." She stepped back, her head to one side as she examined her handiwork. "Yes, that will do. Now the bodice, Henny."

Rosamund gasped as Henny laced the boned bodice at her back. "Not so tight, I beg you."

"You will learn to manage," Ursula said on an unusually firm note. "It's unfortunate you have never been accustomed to it. It is most necessary."

Grimly Rosamund held her breath as the bones cut into her skin beneath the thin shift. She *would* get used to it. She forgot her discomfort when she stepped into the dress. Over the boned bodice it fitted like a glove. The skirts hung in straight, graceful folds over the farthingale. The square-cut neck was edged in seed pearls, and the wide sleeves were lined in ivory damask. The train was heavy, and when she walked, it seemed designed to trap her feet. She stopped in dismay. "How does one walk, madam?"

"You're not wearing shoes," Ursula reminded her. "The skirts are too long without them. Pass me the pink satin slippers, Henny."

The slippers had a small rise at the back, and when

Henny on her knees slid the shoes onto Rosamund's feet, she felt immediately more stately. She stood taller, her shoulders straighter, and she found that the bones beneath the bodice took care of every aspect of her posture. She was encased and could move in only one way. Straight, graceful, elegant.

She experimented, walking across the floor, the train following her. It no longer seemed like a trap for her feet. It behaved itself as well as a lapdog on a leash.

"Excellent," Lady Walsingham pronounced. "You are naturally graceful, my dear. Now, I have one other gown, an emerald green damask. There is sufficient material there I believe to furnish you with a second court dress. Very few of the maids of honor have more than two, so you will not find yourself at a disadvantage. But neither must you arouse envy. The ladies of her majesty's court are such rivals." She was talking in the chatty, gossipy fashion that Rosamund knew meant she was imparting something important.

"Every little thing, even the most insignificant, is a matter for competition," Ursula continued, examining the green damask with a critical frown. "And a new acquisition is immediately the cause for speculation . . . something as trivial as a new handkerchief . . . yes, I think this can be made up in the same style, but with gold undersleeves. Most dramatic, don't you think, my dear Rosamund?"

"Indeed, madam." Rosamund was beginning to wonder if she really wanted to enter this cutthroat world of female rivalry. Her experience of female companionship was almost nonexistent. She had never had a close female friend; even as a child her only companions had been the household maids, and they had little enough time for play and gossip. Her two sisters were so much older than herself and had left Scadbury for their own households before she was out of the nursery. She doubted she would recognize them on the street.

Ursula looked up, hearing the note of uncertainty in her charge's voice. "Now, don't worry, Rosamund. You will do very well if you remember our little discussions, and if you have any difficulty, any questions, then you must come to me at once."

"You are very kind, madam."

"Not at all, child. You have no mother to advise you. I will do what I can. Now, let us see what we can do to refresh your everyday gowns."

Five days later Rosamund had her two court dresses, and her two refreshed dresses for ordinary occasions. Sir Francis summoned her once more to his office.

He was seated as usual at his desk as she came in, but he looked rather less intimidating than on previous occasions, indeed, he even managed something approximating a tight smile. "So, Lady Walsingham informs me that you are fully equipped and ready to be presented to her majesty."

"I am grateful for the opportunity, Sir Francis, and I trust I will not cause you to regret your kindness," she murmured with a deep curtsy.

"I'm sure you will not." His tone was customarily dry. "My wife has only good report to make of you, and I know for myself that you have a sharp mind and an even sharper memory to match, with an unusual talent as a draftsman."

Rosamund said nothing. She could think of nothing to say since this recitation of her abilities, while meager, was perfectly true.

Sir Francis laid his hands on the desk, fingers interlocked, his eyes shrewd and calculating. "This world, Rosamund, runs on favors given and received. Remember that. What you do for someone will be repaid in due time. And the same is true of a disservice. Remember that with your every breath. Nothing is given for free, so the time has come for me to tell you what I wish of you during your time at court in exchange for the opportunity I have given you to make a reasonable match for yourself."

Rosamund stiffened, drew a deep breath. "Yes, sir?"

"Sit down." He waved her to the only other chair in the chamber.

Rosamund took it, settled her quivering fingers in her lap, and fixed the queen's spymaster with a steady green-eyed gaze.

"During your service to the queen you will be party to many conversations. I am not interested in secrets," he said swiftly. "You will not know a secret when you hear it. I don't expect subtlety from you. But I want your accurate accountings of conversations that take place between the queen and her women, those that you are privy to, of course. I do not wish you to hide behind tapestries or in cupboards." Here he assayed a small smile that Rosamund found impossible to respond to.

"I wish to hear what is said among the ladies of the bedchamber when they are at leisure. Whom do they talk of . . . what do they talk of. And I want your drawings." Here he began to play idly with his quill, turning it between his fingers. "Draw me the scenes, Rosamund. Any scene that involves the queen. Any scene at all. I will be the judge of their importance." He looked up, his eyes dark and intent. "Do you understand me?"

"Perfectly, Sir Francis."

"Good." He nodded dismissal and she got to her feet. "I will present you to the queen myself, and I shall see you there from time to time. Remember that this is your opportunity to secure your future. Have the greatest care for your reputation, and I shall do my utmost to make a good match for you."

"My thanks, sir." With a final curtsy, Rosamund escaped, her head in a whirl. She had been given a specific task, well, two specific tasks. How was she to undertake those to the satisfaction of an exacting taskmaster, while trying to placate an army of predatory women?

Chapter Nine

THE CHEVALIER DE Vaugiras slammed the tennis ball into the wall of the court and tossed his racket in the air with a triumphant laugh. "My game, I believe, Delancy."

"Aye, you've the devil's own luck this morning, Arnaud." His opponent wiped his brow with a silk cloth. "I'll have my revenge though."

"I'll be happy to accommodate you, my friend, but, alas, not now. I have an assignation," the chevalier said with a knowing chuckle.

"As I said, you've the devil's own luck," Delancy declared somewhat enviously. Arnaud's reputation as a ladies' man was well honed at court. He was like a butterfly, flitting from one bright flower to the next. "How many hearts have you broken this season at court?"

Arnaud laughed again. He wiped his own sweaty brow and draped the cloth around his neck. "I do not break hearts, Delancy. On the contrary, I treat such delicate organs with the utmost care." He tossed his racket to the page who stood waiting to catch it and left the court, feeling invigorated as always after a bout of any energetic sport, from the bedchamber to the fencing field. He strolled along the path that led from the tennis court back into the palace, then paused as four people crossed the path in front of him.

He turned sideways, propping a foot on a stone bench, pretending to fiddle with the lace of his shoe as he watched the little party out of the corner of his eye. Lord Burghley and Sir Francis Walsingham were no surprise, the two senior members of the queen's council were often to be seen together. Arnaud was more interested in their two companions. Thomas Walsingham and a young woman, who, unless he was much mistaken, had been bred in the same Walsingham stable. She had much of the look of Thomas about her, and something of Master Secretary in the set of her head. Elusive but there nevertheless.

Newcomers were always interesting. So who was she? Well, Agathe would know soon enough if she didn't know now. He was already anticipating a late-afternoon romp with his mistress; he would find out then.

"Will your majesty take a turn around the knot garden?" Mary Talbot, Countess of Shrewsbury and Lady of the Privy Chamber, approached the queen, who was sitting at her desk, her head resting in her hand. "It might help the pains in your head."

"It might, Mary." Elizabeth's smile was weary.

"A little hartshorn in water, perhaps, madam," Elizabeth Vernon ventured. "And then perhaps a rest upon your bed."

The queen shook her head. "No, tempting though that might be. I have to meet with the secretary of state and Lord Burghley later this afternoon. Play something for me."

The young woman sat down at the harp and began to pluck the strings in a soft and haunting melody, and Elizabeth closed her eyes for a moment, before taking up her quill again. Her ladies were gathered around the large chamber, occupied with needlework, listening to another young woman who was reading aloud from a book of French poetry. A fly buzzed against a leaded windowpane.

Joan Davenport, sitting with her tambour frame in a ray of sun, felt perspiration gather between her breasts and trickle down her spine. Her heavy brocade gown was ill-suited to the warmth of early summer, but she had no lighter summer gowns. Her family was not wealthy, and even though court finery was not required for every day, the simpler gowns themselves constituted a significant outlay. Her hair beneath her headdress was limp and damp and she knew the sweat trickling down her face would cause the freckles that were the bane of her life to stand out from her unnaturally pale skin like so many ugly brown flies. She was bored, longing for some distraction, but until the queen dismissed them, her ladies were obliged to keep her company.

Joan had been at court for six months, and her initial excitement had given way to a dismal acceptance. She was the most junior maid of honor in the queen's entourage and was treated with lofty disdain by her peers, excluded from their gossipy cliques, constantly commanded, and given the most lowly tasks by the great ladies of the privy chamber. The daily routine was rarely altered, and only when there were entertainments and revels did the royal household liven up.

Greenwich Palace and Hampton Court were preferable to the stuffiness of Whitehall, where the queen seemed more intent on work than play. At the other two London palaces, she would go riding, there would be archery contests and trips on the river. There was dancing in the evening, sometimes the Queen's players would perform for the court. But here in Whitehall, the queen was always occupied with her advisers, and often unwell, plagued by constant pains in her head and belly, so that her ladies were rarely offered diversions.

The alerting bang of the pikemen's staffs beyond the double doors brought the Countess of Shrewsbury to her feet. She went to open the door and had a whispered conversation. She turned back. "Sir Francis Walsingham and Lord Burghley, madam. Will you see them now?"

"Ask them to attend me in my privy chamber." Elizabeth rose, the rich royal purple damask of her wide skirt settling gracefully around her. The material was so thickly studded with gems that it glittered in the sunshine as she moved to the door. "You may divert yourselves as you please," she said to the assembled ladies as she sailed through the door.

Joan waited for some movement in the chamber, for someone to suggest that they stroll in the gardens. Lady Shrewsbury might even give them permission to go about their own pursuits for a precious time, but nothing happened and the moments slid by until there was a knock at the door.

Countess Shrewsbury looked over at Joan and with an imperative gesture of one plump, beringed hand indicated that she should answer it. The countess only responded to the pikemen's signal, which was used only when the queen was present. Joan rose from her low stool and went obediently to open the door.

One of the queen's chamberlains stood there, resplendent with his gold seal and staff of office. He intoned, "Her majesty requests the presence of the Countess of Shrewsbury in her privy chamber." He turned on his heel and went off on his next important errand.

Joan stepped back and closed the door. The countess regarded her with an interrogatively raised eyebrow. Joan curtsied and delivered her message, then returned to her stool. Lady Shrewsbury left with stately step, and the apartment returned to its dull silence.

In the queen's privy chamber Rosamund Walsingham remained on bended knee waiting for her majesty's permission to rise. Her heart was pounding uncomfortably against the boned bodice of her court dress. When Thomas had left her with the two councilors at the door of the outer antechamber, she had never felt more alone than when progressing between the two silent and intimidating men into the queen's presence. Until the last month she had never in her wildest dreams or blackest nightmares imagined herself here, in the privy chamber, staring at the carpet and the jeweled heels of the queen's shoes.

Now Sir Francis, having made the introduction, stood behind her. Lord Burghley, her majesty's treasurer, a formidable gentleman dressed like Sir Francis in a scholar's black gown and skullcap, looked merely bored with this interruption to his afternoon's council with the queen.

"You may rise, Mistress Walsingham." The queen sat down in the chair of state. "Approach." She beckoned, and Rosamund, rising slowly, stepped forward, careful of the unaccustomed train.

She stood waiting, eyes demurely lowered, as the queen subjected her to an unnerving scrutiny. "Do you read Latin and Greek, Mistress Walsingham?"

Rosamund flushed. "Inadequately, madam."

"So you are not studious?" A tight frown drew the well-plucked eyebrows together.

Rosamund's throat was so dry she had difficulty forming the words to answer a question that was clearly disapproving. "I had little opportunity, madam. There were no tutors in the house. My brothers were all educated in other households. My mother was ill."

"Ah." Elizabeth ·nodded. "How unfortunate. Do you have any particular skill? Music, perhaps?"

"I play a little on the virginals, but I do not consider myself to be skilled," Rosamund added hastily, lest she receive the royal command to demonstrate.

"How is your voice? Is it pleasing? Can you keep a tune? I expect my ladies to know something of the arts of entertainment."

Rosamund had not been prepared for an examination. She swallowed, trying to moisten her throat, then said, "Madam, I have some skill at drawing, and to a lesser degree at painting. I also have a fair hand at italics. If such skills are of use to your majesty." She curtsied again.

Elizabeth looked her over. "There are times when I would find an amanuensis useful. But such a one must have a hand as good as my own. Demonstrate." She indicated a small table in an alcove. "You will find parchment and quill over there."

Rosamund curtsied and went to the table. She stared down at the creamy parchment, seeing it in her mind's eye disfigured with great black ink spots as she tried to form letters on the pristine surface. "Is there anything special I should write, madam?"

"The Catechism, Rosamund." It was Sir Francis who answered, sensing that the queen had had enough of the conversation.

Rosamund smoothed the sheet and dipped her pen in the inkwell. At least she knew the Catechism by heart. She forced herself to breathe deeply, to take her time as she formed the first word, concentrating on the graceful italic curlicues and flourishes that proclaimed excellent penmanship. When finally it was finished, she examined it critically and could find no fault. She sanded the document and glanced across to the queen. Her majesty was deep in low-voiced conversation with her two advisers, and they all appeared to have forgotten Rosamund's presence.

She could hardly interrupt them, Rosamund reflected. Almost automatically she took another sheet and began to sketch a butterfly hovering on a tendril of honeysuckle framing the open window in front of her.

"Rosamund . . . Rosamund."

She looked up with a guilty start at Sir Francis's imperative tones. "I . . . I beg your pardon, sir." She jumped to her feet, nearly knocking over the inkwell. "You . . . you were occupied and I thought not to interrupt . . . I—"

"Bring me your work," the queen demanded, holding out a hand.

Rosamund approached, curtsied, and put the paper into her majesty's hand. The queen stared down at her, her expression thunderstruck. "What is this?" She held it out. Rosamund saw that she had by accident presented Elizabeth with the butterfly drawing.

"Oh, forgive me, madam. I didn't realize . . . I was just . . . Oh . . ." She rushed back to the desk and retrieved the script, forgetting to curtsy in her anxiety as she presented the correct sheet.

The queen examined it with impassive countenance, then looked at Rosamund and nodded. "You have a fair hand, Mistress Walsingham." She looked again at the sketch. "And a fair eye too. Ask Lady Shrewsbury to come to me." This last was spoken in the direction of the door, where an attendant stood awaiting orders.

"You may retire, Rosamund." Elizabeth turned to her waiting councilors. "Lord Burghley, Sir Francis, let us continue. I received a dispatch from my lord Essex in the Low Countries this morning."

Rosamund stepped away from the queen's chair as the two men approached and returned to the table in the window embrasure. Within a few moments, the Countess of Shrewsbury entered and the queen broke off her discussion to say, "Lady Shrewsbury, Mistress Rosamund Walsingham, a cousin of Sir Francis, is to join my household as maid of honor. Will you take charge of her?"

"Of course, madam." The countess looked Rosamund over rather as if she were inspecting a prime specimen of milk cow. "Come with me, Mistress Walsingham."

Rosamund made her final obeisance to the queen, curtsied to her cousin and the gruff Lord Burghley, and backed away to the door, praying her train would not catch under her heel. Once safely outside, she followed Lady Shrewsbury, who said nothing, leading the way through the antechamber beyond the privy chamber and through the swiftly opened doors into a large apartment that, to Rosamund's first bemused observation, seemed crowded with ladies in a rainbow of elaborate gowns all murmuring at once in a continuous hum that reminded her of the beehives at Scadbury.

She was presented to the great ladies of the privy chamber, the Countess of Pembroke and the Countess of Southampton, and understood immediately that these were too great for someone as humble as mere Mistress Rosamund Walsingham to have dealings with. They barely acknowledged her before returning to their own conversations. She was then introduced to the ladies who were her majesty's maids of honor. These women giggled behind their hands and met her friendly smile with chilly, calculating stares. Only Joan Davenport returned the smile with any warmth.

She could think only that at last there was someone more junior than herself.

"You will share Joan's bed. Joan, make sure Rosamund understands the way we do things," the countess declared, then nodded and sailed across the chamber to where her fellow peeresses were gathered beneath the window.

Rosamund sat down awkwardly on a low stool close to Joan. "Should I not take my belongings to our chamber?"

"Oh, someone will have seen to that," the girl said airily. She glanced around. "But I have an idea that might get us out of here for a while." She set aside her embroidery and got up, hurrying across to Lady Shrewsbury. "My lady, may I show Rosamund to our chamber and acquaint her a little with the palace?"

"As her majesty is otherwise occupied and I do not expect her to return within the hour, you may do so." Her ladyship didn't raise her eyes from her own needlework as she continued in slightly louder tones, "Rosamund, change your gown. Now your presentation is complete, you have no need to wear court dress. That is reserved for formal occasions."

Joan dropped a curtsy and went back to Rosamund. "Come, we have permission to leave."

Rosamund followed her out into the antechamber and from there into the long, crowded corridor without. "Is it necessary to ask for leave every time?" Rosamund dodged a jostling footman carrying a rolled carpet.

"Oh, yes. And it's not always granted either. If her majesty is present, then you must request leave first from Lady Shrewsbury, and if she thinks your need is urgent, she will ask the queen, who will give permission, and then you will be called forward and have to make your request directly to her majesty in order to receive her permission."

It sounded rather tedious to Rosamund, but she was too absorbed in the sights and sounds of the corridors and antechambers through which they passed to fret overlong about such restrictions. The richness of the courtiers' clothes, both male and female, the sparkle and dazzle of jeweled embroidery, chains, and necklaces made even Thomas's finery seem shabby. There was so much noise everywhere. Booted feet marching on the stone floors, the clang of iron as sword sheaths swung against the walls in the press of people, the constant loud voices raised to be heard, and the whole pierced every few minutes by a blast on a horn and a crier pushing his way forward, shouting at the top of his voice the name of someone summoned to somewhere for some reason.

Joan deftly threaded her way through the racketing chaos and took a flight of wooden stairs. It was quieter as they climbed, and climbed, and climbed. They emerged into a dusty attic room, furnished with three beds, footed with heavy oak chests, a few stools, a washstand, and several linen presses and armoires. Tiny windows were set high in the plaster-and-lath walls, and dust motes danced in the rays of sunlight.

"It's cold as the grave in here in the winter, and hot as Hades in summer." Joan stood on tiptoe to examine her reflection in a piece of polished tin. She dabbed disconsolately at her brow and cheeks. "These freckles are worse than ever in the heat, and I don't have any powder. Do you have any I could borrow?" She turned hopefully back to Rosamund.

"No, I'm afraid I don't." Rosamund had no knowledge of such things. "We could try to find some flour," she suggested, trying to be helpful.

"No, it just cakes in the heat and makes you look as if

you have leprosy. Anyway, this is our bed." Joan thumped down on one of the beds. "We have to share the chest. The linen press and the armoire . . ." She shrugged. "You have to fight for space there."

"This is where we're to sleep?" Rosamund was stunned. After the simple privacy of her room at Scadbury and the luxurious comfort of her chamber in Seething Lane, she couldn't believe that in a royal palace she was to be reduced to this.

"Oh, this is quite comfortable compared with some of the places," Joan said with a slightly pitying smile. "When the queen goes on progress, we end up anywhere anyone can house us in the manors who entertain her majesty. I've slept above the stables on more than one occasion. It doesn't make life easy when you must always look your best. And the fleas . . . ugh." She gave an exaggerated shudder. "At least in the queen's own residences, they change the straw in the mattresses quite often, and the rushes are changed every month. And we examine each other's heads for lice regularly. There's always lye soap if we need it."

This was palace living? Rosamund perched on the bed, hearing the straw crunch as the mattress yielded to her weight. She had had a down mattress in Seething Lane, and horsehair at Scadbury. And she had *never* shared a bed.

She noticed her traveling chest against the wall. Joan had spoken truly. "I'll unpack my things." She stood up.

"Oh, no, not now. That's a waste of our liberty. Just change your gown quickly. I will help." Joan jumped to her feet and within ten minutes Rosamund was back in her green gown, newly refurbished with a standing collar and a girdle of twisted golden thread.

"That looks so cool and comfortable," Joan said enviously. "How many gowns do you have?"

"Just this and one other," Rosamund answered, remembering Lady Walsingham's advice. She shrugged. "My family is not wealthy."

"Neither is mine." Joan sounded relieved. She bounded towards the door. "I have permission to show you around. Let us go into the garden before someone sends for us."

Rosamund glanced around the dusty, unwelcoming dorter and decided the less time she spent in here the happier she'd be.

Joan led the way back down the stairs and through a bewildering series of corridors, down short flights of stairs, up others, and finally down a staircase that led directly into a paved courtyard.

"I'd never find my way back." Rosamund turned to look back at the edifice of Whitehall Palace. "How long did it take you?"

"Not long. You'll learn quickly enough. This way." Joan headed for an archway in the far wall. They emerged into a pretty garden intersected with hedges. Joan paused, listening. Then she smiled. "Let's see who's at play." She set off down a pathway leading to an arch cut into the far hedge.

Rosamund, following, could hear the sound of voices, the soft strumming of a lute, a voice raised in song. The air was heavy with the scent of roses and peonies and fresh-cut grass. The hedges were clipped into intricate designs, and she paused for a moment to admire a topiary peacock with full tail feathers, just as the real thing emerged from one of the openings in the hedge and preened himself in front of her.

She laughed and hurried to catch up with Joan at the end of the path. She was still a little behind Joan as they went through the arch into another square garden dominated by an oak tree, against whose broad trunk a young man sat playing a lute. It was Will Creighton, with a trio of young women, and two gentlemen, sitting on rugs on the grass.

Joan went boldly across to the group, and Will looked up from his lute, saying with a lazy smile, "Why, Lady Joan, how delightful. You have escaped the clutches of our lady of Shrewsbury, I see."

Joan bridled and fluttered her eyelashes. "Her majesty has excused us for the afternoon and I am instructed to show our new maid of honor around the palace. It wouldn't do for her to get lost." She gestured to Rosamund, who had stopped a few paces behind her.

Will's eyes widened fractionally as he saw her, then he asked with that same lazy smile, "And who is this new maiden?"

Rosamund relaxed, sure now that Will would not betray their acquaintance. She was faintly surprised at how comforting she found his familiar presence on this strangely disconcerting day, even though she couldn't acknowledge it with more than a polite smile. She sketched a curtsy. "Rosamund Walsingham, sir." Her smile moved to encompass the entire group.

Will laid aside his lute and rose to his feet. He bowed. "Mistress Walsingham, Will Creighton at your service. It is an honor to make your acquaintance. You are perhaps connected to Sir Francis?"

A suspiciously conspiratorial gleam was in his eye as he asked this, and she had to conceal her own answering amusement as she played along. "Sir Francis Walsingham is my cousin, sir." Her family credentials were now established for the company. The gentlemen of the group had risen and greeted her with murmured introductions and courteous bows. The ladies remained on the grass, but they smiled with a friendly warmth that was a welcome contrast to the frigid greetings of the maids of honor and ladies of the bedchamber in the queen's apartments.

A striking woman with dark hair and eyes such a deep blue as to be almost purple said, "You are most welcome, Mistress Walsingham. A new face is always a pleasure. Pray sit down here." She patted the rug beside her.

Rosamund sat down in a graceful swirl of skirts, surprised at how easy a maneuver it was to accomplish even with a farthingale. Joan followed suit, dabbing self-consciously at her damp freckles with a scrap of lace handkerchief.

Will indicated his lute. "I am engaged in composing a most melancholy love song to a pair of very fine eyes."

Laughter rippled around the group and one of the ladies blushed faintly. A basket of cherries was passed around and Will Creighton plucked his lute and continued with his composition.

His luxuriant brown curls, artfully disheveled, flopped over one eye as he bent over his instrument. It was for deliberate effect, Rosamund decided. If he thought it made him look romantic, the epitome of courtly love, he was perfectly right. His fingers were long and slender on the strings and his voice was pleasing. She couldn't help a faintly disappointed response to the words and sentiment of his ballad, however. But she told herself it was hardly fair to compare Will's amateur efforts at entertaining a group of courtiers to Kit Marlowe's fierce versifying, or the delicate literary pastorals of Thomas Watson. And she had no objections to sitting in the sunshine listening to him for as long as he was willing to play.

Joan suddenly gasped and scrambled inelegantly to her feet. "Rosamund, we've been away for nearly an hour. We must hurry back. The queen dines in state this evening and there is to be dancing afterwards. We must get ready."

Rosamund found Will Creighton's hand extended to help her to her feet and she took it. He smiled at her, his head tilted slightly, his grip tightening as he pulled her up and she rose in a graceful movement. "I hope you will dance tonight, Mistress Walsingham."

"Of course she will," Joan stated. "The queen does not permit her ladies to sit on the sidelines. She loves dancing too much herself."

"Then it seems that I *will* be dancing, Master Creighton." Rosamund met his smile with a complicit one of her own. "Ladies . . . gentlemen." She dropped a curtsy to the assembled company and turned to follow Joan back to the palace.

"Who is the dark lady, with those extraordinary deep blue eyes?" she asked Joan as they entered the palace.

"Oh, that's Agathe, Lady Leinster. She's half-French but was married to an Irish count. She's been a widow for at least two years. There are bets on all the time at court as to who will get her next," Joan said. "But the queen will make the decision and she hasn't done so yet." Her voice dropped to a mere whisper. "'Tis rumored that Agathe can't wait for a husband and takes lovers all the time. If the queen finds out, she'll banish her, send her back to Ireland, or maybe even France. I don't know how she dares take the risk."

"She seems so young to be widowed," Rosamund observed, fascinated. She had been drawn to Lady Leinster for some reason, something in her smile, a certain wicked twitch to her lips that had intrigued her. "Perhaps after a taste of the marriage bed she's reluctant to give up the pleasure."

Joan stared at her. "She's no younger than many, she

must be twenty at least. And what woman enjoys the marriage bed?"

"It can't be all bad," Rosamund said, reflecting that her
only evidence for the pleasures of carnal intercourse came
from observing her brother and Christopher Marlowe, but it
stood to reason that a man and a woman could enjoy it too.

"That's not what my sisters say." Joan changed the subject. "It's been a week since her majesty last dined in state.
At least when she does, there is entertainment and always
dancing, and we dine in the great hall with the rest of the
company. When she dines privately, we must attend her,
but we have to dine in our chamber beforehand. It is so
tiresome to stand for hour after hour while the queen toys
with her pigeon pie."

Rosamund could well believe it. "Do we change our
dress for the evening?"

"Yes, you must put on your court dress again." Joan
glanced at her. "Do you have another court dress?"

"I have one other," Rosamund admitted.

"Then you are fortunate." Joan sounded a little chilly.

"My court dresses were fashioned from gowns that Lady
Walsingham has no further need for." Rosamund hoped this
confidence would placate Joan, who, it seemed, was her only
potential friend among the queen's attendants. Will Creighton, of course, was a different matter, and she might find a
companionable ally in Lady Leinster in time.

"Most of us make do and mend," Joan responded. "It
helps that her majesty doesn't like her ladies to compete
with her in their finery. She can become very cross and
throw things."

Agathe leaned against the tree, feeling the knobs on the
trunk digging into her back as Arnaud pressed against her,

his fingers pushing up her chin, his mouth closing roughly over hers. She wriggled and his hold tightened, his tongue plunging deeper into her mouth. The inevitable heat crept through her loins, the muscles of her thighs tightening with excitement and the ever present fear of discovery. Arnaud would do this sometimes, take her in the open air, in some part of the palace gardens where anyone could walk past. The danger of discovery drove him to greater passion and her own matched it.

He released her mouth abruptly, put his hands on her shoulders, and forced her down to her knees, her skirts billowing in a corolla around her. She knew what he was demanding and her fingers moved swiftly to untruss his hose. She took his penis in her mouth and he drove deep into her throat as he had done with his tongue, and her eyes streamed as he filled her mouth. He held her head fast, murmuring to her as her tongue moved, bringing him to climax. She could hear through the red mists filling her head the sound of voices in the distance, a laugh, and a wash of panic threatened to swamp her. And then she fell back onto her ankles, her hand at her mouth.

He looked down at her, a smile on his lips. "Do me up."

She obeyed, her fingers fumbling a little in her haste with the laces of his hose. She was to have no satisfaction herself then this afternoon, but that was not unusual. And Arnaud knew full well the heights to which denial and anticipation would drive her.

"Has anyone new arrived at court?" he asked, stepping away from her as she struggled to her feet.

"A new maid of honor. Rosamund Walsingham, I think she said." She looked at him curiously. "Why?"

He shrugged. "No reason. I like to know what's going on, and you, *ma chère,* are in a good position to keep me informed. She must be related then to Walsingham."

"Sir Francis's cousin, she said." Agathe brushed down her skirt.

Arnaud smiled. "You had better go back and dress for the evening."

"Will I see you tonight?"

"It depends. I may play at the tables until late. If I want you, I'll send for you." He gave her a slight mocking bow and strolled away.

Agathe cursed him under her breath even as her body stirred anew at the prospect of their next encounter. He would not deprive her then.

Chapter Ten

THE OTHER MAIDS of honor were already in the dorter when Joan and Rosamund went in. They were chattering together, helping each other with laces and pins, and barely glanced at the two junior members of their group.

Joan helped Rosamund unpack the rest of her gowns, and when she lifted out the dress of rose velvet with its seed-pearl embroidery, the chatter stopped as the other women turned to look.

"It's well enough," declared Arbella Vesey in a none-too-discreet whisper. "But I doubt the rose color will suit that hair. Who could have thought it would?"

Rosamund bit down on her inner cheek to keep from uttering the verbal assault hovering on her tongue. Lady Walsingham's advice was still clear in her head, and she could not afford to make enemies, even by defending herself and her patroness. She pretended she hadn't heard and hung the gown in the armoire, careful not to displace the other gowns as she squeezed her own into a corner. This evening she decided it would be politic to wear the same emerald green damask she had worn for her presentation.

She stowed the rest of her possessions as best she could, then helped Joan with her own court dress, lacing her tightly as Joan clutched the bedpost and urged her to greater effort. "I am determined to have a waist a man's hand can span," she gasped. "A half inch more, Rosamund."

"I'll break a rib if I do." Rosamund tied off the laces. "No one could make a waist any smaller than that."

Joan helped her with the laces of her own gown, while their companions continued with their exclusive whispers until they left the dorter in a bevy, chattering like a flock of starlings. Rosamund was glad to see them go. Their company made her uneasy, as if they had the power to harm her in some way.

Joan stood absolutely still, as if listening for something, then whispered, "Guard the door. Let me know if anyone's on the stairs." She darted across the room to the chest at the foot of the first bed. Rosamund, somewhat bemused, went to the door, her ear pressed to the crack.

Joan gingerly lifted the lid of the chest and took out a small box. She opened it carefully and dipped her lace handkerchief into it. She dabbed the handkerchief on her nose and cheeks before closing the box, returning it to the chest and quietly dropping the lid. She came over to Rosamund at the door. "Does that look better? It's not all blotchy?"

"No, not at all." Rosamund shook her head, biting her tongue. The chalky white powder certainly covered Joan's freckles, but it made her look at death's door. However she didn't think Joan would wish to know that.

Joan patted her cheeks with her fingertips. "Arbella won't notice any missing. It's only a few grains. Come, we must hurry. We have to be in our places before the queen enters."

Rosamund retained vivid memories of that evening for many years. It was a jumble of impressions, some of which made her cringe with embarrassment, as when she took a seat above the salt at the long board below the royal dais in the Banqueting Hall of Whitehall Palace. Joan had gone in

ahead of her, having been summoned by Lady Pembroke
to carry her train, and Rosamund did not immediately see
her at the table when she entered the vast candlelit hall.
She was aware only of a colorful blur and the rich aroma of
roasted meat as she walked up the interminable length of
the hall to where the royal dais stood at the top. The body
of the hall was lined with tables all packed with chattering
courtiers.

Her companions on the board reserved exclusively for
the queen's ladies sniggered behind their hands as she
chose a spot in the middle of the board, but they said nothing until a chamberlain approached and informed her too
loudly that her status did not qualify her to sit above the
salt.

Scarlet with mortification, Rosamund struggled off the
bench trying to manage her wide skirts and long train, and
made her way to the bottom of the table, where she now
saw that Joan was already seated.

"I should have warned you," Joan whispered as Rosamund maneuvered herself onto the bench. "We are the
lowliest of the low here. Never presume, or they'll make
sure you pay for it."

Grimly Rosamund nodded, praying that her scarlet cheeks
would soon cool. She wondered how many in the crowded
Banqueting Hall had witnessed her humiliation and caught
herself praying that Will Creighton had not seen it.

Dinner went on for many hours. The queen, dining in
state with the French ambassador on her right, ate and
drank only sparingly. A lute player strummed behind her
chair and she appeared disinclined for conversation, occasionally looking out over the hall at her assembled court as
if committing something to memory.

At last she rose from the table and the court rose

instantly. She disappeared through a tapestry-shielded door at the rear of the dais, the great ladies of the privy chamber accompanying her.

It was the signal for the court to break up, and Rosamund heaved a sigh of relief. It had been the least enjoyable experience of her entire existence thus far. But other memories as the evening progressed were much pleasanter.

On a dais in another massive hall musicians were playing as the court in a body entered from the Banqueting Hall. A troupe of jugglers and acrobats entertained throughout the evening and the queen sat in state, smiling occasionally at some witticism of her fool, who sat at her feet in his motley, his belled hat tinkling merrily at every movement.

Rosamund looked around the crowded hall, her eyes searching for Will, but she could see him nowhere. "Come on, let's dance," Joan prodded eagerly, and Rosamund, afraid she would be conspicuous if she stood to the side, gave up her search and followed Joan into the line for a stately galliard.

She had had dancing lessons in her childhood and was naturally light on her feet, but the galliard was complicated and she was concentrating so hard on her steps she barely raised her eyes from her feet until a faintly accented voice commented with a laugh, "I must protest, Mistress Walsingham. I may be impossibly vain but I would have thought I might be more interesting than a pair of admittedly very dainty feet."

She looked up into a pair of tawny eyes, deep set in an olive complexion. Startling white teeth were revealed in a slightly crooked and most attractive smile. "Forgive me, I didn't realize . . . ," she stammered, not making much sense even to herself, then she frowned in puzzlement. "You seem to have the advantage of me, sir. I do not recall our introduction."

He laughed, taking her hand and turning her with him along the line of dancers, his own steps enviably sure. "Because we have not had one. I happen to know your name because I asked someone who *has* been introduced to you. Lady Leinster. You will remember, perhaps, that you met her this afternoon?"

His smile was attractive, but so was his voice, with that lilt of an accent, and his eyes seemed to see nothing but her, Rosamund thought, somewhat bemused by this barrage of impressions.

"Yes . . . yes, of course, I remember." She looked up at him now with full attention, a question in her eyes.

"Ah, you are wondering why I would ask for your name, but not for an introduction," he guessed, lifting a perfectly arched black eyebrow. "I am right, yes?"

"Yes," she said frankly. "But if you thought now would be a good moment to introduce yourself and redress the balance, I would not disagree with you, sir."

An appreciative smile danced across his eyes. "I am remiss. My most humble apologies, Mistress Walsingham. The Chevalier de Vaugiras at your service, madam." He bowed, managing to make the movement blend with the steps of the dance. "And I asked who you were because I am always curious about newcomers to the court. I do not like to be behindhand in the gossip, you understand?"

"Oh, I am flattered, sir," Rosamund exclaimed, her own eyes sparkling. "To be considered worthy of gossip on one's first day is such a compliment. I doubt I shall recover my composure for quite some time."

"And I am most effectively put in my place. I did not mean to imply anything so insulting."

She regarded him thoughtfully. "Really, Chevalier. I wonder if I believe that." Rosamund realized suddenly that she was behaving quite unlike herself, and enjoying every minute of it. The air seemed to crackle around them as the music continued, and he turned her slowly as the dance steps took her around him.

Then the music slowed, and the dancers gracefully completed their last steps and came to a halt as the last note died. Rosamund curtsied, her partner bowed.

"Shall we dance the next one?" He took her hand in a light clasp.

Rosamund remembered Ursula's gems of advice. *Do nothing to cause comment, never let yourself be singled out for any reason.* She smiled and curtsied again. "I fear not, Chevalier. I am fatigued."

He released her hand immediately and bowed again as she stepped out of the line. "Desolated, madam, but I trust we shall continue our acquaintance at some other time."

She smiled and walked away, feeling rather pleased with herself.

"Rosamund . . . Rosamund?"

She turned at the urgent whisper. Will was beckoning to her from behind an arras that concealed a window embrasure. She glanced around. No one seemed to be looking in their direction, but that didn't mean that people weren't. She gestured that he should come out into the open. It was one thing to have a conversation in front of everyone, quite another to slip behind tapestries.

"Oh, I would never have believed you to be so timid, Mistress Rosamund," Will grumbled, emerging fully from the arras. He came over to her with a laugh in his eyes. "I was hoping for a secret assignation. I wanted to show you how it was possible to escape the rigid rules at court if one was bold enough."

"I'm not bold enough as yet. This is all so new to me, it seems there are traps at every corner."

"You seemed to be having an amusing conversation with Arnaud de Vaugiras," Will remarked, watching her closely.

"Did I?" she said carelessly, then couldn't help herself. "Well, perhaps it *was* amusing."

Will raised his eyebrows. "I'm sure it was. He is generally considered to be one of the most cultivated of courtiers. Her majesty enjoys his company." Will gestured to the dais and Rosamund saw that her former partner was leading the queen into the dance.

"Then I suppose I must be flattered he deigned to converse with me at all," she remarked. "If it's not too bold for a newcomer to make the suggestion, let us join the dance. They're playing a country dance that I happen to know well."

"I am honored, madam." Will bowed, took her hand, and led her into the dance.

"My brother tells me you have aspirations to be a playmaker," she said when they came together in the line of dance again.

For once Will seemed to lose a little of his self-confident composure. "I have a play almost completed, but I have yet to show my work to anyone," he confided.

"You could perhaps ask Master Marlowe to read it. Or my brother. Thomas is generally thought to be something of a patron of the theatre."

Will's smile was rueful. "I own I shrink from being my own advocate. I'm too nervous myself to ask anyone with influence in the theatre to judge my puny efforts."

"I could ask my brother, or Master Marlowe, for you. If that would be any help."

"Would you really?" His blue eyes seemed to deepen in color with the sudden intensity of his voice.

"Of course," she responded simply.

"But perhaps you should read it yourself first, before you commit yourself?" He smiled that self-deprecating smile again.

"Of course, if you wish it. I should be most interested."

His hand tightened on hers and his eyes glowed with pleasure as he led her out of the dance line. "Will you meet me in the morning in the privy garden? Just after sunup. No one will be around and I will show you my play."

Rosamund's look of dismay was almost comical. "Where *is* the privy garden?"

"I was forgetting, this is your first day." Will frowned. "I will meet you at the bottom of the staircase to your dorter at five. You will not be expected to attend upon the queen until after breakfast."

"How do you know that?"

He chuckled. "I have been at court these last three years, Mistress Walsingham. I am well acquainted with her majesty's routines. You will learn them soon enough."

"I'm sure I shall . . . eventually. It all seems very confusing at the moment." She saw Joan standing to one side of the hall, watching them. "I had better go now," she said swiftly. "I will meet you in the morning. I bid you good night, Will." Without waiting for a response, she walked quickly away.

As Rosamund reached her, Joan said on an accusing note, "You seemed very close with Will Creighton."

"Not so . . . I was merely dancing with him. Is there something wrong with that?"

"Only that he's a terrible flirt. I should warn you that he tries to take up with every female newcomer to the court. But he gets bored very quickly, and just when they think he is making a definite play, he drops them like a hot brick."

"Oh. Thank you for the warning." She looked curiously at Joan. "Did that happen to you?"

Joan's angry flush was answer enough, and as they made their way upstairs, Rosamund was in no doubt of the need to keep her dawn rendezvous to herself.

Robin Poley sat in the taproom of the Red Lion in the hamlet of Chartley. Opposite him Thomas Phelippes nursed a tankard of ale. "You've had no contact with Mary Stuart since you arrived this time?"

Poley shook his head. Good-looking, he was dark-haired, swarthy, richly dressed with cobweb lawn at collar and cuffs, and gold buttons to his crimson doublet slashed to reveal gold undersleeves. Only his eyes, small, close-set, and a pale watery blue detracted from the overall impression. "Paulet said she'd taken to her bed. He will send to me when she's up and about again, and I'll make contact with the girl Barbara Curle, who serves the lady. She will do anything for her since Mary baptized her child when Paulet refused to permit a Catholic priest to perform the ceremony."

Phelippes nodded. "I remember. The lady has courage, one must admit. Paulet's enmity is no light burden to carry." He took a sip of ale. "You look well yourself, Robin, for a man recently released from the dungeons of the Fleet."

Poley chuckled. "'Tis easy enough to get relief in there with coin to grease the jailers' palms. And I made some good conversions. Two priests, terrified out of their godly minds by my tales of Topcliffe's racks and screws, are already on their way to the English College in Rheims to listen in to the plots and conspiracies of the Catholic priests and their followers. They will report faithfully, and I shall follow them there soon enough to ensure that they do." He took a draft of ale. "How is our lord and master?"

"Walsingham spins his webs," Phelippes said. "And he draws in the flies. There is talk of conspiracy, and he listens in. Father Ballard, the missionary priest who hides himself under the name of Captain Fortescue, is at work again, and Walsingham has Barnard Maude stuck closer than skin to Ballard's side. And he has a new man . . . one Christopher . . . Kit, they call him . . . Marlowe. A Corpus man."

Poley nodded. "Walsingham always did cleave to Cambridge men. A scholar is he, this Marlowe?"

"Aye, a scholar, a writer of verse, a playmaker too. And a man who holds heretical views, atheistic views, and when in his cups is not afraid to declare them." Phelippes banged his tankard on the table to attract the wench's attention. "He is often in his cups." He smiled. "He is disinclined to accept his destiny, a Church living that might bring him five pounds a year, if he's lucky."

"So he's ripe for the spider's web."

"Indeed, Robin. Indeed. He works with the young Walsingham, but our master talks of putting him in tandem with Gilbert Gifford to sow some provocative seeds among Ballard's troupe."

A movement at the door drew Robin's eyes and he gave an infinitesimal nod to Phelippes as he rose and crossed the taproom. "Mistress Curle. Do you look for me?"

"Yes, Master Poley. A letter from my lady's majesty. I hardly expected to see you so soon." She glanced anxiously around before sliding the letter into his hand. "Sir Amyas has removed her chair and cloth of state."

"Ah, the poor lady. How she must feel it." Robin's voice was low and sympathetic, but his eyes slipped sideways. That might explain Mary's letter. She had not committed herself to writing to her supporters for many weeks.

He nodded to Barbara, who quickly slipped out of the tavern, and returned to Phelippes. He laid the letter on the table, pushing it across to the other man. "For Scotland. You will decipher it, if it's in code."

"Her codes are too simple," Phelippes said, tucking the letter into his doublet. "I will look at it later."

Robin hid his disappointment. He knew his place in Walsingham's web. It was important, but not sufficiently so for him to be considered a confidant of the master's. He was a tool, no more. But it paid well enough and the work pleased him. He enjoyed the deviousness, the sleight of hand, the confusion he could create. He knew he wasn't wholly trusted by anyone, not even his master, the secretary of state. And that suited him well enough. Robin had only one interest, his own well-being and advancement, and like any mercenary he would take that on whichever side of the fence offered the best opportunity.

He said now, "Paulet has taken away the royal symbols."

"Yes, on her majesty's instructions . . . or rather, Walsingham's. Master Secretary suggested it and I understand that her majesty put up no objections."

"It is a first step then?"

"A first step. Walsingham lays the bricks carefully one upon the other." Phelippes rose. "I am to dine with Paulet. I may have instructions for you in the morning. And I will return the letter to you then for delivery."

Robin bowed his head in acknowledgment and called for more ale. This journey as courier would not be as arduous as many he had taken. Scotland was but two days' ride from the north of England, and it would not, thank God, involve another wretched crossing of the Channel.

Chapter Eleven

AGATHE SHIFTED BENEATH her lover's body. Arnaud seemed to be asleep, his head in the hollow of her shoulder, his chest crushing her breasts, his long legs twined with hers. He had given her everything she could have wished for and more during the long hours of the night, bringing her again and again to the peak, holding there as only he could do, before bestowing the caressing touch that would send her tumbling into the rushing black waters of fulfillment. And when he had finally allowed himself to climax, he had seemed to lose consciousness afterwards, falling heavily, a deadweight, onto her exhausted body.

She stroked down his back, reveling in the play of muscles beneath the taut flesh, inhaling the earthy scent of his hair, a strand of which was tickling her nose. She sneezed, her body jumping beneath him.

Arnaud nipped the soft skin of her shoulder, his lips warm against her skin. Playfully she struggled to heave him off her and he laughed softly, letting her struggle for several minutes before he raised his head and murmured, "You have had enough of me so soon, my sweet?"

"Never," she denied, pulling his head down to hers.

He kissed her slowly, languidly, before rolling sideways to swing himself off the bed. Agathe sat up against the pillows, watching as he poured wine into two silver goblets from a crystal decanter on a gilded table against the lead-paned window. The window was open to catch what breeze there was in the muggy night, and the fishy smell of the river below drifted into the chamber.

Agathe took the goblet he offered her with a murmur of thanks. He took a swallow of wine, then leaned over her, pressing his mouth to hers in a wine-infused kiss that sent a shiver of delight across her skin. He straightened slowly, regarding her with narrowed eyes. "So, *ma chère,* I wish you to do something for me."

She gazed hungrily along the long, lean length of him. Even at rest his penis was thick and powerful in its black nest of tightly curled hair, and as she leaned forward to touch it with a fingertip, it twitched and hardened, rising slowly.

Arnaud chuckled and stepped back. "Not that, *ma chère,* at least not at present. I want you to do some work for me."

Agathe made a moue of disappointment and drank from her goblet. "What work?"

"Nothing too arduous." He turned from the bed and walked to the window, where the night sky was lightening in the east. Agathe's gaze was fixed on his back, the light trail of black hair down his spine and into the cleft between the tight muscles of his buttocks. "I want you to cultivate the new maid of honor, Mistress Walsingham. Make her your friend, offer to teach her the ways of the court, the less formal ways of the court, you understand. Act as her guide and mentor in the generally approved paths of dalliance."

"Why?"

"Because, *ma chère,* I intend to seduce her, and I wish you to prepare her for me." He still didn't turn from the window as he spoke, each word dropping clear as a bell into Agathe's astounded silence.

She managed to speak at last. "Seduce her? Why?"

He chuckled. "I'm minded to take a virgin to my bed."

Agathe swallowed. "Am I not enough then?"

He turned, and a dark concentration in his gaze unnerved her. "You are exquisite, everything a man could wish for, but even so a palate becomes jaded and needs refreshing. I am in need of refreshment."

Agathe felt the first stirrings of unusual rebellion. "I do not like it, Arnaud."

He came over to the bed again, leaning over, resting his flat palms on the pillows on either side of her head, his mouth hovering just above hers. "You will find me all the better for it, *mon amour*, I promise you. I shall pleasure you in ways you have not yet dreamed of."

A delicious shiver ran across her skin. Arnaud always kept his promises. But still she protested, "She is too young and innocent for you, Arnaud. Can you not . . . *refresh* . . . yourself with someone a little more experienced?"

He shook his head. "That would defeat the object." His eyes, the tawny gold of a jaguar, held hers, and she felt her resistance melting. It was not only the power he held over her, the power of sweet pain that was her pleasure. It was not only that he understood her, understood her needs and desires as no one else had ever done, or ever would again. She was quite simply incapable of refusing him anything that would please him, even something as against her self-interest as this.

"I will try," she said. "But perhaps she cannot be persuaded."

His gaze darkened. "Do you think that possible, *ma chère*?"

And of course she did not. Who could resist Arnaud when he set out to charm? She didn't answer.

Arnaud straightened, accepting her silence as consent. He glanced at the window. "It's time for you to leave, *mon amour*, the dawn is breaking."

Agathe set her goblet aside and got out of bed, reaching for her night-robe. She was suddenly cold and, most strangely, didn't want to display her nakedness to Arnaud. Ordinarily she reveled in his eyes on her, but at the moment all she could think was that he wanted another woman in his bed. She drew the robe tight around her and slipped her feet into the backless satin slippers.

Without saying anything she went to the small door at the rear of the chamber that led onto a flight of back stairs, but before she could reach the door, Arnaud caught her against him, his mouth pressed hard against hers in a fierce embrace. She struggled to resist but as always it was futile and she yielded with a little sigh of submission. When finally he released her, she touched her bruised and swollen lips and gazed silently up at him.

He regarded her gravely for a moment, then said, "Indulge me in this, *ma chère*. It has nothing to do with you, this strange desire I have for an innocent. It is but a whim and will in no wise keep me from you." He touched her eyelids with the tip of his tongue, a moist, brushing caress. "Believe me, Agathe, nothing could do that."

"I can refuse you nothing," she murmured, half to herself. "When is this seduction to start?"

"Immediately . . . I shall hope to find you with her by the river this afternoon when the queen's ladies are at liberty."

"Very well," she whispered, and slipped away through the door to the back stairs, which took her down little-used corridors to her own apartments. They were much smaller and less desirable than the chevalier's. The steward of the queen's household allocated accommodation partly according to rank, but more important according to where a courtier was positioned in the queen's favor. Almost always the gentlemen favorites were well housed, the single ladies rather less so.

Rosamund lay awake in the gray light of the false dawn, listening to Joan's heavy breathing beside her, the rhythm interspersed with little snores. The mattress crackled as she shifted on the straw and she tried to lie still, afraid to wake her bedmate. She was going to keep her rendezvous with Will Creighton, but at some point during the night her blithe agreement to the clandestine dawn meeting in the privy garden had begun to seem foolhardy if not downright insane. She had known all along that she must tread carefully in this new life, so what had possessed her to throw that caution carefully acquired at the feet of Lady Walsingham to the four winds?

And yet, cold feet or not, she was somehow compelled to follow her impulse. She slid from the bed, standing the instant her feet touched the bare floorboards. She had left her clothes ready on the chest at the foot of the bed before retiring and dressed quickly, barely breathing in case she disturbed one of the sleeping women. They had all come late to bed after the evening's dancing and seemed to be sound sleepers. Carrying her shoes, she tiptoed to the door, opened it a crack, and slid out onto the landing.

It was deathly quiet up here, the doors to the dorters housing other members of the royal household firmly closed. Rosamund crept to the head of the stairs and paused to put on her shoes. She hadn't bothered with stockings in her haste to escape without notice.

She ran lightly down the stairs and stopped at the

bottom. There was no Will Creighton. She cursed herself for a fool. Either he had never intended to make the rendezvous and was merely making game of her, which seemed the sport of choice in this palace, or he was still sleeping the sleep of the just.

Well, she was up now. There was no point wasting her freedom. She thought for a moment, trying to remember which way to go to reach the garden. A low whistle, like a birdcall, came from an embrasure down the deserted corridor. She turned sharply and Will Creighton stepped into the corridor. He grinned at her and strode towards her, swinging a jaunty hat adorned with a pheasant feather.

He bowed with a flourish of his hat. "I give you good morrow, Mistress Rosamund. I was afraid you'd still be abed after last night's dancing."

He looked none the worse for wear, Rosamund reflected, as she said lightly, "I am not made of such poor stuff, Master Creighton."

"No, of course not. You are of Walsingham stock after all." He was regarding her with close intent, his full mouth curved in a smile whose invitation only a fool would miss.

"I know you're acquainted with my brother, but are you also acquainted with our cousin Sir Francis, the secretary of state?"

"Not as well as I would wish. I would like to be in his service," Will said, serious now, the flirtatious manner vanished. "He employs men such as myself from time to time, and I have already written to him, offering my services, but he has not as yet responded."

"You should talk to Thomas then. Or even Master Watson, the poet. I have seen him in Seething Lane visiting my cousin."

Will looked thoughtful, but said easily, "It seems,

Mistress Rosamund, that you are destined to be my good angel. I will seek out Master Watson this afternoon when I go to the play."

"Oh, you are to go to the play?" She sounded wistful.

"I try to go most days. Of course sometimes her majesty's own players will perform at court, but they haven't done so for several weeks now." He began to walk down the presently deserted corridor towards a flight of stairs. "Will you walk a little in the garden with me?"

"I thought you were to show me your play."

"I have it here." He patted his doublet. "But we will be more private in the garden. 'Tis too early for any but gardeners to be about."

Rosamund nodded and they made their bewildering way down corridors, up and down short flights of stairs, across antechambers, and finally down a flight of outside stairs that led directly into a small, enclosed garden where at its center a fountain surrounded by stone benches played into a fishpond.

As Will had said, the garden was deserted. The grass was still moist with dew and the eastern sky glowed red. The air was fresh and Rosamund wished she had brought a shawl. They sat on one of the benches and after a moment's silence Will said, "So you have a love of the theatre, Rosamund."

"A passionate love," she averred. "I would spend every afternoon there if I could. I love everything about it, backstage, the players' talk, the arguments over the versifying, the swordplay. It is so . . . so romantic," she finished, hearing how lame it sounded but quite unable to think of a better way of expressing herself.

"I understand exactly. 'Tis how I feel myself. But, sometimes I fear I shall never make a play good enough to be performed." He sighed heavily as he drew a packet of papers from his doublet. "When I listened to Master Marlowe reciting that passage from his play, *Tamburlaine,* I think he called it, I knew I would never write anything so powerful." He opened the papers tentatively. "But I hope there will be scope for lesser works."

Rosamund was touched by Will's humility, such a contrast to his customary self-confident swagger. She said swiftly, "My brother says that with all the new theatres coming up the players are going to be desperate for plays. There is one being constructed, the Rose, by a man . . ." She wrinkled her forehead. "Henslowe, I think he is called."

"Aye, Philip Henslowe. He has a finger in many pies, that one."

"Well, will you show me your play?"

Again he hesitated. "I think I'm a little afraid to. You appear to be on easy terms with Kyd and Watson, not to mention this Master Marlowe. Whereas I can do no more than hang on to their coattails."

Rosamund was greatly flattered at this assumption, but honesty obliged her to say, "I am on easy terms with Master Marlowe, Will, but not with the others. My brother has been very reluctant to permit me into their company, and I have always kept silent in dark corners lest I draw attention to myself." She extended her hand. "Show me your play."

"The subject is the archery contest when Odysseus returns to find Penelope trying to decide among her many suitors." He put it into her hand and stood up. "I will take a turn around the garden while you read."

Rosamund read quickly. The verse certainly lacked the power of a Marlowe or a Kyd, but nevertheless had a pleasing cadence. The story was simple and romantic, with scope aplenty for some dashing scenes at the archery butts.

That would surely please the groundlings . . . she had noticed how they reacted to grand flourishes.

"Well?"

She hadn't heard his return across the grass and looked up with a little start. "Oh, I was so absorbed, I forgot where I was."

"Truly?" He looked pleased, turning his hat over between his hands. "Do you like it?"

"There is much to please an audience. The story is full of life and passion. It will stage well, I think."

"And the language? What of my verses?"

"Good," she said simply.

He frowned and took back his sheets. "But it's obviously not the work of Master Marlowe, or Master Kyd."

Rosamund wasn't sure whether it was a rhetorical question or a statement, but before she could respond, Will turned on his heel and strode off across the grass.

After a minute Rosamund decided he wasn't coming back and stood up, wondering how she would manage to retrace her steps without her guide. She wandered across the grass to a gap in the hedge at the far side of the garden, and just as she reached it, Will's voice said from behind her, "Rosamund. Don't go."

She turned around. He came across the grass towards her. "I was churlish to leave you like that, but sometimes I feel so frustrated at my lack of skill, forgive me." He took her hands, enclosing them in his own. He gave her a smile, half-apologetic, half-coaxing, infinitely inviting.

"But indeed I don't think you should be frustrated," she demurred. "It will stage well and has everything in it to please an audience. Rather than showing it to my brother or Kit Marlowe, who will look only at the versifying, why not take it straight to Master Alleyn or Master Henslowe, who will look at it with a different eye? They'll look for the audience appeal, and it has plenty of that, and they'll see what the possibilities are for staging it."

Will frowned, but a flicker of interest crossed his eyes. "Perhaps you're right. Maybe this afternoon I'll summon the courage to show it to Ned Alleyn or Dick Burbage."

"I wish I could be there. I would be a most vocal advocate." Rosamund laughed and shook her head in resignation.

Will grinned, once more the self-confident, slightly risqué young courtier. "If you dressed in disguise . . . let me think . . . " He paused, hands outstretched in triumph. "I know . . . in a page's doublet and hose, hat pulled low, no one would recognize you. Not even your brother."

Rosamund stared at him as if he were on display at Bedlam. "You are not serious, are you?"

"It's up to you whether I'm serious or not," he responded with another wicked grin. "I could procure the disguise, but you would need the courage."

Rosamund felt a momentary fizz of excitement that as swiftly died. It was impossible, of course. Will was only teasing her. "A tantalizing idea, Master Will, but no more than that."

He shrugged. "Not necessarily. If you change your mind, let me know."

She shook her head with a smile, saying only, "I had better return to the dorter, my bedmates will be up and about by now. You must needs show me the way, but go slowly so that I may memorize it." This time she would commit the route to memory, and as soon as time and opportunity permitted, she would map it out with pen and paper. In fact, she would map out the entire palace in time.

Will directed their steps back to the side door. "The

queen's ladies usually take the air in the middle of the afternoon. It is customary for them to mingle with the court in the gardens or, if the weather is inclement, in the Long Gallery. If I don't see you this evening after dinner, I will look for you tomorrow afternoon and tell you how the good theatre masters responded to my play."

"I shall await your news most eagerly." She gave him a quick smile and he responded with a little bow.

The corridors and hallways were busier now and they walked quickly without speaking, trying to avoid drawing attention to themselves, although everyone moved so fast and so purposefully, intent on their own business, that it was unlikely two young courtiers would attract so much as a glance of curiosity. At the end of the corridor leading to the stairs to Rosamund's dorter, Will turned aside, laying a conspiratorial finger on his lips before sauntering away in the opposite direction.

Joan was half-dressed as Rosamund entered the dorter. "Heavens, where have you been? I have been so afraid you would be late, and we have to break our fast before attending the queen."

"I woke early. I went for a walk." Rosamund glanced at the other women, willing to offer a morning greeting, but she was pointedly ignored. "Is there water, or must we fetch it?"

"No, it is brought for us." Joan indicated a basin and ewer on the dresser. "It's not clean because we have all used it."

"Oh." Rosamund looked with distaste at the scummy water in the basin. Clearly one needed to be on one's toes in the morning to get the first wash. But then seniority was probably the rule, so it wouldn't matter what time one awoke. She decided to forgo washing this morning. She'd had the luxury of a bath in Seething Lane the previous day before her presentation to the queen. The benefits would have to last a little longer.

The queen's ladies broke their fast in a small parlor attached to the large chamber where they spent their days in attendance upon her majesty. This time Rosamund stuck close to Joan and took her seat at the end of the table, which was presided over by the Countess of Shrewsbury.

As they ate, the countess discussed the day's events, allocated individual tasks, and delivered several reprimands, which were received with downcast eyes and murmured apologies. "And you, Rosamund Walsingham . . ."

Rosamund almost choked on her veal cheek. She had not expected to hear her own name. "Yes . . . my lady?"

"Her majesty requires your presence in her privy chamber at eleven o'clock this morning. I will conduct you there."

Rosamund was aware of a sea of eyes on her. They were unfriendly, envious, calculating. This upstart newcomer who should be hiding in a corner had attracted the queen's notice. She could be about to face banishment from the court, which would concern them not at all except as a delicious topic of speculative gossip, or she could be singled out for some royal favor. And that was not the way matters were conducted among the queen's ladies.

"I wonder why she wants you," Joan whispered. "Can you think?"

"No." Rosamund shook her head and set down her knife. She had quite lost her appetite.

When Lady Shrewsbury rose, they all followed suit and took their places in the big chamber. There was no sign of the queen. The countess directed someone to read aloud, another to play on the virginals, and instructed the rest to take up their needlework. Rosamund sighed and was about to set her first stitch when the countess spoke her name.

"Yes, madam?"

"The queen has said that you may pass the time in drawing, and you are to practice your calligraphy." The lady sounded none too pleased at this diversion from usual practice, but Rosamund felt sweet relief.

She jumped to her feet. "Thank you, madam. I will fetch my paper and pens."

"You will find everything you need at the desk over there."

Rosamund settled down, and as always her surroundings disappeared as she began to sketch from memory the scene on the royal dais when the queen had dined in state with the French ambassador. The man had had an interesting face, and maybe Sir Francis would find the reproduction of interest.

A few minutes before eleven, the countess called her and Rosamund reluctantly put down her pen. She stood up, smoothed down her skirt, and adjusted the ribbon that held her hair away from her face.

The countess examined her with narrowed eyes, then nodded. "Come."

The door to the queen's privy chamber was opened at their approach and Rosamund once more found herself in the presence of her sovereign. She knelt and waited.

"Rise, Rosamund." The queen nodded amiably as the girl rose from her obeisance, and Rosamund's nervousness lessened somewhat. Her majesty was dressed as richly as ever, gems studding her headdress and gown, a circlet of huge emeralds around her throat. A rather scrawny throat, Rosamund couldn't help noticing. The emeralds merely drew attention to the wrinkles. But such flaws were lost amidst the dazzle of the royal gems.

"I have work for you to do, child." The queen gestured to the table where Rosamund had worked the previous afternoon. "You will find letters there. They are poorly written and I would have you transcribe them in a fair hand for my councilors."

She smiled as she continued, "Some of them, poor souls, have such sadly diminished eyesight that they have difficulty reading anything but the clearest of script. The price of age, I fear."

There was a touch of complacency, Rosamund thought. Her majesty was gloating a little over her elderly councilors' physical frailties. She curtsied in acknowledgment, deciding that any speech would be too risky, and hurried to her allotted station.

Chapter Twelve

"Let's go onto the terrace, Rosamund. Charles Singlebury is playing the lute." Joan tugged on Rosamund's sleeve as the two girls crossed the great hall that afternoon towards the open doors and the sun-drenched terrace that ran the width of the palace facing the river.

Rosamund could see knots of courtiers on the terrace, but not the one who had attracted Joan's attention. "As you wish," she agreed. "Who is Charles Singlebury?"

"Oh, he's a new courtier." Joan blushed and her freckles stood out. Swiftly she unfurled her fan, waving it jerkily in front of her face as if she could thus cause them to fly away on the breeze. "The younger son of the Earl of Redmond."

Rosamund regarded her with a quizzical smile. "And you find him of interest?"

Joan bridled. "No, why should I?"

"No reason that I can see," Rosamund responded, still smiling. "But then I haven't met the gentleman as yet." She followed Joan across the terrace to join a small group of people gathered around a young man, who looked barely bearded, playing his lute with an air of the utmost gravity, quite unlike Will Creighton's easy nonchalance, she reflected.

"Mistress Walsingham, well met." The soft, vaguely familiar voice arrested her. She turned and saw Lady Leinster smiling at her, sitting gracefully on the low wall of the terrace a few paces away. Her dark hair was caught up in a snood of silver thread, and she wore a collar of matchless pearls around her throat, one large pearl hanging pendant to the deep cleft of her breasts swelling softly above the pearl-embroidered neckline of her dark blue gown, almost exactly the color of her enormous eyes.

Rosamund curtsied politely. "Yes, well met indeed, my lady." Lady Leinster patted the wall beside her and Rosamund accepted the invitation, a little flattered by the attention. Joan, oblivious of her defection, had joined the group around the lute player.

Lady Leinster observed as she plied her fan indolently, "It's a beautiful afternoon."

"Beautiful," Rosamund agreed.

Behind her fan Agathe hid her sharp scrutiny of this girl she was to bring to Arnaud's bed. *Why?* There was nothing out of the ordinary about her. She was certainly pretty and her coppery hair was beautiful, quite her best feature, together with the large, oval green eyes. But Arnaud wasn't attracted by simple beauty; if he had been, she would not herself have been his playmate. Apart from her own striking eye color, she was more of a *jolie-laide*, as the French would say. Unusual, neither pretty nor ugly, but attractive in her own unique fashion.

Mindful of her instructions, she said, "Shall we walk a little on the riverbank? There's a pleasant breeze down there."

"I would love to." Rosamund jumped energetically to her feet, her skirt swinging around her. "I feel so confined after a morning inside, I would be so happy to walk a little."

Agathe could not herself see the appeal in walking, a languid stroll was as much as she was prepared to contemplate, but she agreed with a smile and rose from the wall, fastidiously smoothing down her skirts.

"If you enjoy outside pursuits, you will enjoy the hunting parties," she observed. "Not every day is spent in idleness, the court is confined only when the queen has much business to occupy her. She is frequently unwell, with overwork they say, and every now and again she'll decide to shake the megrims and we will all be on the move . . . a hunting party at Richmond, a day on the river . . ." She waved an expressive hand. "It is always enjoyable."

"I can hardly wait," Rosamund said with feeling.

Agathe laughed a soft trill of amusement. "When you have been at court a little longer, my dear, you will discover there are many ways to relieve the daily tedium, even for the queen's attendants."

"It must be pleasant to be a courtier but not in attendance on the queen. You may come and go as you please." Rosamund glanced at her companion curiously. "I understand you're a widow, Lady Leinster."

"Yes, and a merry one at that." Agathe's light laughter ran up and down the musical scale. "If you'll take my advice, you will find yourself a rich and careless husband, one who attends to his own business and not his wife's."

"Easier said than done, I imagine." Rosamund was fascinated. "Is that what you did?"

"Leinster was certainly rich and left me very well cared for. He was not however as careless of my business as I could have wished. However, he was careless of himself and a reckless huntsman. A fall from his horse during a boar hunt put a period to his days, I'm afraid." It didn't sound to Rosamund as if Agathe's husband's loss had caused her much grief.

"And you intend to remain a widow?" It seemed quite

possible to ask such questions of Lady Leinster. Something about the woman invited confidential exchanges, and there was no denying that Rosamund could use a little worldly instruction in courtly life outside Lady Walsingham's carefully instilled precepts.

"Certainly. It's a most pleasant existence, Rosamund . . . I may call you Rosamund? Such a pretty name."

"I should be honored."

"And you must call me Agathe," Lady Leinster declared, slipping her arm into Rosamund's. "We shall be the best of friends, I'm sure of it."

"I hope so." Rosamund returned the smile.

"Independence, my dear, is the secret to happiness," her newfound friend informed her as they walked along a busy avenue of plane trees leading to the river. "You choose your own friends, your own pursuits, and . . ." She paused, casting Rosamund a look of pure devilry. "And your own lovers." She laughed again. "Have I shocked you?"

Rosamund shook her head. "Not really." She was remembering what Joan had said about Lady Leinster's romantic escapades.

"Well, you'll see what I mean soon enough."

And Rosamund did. Her companion seemed to know everyone they encountered. They passed other couples, and sometimes quite large knots of people deep in laughing conversation. Agathe nodded, smiled, and once or twice paused to chat, introducing Rosamund with a warm, inclusive smile that immediately produced an answering warmth. Rosamund began to feel almost at home for the first time since her arrival at Whitehall. The coldness of her reception among the queen's attendants ceased to seem important with the realization that outside that tight circle people seemed to behave with normal friendliness and courtesy.

She noticed that Agathe's manner with the gentlemen they encountered seemed to slip into a light flirtatious mode. She used her eyes and that attractive trill of laughter to best advantage, and Rosamund found that in Agathe's company she too attracted an easy flirtatiousness from gentlemen courtiers. She didn't find a similar response natural as yet, but she watched her companion, and listened, noting the gestures, a mock reproving tap of her fan on the arm of one who had made a slightly risqué comment, a toss of the head, accompanied by a flutter of long eyelashes in response to a flowery compliment. It was certainly a very different kind of education from Ursula's instruction, but it was enlightening and definitely more entertaining.

They strolled on down the avenue until they reached the broad, green sweep of the riverbank. Barges and skiffs plied the wide brown-water thoroughfare, and the sing-song cries of the bargemen filled the air.

Rosamund breathed deeply of the fishy, weedy smell of the river. It seemed infinitely refreshing after the stale, muggy atmosphere within the palace.

"Let us sit on that bench. It looks so cool and green." Agathe gestured with her fan to a wooden bench set beneath a spreading willow a little way along the bank, and Rosamund acceded willingly enough, although she would have preferred to continue walking.

They sat down, Agathe arranging her skirts carefully and making a minute adjustment to her décolletage. Automatic little movements that Rosamund noticed and tried to emulate. "So, Rosamund, my dear, are you finding life as a maid of honor most dreadfully tedious?" Agathe looked at her with a knowing smile.

"On occasion," Rosamund replied frankly. "But I begin to see there are ways to relieve the tedium."

"Yes, many of them. Although dalliance is the preferred entertainment among courtiers." Agathe laughed. "Discreet, of course."

"I gather the queen does not look kindly on such entertainment."

Agathe tapped her knee with her closed fan. "She enjoys it herself, my dear, but frowns on any entanglements among her courtiers unless she's promoted them. But we all become accomplished in the ways of discretion."

Rosamund wondered if she would ever master that accomplishment. She remembered Will's outrageous suggestion that she leave the court in a page's disguise and visit the theatre. Could that be achieved with discretion? It was a novel thought. She glanced sideways at her companion, wondering whether to broach the subject, and noticed that Agathe seemed suddenly preoccupied.

A voice spoke suddenly from behind them. "Ah, what a delightful picture, two young maidens, head-to-head in the shade of a willow tree on a lush riverbank. As always, *ma chère* Agathe, you have an infallible instinct for the perfect composition."

Agathe looked up at him with a cool, composed smile. "Chevalier, as always you flatter."

"Not so." He stepped around the bench, his hands raised in protestation. He swept off his jeweled black velvet hat as he bowed low. "Mistress Walsingham, such an unexpected pleasure."

His eyes were fixed on her face and she held his gaze, determined that he would not discompose her. His eyes were such a strange and fascinating color, neither green nor brown, almost golden. They were almond-shaped in his olive-tinted complexion and gave him an almost exotic appearance.

Agathe said quickly, "Shall we continue our walk, Rosamund? Perhaps you would escort us, Arnaud."

"I would be honored." He offered an arm to each lady. "Shall we proceed along the river, or turn up that inviting-looking path over there?"

"Oh, the path, I think," Agathe said, guessing at what was expected of her. "It does look so inviting, don't you think, Rosamund?"

It looked rather secluded and deeply shaded to Rosamund, but she could see no justification for arguing with her newfound friend and acceded with a smile. Her arm was tucked securely into the crook of the chevalier's elbow, and after a moment she noticed that Agathe had slipped her own arm free. She felt she ought to do the same but wasn't sure how to without its seeming discourteous.

They turned into the cool, green shade of a narrow path that wound its way through the trees leading up from the riverbank and back towards the palace. "I heard a delightful nugget of gossip this morning, Agathe," the chevalier said with a wicked smile, his white teeth gleaming in the dappled light.

"Arnaud always knows the latest intrigue, Rosamund," Agathe said. "If you wish to know who is having a liaison with whom, or who is about to find themselves banished or sent to the Tower for some indiscretion, Arnaud will tell you." She laughed, but Rosamund thought it lacked her customary infectious trill.

"It is as well to be informed about these things," the chevalier said, turning to Rosamund. "The only way to avoid saying something indiscreet oneself is to know absolutely everything about other people's business. Is that not so, Agathe?"

"If you say so, Arnaud." Her tone was a little listless and

he looked at her with a frown that Rosamund could not see.

"Is the heat affecting you, *ma chère*?"

"Not really." She managed a smile. "But if you'll both excuse me, I think I will return to the palace. I would rest a little this afternoon."

"Let us go back immediately," Rosamund said, taking the excuse to slip her hand free of the chevalier's arm.

"No . . . no, indeed, I won't have it," Agathe declared. "You and the chevalier continue your walk." Before Rosamund could protest, Agathe had flitted away back towards the riverbank.

"I should go with her," Rosamund said awkwardly.

"No . . . that would only disrupt her plans," the chevalier said. "Knowing Agathe as I do, she has suddenly remembered an assignation that had slipped her mind, and believe me, Mistress Walsingham, you would only be in the way." He tucked her hand firmly back into his arm.

Rosamund was at a loss. She had to believe him; indeed, from what she had learned from Agathe in the last hour or so, it seemed highly likely. She had little choice it seemed but to continue her walk under the trees alone with the chevalier.

Arnaud began to talk about court, entertaining her with a series of humorous anecdotes, all told in a droll tone that soon had her laughing. He was doing a wonderful imitation of a particular courtier who, in the belief that it was an attractive affectation, had carefully cultivated a lisp, when the path suddenly opened up into a green, sun-dappled glade.

"What a delightful spot," she exclaimed. "Quite hidden away." The only sounds were birdsong and the rustle of leaves as squirrels leaped from branch to branch.

"The world is full of surprises," Arnaud said. He turned to look down at Rosamund's upturned countenance and his expression changed.

She felt the change in the atmosphere as clearly as she saw the change in his eyes. They were no longer filled with smiling good humor but instead held a strange intensity that sent a shiver across her scalp. "We should go back," she said hastily.

"All in good time." His voice had changed too. His expression was grave and intent as he lightly traced the curve of her mouth with a fingertip.

It was the strangest sensation, part thrilling, part terrifying. She stood mesmerized, waiting for something, wanting to see what would happen even as instinct told her to turn and run as fast as she could back to the thronged riverbank, away from this dangerous seclusion under the trees.

He kept his finger on her lips as he held her gaze with his. "I think I could teach you a few things, Rosamund, that would give us both a great deal of pleasure," he murmured. "What do you think? Shall I be your tutor?" He bent his head, and his lips brushed hers, making barely an impression yet leaving a trail of tingling warmth.

Rosamund's throat seemed to have closed. She stood stock-still, staring at him, and suddenly he chuckled. "Oh, dear, I have frightened you. I forgot how unused you are to our ways. But there's nothing to be afraid of in these little games we all play, sweet innocent. You will see." He dropped an avuncular kiss on her brow. "I'll escort you home now."

Rosamund felt the ridiculous urge to stamp her foot and announce that she had no wish to go back to the palace. One minute she had been hovering on the brink of an unknown that was both alarming and exciting, and the next he was treating her like an innocent whose naïveté had amused the grown-ups. He was hurrying her back along the path to the sound of voices and the cries of the bargemen.

"You didn't frighten me," she stated as the familiar inhabited world grew closer and her confidence returned.

He glanced down at her with that amused glimmer still in his eye. "Didn't I? I'm glad. Our next lesson can be a little more advanced in that case."

The promise brought her a frisson of excitement. Why shouldn't she learn to do what everyone else was doing with impunity? If she kept her head, this worldly-wise courtier could set her on the path to achieving the future that was her goal. If she was to find a husband and a life of her own, independent of her family and away from the admittedly nominal supervision of her brothers, then the court was the place. She would learn much from Agathe, but the exotic chevalier had much to teach her too if he was willing to teach and she to learn.

"Is that a promise?" she asked with a tilt of her head and a lift of her eyebrow that she had observed Agathe employing to good effect.

He laughed delightedly. "I perceive I have a most apt pupil." He tipped up her chin with a forefinger and kissed her again, but this time when he raised his head, she felt the imprint of his lips upon hers, warm and tingling.

Several afternoons later Rosamund was sketching in the Long Gallery. The weather had broken, and outside, the rain pounded the windows and the vista was an unrelieved gray. The gallery itself was buzzing with richly clad courtiers gossiping or wagering at the gaming tables, against the background accompaniment of musicians playing at the far end of the gallery.

The queen's ladies were at liberty and had all gravitated to the Long Gallery, where they had broken into intimate groups, the younger ones with a circle of gallants in attendance. Rosamund had hovered for a while, hoping to be acknowledged by her fellow maids of honor, but they had studiously ignored her. Even Joan had defected from Rosamund upon receiving a cool nod of inclusion.

The queen's unusual attention had done nothing to improve Rosamund's acceptance by her peers. She looked for a familiar friendly face, but could see no sign of Lady Leinster or the Chevalier de Vaugiras. She debated leaving the gallery altogether, then decided to stay and draw whatever in the crowded scene interested her. Sir Francis had given her carte blanche, and some interesting faces were in the crowd. There were a lot of profoundly uninteresting countenances too, bland-faced gentlemen and simpering ladies with vacuous expressions.

Will had promised to find her the afternoon after his visit to the theatre, to tell her the result of his efforts to show his play to Alleyn or Burbage, but he had not appeared at court since their meeting in the privy garden, and she didn't know what to make of his two-day absence. Was he ill? Or had he been summoned away on family business? There were any number of plausible reasons, so she tried to quash her disappointment and the slight resentment to which she had no right. Maybe this afternoon he would come.

She looked around for a suitable subject for her pen. Her eye fell on a young man standing with a small group of men deep in a low-voiced conversation that seemed to absorb them completely. He was strikingly handsome, and his ivory doublet embroidered with gold and jet was as rich as any she had seen in this dazzling court. His cartwheel ruff was at the most extravagant height of fashion, and the hilt of his sword glowed with rubies. A very wealthy young man, obviously. At one point he seemed to look directly at her, as if aware of her interest. He had very fine eyes, dark and glowing with a deep light.

Rosamund began to sketch in an outline, as usual forgetting her surroundings as she became absorbed in her work, and she had been drawing for more than ten minutes when Will Creighton joined the group around her subject. She paused, watching covertly, willing him to look over at her, but he appeared too deeply engaged with his present companions for distraction. She could hear nothing of what was said, but their facial expressions were what interested her as she fleshed out the outlines.

"I give you good day, gentlemen." Will smiled easily around the circle. He nodded to the gentleman in the ivory doublet. "Anthony, well met. I have been in search of you all morning. I owe you a noble for last even's entertainment." He reached into his doublet for a leather pouch of coins.

"My thanks." Anthony Babington caught the coin deftly as Will flicked it over with his thumb. "If you are at liberty, I would have speech with you."

"By all means." Will nodded at their companions, who took the hint and drifted away. Will was still triumphant at the success of his meeting with Thomas Walsingham two days ago at the theatre. He had wanted the opportunity to bring up his play, but instead Walsingham had sought him out to tell him that Sir Francis had a task for him if he was still willing to be of service.

Will had stammered that he thought his letter had been lost, and Thomas had merely laughed and told him that

Master Secretary never lost anything, merely waited until the right tool appeared for the right job. Will's job in this instance was to befriend Anthony Babington, a courtier he knew hitherto only slightly. He was to let it be known that he shared Babington's Catholic sympathies. Anthony Babington's passionate championship of Mary Stuart was a significant tool in Francis Walsingham's armory, and Will's task was to keep the flame alight.

Babington had welcomed Will as another Catholic sympathizer into his friendship and his own circle with an almost desperate hunger, and an innocent trust that Will found sadly pathetic. And when Will had realized what fanatical passion drove this group of men, he had almost run from it. It was impossible and could only lead to a bloody end on Tyburn Tree, but he had been instructed to listen, to encourage, to offer his own passionate support. And he was following his instructions to the letter.

Now Anthony moved closer to Will, lowering his voice and speaking rapidly. "There's to be a meeting in the next day or so. Father Ballard is to go into France to discuss the matter with the Spanish ambassador and Mary's agent, Morgan. Will you attend?"

"Readily," Will said in the same undertone, concealing the prickle of excitement. This was a nugget Sir Francis would appreciate. "You are a most faithful friend to Queen Mary."

Anthony shook his head. "I have been her devoted servant since I first saw her all those years ago, when I was a page in Shrewsbury's household and he was her first guardian. She was so beautiful, so lively, and with the most wonderful smile. Ah, you should have seen her then, Will."

Anthony sighed. "Shrewsbury cared for her gently, so different from the treatment meted out to her in these dark days by Amyas Paulet. She has been ill unto death with agues and stomach pains. We *must* gain her release. There is no time to be lost."

Will nodded and laid a sympathetic hand on the other man's arm. "We will succeed, Anthony. Father Ballard will bring the help we need."

"Aye, 'tis to be hoped for. The meeting is to be held at the Plough in Temple Bar. There will be others there . . ." Anthony moved closer in, his voice little more than a whisper.

Rosamund couldn't help but wonder what topic could so absorb Will and his companion that neither of them spared a glance for the throng around them. Surely Will ought to be able to sense her presence just a few feet away. But he didn't look once in her direction. Her pen moved quickly, and when she had finished, she had both Will and the gentleman to life on the paper. She regarded it critically, before tucking it out of sight and taking a fresh sheet, looking for a new subject.

"Mistress Walsingham?"

She looked up startled to find a servant at her elbow. "Sir Francis Walsingham requests your company."

Rather nervously, Rosamund gathered up her belongings and followed the servant out of the gallery into a small antechamber where Sir Francis and her brother were standing together at a rain-washed window.

"Ah, Rosamund, good. You are here." Master Secretary's nod of greeting was curt as she approached and curtsied to them both.

Her brother kissed her cheek. "How are you enjoying court life, little sister?" His tone was hearty, a little too hearty she thought.

"Diverting for the most part," she replied cautiously. She

didn't think her cousin or her brother would care to know of her burgeoning education in the court's less visible and less conventional life.

Sir Francis looked at her sharply, almost as if he could read her mind. "Be careful, child. If you are to find a decent future for yourself, it is here you will find it, and you should be thinking of nothing else."

She curtsied meekly and in silence. After a moment Sir Francis said, "Do you have anything to show me?"

"A few sketches only. I have not seen very much, sir. There is little change of scene or of company in the queen's chambers." She hoped that didn't sound too much like a complaint as she handed over the sheaf of papers, including her most recent drawing.

Sir Francis took them to the window and examined them closely. "Mmm . . . you have indeed a most detailed eye. Ah, why did this gentleman catch your eye?" He tapped her afternoon's work with a fingertip.

"There was something about him . . . I don't know exactly. His dress, his eyes . . ." She shrugged.

"What think you, Thomas?" Francis passed the sheet to the other man. "She has our friend Babington to the life."

"And Creighton too. He seems to be applying himself to the task." Thomas glanced at his sister, who appeared not to be listening.

Rosamund's ears however were pricked. It sounded as if Will had managed to enter Sir Francis's service in the two days since they had last talked and was now at work. Perhaps that explained his absence from court.

Francis said, "This man, Rosamund . . . his name is Anthony Babington. I would have you take note of him, sketch him and his companions whenever the opportunity arises. I am particularly interested in the company he keeps." He folded the sheets and tucked them inside his doublet. "You have plenty of time for drawing, I trust?"

"Yes, Sir Francis. Her majesty has been most kind in permitting me to draw as much as I wish when we are at leisure."

He nodded. "Good . . . good." He touched his neat beard as if searching for words, then coughed and said, "My lady wife is most anxious to know how you are getting on. I will ask Lady Shrewsbury to give you leave to visit us one evening."

Rosamund's face split in a smile of pleasure as she dropped into a deep curtsy. "Oh, I should like that of all things, Sir Francis. I am at Lady Walsingham's service always."

He nodded, murmured another "Good . . . good," and turned from her.

Rosamund took her dismissal and turned to leave, glancing once over her shoulder at her brother, who had resumed his conversation with the secretary. Thomas caught her look and gave her a short nod that she had no idea how to interpret. She returned without much enthusiasm to the Long Gallery.

"Mistress Walsingham, I thought you had abandoned us." Will, arm in arm with the handsome gentleman she now knew to be Anthony Babington, approached her as she entered the gallery. Will's smile was full of hidden meaning, and Rosamund felt the last shreds of her resentment at his absence vanish. He indicated his companion. "My friend Master Babington asks to be made known to you."

"Sir." Rosamund curtsied, wondering what it was about this man that interested her majesty's spymaster.

"Mistress Walsingham." He bowed. "I have not seen you at court before."

"I have been at court less than a week, sir. It is still very unfamiliar to me, Master Babington. I daresay for one who has frequented the court for some time, that is hard to understand."

"I am here infrequently myself, mistress. I am but a humble law student at Lincoln's Inn." His smile was as charming as his countenance.

"You may be a student at the Inns of Court, sir, but I doubt you are humble." She didn't add that no man whose garments were so stiff with jewels they could stand alone could possibly claim humble status.

"I protest, Mistress Walsingham. I can claim to be a mere squire's son. No more, no less." Anthony Babington's eyes twinkled and Rosamund realized that she was being invited to flirt. It really did seem to be the most popular pastime, but she had no wish to accept the invitation this afternoon, she was too interested in Will to give anyone else her attention.

Will Creighton said swiftly, "We were at the play yesterday, Mistress Walsingham, and were lucky enough afterwards to hear Master Marlowe read some further lines of his *Tamburlaine*. It is most moving verse."

Rosamund was instantly consumed with envious longing. It was ridiculous, she knew, but she felt as if she had a proprietorial interest in Kit Marlowe and his play, and the idea that anyone else should be becoming a familiar of Kit's in her absence made her green. She changed the subject. "Have you traveled abroad much, Master Babington?"

"To Paris. I spent some months there. It is a most godly city."

Something about his voice struck Rosamund as strange. She frowned. "*Godly*. I would hardly think that a suitable word, sir. The massacre of the Huguenots . . . one could hardly call that a godly act."

Anthony Babington shook his head. "God works in mysterious ways, Mistress Walsingham."

Rosamund remembered Kit's saying how men used God's name to establish their own power over other men. It was heresy, she knew. But it still made sense to her. She glanced around. No one was within earshot except Will. Softly, she explained to Anthony Babington Christopher Marlowe's views on God and power. And when she'd finished, she wished she had not opened her mouth.

"That is heresy, Mistress Walsingham. The blackest heresy," Anthony declared, mercifully keeping his voice low despite his outrage. "You would propound such atheistical views . . . they will drag you on a hurdle to Tyburn Tree . . . to the stake." He turned on his heel and stalked away.

"Rosamund, has no one ever told you to watch your tongue?" Will inquired in a fierce undertone. "You are at court. You cannot say such things, there are ears everywhere."

"But it is only what Kit says. It is the subject of his play."

"Then let Master Marlowe go to Tyburn Tree," Will said forcefully. "And keep your distance from Anthony Babington."

Rosamund looked at him with interest. "Why? Is there something about him that I should know?"

"What makes you think that?"

Oh, just something the queen's spymaster said. But she kept that to herself. If Will wanted to confide in her about his service with Sir Francis, he would do so in his own good time. Maybe he was supposed to keep it a secret. "Just a feeling."

Will chewed his lip, then said, "Master Babington is a

Catholic. It is unwise to cultivate him, and dangerous to talk religion openly with a recusant."

Because they draw the attention of the spymaster? "Believe me, Will, I have no particular interest in Catholics," she said easily. "And I've no desire to cause trouble. But if it's unwise, why do you cultivate him?" She waited to see if he would tell her the true reason.

"He's pleasant company, and he has a fat purse." Will laughed, seeming to cast off the gravity of a moment before. "My purse on the other hand is lean, and our friend is generous. And we never discuss religion."

It was a convincing enough reason, even though she knew it wasn't true. But if he had been sworn to secrecy, she wouldn't press him.

"I have missed you these last two days," she said instead. "Did you show your play to Master Alleyn or Master Burbage?"

"Not as yet. Some other business arose and the moment passed, but next time I visit the theatre I am determined to do so."

"Maybe next time I'll come with you." Her eyebrows lifted in faint question mark.

He looked at her with his customary glimmer of mischief. "As I said, Rosamund, if you have the courage, I will provide the costume." It sounded like a challenge, and for a moment she was tempted to take it up, but caution prevailed. "Maybe . . . one of these days."

He laughed. "I didn't think you had the courage."

"Oh, just you wait and see, Master Creighton." She tossed her head in a fair imitation of Lady Leinster and with a flutter of her eyelashes turned away, leaving him chuckling.

Chapter Thirteen

"So CREIGHTON IS keeping an eye on Babington," Robin Poley said. "And Barnard Maude is stuck close to Ballard, and Kit Marlowe is to work with Gilbert Gifford to encourage Savage. What am I to do, sir?"

Sir Francis smiled a slow smile. "You and Phelippes will work together. You will return to Chartley together and you will impart to Mary Stuart the details of a secret means of communication between herself and her loyal subjects. She must be convinced that this corridor of information is impregnable so that she has no need watch her words. My cousin Thomas has an ingenious plan involving brewery kegs entering and leaving the castle. He will explain it in detail before you go north.

"Christopher Marlowe and Gifford will ensure that Babington and his little league understand that the corridor of communication cannot be discovered, so that they too will feel free to write openly. And then we will intercept. Phelippes will decipher both sides of the correspondence and, where we deem it necessary, add a few details of encouragement. And then we shall wait to see what springs the trap."

"We are to encourage Scots Mary to believe that an invasion is planned and supported on our shores, and that

Queen Elizabeth will be removed to give her a straight path to the throne? Do I have it right?"

"You do. Barnard Maude tells me there's to be a meeting just outside Temple Bar. An inn called the Plough. Ostensibly it's to bid farewell to Captain Fortescue, otherwise known as our old friend Father John Ballard. The captain is off on military business, apparently, but of course we know better. Creighton and Maude will be there as friends and supporters."

"As inciters?"

"If you choose to call it that."

"And Thomas Walsingham?"

"He is running the operation. They report to him and he will keep me informed."

Poley accepted his dismissal with a bow. Outside, he found Ingram Frizer hovering as only he could do. Picking filthy fingernails with the tip of his dagger, whistling through blackened teeth, eyes as sharp as files, he nodded as Robin came out of the house on Seething Lane.

"Anything to be done?"

"Aye. Arrange a meeting with the young Walsingham as soon as possible. I'll await him in my lodgings."

Frizer spat into the gutter. "Any notion where I'll find Walsingham?"

"No, but you don't usually have trouble nosing people out." Robin looked at him in distaste. Frizer had his uses, but he always left Robin feeling as if he needed to wash his hands with lye after an encounter.

Frizer grinned, as if he understood exactly what the elegant Poley was thinking, thrust the dagger into his belt, and sidled off down the street.

* * *

"There's to be a hunting party and picnic at Richmond tomorrow." Joan bounced into the dorter, eyes shining. "Her majesty has decided, and the whole court is to go."

Rosamund, who was sitting on the bed dolefully examining the fallen hem of her green gown, discarded the mending project with relief as a new issue took precedence. "I need my horse. I wonder if she's still stabled at Seething Lane." She jumped up with renewed energy. "I must send a message to Sir Francis. How does one do that, Joan?"

Joan was delving in the armoire for her second-best gown, and her voice was muffled. "Write a note and give it to one of the heralds. You can always find one in the corridors. They'll take it for you."

Rosamund took her writing tablet and, taking extra care over her penmanship, wrote her request to Sir Francis. She sanded the sheet, folded it, and sealed it with wax before writing the direction on the front. "I'll go and find someone to take this." She hurried from the dorter and down the stairs. The prospect of such an excursion was heady after almost two weeks of a confinement that even the afternoons at liberty couldn't properly relieve.

She found a herald standing at a door leading to a series of antechambers. The heralds were splendidly dressed in the royal livery of crimson and silver and strode through the palace with such purpose and clear importance that she made her request somewhat tentatively, wondering if a courtier as lowly as herself would qualify for such august services. The man took the message without a flicker of objection, however, bowed, and marched away.

Rosamund was hesitating as to what to do next. Her mending awaited her in the dorter but it was not an enticing prospect. She was still debating when she heard a

familiar trill of laughter and spun around just as Lady
Leinster with a small group of men and women turned the
corner.

Agathe saw her and waved. "Rosamund, a fortunate
meeting, we're going to the archery butts for a competition. Do join us if you're at liberty."

Rosamund was quite a skilled archer. Thomas had
taught her several years previously when he'd been in a
particularly accommodating frame of mind. "I have no
bow," she demurred.

"You won't need one. There are bows and arrows
aplenty at the butts." Agathe linked her arm companionably in Rosamund's. "You look in dire need of diversion."

Rosamund acceded with enthusiasm and allowed herself to be borne on the tide of this merry group who
seemed to have not a care in the world. She found it sur-
prisingly easy to slip into the same carefree frame of mind
and relished the sense of inclusion. These people treated
her as an equal, the rigid hierarchy of the queen's personal
attendants didn't apply, and she could only be grateful to
Agathe for her generous friendship that made her immediately welcome.

"There's to be a hunting party tomorrow, I understand,"
she observed to Agathe as they stepped out into the afternoon sunshine.

"Yes, indeed, and they are always excessively amusing."

"Except when the beaters fail to find a hart for the
queen and she gets a little out of sorts," declared one of
the gentlemen. "Let's hope they do their job well on the
morrow."

They made their way to the archery butts situated just
beyond the royal mews. A group of courtiers were already
there, shooting their arrows with a concentrated precision

that indicated they were not merely indulging in leisurely sport. The Chevalier de Vaugiras was one of them, and Rosamund paused to watch him. He had discarded his black velvet doublet and it lay carelessly over a tree stump a few feet from him. As he pulled the bow back, the muscles on his back were clearly delineated beneath the fine lawn of his white shirt.

She became aware of Agathe, who seemed to be watching her closely, as if aware of Rosamund's particular interest in the chevalier. She turned away with a slightly self-conscious laugh and Agathe gave her a knowing smile. "He is a very fine figure of man, the chevalier. Is he not?"

"Yes, I suppose he is." Rosamund tried to sound carelessly indifferent but was rather afraid she had not fooled the worldly Lady Leinster. "He's a skilled archer at any rate."

"There is little at which Arnaud does not excel," Agathe said, and Rosamund thought she could detect just a hint of cynicism in the observation.

"Come, ladies, we are set to begin." The summons came from one of their companions, and Rosamund followed Agathe over to a more distant target where their own group was congregating. She took the bow handed to her and drew it experimentally. It was a light lady's bow and she could draw it with ease. She took an arrow from the quiver and notched it, trying for a practice shot. The arrow flew straight to the target, but buried itself in an outer ring.

"Bravo, Mistress Rosamund."

She spun around to see the chevalier applauding her a few feet away. "You are overly kind, Chevalier. I missed the center by a furlong."

"You exaggerate. But there is a certain trick to holding the bow. Let me show you." He stepped up behind her as she took another arrow and notched it. The heat of his body against her back, his breath on her neck, the brush of his arms against her breasts as he reached around her to reposition her hands on the bow, almost overwhelmed her. She wondered if anyone noticed the extraordinary proximity of their bodies, or if they did, did they think it indelicate, scandalous even?

But no one seemed to be paying any attention. They were all shooting their own arrows, applauding a good shot, laughing good-naturedly at a poor one. She could only conclude that the intimacy of this lesson from the chevalier was not sufficiently unusual to cause comment.

Flustered, she let her arrow fly too soon, and to her chagrin it dropped to the ground short of the target. "I think I do better on my own, sir," she said, feeling heat invading her cheeks. She stepped away from him and went to retrieve the arrow.

He laughed. "Nonsense, you were a little premature, that was all. Come, let me show you again." Once again he took up a position behind her, and she felt her nipples rise against her bodice at the press of his arms against her breasts.

Belatedly she realized that this was not a lesson in archery but in yet another aspect of dalliance. When she felt his mouth lightly brush the nape of her neck, she inhaled sharply, her pulse jumping in her throat.

He laughed softly, feeling her response. "Be still, *ma chère*. Stealing caresses under the eyes of the world is one of the greatest pleasures in these games, as I trust you are discovering."

There was pleasure, Rosamund would freely admit. An excitement, a thrill of danger.

"Arnaud, for shame." Agathe came over to them, her voice soft, but lightly amused. Her eyes however were sharply watchful. "Rosamund is still unaccustomed to our ways, you will frighten her playing your wicked games." She spoke only a little above a whisper. "Rosamund, my dear, take no notice of Arnaud. He loves to play games of seduction. I told you there is no sport in which he does not excel, but I am always telling him he should pick partners who are up to his weight."

Rosamund once again had that annoying feeling of being patronized. She didn't need Agathe's protection. She loosed her arrow before she spoke and this time had the satisfaction of seeing it hit almost in the center. She turned to her companions and intercepted a glance between them that startled her. It was a glance full of meaning, of a shared understanding. For the first time she wondered if the easy friendship they seemed to have was something more than that . . . a liaison? But why, if that was so, would Arnaud flirt with her in front of his mistress? These games were too deep for her, she decided. At least while she was still so new at the play.

The chevalier retrieved the arrow for her. "Much better, Mistress Rosamund. Shall we try this again and see if you can hit the bull's-eye?"

She flashed him a smile, a purely flirtatious smile. "I think the tutoring is over for today, Chevalier." She curtsied and walked away, feeling the eyes of both the chevalier and Agathe upon her back.

Will stirred restlessly on his stool in the private parlor of the Plough, just outside Temple Bar. Anthony Babington beside him drummed his fingers impatiently on the deal table. Three other men were in the room, all showing signs of anxiety. They were awaiting one man, Father John Ballard. A known Catholic missionary, an outlaw who roamed the country offering succor to the religiously oppressed while searching tirelessly for converts, he had a price on his head and those who associated with him were as liable for arrest as he.

Will emulated his companions' feverish impatience, his voice rising with the rising levels of nervous excitement in the room. He drank deep, as did they all. He had received the message from Babington that tonight they would hold the meeting at the Plough, in Temple Bar, and he had faced the prospect with genuine anxiety. It was his first true mission for Master Secretary. Before, he had been instructed merely to gain Anthony Babington's confidence; now, having achieved that goal, he was to penetrate the cabal of conspirators led by Father John Ballard. If they suspected for one instant, they would kill him on the spot. He was under no illusions that while Babington could be blindly foolish in his idealism, Father Ballard was an old soldier in this enterprise. He'd suffered arrest, imprisonment, escaped capture and death by a hair on numerous occasions, and he would be hard to fool. He could probably detect a mole in the room just by smelling the man's sweat.

Walsingham's agents were planted throughout the little circle of Catholic devotees of Scots Mary, listening, watching, reporting. When necessary, on their master's instructions they were to actively encourage the plans and the tentative plots suggested by the conspirators, whose zealotry was hampered by inexperience. Will was to do that tonight if he sensed a moment's hesitation.

The pitcher of wine circulated around the deal table where supper was to be served. As far as the innkeeper was concerned, the evening was a farewell dinner for a certain Captain Fortescue, who was leaving England's shores for France on army business. Captain Fortescue was Father John Ballard's alias while he was on English soil.

A heavy tread heralded the arrival of the evening's chief guest. Father Ballard entered, dressed in soldierly garb, a scarlet-lined cloak swinging from his shoulders. A stocky man came in on his heels. Barnard Maude was also in Walsingham's pay. A much more experienced agent than Will, he had the more delicate task of supporting the conspiracy's mastermind. He didn't exchange so much as a glance with Will, who took his cue and showed only the blank expression of an indifferent stranger.

Will leaned sideways to refill Babington's wine cup. "Drink, my friend."

"Aye," Anthony declared. "A toast to our good captain, and our Holy Father's blessing on his task. May God go with you, Father Ballard." He raised his cup and the others followed suit.

"My thanks, gentlemen." Ballard cast aside his cloak and sat at the table. "I have already had correspondence with Morgan and Charles Paget in Paris and will meet with them in person. Don Bernardino de Mendoza, the Spanish ambassador, has also granted me a meeting. If I can persuade the French and Spanish to combine forces for the invasion, they will be unbeatable."

"An invasion will secure the deposal of Queen Elizabeth?" Will asked casually. "Where should she be housed when this is done?"

"That will be for Queen Mary to decide," Ballard stated, adding carefully, "should she decide that deposal is the right disposition to be made of this false queen."

Will kept his eyes on the table, a cold chill prickling his skin. *Was Ballard suggesting some other way of disposing of the present queen? Was he hinting at assassination?* That would be the darkest treason and Walsingham would rub his hands with satisfaction if it could be proved. They would all end at Tyburn Tree, watching as their entrails were yanked from their bellies, watching them shrivel and burn in the fire before their eyes, before death brought merciful release. Will controlled an instinctive shudder and drank deep from his cup.

"The people are happy with Elizabeth," Babington pointed out rather hesitantly. "Indeed they love her. It will not be easy to depose her without the people's support, and I believe that will be well nigh impossible to gain."

Ballard waved this away with a dismissive gesture. "Have no fear, that will be taken care of. The queen's life will not stand in the way. She will be removed before the invasion and there will be an empty throne for Queen Mary to take as her due by birthright."

Will stored the words verbatim in his memory and resisted glancing at Maude across the table. *The queen's life will not stand in the way.* If it *was* assassination that they planned, then the Bond of Association would condemn Mary for treason in the company of these conspirators, as beneficiary of their plotting even if she had no knowledge of it. Would Walsingham press the queen to take that action?

The weight of responsibility for such an outcome seemed abruptly too heavy, and he decided he needed to pass his information on to Walsingham and relieve himself of the burden. He was an insignificant cog in Walsingham's plots and had no desire to be any more important. He would leave that to Barnard Maude, who was ever hanging on Ballard's coattails. Maude would stay to the end and report anything else of significance.

Will pushed back his chair. "I must ask you to forgive me, gentlemen, but I have business in the palace."

"You will not stay to sup?" Babington laid a hand on Will's sleeve. "I have gone to some trouble to order delicacies for our dinner. Larks' tongues in a pie, a brace of roasted geese, a fish soup whose like you will never before have tasted. The cook here is a master of his art."

Babington was rich. His fellow conspirators were for the most part impoverished Catholic recusants whose estates had been confiscated by the crown. They lived on what they could beg or borrow from sympathizers. Babington's purse was always open and ever ready to fund such journeys as the one Ballard was now preparing for.

"Alas, my friend, I cannot." Will slung his cloak around his shoulders. "This business is urgent." He stretched out his hand to Ballard across the table. "God's speed, Father Ballard, and may the Holy Mother ensure you a fair wind and good counsel in Paris."

Ballard shook his hand, and with a brief bow to the assembled company Will escaped into the relative freshness of the evening air.

The Inns of Court lay alongside the river, and black-robed lawyers hurried across the courtyards that connected them. As Will turned away from Temple Bar to walk along the river, he sensed a man in the shadows behind him. Footpads, murderers, the city was rife with them, and they came out at night. His hand went to his sword and he kept his step even, inching the weapon out of its scabbard. The footsteps kept pace with him. Just ahead, a patch of moonlight fell on the path where there was no tree cover. He waited until the light fell on his face, then spun around, drawing his sword in the same instant. He lunged towards the figure still cloaked in shadow. It jumped back.

"*Creighton.*" The voice was familiar, and just in time Will snatched back his sword point.

He stopped, breathing fast, and said angrily, "Gifford. For God's sake, man, why wouldn't you declare yourself?

I nearly ran you through." Gilbert Gifford was another Walsingham man, and for some reason Will disliked and distrusted him.

Gifford gave a short laugh. "I wished to see how fast you could draw, Creighton. It's always as well to know the mettle of one's friends as well as of one's enemies."

Will controlled his anger at all the assumptions lying behind this statement. Slowly, reluctantly almost, he sheathed his sword. "You were not at Ballard's supper party."

"No, I was at Barnard's Inn working on the young lawyer, John Savage." Gifford smiled a chilly smile. "The young fool needed a spur. What was said at the Plough?"

"Talk of removing the queen before the invasion, so that Mary will mount the steps to an empty throne." Will increased his speed and Gifford kept pace. "I fear I know what they mean."

Gifford gave a short laugh. "Maybe you do. But you're wise to keep the words from your tongue. Ballard and his league have their weapon, though. Young Savage has sworn an oath on the Virgin Mary to remove the queen, but he was in danger of breaking his oath. I have been with him, at pains to give him courage to honor his vow. Master Marlowe is drinking with him now, offering his own form of liquid encouragement."

Will felt queasy. This was not just watching, eavesdropping, hoping to catch the conspirators red-handed, this was the deliberate fomenting of treason to lay and spring a trap. "I like it not."

Gifford shrugged. "Like it or not, my friend, 'tis Walsingham's way and he will as always have his way. How far do you walk? I'll keep you company as far as Aldwych."

Will would have preferred to do without the company, but Gifford proved an amiable enough companion, offering little in the way of conversation. Beyond asking Will to tell him who else was at the meeting, he walked in silence, seemingly deep in his own meditations. At Aldwych they parted company and Will made his way to Seething Lane.

He found Sir Francis still at work in his candlelit study. He greeted Will with a weary nod and waved him to a chair. "So, you have been at the Plough. What transpired?"

Will gave an accurate account of the conversation, and the secretary nodded from time to time, making notes as Will talked. "It is as I thought," he said when Will had ended his recital. He sounded satisfied. "You did well. Phelippes is on his way to Chartley, where Mary is held, so you must collect your payment from Arthur Gregory. He is at work in Phelippes's place."

Will hesitated, getting slowly to his feet. "Will you use the Bond of Association, then, to deal with Scots Mary?"

Walsingham frowned, seeming to hesitate before replying. Finally he said, "I doubt the queen can be persuaded to act in that way. Mary must incriminate herself. And she will do so, we shall make sure of that."

Will felt a cold chill at the plain statement of fact. Sometimes with Walsingham he felt he was in the presence of Mephistopheles. Such sinister power lurked in the shadows around the queen's secretary. He bowed himself from the study and went to claim his payment.

Chapter Fourteen

ROSAMUND AWOKE TO the hum of voices in the dorter as her fellows prepared themselves for the day. It was unlike her to be the last abed these mornings, but she had slept particularly deeply, plagued with strange and unsettling dreams. She felt sluggish as she came fully awake.

"Oh, hurry, Rosamund." Joan was struggling with her stockings. "'Tis the hunt today. Have you forgotten? We must break our fast early. The queen likes to start out by eight o'clock and 'tis already past six."

Rosamund yawned and got to her feet. There had been no word from Sir Francis about her horse. "What happens if I don't have a horse?"

"There are litters, but they can only take you to the picnic. You cannot ride with the hunt . . . lace me." Joan turned her back.

Rosamund grimaced at such a tame prospect as she laced Joan tightly. Maybe Jenny had been taken back to Scadbury. Maybe Thomas had decided his sister no longer had need of her and he'd decided to sell the mare at last. In a somewhat melancholy mood she went down with Joan to the parlor, where they broke their fast.

The Countess of Shrewsbury was already presiding over the table when they trooped in. "Mistress Walsingham, Sir Francis has sent word that your mare is now housed in the royal mews at your brother's expense. She will be at your disposal this morning."

Rosamund's spirits lifted immediately. Thomas would not relish the extra expense, she knew, but if their cousin insisted, he would be hard-pressed to refuse. She curtsied and murmured her thanks before taking her place at table.

The royal mews at the start of the hunt was a seething turmoil of horses, riders, huntsmen, groomsmen, and litter bearers. "We wait here and the grooms will bring our horses. It's not quite as chaotic as it looks." Joan was as always in her element instructing the newcomer, and Rosamund was far too aware of a need for any information that would help her avoid the numerous and random pitfalls of court etiquette to resent Joan's faintly condescending manner at such times.

A groom emerged from the apparent chaos leading Jenny, and with a cry of delight Rosamund plunged through the throng to greet her mare. Jenny whinnied and nuzzled and Rosamund took her head and blew softly into her nostrils in her own greeting. The groom helped her mount, and once seated in the saddle, the horse moving easily beneath her, Rosamund felt all her diffidence in the strange atmosphere of the court disappear. She looked around at what became clear was an orderly chaos and urged the well-mannered Jenny through the crowd to join up with Joan.

Joan looked enviously at Rosamund's mount. "She's beautiful. I don't ride very well, so my family will only let me have the use of a very dull pony."

"As long as you're not riding in a litter." Rosamund gestured to the litter bearers gathering at the edge of the courtyard. Then her eyes widened as she saw Lady Leinster climbing the footstep into one of the litters. Never would she have expected the elegant, sophisticated, amusing, and popular Agathe to go to a hunt in a litter. Agathe turned and caught sight of her and raised a hand in invitation.

Rosamund urged the mare forwards towards the litter where Agathe was disposing herself on thick cushions. "Lady Leinster, are you quite well?"

"Oh, yes indeed, Rosamund . . . and you are to call me Agathe, it was agreed."

Rosamund acknowledged this with a smile. "Forgive me, Agathe. I was just surprised to see—"

"To see me in a litter like some feeble old lady," Agathe finished for her. She lowered her voice, a conspiratorial gleam in her eye. "Don't be shocked, my dear, but in truth, I have some aches and pains from a rather strenuous night, if you understand me."

Rosamund did and was not so much shocked as fascinated. She'd learned a great deal about carnal matters in the last weeks, but was always ready for further instruction. Greatly daring, she questioned with a raised eyebrow, "A particularly energetic lover, perhaps?"

Agathe went into a peal of laughter. "Exactly so, my dear. Take my advice and beware of particularly energetic nights when a day in the saddle is to follow."

Rosamund nodded. "I'll bear it in mind, my lady."

"Do . . . but stay a moment." Agathe leaned sideways to speak softly over the side of the litter. "On the subject of energetic ardor, don't allow a man's enthusiasm to prejudice you against him. You are still an innocent but you mustn't be frightened by . . . by, shall we say, more vigorous attentions than you are used to. Men lack subtlety so often, but it is never wise to turn aside a compliment, Rosamund. If you'll accept a word of advice." She smiled.

"Men trespass, women forgive. It's the way of our world, my dear."

"I'll remember." Rosamund raised a hand in farewell and turned Jenny back to the gathering group of riders. Had Agathe been referring to the chevalier? Had she noticed the intimacy of his position behind her at the archery butts? Perhaps her own discomfort had been laughably obvious to the worldly Lady Leinster.

The clarion call of trumpets produced a sudden silence over the great throng, who all turned as one towards the palace. Queen Elizabeth rode out on a magnificent white palfrey, her gown of forest green encrusted with emeralds spreading over the perfect white flanks of her horse. Two white plumes adorned her crimson velvet hat, and a collar of emeralds encircled her throat. Around her rode a party of horsemen, the gentlemen of her household, similarly clad in green velvet aglow with emeralds.

Rosamund caught her breath. It was a magnificent sight. She recognized Lord Essex and Lord Leicester among the queen's retinue but could not as yet put a name to the other noblemen. Instinctively she etched the scene on her memory. She would commit it to paper later. Sir Francis might find something of interest.

The queen's appearance was the signal for the vast crowd to move off, and Rosamund found all her energies consumed with guiding Jenny among the crush of riders, trying to keep her on a straight course. She caught sight of Joan a few rows back sturdily seated upon a wide-backed, dappled pony who was clearly disinclined for excitement of any kind. The beaters with their dogs would have gone ahead long before dawn to chase up scents and flush out hart or stag, and the huge hunting crowd in their wake made so much noise Rosamund couldn't imagine how they could ever pin a deer in their sights without it running long before the queen and her retinue, bows at the ready, could expect to reach it.

"I give you good morrow, Mistress Rosamund." Will Creighton, on a rawboned chestnut gelding, rode up beside her. His teeth flashed in a white smile, and his lively eyes sparked with the reckless mischief that she found so enticing. He was looking particularly fine in doublet and britches of purple velvet, with a high-crowned hat, adorned with a green-dyed feather set at a rakish angle.

Rosamund was in her tawny velvet gown, which she had refurbished with a gold lace ruff that Lady Walsingham had sent her, together with a pair of soft kidskin gloves edged with matching gold lace. Her russet hair was confined at the nape of her neck in a golden netted snood, and she wore a broad, green velvet ribbon banded around her forehead. Her appearance had pleased her that morning and she could see from the appreciative gleam in Will's eyes that it pleased him too.

"Good morrow, Master Creighton," she returned, narrowing her eyes a little and fluttering her eyelashes as she'd seen Agathe do.

He bowed and his eyes danced. "May I ride with you?"

"Certainly," she said, glancing around, wondering if anyone was watching her. She could see no one looking at her in particular; even Joan was preoccupied with her pony as she tried to get it to move beyond a trundling walk. People seemed to be pairing up, or gathering in small groups, as they rode out of the mews towards the riverbank. "How long a ride is it to Richmond?"

"An hour maybe. It will be a long day, the queen likes to hunt and she is indefatigable, often after such a day we don't return to the palace until nightfall."

"Is galloping permitted?"

"Anything is permitted," he responded with a chuckle. He fixed her with a meaningful gaze. "And in the forest there are many paths, many rides away from the crowd. There are so many people and oftentimes the hunt becomes so confused that no one notices an occasional disappearance."

"I suppose it's easy enough to stray by accident from the main party," she observed blandly, keeping her eyes on the space between Jenny's pricked ears. "Particularly in the excitement of the chase."

"Particularly then," he agreed solemnly.

Rosamund couldn't help it. She went into a peal of laughter, and Will after a startled minute joined her. "Forgive me," she said through her laughter, "but I have no experience of subtle flirtation. It seems so artificial."

"Because it is. But the game is amusing, or at least most people find it so." He regarded her thoughtfully. "You're rather different from most people, though, Rosamund. I think that's why I find you so intriguing."

There was nothing subtle or insincere about this statement, and Rosamund felt herself blush with pleasure. Talking with Will felt so much cleaner somehow than any kind of engagement with the chevalier. There was no edge of danger with Will, and she couldn't deny she found that edge exciting with the chevalier, but Will's ready mischief was a more than adequate substitute.

"Have you shown your play to anyone yet?" Jenny was frisky and Will's gelding responded in kind so that they were moving ahead of the main body of the hunt, following close on the heels of the queen's own party.

"I gave it to Dick Burbage." Will's expression was suddenly serious, his eyes no longer lighthearted. "He said he would read it as soon as may be, but I know he's busy." He drew back on the reins a little. "We shouldn't draw too far ahead of the rest. It's not wise to be conspicuous."

Rosamund eased Jenny to a more sedate pace without comment, glad that Will had some thought for censorious eyes. "I'm sure he'll read it soon. I heard him say how they needed new plays."

Will sighed. "I hope so, but what alarms me is that he has the only copy. If it's lost, or damaged beyond legibility, I don't know what I would do."

"I'm sure Master Burbage will take good care of it. He lives and breathes the theatre, he knows how important a new play is."

Will nodded. "I know you're right, of course, but I feel like a new mother whose baby has been put to a wet nurse."

Rosamund laughed. "An unusual analogy, Will. You have a knack with words and Burbage will recognize it, I'm sure."

He looked pleased and the gravity left his expression. They were riding along the broad riverbank, stately swans gliding by beyond the rushes, treating the boat traffic with regal indifference as befitted royal property.

The queen's party was moving quickly and was probably a half mile ahead, getting close to the great green expanse of Richmond Forest. It had been the queen's father's favorite hunting ground, and Elizabeth's fondness for it went back to her childhood, when her father, during those random periods when he had looked kindly upon her, had occasionally taken her up with him on his magnificent charger while hunting for his favorite game, the wild boar.

Thomas Walsingham was riding with Kit Marlowe in the rear of the hunting party. He had spent little time at court in the past months; he was fully occupied these days on his cousin's affairs now that the business of Scots Mary had become so urgent. Between visits to France and immersing himself in the plots of Babington and his fellow conspirators, he had little enough time for the manifold pleasures of bedsport with Kit and the literary delights of the theatre and the poets and writers whose company he loved.

Kit was reciting from his translation of Ovid as they rode and Thomas was torn between amused admiration for the skill of the translation, and the fear that someone around them would recognize it for the publicly condemned obscenity that it was. But Kit was merrily oblivious as he took frequent pulls from the leather flask at his belt and in between bursts of recitation made lyrical observations on the beauty of the morning.

"Where is the fair Rosamund these days?" he inquired, standing up in his stirrups to look over the crowd of riders. "You neglect her most dreadfully, Thomas."

"She has no need of me," Thomas declared. "She's well established, and Sir Francis keeps his eye on her. Her tastes are too simple and unformed for her to get into any trouble. Her innocence will protect her from predators. The sophisticates at court have no interest in the innocent, they provide no sport."

Kit raised an eyebrow, privately thinking that his friend was a little too blasé. He himself was convinced that Rosamund was probably no longer the uninitiated ingenue her brother so fondly believed. She was far too quick-witted and observant not to pick up the trappings of sophistication if she felt it necessary to make her way at court. But then, he reflected, we often know least the people we ought to know best.

The queen's party had reached the edge of the forest

now and had halted for a brief consultation with the chief huntsman and the master of hounds. Then a horn blew and the horses charged forwards after the hounds. The main body of the hunt put spur to their horses.

Rosamund and Will were still a little out in front, and with a spontaneous cry of glee Rosamund set Jenny to a gallop, Will on her heels, as they raced for the entrance to the forest that the queen's party had taken. It was cool and shady under the trees and they could hear the beat of hooves both in front and behind them.

"Keep up with the queen," Will shouted as his gelding passed Jenny on the broad ride, and Rosamund urged her horse to greater speed, filled with exhilaration and the freedom of the chase.

Behind them the rest of the hunt crashed through the trees in a melee with curses and confused shouts as horses bumped into one another until a natural order had reasserted itself. Jenny faltered as her front hoof slipped on a patch of mud, and Rosamund pulled her up, leaning over to pat her steaming neck, waiting for the animal to regain her equilibrium. She had lost her place at the front of the pack and there was no sign of Will now. But that was often the way with hunts, and she drew Jenny aside to let the pack thunder past, reflecting that a narrower ride probably ran parallel with this one and she could gain some speed then.

She rode along the edge and soon found an opening in the trees that appeared to lead onto a narrow, grassy path parallel to the main ride. It was clear although the trees hung low, but she kept low in the saddle and encouraged Jenny into a canter, hearing the sounds of the hunt reassuringly close through a band of trees and shrubs that separated the path from the main ride.

The sound of hoofbeats behind her brought her heart into her throat. Despite the real closeness of the hunt, the path she had chosen was deserted as far as she could see, and the trees were dark and thick on either side. She urged Jenny faster but the hooves grew closer and closer, and she knew she was being followed by a more powerful beast than her own mare. A shadow fell across her as the horse came up on the mare's hindquarters and gradually drew level. She kept her eyes on the path ahead, her heart racing, sweat breaking out on her forehead, as she leaned low over Jenny's neck.

"Sweet Jesus, Mistress Rosamund, why are we racing?"

The chevalier sounded amused as well as puzzled, and Rosamund with a wave of relief looked sideways. His smile was quizzical, his eyes full of amusement. "May we draw rein a little?" he asked in a mock-plaintive tone. "I'm afraid my horse will founder if we must continue at this pace."

That made Rosamund laugh at the absurdity of his deep-chested, powerfully shouldered stallion succumbing in such fashion. She drew rein, slowing Jenny to a gentle canter. "You'll have to forgive me, Chevalier, if I find that hard to believe. He's a splendid creature."

"He is," he agreed simply. "And he's not met an animal yet that he cannot outrun. But tell me, why were you trying to outrun us?"

Rosamund felt a little foolish, but she told the truth. "I had no idea who was following me. It never occurred to me that someone from the hunt might have decided to take the same path."

"I saw you take it and I was curious. Curious as to why a young woman should choose to go off on her own down a deserted path in the middle of the forest. Do you perhaps have an assignation? Will I be in the way?" His eyebrows waggled comically as he put the question and she had to laugh.

"Of course not."

"Why of course not? You're a very desirable young woman, Mistress Rosamund. There must be many men at court who'd count themselves fortunate to draw your favor."

It was there again, that frisson, that sense of playing with hot coals. If she could keep them in the air all would be well, but if she held on too long she would be burned. "You flatter me, Chevalier." She tried to keep her tone matter-of-fact, but knew she sounded flirtatious instead.

"I swear I do not," he declared, hand on his heart. Then his expression changed, became serious, his gaze intent. "You stir *me,* Rosamund, and believe me, I am not easily stirred." His voice was low, as if, despite their present seclusion, he was afraid they might be overheard. He reached over and touched her hand as it rested on the pommel, and Rosamund felt the touch like the hot coal she had imagined.

"I have no desire to stir anyone, Chevalier," she managed to say. "But I am complimented, and grateful for it." She tried for a light laugh, but it sounded more like a donkey's bray to her ears.

He drew rein, bringing his horse to a stop as he leaned over to catch Jenny's bridle above the bit. "Let us walk a little, Rosamund." He dismounted, knotting the reins of both animals before reaching up to lift the startled but unresisting Rosamund from her saddle.

She thought she should resist this firm handling, but that would make her seem a naive simpleton. It wasn't as if he was going to rape her under the trees. He took her hand and led her a little way along the path to where a patch of sunshine blazed down through a break in the tree cover. The sounds of the hunt seemed to be rather far away, Rosamund thought.

Arnaud stopped and gently positioned her against the broad trunk of an ancient oak. He pushed up her chin with a forefinger and looked long and deep into her eyes. Then he kissed her full on the mouth. She tasted sweet and fresh. He kissed the tip of her nose, ran his tongue in a flickering caress over her eyelids, turned her head slightly to nibble on her earlobes. And Rosamund shuddered with pleasure beneath the careful education of his lips and tongue.

Arnaud was careful. Slow seduction was often its own reward, and something about this girl, something delightfully new-fledged, a little brave, a little timid, pleased him deeply. He would enjoy taking his time. He allowed himself a brief stroking caress across the swell of her breasts over her décolletage, and when she didn't jump back, he let his lips follow the path of his fingers.

Rosamund was holding her breath, all the better to savor the exquisite sensations. Alone with the chevalier, she found her misgivings drifting away. He found her attractive, he wanted to kiss her, and she enjoyed those kisses . . . more than enjoyed them. It was new and wonderful and if she was careful she could indulge in the experience and learn from it.

After a minute, Arnaud stepped back. He held her waist as he smiled down into her flushed face, her dreamy eyes. "I didn't scare you then, *ma fleur.*" It was a statement, not a question, and Rosamund shook her head, entranced by the unusual endearment. She wasn't accustomed to thinking of herself as a fragile, sweetly perfumed blossom.

"We should return before someone misses you," he said. Rosamund nodded, reassured that he had her reputation in mind even though for a moment back then she seemed to have forgotten it herself.

He helped her mount and they continued along the path in a silence that for Rosamund was charged with remembered sensation. Her lips still tingled, the crowns of her breasts pressed hard against her bodice, and there was a tension in her belly she couldn't identify.

After a moment a side path opened up ahead. Arnaud pointed with his whip. "That will lead us back to the main ride." He drew back so that she could ride ahead on the narrow path. He followed her at a little distance as she emerged into the stragglers on the broad ride.

There was no sign of Will, or indeed of anyone Rosamund knew, until she saw Joan on her dappled pony plodding along just ahead. She glanced over her shoulder and Arnaud merely gave her a nod and a half smile. She trotted up to Joan, greeting her with a cheerful salute. Joan looked astonished to see her.

"What are you doing back here? I thought you must be up at the head of the party."

"I thought Jenny seemed lame, so I stopped to check her hooves for stones. But she seems fine now." Rosamund fell in beside Joan, slowing Jenny to the pony's steady plod. She had had enough excitement for one morning and was quite happy to keep Joan company while savoring the two delicious encounters. The two men were so different, and if truth be told, she was much more comfortable with Will, enjoyed her banter with him without reservation. The chevalier made her uneasy even as he excited and challenged her in some way. She felt on her mettle and on her guard the entire time in his company. But she also loved every minute of it.

* * *

Thomas, deep in conversation with Kit, had fallen way behind the main body of the hunt. He looked up in surprise
to see how far back they had fallen. At this rate they'd be
lucky to beat the litters to the picnic ground. He shaded his
eyes, peering down the ride, then suddenly stiffened. He
thought he saw Rosamund emerge from a side path. What
the devil was she doing off the ride? Maybe a call of nature,
he reasoned, until he saw a man emerge a couple of minutes
after her.

His temples began to pound and he felt the blood rush
to his face. What the hell was *he* doing here at the English
court?

Kit looked at him in astonishment. "What, Thomas?
You look as if you're about to have an apoplexy."

"No, not that," Thomas said, staring ahead. "There's an
old friend up yonder, whom I haven't seen in an age. I'd
renew our acquaintance."

Kit, still staring at him, gave a shout of exultant laughter. "An old friend, is it? Well, if it's an old friend to be
greeted on a sword point, I'm with you, Thomas. Let's have
at him."

Thomas hesitated for barely a moment, then he put
spur to his horse. It jumped forwards and Kit with another
exultant cry set his own horse in pursuit. He had no idea
what Thomas was up to, but it felt like a scrap and Kit
loved nothing more.

Arnaud heard the beat of the hooves and glanced in
surprise behind him. His face was abruptly wiped clean of
expression. He drew rein and turned on the path, waiting.
His hand rested on his sword hilt.

Thomas drew up a few feet from him. The stragglers
had continued placidly on their way and the ride was
quiet, deserted, behind them. "Chevalier, I give you good

morrow." He bowed in his saddle. "Are you acquainted with my sister?"

Arnaud blinked in bemusement. "Your sister, Master Walsingham? I was unaware you had such a one. But if you believe you have a score to settle, then I am more than willing to accommodate you . . . even if you feel it necessary to bring reinforcements." He flicked a scornful glance at Kit.

Thomas's countenance was brick red, his breathing swift. He drew his sword in one clean movement and, as Kit made to draw his own, said in a fierce hiss, "No. This is mine alone."

The chevalier drew his own sword and they sat their horses on the path, facing each other and yet neither making a move to dismount.

"For God's sake, Thomas, have at him, or let me do so," Kit exclaimed.

In silence, Thomas swung down from his horse and the chevalier followed suit. "There's a clearing back there." Arnaud gestured with his sword to the path through the trees.

"Stay with the horses, Kit." The instruction ill-suited Marlowe but restraint prevailed for once despite his frustration. He took the bridles of the two riderless animals and, fighting impatience, sat and waited.

The two men emerged into the small clearing. The ground was uneven, tree roots twisting in an untidy obstacle course beneath the moss. They took up positions, made the formal pass through the air, and Thomas lunged, aiming for the chevalier's unprotected underarm. Arnaud parried and their blades clashed. It was clumsy swordplay on the uneven ground, but none the less determined for that. Thomas drew first blood, his blade slicing into the chevalier's forearm as Arnaud was wrong-footed by a tree root. Arnaud grimaced as blood dripped to the ground, but it was instantly absorbed and presented no danger of slipping. Thomas dropped his point and stepped back. "Bind it."

Arnaud tore a strip of his shirtsleeve with his teeth and twisted it around the slash, using his teeth to hold the knot. He stepped back, sword point up. Neither of them was aware of Kit, who, unable to stay out of this scrap whatever it was about, had tethered the horses roughly and come up quietly into the glade. He watched, realizing that, for all its ferocity, this was not a fight to the death. A score was to be settled, but they weren't going to kill each other over it. Or at least, not here.

Arnaud feinted, danced back, lunged, and his sword point slithered across his opponent's ribs, causing Thomas to curse and fall back, blood soaking his shirt.

"Honors even?" Arnaud gasped, dropping his sword point.

"For the present," Thomas returned coldly, pulling his shirt free of his trunk hose to wad it against the wound. "But if I ever see you near my sister again, de Vaugiras, there will be no honors even."

Arnaud laughed and picked up his doublet from the tree stump where he had thrown it. "As I said, Walsingham. I didn't know you had a sister."

"Come, Kit. The air is poisonous here." Holding his side, Thomas walked from the glade, leaving Kit to pick up his doublet and follow.

He mounted with difficulty, one hand still pressed to his side.

"We had better return home," Kit said. "The wound needs tending."

"'Tis only shallow," Thomas muttered.

"Maybe, but you risk infection if you leave it untended."

Thomas turned his horse back the way they had come without saying anything and rode in the same furious silence until Kit finally asked in jovial tones, "So what is this business between you and the Frenchman? Is it a matter of love perhaps? Requited . . . unrequited?"

Thomas cast him a scathing glance. "'Tis not a matter for your ill-placed jests. And it lies between me and the Frenchman."

Kit shrugged, not in the least put out by this dismissal. "As you will, my friend. It matters naught to me."

Arnaud remained in the glade, sitting on the tree stump tightening the torn sleeve of his shirt around the wound on his arm, until he was sure Walsingham and his companion had departed. He would be hors de combat for the rest of the day, and the prospect of riding back side by side with his opponent to have their wounds tended was so laughable it couldn't be considered. But his morning had not been unsatisfactory on the whole. It had been inevitable that at some point he and Walsingham would come face-to-face.

Chapter Fifteen

THE CHOSEN PICNIC ground was set on the brow of a small hill crowned by a coppice of beech trees. A stream gurgled musically at its base, competing with the musicians' lutes. Rosamund drew a breath of astonishment as she and Joan emerged from the trees. She had had many picnics in her life, but never had she seen an alfresco meal served in such grandeur.

The queen sat in her chair of state surrounded by the senior ladies and gentlemen of her household seated on padded stools. A canvas pavilion had been erected to shade long trestles, their pristine damask cloths laden with food, flagons of wine, kegs of ale. People were seated on canvas stools or rich Turkey carpets laid upon the grass, and servants scurried between them with laden chargers and jugs of wine, filling goblets and silver platters. It could not have been more elegant if it had been a state banquet in the great Banqueting Hall of Whitehall Palace.

"The queen will not have anything unceremonious, however casual the setting," Joan informed Rosamund, guessing accurately at her amazement. Joan dismounted as a groom came hurrying up to take their horses, and Rosamund followed suit, handing Jenny's reins to the groom, who took the animals away to water them at the stream.

"Let us find somewhere to sit on the grass." Joan looked

around at the throng, seeking a familiar face. "Oh, look, there's Will Creighton and some of the younger folk. Let's join them."

Nothing loath, Rosamund followed Joan across the grass to where a large party of young people were sprawled, in the case of the gentlemen, and elegantly disposed in the case of the ladies, their skirts billowing around them, the deep, rich colors blending with those in the thick carpet beneath them.

Will was stretched out, his head resting on one elbow-propped palm, a thick turkey leg held in his other hand. He sat up as Rosamund and Joan approached. "Ladies, come and join us," he called. "Mistress Walsingham, what happened to you? You disappeared as if spirited away by demons."

"My horse stumbled and I took her out of the path for a few minutes, and by the time I looked up, you were long gone," Rosamund said lightly, sitting on the rug beside him, arranging her tawny velvet skirts to best advantage with a deft twitch and a pat.

With an air of carefree informality the group was seated around baskets and platters of food from which they helped themselves liberally. They greeted the new arrivals in friendly fashion and Will waved his turkey leg at the food. "We stand on no ceremony on this carpet. Eat, ladies."

He leaned forward and took up the basket of manchets, offering it to Rosamund. His eyes flickered in a conspiratorial half wink that sent the strangest jolt of warmth through her belly. It was as if he were underscoring a secret understanding that they shared, yet nothing had happened between them. He hadn't even attempted to kiss her. But perhaps youth held him back, where it could not hold back the chevalier. She smiled and touched a finger to her lips in a fleeting gesture before taking a manchet from the basket.

Someone passed over a wine cup filled to the brim with canary wine, someone else a platter of sirloin. Joan was sitting beside her, eating hungrily, but Rosamund noticed that her gaze was concentrated on Will, who didn't appear to notice her. His eyes were all for Rosamund.

"Master Creighton, I haven't heard you play for some time," Joan declared through a mouthful of cheese tart. "Have you given up the lute?"

Will looked startled at this strangely abrupt non sequitur. "Why, no, Mistress Joan. I've been playing as much as usual, I'm sure. Have I not?" He looked a question around the company.

"Aye, Will, you've been plaguing us with your sorrowful, romantical lyrics as often as usual," one of the gentlemen said with a grin. Will threw a cherry pit at him and he laughed and threw a cherry back. It caught Will on the cheek, leaving a scarlet smear. Will cast an oath at his assailant, but it was in jest and greeted with general laughter.

"Here." Rosamund twisted to wipe the smear from his cheek with a lace-edged handkerchief. It seemed such a natural gesture in the present atmosphere, and no one appeared to see any significance in it, except that suddenly she was aware of Joan's sharpened gaze.

"My thanks, Mistress Rosamund." Will stretched out again on his side, idly chewing on his turkey leg. "Shall we play a word game?"

There was a ready chorus of agreement and Will, frowning in thought, began to tell a story. After two lines he stopped and looked at Rosamund. "Your turn, Mistress Rosamund."

"To do what?"

"You must tell the next bit of the story," Joan explained. "It's a game often played at court. But then you haven't been here very long."

Rosamund was prepared to forgive the condescension, guessing at Joan's chagrin over her failure to engage Will in conversation. She frowned in thought and Will said, "No, no, Rosamund, you must not think, you have to say the first things that come into your head."

"I see." She obliged with a piece of utter nonsense that had them all laughing, and they played companionably for the next half hour.

"I must take a stroll. . . . If you'll forgive me, ladies." One of the men rose from the carpet, glancing towards the coppice. The rest of the men rose with him and they walked off in a purposeful group into the trees.

"I wish we could gain relief as easily," one of the women said to a groaning chorus of agreement. "I daren't drink very much on this kind of excursion in case there's nowhere to go."

"There's a line of bushes over there." Rosamund, who was anxious for relief herself, pointed to what looked like a shrubbery. She got to her feet. "I'll see how private it is."

She stood for a moment looking around the hillside. She could see Agathe in a group seated comfortably on stools a few yards from the queen's party, but there was no sign of the chevalier anywhere. Perhaps the hunt had lost its savor and he'd left. Rosamund was not sorry that he was absent, she found that the intensity of their encounters was too high to be experienced too often.

She set off across the hillside and ducked behind the bushes. They provided a screen of sorts, and she could hear no close voices on the other side. It was as always a struggle with skirts and petticoats and the wretched farthingale, but she managed and feeling greatly relieved she adjusted her gown and moved casually away from the screen.

"Feeling better?" Will's laughing voice came from just behind her and she spun around.

"Were you watching?"

He shook his head, raising his hands in protestation. "No, I wouldn't dream of it."

She regarded him suspiciously, not quite convinced. He looked like a particularly mischievous boy at the moment. "I'm not sure I believe you."

"I swear it." He held out his hand. "Come walk with me a little."

Rosamund glanced around. Couples were strolling across the hill, some people seemed stretched in sleep upon the carpets, others gathered in chatting groups. The queen was still seated in her chair of state among her household listening to the musicians as she sipped from her crystal goblet. It was a delightfully pastoral scene that showed no signs of breaking up.

She took Will's hand and walked with him over the brow of the hill. The far side was deserted, almost as if no one had realized that a hill had two sides. A scattering of trees littered the hillside and they walked down to the stream, the crystal clear water bubbling over large white stones. Will sat on the bank and pulled her down beside him. He put an arm around her shoulders and turned slightly to face her. His eyes glowed with purpose and she knew he was going to kiss her.

She tilted her face up, her mouth curving in a smile of invitation, and he brought his lips to hers. It was a very different kiss from the chevalier's, less assured perhaps, but also stronger, more passionate, and Rosamund found herself responding with a ready instinct.

When he raised his head, he looked at her as if seeing her for the first time, and Rosamund wondered for an uneasy moment if her willing response had somehow transgressed a rule she knew nothing about. But then she saw that the glow in his eyes had deepened.

"You are lovely," he said, and she was suffused with a wonderful feeling of triumphant satisfaction. Even Agathe could not have been paid a stronger or more sincere compliment.

Will regarded her for another moment, then the glow in his eyes was replaced with the wicked gleam of mischief she had come to expect. "Shall we go to the theatre?"

She remembered his earlier suggestion, a suggestion she had thought made mostly in jest. She had certainly responded to it as such. But now, after the wonderful adventures of the day, the clandestine encounters that still infused her with a sense of power, she thought, *Why not?* She could do anything. She had learned that there were ways around every rule, as long as the rules were broken with discretion. And what a wonderful adventure it would be.

"When?" she asked, and he laughed delightedly.

"So you *do* have the courage, after all."

"Of course I do," she stated with mock indignation. "I just wasn't sure I had the inclination before."

That made him laugh anew, and then he became serious. "I understand the court is removing to Greenwich in three days just for the night. The queen is to receive her ambassadors there. If you could contrive some excuse to remain behind at Whitehall . . . ?" He raised an eyebrow.

"I suppose I could have an ague . . . some woman's complaint . . ." She was thinking out loud.

"I will procure the disguise if you procure your freedom," he promised, getting to his feet.

"Oh, I will." She took the hand he held out and let him pull her to her feet. Briefly he pulled her against him and she felt the heat of his body, then he released her quickly as the sound of voices reached them from the hilltop.

"It sounds as if we're on the move again. Stay up with me this afternoon, if your horse has the strength." He was climbing swiftly as he spoke.

"She can stay the course." Rosamund spoke with confidence. An afternoon with no romantic interludes would be a pleasant change, two a day seemed more than enough. Now she was ready to enjoy just the simple pleasure of riding fast to hounds.

Kit Marlowe was on his own at the theatre. Thomas was off on some business with the unsavory Frizer, and Kit was not sorry to be excluded from that encounter. His own present assignment was unpleasant enough, working with Walsingham's man Gilbert Gifford to prod a naive and impassioned young man who went by the name of John Savage to declare himself openly for the Scots queen's cause. Once he'd made an unequivocal declaration, then he would instantly be open to arrest whenever it suited Walsingham to move.

Kit resented the necessity for his involvement with Walsingham's secret world, yet he was honest enough to admit that he enjoyed its fruits. His garments today were all his own. Each of the fourteen gold buttons marching down each deep brown velvet sleeve of his doublet represented his own labor in the service of his country. He relished the orange taffeta lining of his doublet showing through the slashed sleeves, and the delicate cobweb lawn of his shirt collar and cuffs. An affectation taken from Thomas, he freely acknowledged, but it looked good and marked a man as one of status.

He drank deep at the tavern hard by the Curtain before making his way, a welcome visitor, backstage to commune with the actors as they readied themselves for the stage.

"Eh, Kit, that's a whore's color you're wearing," Ned Alleyn declared, painting his face at a small silvered mirror. "Is it a whore's work you've been about?"

Kit buffeted Ned's shoulder, rather harder than was strictly necessary. "My tastes do not run in that direction, as well you know. Besides, I see nothing of a whore in brown velvet."

" 'Tis the orange beneath, he means," Burbage said from his stool at the side of the tiring room. "Where's Thomas?"

"He had business." Kit straddled a stool and felt in his pocket for a coin. "Hey, lad . . ." He crooked a finger at one of the indentured apprentice actors whose fresh faces graced the female parts in the plays. "Fetch a pitcher of ale, Robby."

"Yes, Master Marlowe." The lad snatched the coin and ran off.

"There'll be no drinking until after the play is done," Burbage announced. " 'Tis hard enough to have decent takings when the audience is in its cups. My actors will be sober until after."

A chorus of groans greeted the proscription but they were not in earnest. Kit said, "Ah, well, I shall drink now, and if there's any left, it shall go to the rest of you."

"There'll be none left," one of the actors said sotto voce. He glanced at Kit, hoping he hadn't heard him. Master Marlowe's uncertain temper was now well-known among the theatre folk. But if Kit had heard him, he appeared untroubled by the comment. The arrival of Tom Kyd distracted him, and when the lad brought in the pitcher of ale, he flung an arm around Kyd's shoulders and said they should take their stools on the stage and sample the ale, while Kit pointed out some infelicitous verse in *The Spanish Tragedy* that he had long been intending to bring to Master Kyd's attention.

Tom Kyd did not look best pleased at this, but he followed the ale like a horse following a nose bag, and they took their places onstage.

Kit drank from the pitcher and passed it to Tom. He let his gaze roam around the filling theatre. The groundlings were packed into the pit before the stage, and the galleries looked as if they would buckle under the weight of the audience. His eye fell on a fresh-faced youth, leaning on the rail at the front of the gallery. Pink cheeks, delightfully rounded, a lock of russet hair falling onto a white forehead from beneath the brim of his hat.

Kit smiled, contemplating the sweetness of a fresh youth just out of boyhood. He had tumbled with a young stable lad a couple of days earlier, which had reminded him of the pleasures to be had apart from the full-grown passion he shared with Thomas Walsingham. There was all cut and thrust, violent conjugations, glorious triumph and equally glorious submission, but a man needed a taste of honey on occasion.

He kept his eye on the youth as the players assembled onstage, enchanted by the lad's wide-eyed delight. Was he alone? But, no, a man was beside him. Kit's eyebrows lifted as he recognized Will Creighton. He had never thought that that young man shared his own predilection for the delights of a young boy, but there was something proprietorial in the way his hand rested on the youth's shoulder, as if he saw himself as a protector. Maybe there was another explanation. Maybe the lad was a relative of some kind.

Kit resolved to discover for himself when the play was done and turned his attention to the action onstage.

Rosamund could hardly believe she was here in the gallery of the Curtain. It had been astonishingly easy to fake a pain in her belly so severe she couldn't leave her bed. It hadn't occurred to anyone that a maid of honor would willingly forgo the delights of a trip on the river to Greenwich in one of the royal barges, followed by a state banquet and dancing, and a night spent in the almost palatial accommodations made available to them at Greenwich.

A sympathetic Joan had conveyed news of Rosamund's indisposition to the Countess of Shrewsbury, who had decreed Mistress Walsingham was to remain abed so that she would be sufficiently recovered to return to her duties when the queen and her household returned to Whitehall on the morrow. Rosamund had waited, watching from the high window in the dorter, until the last stragglers had reached the river and boarded the last of the long line of barges. The silence in the palace had seemed almost eerie, and on the high attic floor it was so silent she could hear the mice scratching behind the walls.

Will had been waiting as arranged at the foot of the stairs with a bundle of clothes. In urgent silence he had handed her the bundle and she had disappeared upstairs, reappearing a short while later in the black homespun doublet and hose of a page, her hair knotted securely beneath a flat cap, shoes with pewter buckles on her feet.

She smiled now remembering Will's wide-eyed expression as he'd taken in her appearance. They'd left the palace, with Rosamund riding pillion behind Will on his chestnut gelding. It was too risky for her to draw attention to herself by taking Jenny. Now here she was in the gallery of the

Curtain, relishing the sights, the sounds, even the powerful smells of packed bodies around her.

She had not seen the play before, but she recognized the actors. She saw Kit Marlowe on a stage stool, but there was no danger of encountering him. There would be no mingling with the actors after this play.

Will leaned in beside her and said into her ear, "Don't move. I'll be back in a minute." He stepped away and she felt instantly vulnerable. People flowed like lava into the space left by Will, and she was suddenly overpowered by the stench of humanity pressing around her, rotten breath, stale beer, raw onions, and ancient sweat. The voices were rough and raucous and someone pushed heavily into her back, forcing her forward against the gallery rail. She pushed back, trying to breathe, and then Will was there again, somehow managing to re-create sufficient space beside her.

"I thought you might be hungry." He handed her a meat pie as he took a hungry bite of his own, gravy spurting onto his chin. He wiped it off with the back of his hand and gave her his wide grin.

Rosamund felt instantly better. She was here with Will and no one knew it. She was part of this boisterous crowd, and she could revel in her anonymity. She took a big bite of her pie and, when the gravy spurted, followed Will's example and swiped it away with the back of her hand. The pie was manna. She didn't think she had ever tasted anything so succulent and toothsome. She looked across at Will and grinned like the urchin she felt herself to be.

The play as always unfolded before her, laying out its riches as if onto a magic carpet, transporting her to a world far from her own. At its end, she applauded wildly, her eyes dazed with wonder.

"You enjoyed it." Will stated the obvious with a pleased smile. He couldn't take his eyes off her radiant countenance and her light-filled green eyes. The page's costume excited him with a sense of the forbidden. It revealed the lines and contours of her body in a way that thrilled him. She was so small and shapely, her hips and buttocks curving in a soft swell in the trunk hose, her bosom a mere hint beneath the doublet.

"What are you looking at?" Rosamund had never seen that hungry, lustful look on a man's face before. She had seen appreciation, but it had been almost decorous compared with the look in Will's eye now. It made her feel hot, her skin tight and prickly, but it excited her too, gave her a feeling of power even as her body stirred beneath it.

"You." Will shook his head as if he could thus dispel his disturbing fantasy. "Sweet heaven, Rosamund, if I'd known what those clothes would do . . ." He broke off abruptly. "Let us get away from here before we're engulfed."

It was a realistic fear, Rosamund realized, forgetting what he had said as they battled their way to the stairs at the corner of the gallery. She stumbled on the way down, people pressing her forward while others in front of her were for a moment unable to proceed themselves. Then the throng heaved, surged, and she was catapulted down the stairs and out into the air like a cork from a bottle.

She stood, gasping for breath, trying to get her bearings as the mass of humanity heaved around her. She couldn't see Will anywhere. At first she took no notice of the feeling of someone behind her; she had been shoved and touched so much in the rush to leave the gallery that this seemed no different. Only slowly did she realize that something deliberate was going on at her back. A hand was moving lightly over her backside. Instinctively she reached a hand behind her in a vigorous chopping motion. In response a soft laugh whispered against her ear, and a voice murmured, "Gently, gently, ladikins. You're too sweet a morsel for such unfriendliness."

Rosamund froze. Slowly she turned and looked into the laughing face of Christopher Marlowe.

Kit's laugh died with his smile as he stared at her. "God in heaven . . . Rosamund, what in the devil's name . . . ?"

"I might ask the same of you," she returned, trying to cover her embarrassment with a snappy riposte, but she knew her face was scarlet, and she remembered Will's words up in the gallery, and the look on his face. Was this disguise that provocative?

Kit held up his hands in a gesture of submission. "I saw what I thought was a delicious morsel just waiting to be plucked. I did what any red-blooded male would do in the circumstances."

"Hardly *any* red-blooded male," she muttered.

"You may have a point there." He had regained his composure and now was both amused and intrigued by the situation. "Are you with Thomas? No, of course you're not. He's busy on Master Secretary's business. I saw you with Master Creighton. Is he your escort?" He looked around and came eye to eye with Will Creighton.

"Master Marlowe." Will bowed awkwardly. He'd been frozen in horror, his stunned gaze not missing a single one of Master Marlowe's roving pats on Rosamund's delightfully outlined bottom.

"Master Will. I saw you earlier in the gallery." Kit glanced at Rosamund and smiled. "So that's the way the wind blows. I see it all now. Where better for two lovers to tryst than in the gallery of the theatre among the unwashed?"

"It's not . . . it's not a tryst," Rosamund protested. "Will knows how much I miss the theatre, and we contrived this together. The court has gone to Greenwich and I am at Whitehall on my sickbed." She realized how silly that sounded only when she'd said it.

Kit laughed. "Well, you look well recovered, Mistress Rosamund, and your secret is safe with me, whatever it may be. I suggest we find a pleasant hostelry where we can eat, drink, and be merry together. What say you?"

"Not with the players. Rosamund's brother must never know of this."

Kit regarded Will with a half smile. "Oh, I think Thomas's objections would only apply if his sister's escapades reached the ears of Master Secretary and his cohorts. I doubt he has the will to fret otherwise. 'Tis highly unlikely that Ned Alleyn and the rest of 'em rub shoulders with courtiers, apart from Thomas himself, and our friend Master Watson, that is."

Will looked askance at Rosamund, who suddenly tossed the last vestiges of caution to the four winds. What could it possibly matter now? "Master Marlowe is right. Thomas will not care as long as his own life is not affected adversely by what I do. And the court is disporting itself at Greenwich. So do let us go, Will."

"I think we should give you a name more suited to your costume," Kit said solemnly. "Ganymede would be most appropriate. But I think something a little less flamboyant. How about Pip? You look like a Pip to me. As fresh and green as a pippin." He was highly amused by Rosamund's escapade and, he had to admit, deliciously aroused by the image she presented of a barely fledged youth.

Rosamund made a face. Kit was making jest of her, but it didn't have the malice of court mockery, and after Will's reaction to her costume she could see his temptation. She looked at Will, who was looking uncertain.

Will was torn. He didn't wish to share Rosamund with the rowdy players and the so lascivious Kit Marlowe on this precious evening alone, but he was drawn to the players himself, and he knew how much Rosamund wanted to join them. "Of course," he said finally. "We'll just hope that it never comes to the wrong ears, I've no wish to fight a duel with your brother on Finsbury Field."

Rosamund tucked her hand into his arm and squeezed. "I won't let that happen, Will. If necessary, I'll cut Thomas's throat in his sleep."

"Oh, what a bloodthirsty lad it is," exclaimed Kit, leading the way backstage.

Chapter Sixteen

BACKSTAGE, THE PLAYERS were counting the evening's takings, and Burbage was grumbling as usual as he took the leather pouch from the doorkeeper and shook out its contents. "Five bad coins. Thieves, God rot 'em." He looked up as Kit and his companions entered the tiring-room. "Eh, Master Marlowe, any complaints today as to the versifying?" His tone was sour and challenging.

Kit was untroubled, understanding the worries that plagued Burbage. He merely chuckled. "Not to speak of, Burbage. But I bring companions. Will Creighton you know, but I doubt you are acquainted with young Pip here." He pushed Rosamund forward with a hand between her shoulder blades.

"Another ladikins, eh, Marlowe?" Ned pulled off his wig, laying it carefully over its hanger. "I'd have thought you'd enough to keep your sword busy at home without going a-hunting."

"I plead innocence on this occasion." Kit perched on a stool. "Our friend Will has first option."

Will opened his mouth to protest as the men in the tiring-room turned with interest to look at Rosamund, who, deciding she would play this part to the hilt, tugged at her doublet and set her hat at a rakish angle, striking a pose with one hand on an outthrust hip.

Laughter rocked the rafters as the men recognized in this cocky youngster Thomas Walsingham's usually timidly reclusive little sister.

Will relaxed, his protests unborn. If Rosamund wanted to play this game, then he too would play. He bowed with a sweeping flourish of his plumed hat. "If you gentlemen would permit the company of a pair of young gallants for the evening, we would gladly furnish the feast with a pitcher of burgundy."

"Well said, Will." Kit slapped his shoulder. "Come, gentlemen, let's repair to the White Horse, and Pip here shall put pen to paper and re-create the scenes of this afternoon. I have some suggestions to make as to the staging of the lovers' tryst. I will demonstrate more easily with a sketch for reference."

Rosamund remembered little of that evening. At some point she saw Will and Burbage in earnest discussion and hoped they were talking of Will's play and hoped more fervently that Burbage was giving him encouragement. Will didn't look downcast at least, but she had no opportunity to talk to him privately until finally they staggered out of the White Horse in the company of the others, all of whom were far from sober, but in good enough mood, laughing, tossing lines of verse at each other, while Kit, prancing like a pony down the street, burst into ribald song, waving his hat in time.

They reached a corner and Will nudged Rosamund to the left, while the rest surged drunkenly to the right, following Kit as if he were the Pied Piper. "We must go this way, Rosamund. I have to collect my horse from the livery stable."

His voice was slurred and Rosamund giggled as she looked at him. "I think you are overdrunk, Will."

"I may be, but so, my dear Pip, are you." He caught her arm as she swayed against a wall. "Come, we have to get you back into the palace."

That made sense to Rosamund, and she clung to his arm as they staggered together down the lane, with Will trying to remember where he'd left his horse. "I think it was this way . . . no, that way . . . Oh, sweet heaven, Rosamund." He leaned against a wall, closing his eyes. "I don't know where the hell I left him."

Rosamund squinted as if it would somehow concentrate her memory. It was very dark, even the stars offering little enough light from the overcast sky. And she knew, as did Will, despite their uncertain state, that the streets of night-time London were no place for two well-to-do drunken stragglers.

"That way." She pointed decisively to the right. And, indeed, she could just make out the turrets of the Curtain theatre at the end. "The stable is close to the theatre."

Will seized her hand and together they plunged down the lane. Footsteps sounded behind them. Will put his free hand on his sword, urging her forward. She was almost running when the footsteps were joined by others. Will suddenly dived sideways, dragging her with him, into pitch-darkness. He clanged a heavy door behind them and stood leaning against it as the footsteps outside stopped. The door heaved as someone pushed hard against it.

Will swore, then with an almighty effort he brought the door's heavy iron bar down into its bracket. The door stood firm against the first onslaught. Rosamund held on to the door for dear life beside Will, even though she knew her counterweight was no help. She was suddenly clear-headed and terrified, but also determined that the door would hold. She and Will together would hold it.

At last the outsiders gave up and the sound of their receding footsteps was like the sweetest music. Rosamund took a deep breath and whispered, "Where are we, Will?"

"I hope we're in the stables," he replied softly, pushing himself away from the door, peering into the darkness. Their eyes were growing accustomed now and they could make out the shape of a building just across the small cobbled yard. "I think it is."

He walked to the building, Rosamund on his heels. She could smell stable, manure, leather, horseflesh. But quite a few of them were in the area serving the local taverns. Will whistled softly and a horse whickered from behind the door.

"It's Sam." He lifted the latch on the door and pushed it open. It was warm inside, thick with the smell of horses and hay. Rosamund followed as Will felt his way down the stalls until he found his chestnut in a stall halfway down. The horse whickered again, pushing his nose into Will's hand as he leaned over the partition.

"I think we had better stay here until it's light." Will peered at Rosamund in the darkness where no starlight however faint could penetrate. "We could try to make a bed of hay if we can find an empty stall."

Rosamund nodded, taking this as her task. She felt her way down the stalls and found an empty one at the far end of the row. It was swept clean, but a ladder led up to what she assumed was the hayloft above. She climbed the ladder, with the exultant thought that such a maneuver would have been near impossible in skirts and farthingale. The hayloft smelled sweet, and best of all a small, round window offered the sky's faint illumination.

"Will . . . up here," she called softly, hitching herself up into the loft.

Will followed to find her spreading hay with a pitch-fork to make a mattress under the window. "If we put our cloaks over it, it will keep the straw from pricking." She had discarded her own and was spreading it over the pile. Then with a moan of exhaustion, she collapsed on the makeshift mattress. "I can't move, Will. And my head's spinning."

Will took off his own cloak and threw it over her. He hesitated for a moment, looking down at her, then said, "I'll make a bed over there . . . unless, of course, you're cold?"

Rosamund opened her eyes, gazing straight up at him. "I *am* cold, but we could bundle." She moved his cloak aside. "There's room aplenty on the hay here."

He hesitated for only a second, then slipped beneath his cloak to lie beside her. The sweet smell of hay, the faint crescent of the new moon in the window, the shuf-flings and snufflings of the animals below, created a world of its own. Will slipped an arm beneath her, rolling her into his embrace. His eyes were wide and shining in the gloom, as silently he brought his mouth to hers. He mur-mured against her lips, "Dear God, I want you so much, Rosamund."

She inhaled his mingled scents of wine and sweat, of the faint lingering aroma of lavender in his linen, of a hint of leather and horseflesh, feeling the roughness of his night-time beard against her cheeks, and she stretched against him with an unnamed urgency of her own. Her own words were a jumble of confusion as she spoke against his mouth. "I need . . . I feel . . . oh, Will, I don't have words for this. I've never felt like this before."

She lay on top of him, moved against him, feeling his body delineated against her own, felt the hard, upward press of his loins. Her own body felt much more open, more available in the page's garments, and she delighted in the sensation.

Will cupped her face between his hands and kissed her again, then he rolled sideways, bringing her with him so that now she lay beneath him. He hung above her, that same light glowing in his blue eyes. "It's something about these clothes," he muttered. "Sweet Jesus, Rosamund."

"I should wear them more often," she whispered, moving beneath him with more urgency. They were existing in a world apart, their own little space in the universe. Nothing was real but this, the feel of his body, the shape of him, his scent, and the surging, indescribable need to possess him, to have all of him, a part of her.

His hand brushed across her breasts beneath the doublet. His fingers worked the buttons, spreading the sides of the doublet wide. Her breasts, unsupported by a boned bodice, were warm and soft beneath the linen shirt, and her nipples peaked hard against the slightly rough material. He whispered into her ear and her body responded again, moving urgently against him, following its own path. With rough haste he unlaced her hose, and she wriggled out of the garment, giving a little sigh of satisfaction as at last she felt the nakedness of his loins against hers.

Their bodies merged, melded, their limbs intertwined, and Rosamund after a moment's piercing pain floated on sensation that was and was not part of a dream. She was aware of the moment when he left her body, aware of a stab of loss, then she curled against him, his arm holding her close, and slept, her head buried in the hollow of his shoulder.

Rosamund awoke to the first glimmer of daylight, aware of a crucifying headache and completely at a loss as to where she was. She turned her head with a groan and gazed with incomprehension at Will sleeping beside her, one bare arm flung above his head. She edged up on an elbow and looked gingerly around. Their shoes, stockings, hose, were tangled at the end of the mattress. And Rosamund remembered. Remembered with a flood of delight despite the pain in her head.

She lay down again, touching herself, aware of a soreness now. Her fingers came away sticky with a smear of blood. She was no longer virgin. She must be wicked and destined for hell, but those dreamlike moments in the straw had brought her nothing but pleasure. How could she regret the feel of his body on hers, *in* hers. The scent of his skin, still in her nostrils, the taste of his tongue, the astounding moment when she felt she had hovered on the brink of some exquisite sensation, and the moment when she had fallen from that brink. Rosamund could think only of how soon she could repeat those moments.

She rolled on her side and touched Will's eyes in a gentle, fluttering kiss of her tongue.

He woke instantly, looked at her in bemusement, and then slowly recollection flooded him. "Rosamund?" He struggled to sit up. His eye fell on their tangled garments.

Rosamund's smile was a little uncertain as she read his expression. He looked shocked. She touched his arm, fixing him with her candid gaze. "Is something wrong?"

Will shook his head and winced at the sharp stab of pain through his temples. "No, my sweet, no . . . but, yes, everything. I have taken your virginity. It's unforgivable."

"You didn't take it, I gave it," she said quietly. "I gave it willingly, Will, and I don't regret it. Do you regret it?"

He looked at her, her grave expression, the tangled curls tumbling around her pale face, the large, oval green eyes filled with uncertainty. "No, how could I?" He drew her against him, kissing her eyes. "You are lovely. But I have the devil of a headache, and everything looks bad in the morning after a serious bout of overdrinking." His tone was ruefully humorous, and she couldn't help a feeble responding smile.

"I have never felt this ill before. It's horrible."

"Yes, it is, and I *have* known it, so I should know better." He reached for his clothes. "Lord, I must smell as rank as an old beer keg."

"Me too." Rosamund breathed into her cupped hands with a grimace. "We need to get back to the palace. My head aches as if Thor's hammering on his anvil behind my eyes."

Will fastened his britches. "No one's about as yet. We may be lucky and manage to take Sam and get out unseen before the first grooms come to work." He slung his cloak over his shoulders, ignoring the straw clinging to it. He shinned down the ladder and Rosamund followed, having first brushed the straw from her own cloak.

"How will you pay them?" She watched as he led Sam from the stall and saddled him.

"I'll leave coin in the stall." Will reached into his pocket for his purse. It was lamentably lighter than it had been at the start of yesterday's excursion, the burgundy pitchers had frequently been refilled, but he found a shilling and laid it carefully on the ledge beside the partition door to the stall.

He led the horse out into the yard, blinking painfully in the growing light, and swung himself into the saddle. Rosamund went to open the barred door and, once Will had walked Sam into the lane, grabbed his hand and he hoisted her up behind him.

The lane held no terrors this morning. A few folk were about, a few doors opened to the street as women swept yesterday's debris into the kennel. Will moved Sam sideways briskly as a cry of "Gardyloo" came from above. He was a little too slow and the night soil contents of the chamber pot splashed up from the kennel.

"God rot their black souls," he said, wrinkling his nose at the stench. Rosamund, her own nose buried against the fine velvet of his cloak, made no sound. She was thinking of a bath. Of how to contrive such a thing in the corridors of Whitehall Palace. Of the joys of a long afternoon's sleep in a bed she would have to herself until Joan returned that evening.

Whitehall Palace took shape in the early morning, a light mist rising from the river, softening its lines, dampening the lush green sweep of the lawns. They took a narrow lane running along the side of the palace and entered the grounds through a relatively unused gate.

Will dismounted and lifted Rosamund down. He held her for a moment, his hands firm and warm at her waist. His expression was troubled. "Can you manage to get in unobserved, sweet?"

"I'll slip in through the side door," she said confidently. "There's no need to worry, Will."

"No," he said, but he didn't sound reassured and it puzzled her.

"Truly," she said.

He nodded, but the troubled look in his eye didn't dissipate. "I'm sure you're more than capable." He glanced around to ensure they were unobserved, then bent and kissed her quickly on the lips. "Hurry in and sleep well."

"Oh, I will." She reached up and traced the curve of his mouth with her finger. "Until later, Will."

"Yes, until later." He watched her flit down the path that would take her to the side door to the palace. He tried to explain away his feeling that something had started that he could neither control nor continue, by blaming it on the depressing effects of too much wine. A solution would present itself. He walked away in search of his own bed.

Rosamund hurried along less-well-used corridors and up to the dorter, seeing no one who might remark upon a hurrying page.

She reached the peace of the attic chamber confident that she had drawn no attention. And then she saw on the dresser a platter of bread and cheese and a cup of milk. Someone had been in to check on her. Would the person wonder where the supposed invalid had gone? Had the person come back more than once, to find the chamber still empty?

Her heart began to pound in time with her head, and for a moment she stood paralyzed by the horrendous implications of such a discovery. Then with an effort she threw off her clothes and washed herself with the cold water remaining in the ewer. It refreshed her enough to clear her head a little. There was no point imagining problems that might well not materialize. She scrambled back into her shift before bundling the page's garments tightly and burying them in the bottom of the trunk that had accompanied her to the palace. Maybe she would have the opportunity to use them again. She sank back onto the bed, pulling the coverlet over her, closing her eyes. She would sleep, and with any luck when she awoke, blissfully free of headache, she would be able to think of a convincing reason for her absence from the dorter should it be questioned.

*   *   *

Rosamund was awakened from a deep slumber early that evening by the chatter of women as the maids of honor returned from their excursion to Greenwich.

"Are you still abed, Rosamund?" Joan flopped onto the edge of the bed. "Are you still unwell? Lady Shrewsbury will insist on sending for the leech if you cannot get up tomorrow."

"I am better, thank you." Rosamund propped herself on an elbow and gazed bleary-eyed around the familiar attic, where the other women were putting away their clothes, the same magpie chatter filling the air. "Did you have a good time?"

"Oh, it was wonderful. The boat ride was delightful and the dancing last night was, oh, heavenly." Joan jumped to her feet and twirled. "Such a shame you had to miss it, Rosamund."

"Our dear Joan has a lovelorn swain," Lettice Asherton said with a sardonic chuckle. "You had better be careful the queen doesn't get to hear of it, Joan. She does not like it when her ladies find lovers for themselves, even though she tolerates flirting."

"She does enough of it herself," Frances Darcy murmured, almost sotto voce. "Essex is young enough to be her own son. And she preens and paints herself for him as if she were a girl of twenty."

"That's treasonous talk, Frances," Lettice warned.

"'Tis but the truth and everyone knows it." Frances pouted as she removed her heavy diamond earrings and hung them on the little silver tree on the dresser.

Lettice regarded her crossly. Frances was related by her father's third marriage to the Howards, the family name of the dukes of Norfolk, and thus destined for a great marriage of her own, despite her rather plain countenance where the pox scars were clearly visible and her poor teeth, three of which blackened her smile and gave her great pain, which made her irritable and poor company.

But once her family had decided on the alliance that would bring them the most influence and wealth, she would be married, neither bride nor groom consulted in the matter. She had no shortage of jewels or of coin, and when she needed a new gown, it was instantly provided. But her very status and privilege inured her from the envious malice of her fellows. No one dared even gossip about her.

Rosamund had got up from the bed. She hadn't eaten since the previous evening in the White Horse and she was famished. The now-stale bread and dried-up cheese so thoughtfully left for the invalid was all that was on offer and she began absently to eat. The milk was sour, but she drank it anyway. Who had left this for her? Her stomach began to flutter with fear. Would her absence be reported? If she could discover who had been up to the dorter, she could perhaps persuade the person, bribe the person, to keep quiet about it.

But there was nothing to be done tonight. She finished her supper, such as it was, and returned to bed.

When she awoke in the morning, it was to a familiar cramping ache in her belly. The arrival of her monthly courses would add verisimilitude to her make-believe indisposition, she reflected. Joan, seeing her bring out thick linen clouts from the chest, gave her a look of sympathy. "Do you still have the bellyache?"

Rosamund nodded but said swiftly, " 'Tis not as bad as yesterday." She thought longingly of the remedy she had always had at home. Hot, spiced gruel mixed with wine. "A caudle will help. If such a thing is available."

"Oh, yes. The maids will make you some if you ask them at breakfast. . . . Will you do my laces?"

Rosamund obliged and Joan helped her in turn. They went down to breakfast, where Lady Shrewsbury as usual presided. She gave Rosamund a sharp look. "You are better, I trust, Rosamund. You look a little pale."

"I am better, thank you, madam." Rosamund curtsied as she answered before taking her place at the table. "May I ask the maid for a caudle?"

The countess nodded with instant comprehension. It was a universally understood remedy. "That is probably why you were unwell." She signaled one of the serving maids. "You, girl, fetch a caudle for Mistress Rosamund."

The morning dragged by. Rosamund ignored her bellyache as best she could, trying to lose herself in her sketching, half hoping that the queen would summon her to her privy chamber to do some secretarial work, which would at least give her something concrete to do. But no summons came and she watched the clock, waiting for the moment when the queen's ladies would be free to join the rest of the court in the gardens and galleries. She was certain Will would be at court this afternoon. He wouldn't miss a chance to see her. Their farewell had been of necessity hurried, but she longed for the opportunity to linger a little with him, to exchange the secretive little gestures and glances that made their public encounters so special and would invest them with so much more meaning now.

At last Lady Shrewsbury gave the signal that the queen had no further need of their company and they were at liberty. The ladies flowed in a brightly colored, chattering stream from the queen's apartments. Rosamund hung back a little, seeming to be part of the group but trying to be inconspicuous. When they reached the head of the stairs that led down to the central hall of the palace, she paused, scanning the groups of courtiers gathered below, searching for·Will. Minstrels played from the gallery above the hall, the strains of their music struggling to compete with the rise and fall of voices. Realizing the others had reached the bottom, leaving her standing conspicuously alone, she hastened down the stairs, her gaze still skimming the assembled company.

At first she was disappointed. There was no sign of him, but then through the doors that stood open to a wide terrace she caught sight of a group of younger men.

"Where's Rosamund Walsingham going?" Lettice Asherton demanded, seeing Rosamund moving towards the terrace.

"I expect she thinks she's too good for our company now that the queen has noticed her," Frances Darcy declared.

"She's only a Walsingham," one of the others put in. "Her cousin may be the queen's secretary, and there may be some distant connection with the Boleyns, but that's no reason to give herself airs."

"I don't think she really does that. She never mentions the connection," Joan offered timidly, and immediately wished she'd kept her mouth shut. Her companions looked at her with annoyance mixed with derision, then, as one, they turned their shoulders and began to chatter in an excluding undertone.

Joan's lip trembled. Things had been better for her since Rosamund's arrival and she had felt she was on the way to being accepted, but she should have known better than to have contradicted the group leaders by standing up for the outsider. Safety in this court lay both in numbers and the acceptance of one's peers. Without them one was easy prey to malice and gossip. She stood awkwardly alone on the outskirts, then forlornly followed Rosamund out to the terrace, which basked in the warm sunshine.

Rosamund had spotted Will talking with the man she now knew as Anthony Babington. She crossed the terrace willing Will to turn and acknowledge her. However, Anthony Babington saw her first. He swept his hat with a flourish as he bowed. "Mistress Walsingham, I give you good day."

Rosamund curtsied. It would seem that Master Babington had either forgotten or chosen to ignore the edge to their previous conversation about religion and power. "And I you, sir . . . Master Creighton." She smiled at Will, who bowed his own greeting, the gravity of his countenance belied by the glint in his eye and the twitch of his lips.

"A beautiful day, Mistress Walsingham."

"It is. I've a mind to stroll down to the river." She gestured to the sweep of lawn leading down to the silver glimmer of water. "I sorely missed the opportunity to go by water to Greenwich with the court."

"Then allow me to escort you, Mistress Walsingham." Anthony offered his arm.

That was not quite what Rosamund had intended, however she could hardly refuse. She accepted the arm with a smile. "Do you accompany us, Master Creighton?"

"With alacrity, ma'am." He fell in on her other side as they walked down the wide, shallow steps leading to the lawn. "I understand you have been unwell. You are better now, I trust?"

"Oh, yes, quite better, I thank you, sir. A day abed can be most restorative."

"I'm sure it can," Will agreed, a smile playing over his lips as he held out his hand to assist her down the last step onto the lawn. He invested the four words with so much undercurrent of meaning that Rosamund was hard-pressed to keep a straight face. She glanced at Babington to see if he had noticed anything, but his polite smile seemed preoccupied.

Joan stood on the terrace watching the three of them move away. Rosamund must have known she was there, and she had ignored her, too intent on keeping both her escorts to herself. It was unseemly and unfriendly, particularly when Joan had gone out of her way to introduce her to the younger members of the court who were not attendant upon the queen. She stood at the edge of the terrace watching them as they strolled to the river. Rosamund and Will were laughing, and Joan wished with all her heart that she had not introduced them. Will showed much more interest in Rosamund than he had ever shown in her, and it had been many weeks since Joan had decided that Will belonged to her, even if he didn't as yet know it.

To Rosamund's relief Anthony excused himself after a few minutes of strolling along the riverbank. "I am engaged to go coursing on the heath with some friends and they'll be sorely put out if I keep them waiting. I beg your forgiveness, Mistress Walsingham." His words were as flowery as the richly colored garlands embroidered on his sky blue doublet.

Rosamund decided to withhold judgment on Master Babington. Will had told her to steer clear of his company, a piece of advice he clearly didn't take himself, and the ferocious intensity in Babington's dark eyes made her uneasy. Sometimes he seemed to be ready to burst into flame even as the words that came out of his mouth were perfectly unobjectionable.

He walked away, leaving Rosamund and Will at long

last alone. "I have missed you," Will said simply, taking her arm. "Let's go around the bend in the bank. We're too likely to be observed here."

They walked around the curve in the bank out of sight of any wanderers from the palace. "I missed you too," Rosamund said. "It seems like such a wonderful, sensual dream now, Will. I wish we could do it again . . . when can we do it again?"

"Hush," he said softly, although his eyes said something different. "It was madness, my sweet. We mustn't let it happen again."

"Why ever not?" she exclaimed. "As I understand it, people take lovers all the time at court. 'Tis said that the queen herself has taken the Earl of Essex as her lover—"

"*Hush*," Will exclaimed again in a fierce undertone. "You'll find yourself in the Tower if you're not careful."

"But as long as one's discreet, there seems no—"

She fell silent as Will pressed a finger against her lips. "It's easier for some than for others," he said, his voice still soft, but none the less determined. "For those of us making our way in the world, as we both are, Rosamund, it's a very different matter. What is acceptable with the rich and ennobled is not for those who have a mark to make on the world."

"But you were the one who chided me for lack of courage," she said, puzzled by this apparent volte-face.

"Oh, that was for a little adventure, a little excitement, harmless really. What we did together was not harmless. You lost your virginity . . . what will happen if you conceive?"

"Well, that didn't happen. I have my monthly courses."

He pursed his lips in a silent whistle. "Then we may yet pull this coal out of the fire." He glanced around and, seeing no one, put his hands on her shoulders, looking deeply into her eyes. "Rosamund, my sweet, I would like nothing more than to love you again. But we cannot, we *cannot.*"

He sounded almost desperate in his anxiety to convince her, and, although she did not know this, even more himself. "If we are discovered, it will be the end of both of us. We will be banished from court, and . . ." He shook his head miserably. "I have no fortune, Rosamund, almost nothing to my name. My family are counting on me. They gave everything they have to give me this opportunity. I have to make my own way, and I am determined to do so."

"To marry for position and fortune, you mean." She felt cold, as if an icy draft was blowing against her back, and shivered, suddenly remembering what Joan had said about Will in those early days . . . about what a terrible flirt he was, about how just when a lady thought he was really interested in her, he dropped her like a hot brick and went on to pastures new. But surely that wasn't what was happening here. Not after what they had had between them.

Will's hands on her shoulders tightened their grip. "Is it so very hard to understand?" His voice was pleading, his eyes filled with something akin to pain, and Rosamund knew that he had not merely been playing with her.

She shook her head impatiently. "No. I understand . . . I understand the reality, but I don't see why we cannot enjoy each other discreetly until you find the wife who will bring you what you need. After all, we have had one night together, why can't we have others?"

He groaned. "Rosamund, sweetheart, think . . . think what we risk. You will lose everything if you are touched by scandal. A woman's reputation is all she has. A man can recover from scandal . . . a woman, never."

"Then isn't it for me to decide whether the risk is worth taking?"

He shook his head vigorously. "You're not thinking clearly. You don't know what it means. Listen to me, love. We can play the game, as everyone does, flirt, enjoy each other's company, but more than that . . . we *must* not. Trust me, my sweet. I know what I'm talking about."

She looked at him in silence for a minute. They were talking only of physical passion, of the impossibility of satisfying the desire they both felt so strongly. But was there more than that? Was she talking of being together, talking, laughing, as they had so often done? Sharing little conspiratorial moments of secret understanding? Were those things as dangerous, as potentially scandalous, as clandestine loving?

"Why don't you go back ahead," she said. "I'll wait here a little. Perhaps it would be best if we weren't seen returning together." She wanted him to laugh such a consideration out of court, but somehow she knew he wouldn't. He traced the curve of her cheek with his fingers, then moved away, heading quickly up to the palace.

Rosamund waited awhile, staring out at the river, watching a skirmish between two ducks, before she turned and made her own way back.

She saw Joan on the terrace as she approached and waved a hand in greeting. Joan didn't appear to see her and turned back inside.

Chapter Seventeen

ROSAMUND PAUSED ON the terrace for a moment watching a group of young courtiers who were playing bowls on the lawn below the terrace. Will had joined them. He had discarded his doublet and pushed up the sleeves of his white lawn shirt. He was poised to roll his ball, and she felt a surge of pure physical longing for the feel of his body against hers. It couldn't be possible that she would never have that again. Could it?

She bit her lip hard at the threatening prickle of tears behind her eyes and resolutely turned to go back into the hall.

The queen had come down during her absence and was enthroned in the great chair of state beneath the cloth of state on the dais at the far end. She was laughing behind her fan with the Earl of Leicester, her Master of Horse, who stood beside her, his lush white beard and mustache the only signs of his age. His soldierly posture was as erect as it had ever been on the battlefields on which he'd fought for his queen in his youth.

Rosamund moved closer to the dais, watching them with interest. Robert Dudley, Earl of Leicester, drifted at will in the tide of the queen's favor since his unsanctioned marriage. She would refuse to see him or talk to him for weeks at a time and would not permit his wife to appear at court, then suddenly she would treat him with all the loving friendship that had marked their long association, although his wife remained in exile. Rosamund knew the rumors about the long-ago love affair between the queen and the earl, but at this moment she could see only the ease and intimacy of old friends.

The crowd around Rosamund stirred and parted as a young man pushed his way through to approach the dais. He knelt before his queen, one hand on the hilt of his sword, the other holding his hat to his breast. His golden hair glowed in the sunlight. He was magnificently dressed in red velvet, the sleeves of his doublet slashed to reveal their ivory silk lining. Rosamund was close enough now to hear the conversation.

"Madam, my queen, I am come to bid you farewell."

"Why, Robert, are you to go so soon? You are only just returned to us." The queen smiled at Robert Devereux from behind her fan. "Come up, dear boy, come up." She beckoned him, and the Earl of Leicester with a pained look yielded his place beside the chair of state.

Rosamund, fascinated, inched closer without appearing to do so. The Earl of Essex had supplanted Leicester in the queen's affections it was said. And judging by Leicester's glum looks, there was some truth to it.

Essex bowed and kissed the queen's hand as she extended it to him. "I am desolated to leave you, madam, but I am wholly at your service and I obey your commands."

At this the queen frowned. "That goes without saying, my lord."

Essex went down on one knee again. "Forgive me, madam, I did not intend any impertinence. I pray you send me away with one smile that I may treasure the memory."

Elizabeth smiled again and, leaning forwards, tapped his

shoulder with her fan. "Rise up, Essex. You are pardoned. Much may be forgiven in such a remarkably pretty youth."

Essex offered a boyish smile in return. "Alas, madam, I wish I had some keepsake of my queen for my journey, something that I might look upon before I sleep."

"Oh, such flattery." She waved her fan in dismissal. Then her eye fell upon Rosamund, who was now standing close to the dais. "Ah, I have the answer. Rosamund Walsingham, approach."

Rosamund's heart pounded against her breastbone. She came up the steps to the dais, then dropped to her knees. "Yes, madam?"

"Draw me, child."

"Draw you, madam?" Rosamund felt her mouth opening and closing like a fish on a slab.

Her majesty frowned. "That is what I said. You shall do a miniature that my loyal servant, the Earl of Essex, may carry next to his heart and look upon before he sleeps."

It seemed simple enough, but Rosamund could feel the eyes of the court upon her as she knelt. "I have neither paper nor pen, madam." She kept her eyes on the hem of the queen's silver gauze gown as she spoke.

The queen turned her head and beckoned to one of her gentlemen. "Find Mistress Walsingham the necessary tools for her task, Gerald."

The gentleman bowed and left. Rosamund remained kneeling, unsure what to do next.

"Rise, child." Elizabeth sounded a little impatient. "You may sit on that stool to do your drawing." She gestured to a three-legged stool in the corner of the dais. "Find the place where you will have the best view of my profile. The right side."

"Yes, madam." Rosamund stood and surveyed the scene. The queen's chair was in the center of the dais, her gentlemen grouped around her. She fetched the stool, chose a perch a little to the right, and said hesitantly, "Would it be possible, madam, to ask the gentlemen to move to the other side of your chair?"

"Go away . . . go away, all of you. Give Mistress Rosamund an uninterrupted view." The queen waved a hand and the gentlemen all stepped aside. "Now, child, will this do?" She set her head, twitched her lips into the merest hint of a smile.

"You look magnificent, madam." Rosamund found the words tripped easily off her tongue. *Magnificent* was a good word to describe the queen's attire. Her gown of silver gauze had sleeves slashed with crimson taffeta. The square bodice was cut very low, and a great chain of rubies and pearls drew the eye perforce to the swell of her breasts.

Too much accuracy there would be a mistake, Rosamund decided. Her majesty would not be best pleased to have the wrinkles delineated on the sagging flesh. She would be safest concentrating on the high-standing collar that rose behind the queen's neck, its lining studded with myriad tiny pearls and rubies, and the thick curls of her red-gold wig that hung down to her shoulders.

The gentleman returned with a japanned standish containing vellum, quill, and ink. Rosamund thanked him and arranged her materials. She was aware of what felt like a thousand eyes upon her and for an instant was unable to move, paralyzed by anxiety. What would happen to someone whose drawing of the queen failed to give satisfaction? What if the queen considered herself ill-drawn, unflatteringly so? She could spend the rest of her life in the Tower.

Concentrate, she told herself firmly. *Look at her as if she were any other subject.* A butterfly on a flower, a haymaker in a field. The nose was a dominant feature, particularly in profile. The eyes were a good beginning, black and sparkling. Ignore the teeth, the few that she had were black.

Rosamund began to sketch her outline. She knew there would be no opportunity to redo this portrait, so every stroke must be true. The queen sat still for the most part, but she would occasionally pass some remark with Essex or one of her councilors, and Rosamund used those interludes to imagine her subject as her subject wished herself to be portrayed. She had to be careful, though. Too much dissembling and it would look like a mockery. The queen needed to look like herself, but with the glaring faults of age diminished.

After a while, Rosamund's audience grew bored with the spectacle and she began to relax. She was only vaguely aware of Sir Francis Walsingham's arrival on the dais. By then she no longer needed to study her subject. She had committed what she needed to memory.

"Well, Mistress Walsingham, are you not finished yet?"

The queen's voice broke the spell. Rosamund looked at her sketch before answering, then she made a tiny adjustment to the neck, softening it with a touch of shading. "I believe so, madam."

"Well, bring it here." The queen's voice was as impatient as a child's for a toy. "Let us see it."

Rosamund stood up, smoothing down her skirt, and approached the chair of state. She curtsied, proffering the sketch. Then stepped back. Oddly she was not afraid of what Elizabeth might think. It was good, Rosamund knew it. If the queen didn't care for it, then there was little to be done. She had been careful to diminish any unflattering angles, had concentrated on the strength of the features, and had made the most of the jewels.

Elizabeth examined the portrait, then passed it to Essex. "Well, Essex, what do you think?"

"Magnificent, madam. A most accurate portrait of a most majestic and beautiful monarch." He bowed, his hand on his heart.

Hypocrite, Rosamund thought. Essex had eyes, he must have seen what she had avoided. But she supposed she couldn't blame him. Their queen was one of the vainest women on earth.

"Francis, what think you of your protégée's skill?" Elizabeth turned to her secretary of state.

Walsingham took the drawing from Essex and examined it, head on one side. He shot Rosamund a quick, comprehending glance in which she detected approval, before he handed it back to his sovereign. "Masterly, madam. She has you to the life."

"I will treasure it, my queen." Essex took back the paper and folded it carefully, inserting it within his doublet. "And now I am for Ireland on your majesty's service."

"Go with God, Essex." The queen gave him her hand to kiss. He left the dais, and Rosamund after a moment decided that she had been forgotten and slipped back down the steps into the anonymity of the hall.

"You have an uncommon skill, Mistress Rosamund."

She turned abruptly to see the chevalier watching her from a few paces away. "How . . . how could you know that, sir?" She stammered slightly. The unexpected sight of him had thrown her off course. She had forgotten all about him in the heated delights of her time with Will, but now the full flood of memory returned and she was back in the clearing, the chevalier's lips pressed to hers. His eyes were dancing as if he could read her mind.

"Your sketch pleased the queen. Therefore you must

have an uncommon talent." A smile flickered across his eyes. "You were not at Greenwich yesterday?"

"No, I was indisposed." Rosamund had the familiar sensation of playing with fire, and the familiar thrill in the play.

Arnaud stepped closer. "I'm glad to see you have recovered, *ma fleur.*"

The endearment caressed her, his eyes seemed to delve into her innermost self, and the crowded hall seemed to become distant, leaving them standing alone in their own space. "Shall we walk a little?" He held out his hand. He still wore a bandage over the almost healed wound on his forearm, but the white cloth was tightly wrapped and well concealed beneath his shirt and the closely fitted sleeve of his turquoise and silver satin doublet.

Rosamund hesitated. How could she feel so drawn to this man when all her feelings were inextricably linked with Will?

"Come." His voice was softly insistent and she was about to put her hand in his when Lady Leinster emerged from the faceless throng, taking shape and substance as she stepped up to them, resplendent in a gown of ivory damask opened over a gold underskirt, crimson undersleeves embroidered with jet. Her eyes were deepest purple in the candlelit hall, and a jeweled headdress set far back from her forehead set off the richly luxuriant blue-black lights in her hair.

"My dear Rosamund . . . Arnaud. Do I interrupt?"

"How could you, *ma chère* Agathe?" Arnaud casually moved the hand that Rosamund had been about to take and took Agathe's hand instead. He bowed, raising it to his lips. "There isn't a moment in the day that is not enhanced by your presence."

"You have such a sweet tongue." Laughing, she tapped his arm with her closed fan. "Be careful, Rosamund. Arnaud could charm the bees from the hive."

"I don't doubt it, Agathe." Rosamund's light laugh concealed a disappointment strongly mingling with relief at this interruption. "But if one enjoys the game, then one can only appreciate a superb player."

"Oh, beautifully said, my dear." Agathe nodded her approval. "What think you, Arnaud? Mistress Rosamund is learning our little ways remarkably quickly for one so new to court."

"Indeed," he agreed, looking between them. They were so different, yet each had a most powerful allure. "And with two such beautiful women, what is a man to do but retire defeated by beauty and wit." He bowed and moved away, wondering why Agathe had moved in like that. Had she seen . . . intuited . . . something he had missed? Or had it simply been impulse? She was not a jealous woman. She had certainly never given him reason to think so, and she would never do anything to spoil a conquest for him.

Agathe watched him go. He had not seen Will Creighton's gaze so fiercely fixed upon him as he talked with Rosamund. The hunger in the younger man's eyes spoke volumes to the more experienced Agathe. She had seen Will and Rosamund together at the picnic, had seen them wander off to the other side of the hill, and had watched them return. At first she had thought it was simply two attractive young courtiers taking advantage of the relaxed atmosphere, but now she was not so sure it was that simple. Arnaud would certainly not like the idea of being in competition with such a green and relatively insignificant young courtier, and if Creighton chose to confront the chevalier, it would be an ugly scene.

Will was approaching them, threading his way through the crowd. "Lady Leinster, Mistress Walsingham." He bowed as he reached them. Perspiration still glowed on his forehead from the game of bowls. He glanced up at the dais, saying with a smile, "You seem to have pleased her majesty, Mistress Rosamund. What did she wish you to do for her?"

"She wished me to make a drawing of her . . . a portrait for Lord Essex to keep next to his heart on his mission to Ireland," she returned, keeping her tone lightly conversational.

"Of course," he said. "I was forgetting about your uncommon artistic talent." Of course he'd only seen it displayed in relation to the theatre, but Lady Leinster was not to know that.

"Indeed," Agathe said. "It's a talent you keep well hidden, Rosamund. One should not, in this court, hide one's light under any bushels." She gave her musical trill of laughter. "Believe me, my dear, it's every man and woman for themselves here, and whatever will make you noticed must be cultivated. . . . If you'll excuse me, I see Lady Markham beckoning to me." She bestowed a smile between them and walked away.

"Lady Leinster gives good advice." Will's gaze flickered across Rosamund's countenance. "You seemed to be very engaged with the Chevalier de Vaugiras earlier. I didn't realize you were so closely acquainted with him."

To her chagrin Rosamund felt herself blush. "Indeed I am not. Lady Leinster introduced us, and I have some occasional conversation with him. I would not count him a close acquaintance by any means." That was not exactly a lie, she reflected. She certainly didn't feel a close friendship with the chevalier despite the stolen kisses. He affected her most powerfully, it was true, but not in the comfortable way one would associate with friendship. Nothing at all was comfortable about being in the chevalier's company, there was too much dangerous excitement for comfort. And that of course was exactly where his power lay.

Will frowned, sensing something wrong with her denial . . . and why would she deny it anyway? She had every right to be acquainted with de Vaugiras, every right to enjoy a little dalliance with such an accomplished courtier. He himself had no rights, particularly after what he had said to her down by the river. But she looked almost guilty.

Rosamund averted her gaze from the puzzled question in Will's. She looked to the dais again and caught Master Secretary's eye. Sir Francis crooked a finger at her.

"My cousin summons me," she said with ill-concealed relief. "Excuse me, Will." She pushed her way to the steps to the dais where Francis came down to her. "A word in private," he said in his curt fashion. "Follow me."

Rosamund followed him through a narrow door next to the grand staircase. It led into a small antechamber, little bigger than a closet.

"You pleased the queen this afternoon. It is good," he stated without preamble. "You must keep in her favor if you've a mind to make a decent match for yourself."

Rosamund hesitated before saying, "Forgive me, Sir Francis, but how am I to make a match without a dowry?"

She was afraid he would be offended, but instead he nodded. "That is a difficulty, I agree. But if you keep the queen's favor, and she approves a match for you, then she may well be persuaded to make you a wedding present."

"But not if she doesn't approve the match," Rosamund said slowly.

Her cousin's expression darkened. "If the queen does

not approve the match, it will not be made. Don't ever imagine for one minute that you will be left to make your own choice in such a matter. Her majesty disposes of her ladies as she chooses. If you keep her favor, she may well agree to keep you at court after your marriage. Something devoutly to be hoped for."

Rosamund wondered if this devout hope was for her own sake, or his, because she could continue to work for him. She wasn't at all sure she hoped to remain a maid of honor, married or unmarried, for the rest of her existence. But she knew that once appointed she served at the queen's pleasure. It was not for her to decide when that service should end.

"You understand, Rosamund?"

"I understand, sir."

"Good. Well, as I said, you are doing well and the queen is pleased. Have you any further sketches for me?"

"I have several, sir, but nothing of significance, I believe."

"I will be the judge of that. Fetch them for me, I'll await you here."

Rosamund hurried to get the sheaf of sketches from the chest in the dorter, reflecting that she should have known better than to offer any opinion to Master Secretary. She returned in a few minutes to the antechamber, where her cousin awaited her, impatiently drumming his fingers on a small inlaid table. Rosamund handed over the papers with a curtsy.

Francis riffled through them, a deep frown corrugating his brow as he absorbed the subjects. One in particular caught his eye. He examined it closely, his frown deepening, then he folded it and tucked it inside his doublet. The rest he handed back to Rosamund, saying sharply, "Why were you not with the court at Greenwich? I had some work for you to do there. The atmosphere is more relaxed and people are not always on their guard. I was interested in capturing the movements and exchanges of Châteauneuf, the French ambassador. But you were not there."

"I was unwell, sir. I kept to my bed."

Sir Francis frowned. "That was unfortunate. Try not to let it happen again."

As if I would have any choice in the matter if my sickness had been genuine. Rosamund said merely, "I will do my best, sir."

He grunted and turned to the door. "By the way, Lady Walsingham has requested that you visit her on Wednesday afternoon, three days hence. Lady Shrewsbury has given leave. I will send a litter for you."

"Could I not ride, sir? My horse is in the royal mews."

He shrugged his angular shoulders. "It matters not to me. Thomas must escort you. You will be ready to leave at three o'clock."

Rosamund curtsied and said to his departing back, "I haven't seen Thomas at court since I arrived."

"You'll see him in three days." The words drifted over his shoulder as he left.

Rosamund looked through the drawings, wondering which one had interested her cousin sufficiently for him to abstract it. But she couldn't remember what sketches had been there in the first place. She was always drawing, from memory as well as from life, following her instructions to the letter. Anything, any individual, any time, was grist to her mill and by definition Master Secretary's.

At this moment, Thomas Walsingham was in the north, in the village of Chartley, talking with a brewer on the ale bench outside the tavern. Robin Poley listened to the conversation, one hand circling his tankard, the other idly flicking at his boots with his riding whip. Nothing that was being said was news to him.

"The deliveries are every Friday, sir," the brewer was saying. "I takes fresh kegs in an' brings out the empty ones."

"And it is possible to create a hiding place in the bung of one of the kegs?" Thomas twisted to pick up the ale jug behind him and winced as the movement pulled at the newly healed sword scratch across his ribs. It was a shallow enough wound and had bled little, but it was still sore. He harbored the vicious hope that de Vaugiras had contracted an infection in the cut Thomas had inflicted on his forearm.

"Aye, Master Walsingham, sir." The brewer reached into his britches pocket and took out a small leather pouch. "This 'ere, see, can be inserted easy enough before the cork goes in. It's been pitch-tarred to keep out the wet." He dipped it into the rain barrel standing beside the ale bench, lifting it out to show how the water ran off. "An' then the barrels come out, or go in on my drays, and no one need be the wiser."

"Not quite no one," Poley murmured with a soft chuckle. "You have talked with Paulet, Thomas?"

"Aye, he's ready for our good honest man here to play postman."

"That I'll do right readily." The brewer tugged at his cap. "As a good honest servant of her majesty, Queen Elizabeth."

"You are indeed an honest man," Thomas declared. "The queen will not forget your service." Even as he promised this, he doubted its truth. The queen would not want to know anything about this clever trap for traitors and her queen cousin.

The man stood up. "Well, I'll be leavin' you gentlemen to your work. Send word when I'm to start." He strode off out of the yard.

"Salt of the earth," Poley murmured with a touch of sarcasm.

Thomas merely raised his tankard and drained it. "Without men such as he, Poley, we'd be hard-pressed to keep the realm safe. Mark my words, this listening device will bring this troublesome matter of state to an end. I go to Paulet now."

"And I to good Queen Mary." Robin uncurled himself from the bench. "Paulet has given permission for her to take the air for half an hour a day in the orchard. There is a brick in the wall that can be pried loose and we whisper through it, a veritable Pyramus and Thisbe." He laughed without mirth. "Sometimes I can find it in my heart to feel sorry for the lady. She has no idea how she is beset at every turn."

"Your sympathies are misplaced, Poley," Thomas said curtly, rising and settling his sword more comfortably on his hip. "I return to London in the morning. You?"

"I have our master's instructions to assist in the encouragement of Babington. Will Creighton is doing well enough, but Master Secretary wishes to close any possible breaches in the wall."

Thomas nodded. The two shook hands and parted company. Thomas rode to the imposing front door of Chartley Hall and was greeted as an honored guest by Sir Amyas Paulet. Robin Poley took the lane that led to the far edge of Chartley Hall property.

Mary Stuart was walking in the orchard, her ladies accompanying her, the little Skye terrier bounding ahead, rooting in the undergrowth. The day was warm and dry and Mary felt the sun warming her bones, easing the ague that plagued her year-round. She was reading aloud from her book of psalms as she walked, relishing the words on her tongue, the comfort of their familiarity. But her steps were deliberate, taking her to the far corner of the orchard. Her ladies followed at a discreet distance, talking softly among themselves.

"I pray that there will be some hope for our lady today," Charlotte murmured. "Every day for the last two weeks she has come to the wall and been disappointed."

"God's son will bring her comfort," one of her companions said, making the sign of the cross.

"If he doesn't, there is no one else to provide," Charlotte said rather tartly. She paused as Mary reached the wall at the end of the orchard. "Stay back." The other women took a step back and they all waited under the trees, watching as Mary stepped up to the wall.

"Master Poley?" Mary whispered, not daring to hope that he would be there, but her heart lifted as a brick slid out, leaving a gap.

"Madam, I am here. Are you well?"

"As well as may be, Master Poley. What news?"

"Listen well, madam. We have established a safe means of communication between you and your supporters. It is impregnable."

Mary leaned in closer, her ear close to the gap in the wall, as she listened. "Every Friday, you say?"

"Rain or shine, madam. The brewer is a most loyal Catholic and loves your majesty dearly. He will ensure the safe delivery of all correspondence."

"My maid Barbara, she will act as go-between. She will secrete my letters in the pouch in the keg and will retrieve the others. Her presence in the buttery will draw no remark."

Mary's voice was stronger now, filled with hope. So often hopes had been dashed during her long imprisonment, but always someone had come to her aid with a fresh plan. "My dear Thomas Morgan in Paris works tirelessly on my behalf. Does he know of this secure means of communication?"

"I have written of it myself, madam. He has not yet replied, but the courier is a most trusted subject of your majesty, and I expect him to return with a reply any day now."

Mary leaned her forehead for a moment against the rough brick wall. She wanted to believe this, but experience warned her to be careful. "Are you certain, Master Poley, that this is impregnable?"

"As certain as 'tis possible to be, madam. The brewer is your most devoted friend. As long as you can ensure that your maid is both discreet and clever in the depositing and retrieval of the pouch, no one will have any idea."

"And how soon will this mail delivery begin?"

"From now, madam. Make sure your maid checks the kegs every Friday from now on. Should you wish to send to your supporters, here is the pouch to be used."

Mary took the little leather pouch that was pushed through the wall. She examined it carefully before saying, "Thank you, my friend. I wish I could reward your loyalty and devotion."

"Your safety and the success of our enterprise is all the reward I need, madam." Robin slid the brick back.

Mary tucked the pouch into the pocket of her skirt and walked back to where her ladies remained on the path.

Chapter Eighteen

LETTICE ASHERTON WAS alone in the dorter changing her stockings. A hole in the heel was causing a painful blister, and Lady Shrewsbury would not look sympathetically upon a hobbling maid of honor. She had only three pairs of stockings and examined the hole with a rueful grimace. It was almost too big to darn, but it would probably survive one more mending. She sat on a stool and eased the clean stocking over her foot.

The click of the door latch startled her and she glanced over her shoulder. A young maidservant came in carrying the chamber pots that she had emptied that morning. She curtsied. "Your pardon, madam. I didn't know anyone was 'ere."

"I won't be in a minute," Lettice said carelessly, taking up the second stocking.

The girl bent to push the chamber pots beneath the beds. "Is the young lady what was supposed to be sick better now?" she ventured from beneath Joan and Rosamund's bed.

"Who was that?" Lettice looked over at her.

"The young lady what was supposed to be in this bed when you all went to Greenwich." The girl backed out. "I was told to look in on 'er a couple o' times, bring 'er some food. I brought milk an' cheese, but she weren't 'ere. An' when I looked in again, she still weren't 'ere and the food not touched." She stood up, brushing a lank lock of hair from her perspiring forehead. "Ain't it 'ot in 'ere."

"Yes," agreed Lettice impatiently. "When did she come back?"

"Never, not while I was lookin'. . . . Will that be all, madam?"

"Yes . . . no, get rid of those cobwebs in that corner. They've gone black with age. Aren't you supposed to keep this place clean?"

The girl curtsied and hurried to deal with the offending cobwebs. Lettice fastened her garters and with a tiny little smile left the dorter, returning to the queen's chamber.

Her majesty was working on a tapestry, talking softly with the Countess of Shrewsbury and Lady Pembroke while a young minstrel, seated on the wide window seat behind them, plucked a lute to accompany a sweetly youthful voice:

> *Doubt you to whom my muse these songs intendeth,*
> *Which now my breast, o'ercharged, to music lendeth?*
> *To you, to you, all song of praise is due;*
> *Only in you my song begins and endeth.*

"Sidney . . . such a poet," Elizabeth said. "A poet and a soldier. A goodly combination, I think."

"Sir Walter Raleigh is also blessed with both talents," Lady Pembroke said.

The queen smiled. "My dear Raleigh, such a gallant gentleman." She looked up from her tapestry. "Rosamund, have you a picture in your head of Sir Walter Raleigh?"

"Yes, madam."

"Then do me a likeness."

"Yes, madam." Rosamund took a fresh sheet of paper.

Lettice leaned across to Frances Darcy. "Such airs. Who does she think she is? But I know something rather interesting about Madam Favorite. There's rather more to Mistress Rosamund than meets the eye."

"What?" Frances leaned forward, her sharp eyes bright with interest.

Lettice put a finger to her lips and whispered, "Later. In the dorter."

Rosamund was overjoyed to find her brother waiting for her in the royal mews at three o'clock that afternoon, holding Jenny's reins.

Thomas dismounted and embraced her warmly. "Are you well, little sister?"

"Well enough," she returned, lifting her face for his kiss. "All the better for seeing you." She buried her nose in the mare's mane, stroking the velvety nose. "I cannot thank you enough, Thomas, for paying for Jenny's keep in the mews here."

Thomas made a wry face. "I had little choice, but I count the expense as little if it brings my sister pleasure."

She turned her head against the mare's neck to smile at her brother. "Such gallantry. But what of you, Thomas? Where have you been these last weeks?"

"Oh, around and about." He shrugged. "I roam far and wide on our master's business."

"To France?"

"Questions are unwise, my dear girl. And answers even more so. Come, mount up. Lady Walsingham awaits you most eagerly."

Rosamund mounted and settled into the saddle with a wonderful feeling of freedom. She reflected on how very different she was now from the virginal young girl who had ridden with such excitement and such hopes to London. She glanced covertly at her brother as they rode side by side out of the mews. Thomas could never imagine the change in his little sister. At least, she amended with a secret grin, he had better not be able to.

"There are to be other guests at dinner," Thomas informed her. "You would be well advised, Rosamund, to show off your courtly manners. That is, if you've acquired any," he added with a chuckle. "Although I must say in that gown there's little left of the scapegrace I used to think you."

"Lady Walsingham has been most kind," Rosamund said. "She had two of her own court gowns remade for me and refurbished my other day gowns. And this gown arrived for me just the other day." She ran a hand over the turquoise taffeta skirt, adjusting the position of her bent knee over the pommel of the side saddle. "It is most elegant. But I am in sore need of stockings, Thomas, and no money to buy them."

Thomas grimaced but said, "I'll see what I can do. Edmund should be providing for you, but even if he can be pried from between the thighs of his latest harlot, I doubt he'll be sober enough even to see me, let alone part with so much as a groat."

"Well, if you can persuade him to do so, I need another pair of shoes also."

Thomas shook his head. "I can but try."

Rosamund let the matter drop. She had no more confidence in Edmund's honoring his brotherly obligations than did Thomas, but Thomas, if she didn't nag at him, might well feel a prod of conscience. "So who are the other guests, do you know?"

He glanced sideways at her, a curiously speculative

glance. "Oh, a simple enough group. Lady Sidney, Sir Francis's daughter, is to be present, I believe, and my friend Thomas Watson. And Sir Roger Askew, an old friend of Sir Francis and Lady Walsingham."

Rosamund frowned. "I do not think I have heard his name before. Is he at court?"

"He was with Sir Philip in the Low Countries until very recently. His wife died in childbed during his absence, and he's been attending to matters on his estate in Shropshire since his return. He is but newly arrived in London. I am sure he will attend at court. The queen looks kindly upon him."

Thomas rattled off the details in careless fashion, but Rosamund's curiosity was piqued. "Does he also acknowledge Sir Francis as his master?"

"Why would you think that?"

She shrugged. "For two reasons. Firstly because it seems to me that almost everyone known to you, Thomas, is in some way involved with Master Secretary's secret service. And secondly Sir Francis is always working. I doubt he would invite guests to his table who were not in some way connected to that work. It would be a waste of his time."

"Once again, little sister, I will tell you that questions are as unwise as answers."

"Then I will draw my own conclusions." She smiled to herself. She really didn't need Thomas's affirmation of her suspicions. "Is Master Marlowe to be there?"

"I don't believe so. How goes it with your fellow maids of honor?"

"I confess I don't much care for their company, except for Joan Davenport. But fortunately one is not obliged to be in that company for too many hours in the day. And I do find court life immensely diverting at times."

Thomas glanced at her with a touch of suspicion. "Not too diverting, I trust. You are here to find a husband, don't forget. Once you have one, your status will change immediately even if you continue to serve the queen in your present position. No one will trouble you as a married lady."

"Except for the husband."

Thomas gave her a hard look. "You must learn to curb your tongue, miss. If you say things like that in company, you will ruin yourself. This evening you must be especially careful."

Rosamund didn't argue. She had no intention of letting her tongue loose at the Walsingham dinner table.

When they reached Walsingham's mansion on Seething Lane, Thomas helped Rosamund dismount and gave the horses into the charge of the groom who had accompanied them. They were shown immediately into the large apartment that Rosamund knew was used when nonfamily guests were invited.

Lady Walsingham came forward to greet them, embracing Rosamund warmly. "I have sorely missed your company, my dear. Let me look at you." She stood back, surveying the girl. "The gown becomes you very well. I'm so glad. Now you must come and meet my daughter, Lady Sidney." She drew Rosamund towards a tall, rather angular young woman, somewhat older than Rosamund.

Rosamund curtsied. "Lady Sidney, I'm so happy to meet you. Lady Walsingham has told me much about you."

"Only good things I trust." Frances Sidney had her mother's warm smile. "And indeed, my mother has been singing your praises."

Rosamund murmured something suitably modest and acknowledged Thomas Watson's bow with a demure curtsy. "You are already known to Master Watson, I understand," Lady Walsingham said. "But not I believe to our old friend, Sir Roger Askew."

Rosamund made her curtsy, keeping her eyes lowered, raising them only as she rose from her obeisance. Sir Roger, dressed in rich black velvet slashed with silver damask, was tall and held himself erect with the posture of a soldier, a posture accentuated by the very modest ruff at his sun-browned throat. He had, of course, been in the Low Countries with Sir Philip, so presumably he had seen battle. His dark brown hair was thick and slightly curly, a frivolity that seemed at odds with the gravity of his gray eyes and the rather stern set of his mouth. Not so much stern, she thought, as saddened. Perhaps his marriage had been a love match.

"Mistress Walsingham, I am honored." He bowed over her hand and she noticed the single emerald on his finger. An understated gentleman. He had the air of an elder statesman and she thought he must be more than thirty years of age. Almost in his dotage, although apart from the solemnity of his expression he didn't look particularly elderly.

"I bid you welcome, Rosamund." Sir Francis nodded at her with his usual lack of expression and she curtsied demurely.

"Let us go to table." Lady Walsingham walked to the door. "Rosamund, I have placed you beside Sir Roger. Master Watson, you will be seated beside Lady Sidney."

They took their places and dishes began to appear on the long board. It was a lavish feast, more so than Rosamund remembered from her days as houseguest, and she wondered in whose honor the roast swan and the glazed leg of kid were presented. There were greens cooked in almond milk and a rich oyster stew, all accompanied by asparagus and mushrooms in butter. The wine flowed copiously and she thought how merry Kit Marlowe would have been. Too merry for *this* company certainly. She couldn't suppress a smile as the words of one of his raunchier songs came to mind.

"Something amuses you, Mistress Walsingham?"

She turned to her neighbor. "Oh, just a memory, Sir Roger. The words of a song."

"Oh, pray share them."

Her cheeks warmed and she said hastily, "I cannot remember them very well."

He looked at her with a half smile. "I think you prevaricate, mistress."

The smile was somehow reassuring and it lightened his somber expression. She confessed, "In truth, sir, the words are not suitable for dinner-table company," and waited to see how he would react.

His eyebrows lifted. "Do you keep tavern company, then?"

"No, sir." Rosamund managed to inject a degree of indignation into the fib. "But sometimes it's difficult not to overhear the stable boys, particularly in the country."

"Doubtless" was his only response, but then he smiled again, deftly changing the subject. "You are at court, I understand, attending upon the queen."

She nodded, pushing a mushroom around her plate with her three-pronged fork. "It's still very new to me."

"And not much to your liking?" he hazarded, leaning forward to slice meat from the leg of kid with his knife. He put a slice on her plate before taking some for himself.

"Some of the time I like it very well, sir." She left it at that and forked the meat into her mouth. She chewed and swallowed. "How was your time in the Low Countries, Sir Roger? You accompanied Sir Philip Sidney I believe."

He accepted the new direction without hesitation. "The Spanish must be driven from there, their persecutions are appalling. The Inquisition is in every town and its spies are in every hamlet." His voice was passionate, although he still spoke as quietly as before. "We *must* prevail for the sake of the people."

"And surely more importantly to keep the Spanish from establishing a foothold so close to our shores. It would be easier to launch an invasion from the Low Countries than from Spain." Rosamund had put her time acting as the queen's amanuensis to good purpose, her ears attuned to every conversation. The members of the queen's council had frequently discussed the Spanish threat from the Low Countries.

"That is certainly the short-term aim. But I believe the human issue of rescuing a population from persecution to be of greater importance."

"Have you seen any plays at court, Mistress Walsingham?" Thomas Watson, sitting opposite, leaned across the table, his knife point poised to capture a piece of roast swan on the dish in front of him.

Rosamund welcomed the interruption. "Not as yet, Master Watson. There was a play performed by the Earl of Leicester's company at Greenwich last week, but unfortunately I was unable to attend."

"You enjoy the play then, Mistress Walsingham?"

Rosamund turned back to her neighbor, her eyes shining. "Of all things, Sir Roger. I would attend every night if it were possible."

"I daresay traveling companies put on entertainments for your family in the country. Tell me what it is about the plays that you enjoy so much."

Rosamund needed no second invitation. She launched into a vivid description of the plays that she had seen, of the magic of the words, the wonder of the fights and the comedy, the ingeniousness of the plots. Only when she fell silent, aware that everyone around the table was regarding her in some astonishment, did she realize that she had given herself away. Only someone who had frequented the public theatre on more than one occasion could have launched into such a detailed rhapsody.

She dropped her eyes to the table in confusion. Sir Francis knew she had attended, as did her brother and Master Watson, but the two ladies and her present neighbor would have had no idea.

"You have a most vivid imagination, Mistress Walsingham," said Lady Sidney, coming to her rescue. "You make me long for the experience myself. Next time there is to be a play at court, I am determined to attend."

"Yes, indeed," murmured her mother, still regarding Rosamund with a degree of bewilderment.

"You paint a most detailed picture, mistress." Sir Roger smiled but his eyes looked askance.

"Rosamund has a great talent with pen and parchment," Sir Francis said drily. "She can render the most accurate portraits or scenes entirely from memory. Her brother is a devoted patron of the theatre, and I daresay she augmented her own childhood experience with Thomas's descriptions of the scenes in the public theatre that he has particularly enjoyed. Eh, Rosamund?"

"Yes, sir." Rosamund reached for her wine cup and drank deeply. She caught her brother's eye, and he didn't look best pleased.

Somehow dinner was completed with no further disasters. Rosamund kept her remarks to the most anodyne, and her neighbor seemed content to turn his attention to others around the table.

At last Lady Walsingham rose. "I'm sure you gentlemen have business to discuss, so we shall leave you. Come, Francis, Rosamund."

The ladies left the dining parlor and Ursula led the way to the intimacy of her own private apartment. Bowls of roses scented the air and the windows were open to the garden and the soft summer-evening air. Ursula took her usual chair and picked up her embroidery frame. Her daughter sat down and retrieved a tambour frame. "Rosamund, my dear, if you wish to draw, there are drawing materials on the table as usual. I know that you do not enjoy needlework." Ursula's smile was serene.

Rosamund thanked her and took a seat at the table as she had done so often in the past. She had wondered if Ursula would question her further about her theatrical knowledge, but it seemed that Lady Wal-singham was prepared to let sleeping dogs lie. Her husband had made it abundantly clear that he knew all about it and had raised no objection. It was not for her to question her lord's decisions.

"Sir Roger is such a charming man," Frances observed, setting her stitches with great precision. "Did you not think so, Mistress Walsingham?"

"Most charming. But he seemed sad to me. I understand he lost his wife in childbed recently."

"Last year," Ursula said. "It was a great loss, there was great affection between them."

"Did the child survive?" Rosamund glanced up from her sketch.

"No, he was born too early." Lady Walsingham sighed. "'Tis so often the case."

She glanced wistfully at her daughter. Frances had been married to Sir Philip for almost three years and so far there had been no hints of a pregnancy. Of course with Philip governing Flushing, in the Netherlands, there was no present opportunity for conception. He had been adamant that his wife not accompany him, maintaining that the Spanish threat to the Low Countries made it too dangerous. Ursula kept to herself the wish that her daughter had stood against her husband. But of course Frances was too well schooled in a wife's rightful place to argue with her husband. And who other than her mother was to blame for that?

"It is indeed very sad," Frances said tranquilly. "I find him a most sympathetic man."

"He must marry again, and soon," Ursula said, returning to her needlework. "He will make a good husband." She paused, then continued, "I do not believe he is interested in a woman's fortune, since he has ample of his own."

Something in her voice made Rosamund look up again. But Ursula was continuing placidly with her sewing.

When Thomas came to fetch Rosamund to escort her home, Lady Walsingham and Frances both kissed her affectionately.

"I hope to see you at court soon, Rosamund." Frances pressed her hand. "I must wait upon the queen in the next day or two."

"I look forward to it." Rosamund smiled, grateful for this genuine offer of friendship. She couldn't imagine Frances Sidney engaging in the malicious backbiting of the other ladies-in-waiting.

Sir Francis and his two other dinner guests were not in evidence as she left the house with Thomas. "Where are Master Watson and Sir Roger?" she asked as Thomas helped her mount Jenny.

"With Sir Francis, talking business." He swung onto his horse. "What did you think of Sir Roger?"

"He seemed pleasant enough." Rosamund frowned. There seemed to be rather a lot of interest in her reaction to Sir Roger Askew. "Why do you ask?"

He didn't look at her as they rode side by side, the groom following. "He is a widower in search of a wife. He is somewhat in Sir Francis's debt for some past favors, and he's not overly particular about a dowry."

Rosamund's eyes widened. "Does he look for a wife in Seething Lane?" she asked carefully.

"Perhaps." Her brother looked at her now in the waning light of evening. "You would do well to consider your position, Sister. Edmund will do nothing for you, and I certainly can't. Sir Francis is offering you the chance to establish yourself. Askew is wealthy enough not to need a rich wife. He's a solid Protestant with good connections, the queen looks favorably upon him, and if you're fortunate enough that he takes an interest in you, and the queen is pleased to agree to such a marriage, then you should be on your knees with gratitude."

Rosamund stared at a point between Jenny's ears, feeling suddenly overwhelmed. She was learning to enjoy the manifold pleasures of dalliance and clandestine liaisons, and now a potential husband was in the offing, not just the remote possibility at some point in the future, but a real man, right now. She couldn't begin to unravel her feelings, but knew that she must somehow delay this.

"Thomas, he's old and he's a widower." It was a feeble protest but she had to make some kind of rational objection.

"Old? I doubt he's even five and thirty," Thomas scoffed. "He's hale and hearty, in the prime of life. Did you not consider him well-favored?"

"Well enough," she was obliged to admit. "There is nothing objectionable in his appearance. But I do not *know* him, Thomas."

"That will be remedied in good time." They were approaching the palace now and Thomas let the subject drop as they rode into the mews. He escorted his sister inside, parting company with her at the bottom of the stairs leading to the dorter. "Rosamund, do not look this gift horse in the mouth. Sir Francis has worked this on your behalf. I know how headstrong you are, but I tell you, if Sir Roger is willing to marry you, it will be the greatest good fortune. If you refuse, you will offend Sir Francis and do yourself irreparable harm. Have a care."

Rosamund nodded and was for an instant tempted to tell her brother the truth. But it was only an instant. Thomas might seem sympathetic, but he would never act against his own self-interest. If he could help his sister without damaging his own cause, then he would do so with the careless amusement he brought to so much of his life. But let her do anything to damage him and he would abandon her in the blink of an eye. She didn't hold it against him. It was the way he had always been.

"I understand. Good night, Thomas."

He looked relieved. "Good girl." He kissed her forehead. "Sleep well. I understand the court is to remove to Greenwich for several months during the heat of the summer. There is rumor of plague in the city and Whitehall needs cleaning." His smile was cajoling as he lifted her chin on his forefinger. "Life is much pleasanter at Greenwich, you will see. There will be plays and hawking parties, dancing and picnics on the river. The queen takes more leisure at Greenwich."

Rosamund smiled. "It sounds delightful. I own it will be good to have a change of scene." She ran up the stairs, pausing halfway up to blow him a farewell kiss.

Thomas, relieved that his sister had not proved difficult,

went off in search of congenial company. If this marriage could be secured for Rosamund, it would be an enormous weight off his shoulders. Legally he was not responsible for his little sister's welfare, that lay with Edmund, but he had always been fond of her and in some way recognized a kindred spirit. Like himself Rosamund chose the path less trod.

Rosamund paused outside the door to the dorter listening to the rise and fall of voices within. She knew that no one would acknowledge her when she entered the chamber. The conversation would continue, shoulders would be turned, and it would be as if she didn't exist.

With a sigh, she braced her shoulders and lifted the latch.

She had been wrong. The minute she walked in, all conversation stopped and everyone looked at her. Only Joan looked away.

Chapter Nineteen

ROSAMUND STOOD NONPLUSSED. "Is something the matter?"

"That rather depends." Lettice was sitting on her bed, filing her nails. She had an ominous smile on her face. "Where have you been this time, Rosamund?"

"What do you mean, this time?" But the cold fingers on her spine were telling her all she needed to know.

"Oh, just that when you were supposedly sick abed while we were all at Greenwich, you weren't. The maid says she never saw you, although she came in several times. We thought perhaps you had gone adventuring again this afternoon."

"I was at my cousin's house. Sir Francis Walsingham." She crossed to her bed, beginning to unlace herself with trembling fingers.

"On both occasions? I think not." Frances Darcy was brushing her hair with long, smooth strokes. Her hair was her best feature, a rippling black cascade falling down her back.

"I felt a little better and went for a walk in the gardens." Rosamund improvised desperately but she knew it was futile. She had no talent for lying, and the atmosphere in the dorter was so poisonous it made her feel truly sick.

"All night?"

Anger came to her aid. "I fail to see what business it is of yours. Of any of yours." She hung up her gown in the armoire and went to the basin to wash her face. The cool water cleared her head. "I was sick, and then I felt better and in need of air. It's hot as Hades up here." They couldn't dispute that at least. She climbed into bed, turned on her side, and closed her eyes.

"Well, we heard tell that you enjoy the company of gentlemen overmuch." Lettice's voice was insinuating and muted laughter greeted her statement.

Rosamund sighed and sat up. "Who told you that?" She saw Joan redden, and she bit her lip. She had been all too aware of Joan's interest in Will, but had foolishly dismissed it as unimportant. It certainly hadn't occurred to her that in a fit of pique Joan might say something to cause her trouble.

"That hardly matters." Critically, Lettice extended her hands to examine her fingernails. "The queen does not look kindly upon her ladies who like the company of gentlemen overmuch. Come, ladies. To bed."

Rosamund lay down again, chilled. The mattress dipped as Joan got in beside her. The candles went out and she lay in the stuffy darkness. Had Lettice just threatened her, or was it simply another piece of malicious mischief?

She slept poorly and awoke early while her companions still slept. She lay for a minute trying to identify her unease, then remembered. She slipped from the bed and dressed rapidly, needing to get out in the air, somewhere she could think clearly. Her absence would be remarked upon when the others awoke, but what further damage could be done?

The corridors were already busy but no one seemed to give Rosamund a second glance as she joined the flow of people, all intent on their own business. She emerged into the welcome early-morning freshness of the gardens and made her way along the paths lined with ornamental hedges to the small privy garden.

It was deserted when she slipped through the gap in the hedge, and she went to sit on a stone bench, watching the great goldfish swimming among the lily pads.

She didn't hear the soft footfall on the grass, and when he spoke her name, she jumped. "Will . . . ?" She turned on the bench as he walked across the dew-wet grass to where she sat. "You're up early." She smiled, trying to conceal the sudden surge of pleasure she felt at the sight of him.

"As are you." His voice was light but his eyes were troubled. He stood behind her, looking gravely into her face. "I don't know what to do," he said simply. "I know what I *must* do, but it's not what I want to do."

"What do you want to do?" Rosamund stood up slowly, her blood pounding in her ears.

"You know the answer to that. I want to take you in my arms and kiss you, I want to throw you down on the grass, I want to see you naked, I want to make love to you. . . . Dear God, just talking about it is madness, Rosamund." He ran his hands through his hair almost as if he would tear it out by the roots. "Just imagining it is driving me insane. But you know what we risk . . . complete disgrace . . . banishment from the court, the end of any future."

"I know it." She stood up. "The end of ambition."

She gave him a rather sad little smile, and with a groan he cupped her face between his hands. "That sounds so harsh, and yet, it's *real*, my sweet."

"I know," she repeated, then without volition she moved against him, running her flat palms down his chest as she leaned back, her hips pressed against his loins.

Will kissed her with an almost frantic passion. The

softness of her body against him, the sweet scent of orange flowers in the gorgeous russet mass of her hair, the sweet taste of her mouth, overwhelmed him. Hungrily he ran his hands over her body, gripped her buttocks, pressing her ever harder against his own arousal. And she responded with little murmurs of pleasure, stroking his back as her hips moved against him.

When finally they drew apart, her eyes shone, her lips were swollen, kiss-reddened, and she was filled with an urge so powerful she could have ripped off her clothes there and then.

Will struggled to catch his breath. "Sweet Jesus, you are so passionate." His fingers moved over the swell of her breasts above the low neckline of her gown, palmed the soft shape of them beneath her bodice, and her engorged nipples pressed almost painfully through the material into his palms. Desire deepened the blue of his eyes so that they glowed like sapphires in the sun.

Rosamund exhaled slowly, steadying her breath, struggling to regain her sense of self, of her place in the world. She combed her tousled hair with her fingers and gave him a weak smile. "You are right, this is madness, Will." As if to underscore the statement, a crunch on gravel heralded the arrival of a pair of gardeners wielding secateurs.

"I will leave first," Will said swiftly. "Wait five minutes before you follow me."

Rosamund nodded and, with a quick glance at the gardeners, who at present seemed not to have noticed them, moved away from him, strolling casually over to a sundial at the far side of the garden.

She stood deep in thought watching the beam of sunlight move fractionally on the smoothly raked gravel at the sundial's base, then reluctantly she headed back to the palace. She must make an appearance at breakfast or draw more pointed comments on her absences.

For once Lady Shrewsbury did not preside over the breakfast board, and the maids of honor were left to themselves. Rosamund was not included in their chatter, but she was aware of covert sidelong glances, and every now and again her companions would exchange knowing smiles. She felt as if everyone knew something, and she alone was in ignorance. Her sense of foreboding increased when a messenger announced that Lady Lettice Asherton was wanted in the queen's presence chamber. Lettice rose instantly, exchanging another complicit smile with her friends before hurrying away.

Rosamund glanced at Joan, who immediately lowered her eyes to her plate, her cheeks pink. She was the picture of guilt, Rosamund thought, cold fingers marching along her spine. What could they have discovered? They could know nothing beyond her seeming absence from the dorter when she was supposed to be sick in bed. And no one could know for sure how long she'd been gone. But somehow she was not reassured.

Lettice did not return until they had taken up their usual places in the queen's apartments. Lady Shrewsbury was still absent when Lettice came back. She cast Rosamund a quick look, then huddled with Frances and several of the other women in a whispered colloquy. Joan, excluded from this congress, sat with hunched shoulders over her tambour frame. She radiated misery, and if Rosamund had not been so agitated herself, she would have felt sorry for her.

At last Lady Shrewsbury returned. The rich, deep blue velvet folds of her gown swayed with her wide Spanish farthingale as she marched rather than walked into the room. Her face, framed by her large, open, lace-edged ruff was set in lines of cold anger. "Mistress Walsingham, come with me."

In many ways it was a relief when the sword finally fell. Rosamund set aside her pen and without a word followed the countess from the room. Lady Shrewsbury said nothing to her, marching ahead of her through the antechamber and into the queen's presence chamber. Rosamund felt an instant of relief when she saw that the queen was not in her chair of state. But it was short-lived.

"I advise you to be honest in your answers," the countess stated without preamble. "Any prevarication, any outright lies, will be discovered, I can promise you that. Where were you when the court was at Greenwich?"

"I was here, Lady Shrewsbury." Rosamund stood holding her clasped hands tightly against the front of her gown. She tried to meet the older woman's eye but the blazing fury seemed to scorch her. "I did leave the dorter several times when I needed some air. It was very hot up there."

"I do not believe you. But if you will not confess the truth to me, then you will confess it to those better able to get the truth from you." Her voice was as cold as her eyes were hot.

Rosamund felt a nut of nausea lodge in her throat. There was no mistaking the threat. She understood that the countess was responsible for the conduct of the maids of honor, and any lapse in morals would be laid at her door. It explained her rage, but it didn't make it any the easier to experience.

If she stuck to her story, they could prove nothing. No one had seen her leave or return, she was sure of it. It was just innuendo and spiteful tale-telling at this point.

"Madam, I don't understand what I'm accused of." She

kept her voice low and moderate, trying to keep it steady. "I cannot defend myself or answer a charge without knowing what it is."

"Do you deny you left the dorter that night?"

"I left it in the afternoon for a while."

"To do what?"

"To take the air."

"And when did you return? Be careful how you answer. We have the evidence of the maid who was to look in on you. She said you were absent on the three occasions she went to the dorter. Three occasions separated by several hours."

Tread carefully, Rosamund told herself. "I do not recall how many times I left my bed, madam. But I was restless and feverish. I lost count of time."

The countess closed her lips to a thin line. "You have been seen in intimate conversation with certain men. You have been seen walking alone with these men, in circumstances that lend themselves to lewd conduct. Will you deny it?"

"I deny the lewd conduct, Lady Shrewsbury. I cannot deny the conversations or the walks. I made no attempt to conceal them. They all took place in full view of the court."

"You will explain yourself to her majesty. Remain here." The countess made her way to the door at the far end of the presence chamber that led to the queen's bedchamber. Rosamund stood in petrified stillness where she had been left. Everything was unraveling and she cursed her stupidity for ever imagining she could keep anything secret in this court so rife with gossip and malice. Lady Walsingham had warned her clearly enough, and she had not heeded the warning closely enough.

The door to the queen's bedchamber opened and the countess called sharply, "Mistress Walsingham, come here."

Rosamund crossed what seemed a vast expanse of parquet floor where scattered Turkey carpets lay like little bright-colored islands in the sea of glowing wood. She followed Lady Shrewsbury into her majesty's bedchamber and immediately knelt with head bowed low.

She was left in that position for what seemed an eternity, then Elizabeth spoke, her voice harsh. "Stand up, girl."

She stood slowly, but did not raise her eyes. Humble submission seemed the most politic position at present.

"So, you deny these accusations?"

"Madam, I have been accused of nothing that I can deny. I have walked and talked with courtiers, but in full view of Lady Shrewsbury. I have done nothing of which to be ashamed, and I have nothing to hide." Her voice was low but clear.

"Look at me."

She raised her eyes at last. The queen was sitting beside the empty grate, her beringed fingers tapping the carved arms of her chair. This morning she sparkled with diamonds. A thick choker around her throat, heavy bracelets on her arms. The lining of her sleeves was studded with pearls. The lining of her open ruff was sewn with sapphires, and at her waist she wore a loose girdle made entirely of the same stone. The sight of her dazzled the eye and Rosamund blinked. Then she saw that Lady Pembroke was also in the chamber, standing just behind the queen's chair.

"You have been absent from your dorter without explanation or permission. You have been seen in intimate conversation with my courtiers, do you deny that?"

"Not intimate, madam. Merely playful."

"Playful?" Scorn throbbed in the royal tones. "Are you virgin?"

The question was so sudden and unexpected, Rosamund couldn't catch her breath for a moment.

"Well, girl? Are you?" The rings on the fingers played percussion to the impatient question.

"Of course, madam." Rosamund closed her eyes on the lie and prayed as she had never prayed before.

There was a long silence, then the queen said, "I don't know whether you are telling the truth or not. But there is a simple way to discover, and we will put this matter to rest. Lady Shrewsbury, send for the midwives."

Rosamund thought she would vomit where she stood as she saw the trap that had been laid for her. "No," she gasped. "I beg you, madam, *please.*"

But her pleas fell on deaf ears. Lady Shrewsbury seized one arm and Lady Pembroke the other, and between them they half marched, half carried her from the queen's presence. In a few minutes she found herself alone, locked in a small inner antechamber where the only furniture was a long bench against the wall, the only illumination a sconced candle high on the wall.

She was shaking with fear, fighting back tears. At first she could think only of Thomas, of how her disgrace would reflect upon him. He would never forgive her. And her cousin . . . his reaction didn't bear contemplating. Everything he'd done for her, even if it had been done for his own benefit, she'd squandered, and Ursula . . . Ursula would see her kindness thrown back in her face. Rosamund could no longer hold back the tears and they poured down her cheeks. But after a while she began to get a grip on herself. She would not let them find her here in abject terror, drowning in a sodden puddle of tears.

She began to pace the small space, thinking, trying to see a way through this, as the tears dried on her cheeks. Of course they could do anything to her. They could send her to the Tower to enjoy the ministrations of the queen's torturer, Master Topcliffe. But she had not committed treason. Losing her virginity outside the marriage bed wasn't treason, unless one was of royal blood. She had done nothing to deserve the rack.

And somehow she had to keep Will out of it. There was no point embroiling him in the scandal, no need for both of them to suffer disgrace. But could she keep his name out of it? Would she have the strength to withstand whatever pressure they brought to bear?

When she heard the key turning in the door, her heart began to beat wildly, fear and horror engulfed her anew. Lady Shrewsbury and Lady Pembroke came in, and with them three elderly women dressed in black, with white coifs. They could have been nuns, but of course they weren't. There was no place for a nun in the Protestant queen's court.

Rosamund found herself backing up to the wall, holding her hands in front of her as if she could ward them off.

"Don't be stupid, Rosamund." Lady Shrewsbury's voice was less harsh now. "The midwives will examine you. If you fight them, it will hurt more."

"I . . . I have my monthly courses."

"That is fortunate," one of the midwives said. "It will make the examination easier for you."

Easier, but doubly degrading. Rosamund couldn't believe this was going to happen to her, but she knew that it was.

Unless she confessed.

"There is no need for this," she said in a low voice as the midwives grasped her arms. "I will confess. I am no longer virgin."

Their hands dropped and they looked to Lady Shrewsbury, who stared at Rosamund in silence. It was Lady Pembroke who said, "Who has known you?"

"I cannot say, madam."

"You will do so." Lady Shrewsbury's voice was frigid and
confident. She nodded to the midwives. "We have no need
of you now."

The women left in a rustle of black robes and the two
countesses regarded Rosamund with hard eyes. "You little
fool," Lady Shrewsbury said. "To throw away such an opportunity. Do you have any idea how many families solicit
the queen for a position? You have ruined yourself, brought
scandal upon your family, and for what?"

Rosamund had no answer. It all seemed absurd now,
and for the first time she wished that that dreamlike cou-
pling in the hayloft *had* merely been a dream. But she
would not bring Will down with her. She stood silent and
waited for what was to happen next.

"You will remain here." The two ladies swept from the
room, and the key turned in the lock, leaving Rosamund
alone in the cell-like antechamber. She sat down on the
long bench, resting her head against the wall, closing her
eyes.

The candle burned low as the hours passed, but in the
hot and airless room Rosamund thought that the quiet
was the hardest to endure. She was so accustomed to a
constant buzz of noise and bustle that she began to feel
as if she were buried deep in some underground cavern.
Her world had collapsed around her. She had thought she
was in charge of her life, that she could direct its path. And
now she saw with bleak certainty what a chimera that had
been. She had listened to Agathe, to the seductive tidbits of
advice about discretion, about how to manipulate the rules

and protocols for one's own pleasure, and the chevalier had shown her how easy it was to put those tidbits into practice. And she had so naively assumed that what those sophisticated, experienced courtiers could do, she could do too.

When eventually the key turned in the lock, the sound was startling in the silence. She jumped to her feet, bracing herself for what was to come.

Lady Shrewsbury stood in the doorway. "Come with me."

Rosamund followed her out of the antechamber, blinking in the brilliant sunshine of what had to be midafternoon. She was desperately thirsty, her tongue cleaving to the roof of her mouth, her throat so dry she didn't think she could speak clearly. The countess opened the door to a sparsely furnished paneled chamber and gestured curtly that Rosamund should enter.

Sir Francis Walsingham and her brother were the only occupants of the chamber. They stood side by side in front of a long window that looked out over the river. Rosamund curtsied in silence, aware that Lady Shrewsbury had not followed her in. The door clicked shut.

"Who is the man?" Thomas demanded. His face was red with anger, his eyes hot. "You are an ungrateful wanton, Sister, a disgrace to the family. You will tell me now, who is the man?"

Rosamund swallowed painfully. "May I have a drink? My throat is parched."

If Thomas heard her, he chose to ignore it. He glared at her. "*Answer me.*"

Rosamund shook her head helplessly. Thomas advanced on her and she backed away.

"Wait, Thomas." The curt instruction stopped her

brother in his tracks. "You may vent your own spleen later." Sir Francis walked to a small table in the corner and poured wine from a flagon into a pewter cup. He brought it to Rosamund. "Drink this, and then you will talk."

There was such confidence in the statement a graveyard chill ran up her spine. She didn't fear Thomas so much. His temper when roused was fearsome, and his reactions would be primitive and punitive, but she had faced that before, and it was usually short-lived. But Sir Francis was a different matter altogether. She had no idea what he would do to her if she didn't cooperate, but she knew full well what he *could* do.

She drank gratefully, draining the cup in a few swallows. When she had finished, he said, "Now answer me, Rosamund. Who was the man?"

"I cannot say."

His expression didn't change. "Don't be a fool, or any more of a one than you already have been. The queen insists upon knowing the identity of the man who lay with you. And believe me, girl, you *will* tell her what she wishes to know."

"*Why?*" Thomas exploded. "Just tell me *why* you would do something so *stupid*. You have thrown away the opportunity of a lifetime. Just tell me *why*."

She shook her head. It was impossible to describe that night with Will in the hayloft, impossible to explain the overwhelming desire that had caught them up, swept them along on a tide of delight so wonderful it could not possibly have been wrong.

"Thomas, leave us." Again a curt instruction that could not be gainsaid.

Her brother hesitated, looking at his sister with pent-up fury, his hands clenched at his sides. Then he shook his head. "God's blood. When I get my hands on you—"

"*Go*, Thomas. *Now.*"

Thomas stormed out, slamming the door behind him. Sir Francis surveyed Rosamund in grim silence and with an air almost of repugnance. Then he walked back to the window, looking out, punching one hand into the palm of another, seemingly deep in thought.

Rosamund waited. At last he spoke, his voice cold and without expression. "Either my wife sorely neglected some part of your education in the rules of the court or you're more stupid than I thought. Was it not explained to you that the queen is jealous of her gentlemen courtiers' favors? She likes it not when there are understandings between them and her ladies without her blessing. She will not sanction marriages that she has not arranged herself, or at least *believes* that she has." The emphasis was slight, but the meaning was clear. "Tell me, were you not aware of these facts?" He swung round to face her, his black eyes fixing her with a fierce glare.

Rosamund swallowed and finally managed to say, "I was aware of them, Sir Francis."

"And you deliberately chose to flout them?" He shook his head in disgust. "I can't think why I bothered with you. As a favor to me, the queen took you into her service and, as I understand it, has paid you particular attention."

"That is the root of the trouble," Rosamund burst out, unable to keep her humbly penitent silence a minute longer. "If she had not singled me out, the other women would not have made mischief."

"That is no excuse. You gave them the ammunition and you must now pay the piper." He turned away again, as if he couldn't bear to look at her.

Rosamund said nothing, there was nothing to say. If Sir Francis hadn't wanted to use her skill with pen and paper in his own interests, he wouldn't have made such a point of her aptitude to the queen, and she would not have paid such particular attention to her newest and lowliest maid of honor, and none of this would have happened. But she had not the courage to point that out.

After a moment he spoke again, his back still averted and his voice once more expressionless, the cold anger no longer apparent. "The queen, as I said, does not tolerate liaisons between her courtiers and her ladies. Now I ask you again, and think very carefully before you respond. Who is the man?"

Rosamund thought, playing his words back in her mind. Then she understood. "It was at Scadbury," she said in a low voice. "Last summer. A troupe of minstrels and jongleurs. They came to the village. There was one . . . one in particular. I . . . we . . . it was just one time." She fell silent.

Sir Francis turned to face her, his eyes raking her countenance. "Maybe you have not lost your wits after all, and fortunately for you I still have a use for them. Remain here, while I see what chestnuts I can pull out of this fire." He left her alone once more with only her thoughts for company.

Chapter Twenty

SIR FRANCIS ENTERED the queen's privy chamber without undue ceremony, knowing he was expected. Elizabeth was reading in her chair by the window overlooking the river where she got the best light. She folded the book over her finger as her secretary of state entered and bowed.

"So, did you get it out of her, Francis?"

"It would seem, madam, that unbeknownst either to myself or my lady wife the girl arrived at court unchaste. She lost her virginity to an itinerant player at Scadbury last summer. A sadly motherless girl with no female supervision in the first impulsive flush of womanhood." He opened his hands in a *What will you?* gesture. "I can assure you that nothing untoward has happened in her time at court. A little harmless flirtation, perhaps, but nothing more than that."

Elizabeth turned her head to look out at the river. She made no response for a moment, as she remembered her own youthful indiscretion with the admiral. Even at this great distance she could still relive that heady, belly-deep surge of excitement when Seymour had touched her, when he'd wake her in the dawn, tickling, slapping, playfully seeming always, but even as an untried girl of fourteen, she had known it was not at all playful. And she had not tried very hard to turn him away.

"You are certain nothing has occurred with any gentle-men of the court?"

"Believe me, madam, I would know it."

"Yes, of course you would, Francis." She knew her sec-retary's methods. She turned her gaze away from the river, back to Walsingham. "So, what do you suggest be done with her? She cannot remain after such a deception. I insist upon absolute honesty and chastity in my ladies. She must be banished from court."

"Yes, of course, madam." Sir Francis bowed his acknowl-edgment of the justice of the edict. "But if I might venture to suggest a way in which her banishment might be turned to good use?"

Elizabeth smiled, but her tone had an acid edge to it. "You see an opportunity in everything, Francis."

"I certainly make it my business to try, madam."

"What have you in mind? Pour wine, will you? And for yourself if you wish it." She waved towards a flagon on a sideboard against the far wall. "And then take a seat."

Francis obliged, pouring the golden wine into the deli-cate crystal goblets, bringing one to his queen and taking his own to a low chair across from her. He sipped, then set the glass on the table beside him.

"I am suggesting that you send Rosamund to your cousin Mary. As a gesture of goodwill. Her entourage is sadly diminished and another lady would bring a breath of fresh air, fresh companionship, for them all."

"My cousin would hardly trust a companion from *my* court," the queen pointed out, frowning over her glass.

"This one she might, madam. Rosamund will have little difficulty convincing Scots Mary that she has been sent away from your court in disgrace, since it is only the truth. But she will offer the reason for her banishment that she was discovered practicing the Catholic religion in secret. I venture to think that Mary will find the prospect of a persecuted convert irresistible."

Elizabeth regarded him with interest. "Perhaps so. But by no means certain."

"I think she will if Rosamund makes it clear that serving Mary was her idea, that she is a sympathetic Catholic, forced to hide her true sentiments, desperate to find herself in like-minded religious company free to practice her religion in the manner of her convictions."

"You think Rosamund capable of such a deception?" The queen's interest sharpened. "She has an extraordinary memory and considerable talent at reproduction, I grant you, but she is so young, so naive, almost a simpleton. If she were not, she would not find herself in her present disgrace."

"Madam, she is a Walsingham." Francis took the scent of his wine again.

Elizabeth shook her head. "You are a rogue of the first water, Francis. You will force the girl to toe the family line, just like her brother."

"Oh, I do not force Thomas, madam. The work suits him. And I think it likely that it will suit his sister. Her wits make up for what she lacks in experience."

"You are confident of that?"

His curt nod was answer enough.

"And you will use her to gain information while she is part of my cousin's retinue?"

"Yes, madam."

"Then I have no objection. But she must depart the palace immediately. I do not wish to see her again."

Francis rose and bowed. "It will be done, madam." He backed to the door and let himself out.

* * *

Rosamund had finished the wine in the flagon, which on an empty belly made her feel a little muzzy. She knelt on the window seat, pressing her forehead against the diamond panes, gazing out at the river where the barges and skiffs plied their oars with such freedom. The chamber was stuffy and after a moment she opened the casement, leaning on her folded arms to look down into the garden just below. She could hear the murmur of voices as people strolled along the path beneath the window, and her attention was suddenly seized by the sight of Agathe and the chevalier walking arm in arm across the sweep of lawn beyond the path. They were heads together deep in a conversation that looked to be absorbing them completely. She thought Arnaud looked angry, and Agathe once or twice placed a hand on his arm as if to placate or soothe him. Once he unceremoniously pushed the hand away.

Rosamund, despite her own misery, was intrigued. What were they talking about? They continued walking towards the path below her open casement and she drew back a little, not wanting to be seen if they should look up. She had no wish to show herself in her present disgraced imprisonment to anyone she knew. They reached the path below her window and she heard Agathe's voice for a moment quite clearly. "I do not think you can blame me, Arnaud. I did what you asked. I encouraged her, I taught her how to play, it is not my fault if she used the lessons on someone else."

Rosamund leaned out farther but she couldn't make out Arnaud's response. It was in French and too swift for her to follow, but his tone was unmistakable. He was very angry. She withdrew into the chamber, momentarily diverted from her own troubles, but not for many minutes. The key

turned in the lock behind her and her heart began its er-
ratic thumping again. She stood up, facing the door.

Sir Francis came in, followed by two men in the crimson livery of the queen's personal guard. They stood at
either side of the door.

"You will go with these men. They will escort you to
your dorter, where you will pack your belongings. Your
trunk will be collected later and taken to Seething Lane,
where you will stay until you begin your journey."

"My journey where?"

"That will be explained to you when I deem it necessary." He stood aside, gesturing that she should go with the
guards.

Rosamund obeyed in silence, moving past him into the
corridor. The guards fell in beside her and the long walk
began. Rosamund felt the curious stares of those they
passed. She was obviously under guard, even though neither of her escorts laid a hand upon her. She walked with
her head high, eyes straight ahead, refusing to meet anyone's eye. She heard the whispered buzz rising like swarming bees and knew that the story would be on everyone's
lips within half an hour, if it wasn't already.

They turned a corner leading to the dorter and her
step faltered. Will Creighton and two other courtiers were
coming towards them along the corridor, laughing at
something. The laughter died on Will's face when he saw
her, his eyes darting between her liveried escorts. The color
drained from his cheeks and he took a step towards her, his
hand outstretched.

Rosamund shook her head at him and moved one hand
in an unmistakable gesture of rejection. Her eyes were
fierce as they fixed upon him, trying to burn her silent
message into his brain. He looked astounded, bewildered,

then stepped back as she and her guards passed down the corridor.

It took all her willpower to keep from one last look over her shoulder as he walked away from her. Her way lay far from here now, far from the world that was still his. Their paths would probably never cross again. It was right, it was sensible and practical, to salvage something from this catastrophe. There was no reason to ruin Will's chances for advancement, yet the thought of Will continuing his life as if nothing had happened while she faced whatever drear future they had planned for her filled her with a dark resentment that she despised, but could for the moment do nothing to alleviate.

She packed her belongings in the trunk under the watchful if bored eyes of her escort and looked around, making sure she had forgotten nothing. One thing she would not regret would be this wretched space with its lumpy, prickly, flea-ridden mattress, and its vile, vindictive inhabitants. *May the evil eye fall on them all.* On which silent curse, Rosamund shook the dust of Whitehall Palace from her feet and stalked past her guards.

She was escorted to the stables, where Thomas, black-faced as before, waited with Jenny and his own horse. "You can consider yourself fortunate Sir Francis has you in charge," he said, almost throwing her into the saddle. "If you were left to me, you'd be regretting the day you were born."

"I don't doubt it," Rosamund muttered, reflecting that at least she had one reason to be thankful for her cousin's protection. As they rode to Seething Lane, her mind focused miserably on the upcoming meeting with Lady Walsingham. What would she have been told? Presumably the truth. What would she think of the girl she had taken into her house with such kindness and generosity?

Would she see only monumental ingratitude? Would she cast her former protégée aside as a wanton? Beyond the pale, a waste of all her efforts? Beside the prospect of Ursula's disappointment, Thomas's barely controlled rage was nothing to bear.

At Seething Lane, Thomas told her curtly to go inside. He was not to accompany her. She dismounted without his assistance, handing him Jenny's reins, then, full of trepidation she knocked on the door.

It was opened almost immediately by the familiar Mortlake, who held the door for her. She stepped into the hall, with its wonderfully familiar scents of beeswax and lavender.

"Lady Walsingham is in her parlor. You're to go to her there," Mortlake said behind her.

She nodded, took a deep breath, and went to the parlor, where she had so often freely entered at will. Now the door was closed and she knocked, tentatively.

"Come in, Rosamund." Ursula's voice was soft and pleasant as always, but her eyes were grave as she regarded Rosamund, who, after opening the door, curtsied, then stood silent in the doorway.

Ursula beckoned. "Close the door." Rosamund did so.

"Come and sit down. You look as if you've had a very difficult day."

At the note of sympathy Rosamund was afraid she would burst into tears. It was the first kind word anyone had spoken to her since she had left Will that morning, which seemed to have happened in another lifetime. She sat down on a low stool in front of Lady Walsingham.

"Well, what a pickle you seem to find yourself in," Ursula said matter-of-factly. "You shall tell me the whole shortly. First, when did you last eat?"

"This morning, at breakfast, madam."

"Good God, have they kept you all day without food?" Ursula reached for the bell and rang it vigorously. When a servant answered, she gave order for bread, meat, and wine to be brought immediately. Then she leaned forward, tilting Rosamund's chin on her forefinger. "Poor child. It is a den of thieves, I did try to warn you."

"Oh, madam, you did," Rosamund exclaimed, horrified that Ursula should blame herself for any of this disaster. "I couldn't quite believe in how truly, truly *horrible* the women can be. It was all my own fault. I was stupid and I should have known better. I am so very sorry to have let you down. I must seem so ungrateful, but I am not, I am so grateful to you for all your kindness." She seized Ursula's hand in a fervent clasp. "You must believe me."

"Oh, I do, my dear. I know what traps are there for the innocent and unwary." She sighed, patting Rosamund's hand. "Now you shall eat and drink, and then, when you feel refreshed, you had better tell me the whole, because I do not believe that my husband has done so."

The servant had laid a cold roast fowl, a loaf of bread, and a flagon of wine on the table and Ursula gestured to Rosamund. "Go to, child. Go to. You will feel better directly."

Will Creighton forced himself to go through the day as if nothing had happened to disrupt his usual easygoing nonchalance. The morning's scandal was on every tongue, the disgrace of the newest maid of honor a delicious morsel to be savored, chewed over, speculation as to the identity of the lover a delightful topic. His anxiety for Rosamund was sometimes greater than the fear for himself, and sometimes took second place.

Part of him wanted to leave the palace, flee to his lodgings and bury his head, as if that would keep him safe from the chamberlain's knock, and the order of court banishment. Would the queen order him to the Tower? However often he told himself he was too insignificant for such draconian measures, he couldn't convince himself. But then he would see that urgent movement of Rosamund's hand, her eyes burning their message into his head, and he would want to weep for her selflessness, for her courage. No one knew her fate, except for the simple fact of banishment.

Will agonized over possibilities. Had she been sent home, back to Scadbury? Had her family cast her out, a disgrace to the name? Where would she go? Where *could* she go?

As the day wore on and there was no hand on his shoulder, no harsh summons, he began to allow himself to hope, and he comforted himself with the thought that as long as he could stay above the scandal, keep his position and his freedom, then he could perhaps at some point be of service to her.

Yet it seemed impossible that she had withstood interrogation by Sir Francis Walsingham. Had she managed a convincing lie? It seemed unlikely, but as the hours passed and he remained unmolested, his hope grew into conviction. By the evening, when the queen appeared in the Great Hall and seemed perfectly good-humored, willing to be pleased by dancing and music, he knew that Rosamund had stayed true.

He saw Joan Davenport standing alone and threaded his way through the lines of dance to her side. She looked up with a pathetically eager smile as he bowed.

"I give you good even, Mistress Davenport."

"Master Creighton." She curtsied, blushing.

"Will you join the dance?" He offered his hand and she took it instantly.

He led her to the floor, to join the couples in the vigorous movements of the galliard, and for a few measures the lively triple tempo offered no opportunity for conversation, but finally he was able to comment casually, "I daresay the queen's ladies have been agog with the scandal concerning Mistress Walsingham."

"Oh, such excitement, Master Creighton, as you wouldn't believe." Joan was slightly out of breath with the dance, but more than ready for gossip. She lowered her voice conspiratorially. "'Tis said the queen has banished her from court for life. She's to be imprisoned somewhere, not in the Tower, but some other prison, for deceiving the queen. I always knew there was something not quite honest about her."

Will felt his hackles rise, but he kept his voice cool as he said, "What made you think that?"

Joan tossed her head. "Oh, she was a sly one, disappearing from the dorter before anyone was awake, and then pretending she'd gone for a walk, when it was clear as daylight she'd been up to something . . . meeting some man, I'm sure. And she thought she was better than any of us because the queen favored her for her drawing and penmanship. 'Tis good riddance, if you ask me. We all think so."

Will closed his lips firmly on a heated response, saying instead as casually as before, "So no one knows where she's gone?"

"Only that Sir Francis Walsingham, her cousin, had a hand in her removal." Joan put her hands on her hips, performing the quick series of hopping steps demanded by the dance.

Will decided he'd better leave well enough alone now.

He had no wish to draw attention to himself with undue curiosity about the fate of an ordinary maid of honor. If Rosamund had protected him, then he couldn't risk undoing her good work. But nothing could reassure him as to Rosamund's fate, and as soon as he could, he left Joan and went to find friends in whose company he could slip into the burgundy waters of Lethe.

He caught sight of Thomas Walsingham late in the evening, looking morose, his mouth set in a thin line, his eyes hard. Walsingham beckoned him with an imperative gesture. Will instantly felt queasy. If Walsingham had heard of his sister's clandestine afternoon at the theatre, dressed as a page in Will Creighton's company, he would draw the inevitable conclusions. Will made his way over to him.

"You wanted me, Walsingham?"

"Aye. Where's Babington this evening?"

Will reported directly to Thomas Walsingham in this affair of Scots Mary, and Will felt a wave of relief at this straightforward question.

"He told me he was going into the country for a few days. His father had a bad turn and summoned him. A summons Babington can ill afford to ignore without cutting off the purse strings."

Thomas nodded. "If he's gone more than two days, you're to go after him. Impress upon him the urgency of returning to London. He needs to be here when Ballard returns from France and I've been told to expect the good father within the week." With a curt nod, Thomas turned and walked off.

Will decided he'd had sufficient scares for one day. He returned to his lodgings and drank until oblivion claimed him.

*   *   *

Thomas was in a foul mood that evening. If he'd been permitted to vent his fury at his sister's perfidy, and he considered it nothing less than a betrayal of him and everything he had done for her throughout her short life, he would by now have recovered some of his habitual insouciance at life's vagaries, but he had been balked from exacting the vengeance he considered his just due, and as soon as he'd passed on his instructions to Creighton, he left the court.

As he stalked down the corridor to the side door that would provide the shortest access to the mews and his horse, Chevalier de Vaugiras rounded a corner ahead. The two men stopped, hands automatically going to their sword hilts. Thomas felt a jolt of savage satisfaction at the prospect of taking his anger out on such a worthy target. He had half slid his sword from its sheath before he remembered that it was treason to draw a sword under the same roof as the queen.

The chevalier saw Thomas's hand drop from the weapon and a thin smile flickered across his mouth. He continued walking forward.

"We will have our meeting, de Vaugiras." Thomas spoke through barely opened lips. "But I'll not commit treason under her majesty's roof . . . you're not worth it." Deliberately he spat on the ground at the chevalier's feet, then shouldered him aside and continued on his way.

Arnaud, white-faced, stood very still for several minutes. He breathed slowly until he had mastered himself. It had been a day of reverses, but when one door closed, another always opened. The time would come. He walked on following the sounds of music and revelry emanating from the great hall.

*   *   *

Thomas mounted his horse in the mews and with a vicious slash of the whip set him at a canter out into the street. He rode beyond the city walls to a district called Norton Folgate, in the liberty of Shoreditch. It was close to the theatres, and its rooming houses, tenements, and mean cottages offered the kind of cheap lodging affordable for theatre folk, the playmakers and actors, the apprentice actors and the managers.

He stopped outside a rooming house set just off Hog Lane and still sitting his horse looked up at a first-floor window. A light burned despite the late hour. Kit was up then.

Thomas dismounted, tethered his horse to a post at the door, and picked up a handful of stones from the dusty lane. He hurled them at the window in a satisfying scatter-shot and within seconds the window was flung open and Kit leaned out.

"Who's so rudely disturbing the muse?" he demanded in the thick but jovial voice that Thomas recognized as indication that the playmaker was more than two sheets to the wind.

"Let me in, you drunken sot," he called up. "I've need of brandy and your company, my friend."

"Oh, ho, so that's the way the wind blows." Kit's muffled laughter faded, then the narrow front door squeaked open on unoiled hinges and Marlowe peered out, blinking in mock bemusement. "Why, if 'tis not the most honor-able Master Walsingham who deigns to grace my humble abode. Is it a tumble in the sheets you've come for, a little ride-a-cock-horse, then?"

"Hold your tongue, you foulmouthed loon." Thomas pushed past him and stormed up the stairs into the single chamber where Kit wrote, and occasionally slept, and even

more occasionally ate. A half-eaten loaf of stale bread stood
on the table with a moldering piece of cheese; beside it two
empty flagons of wine lay on their sides, two more upon
the floor. An overfull chamber pot half-hidden beneath the
narrow cot lent its aroma to the general stink.

Thomas looked at Kit as he lounged in the doorway. His
hair was a tangled mess, his eyes bloodshot and sunken in
his thin cheeks, his countenance bearing an almost febrile
flush. "Are you ill, man?" For a moment something other
than his own concerns penetrated his anger.

"Not a bit of it." Kit passed a hand through the air in a
nonchalant gesture. "But I have penned some goodly lines,
Thomas. You shall hear them." He went to the rickety table,
took up a sheet of parchment, and began to declaim:

> Now hast though but one bare hour to live,
> And then thou must be damned perpetually.
> Stand still, you ever-moving spheres of heaven,
> That time may cease, and midnight never come.

Despite himself, Thomas was riveted. "That does not
come from your *Tamburlaine*," he stated with conviction.

"No . . . no, of course it does not." Kit picked up an
empty flagon and tipped it up with a mournful air. "Damn
it to hell!" He hurled it to the floor. "It comes from my play
I shall call *Faustus*. I have it in mind to write of the devil."
He flung up a hand and cried, "*The devil will come, and
Faustus must be damned.*"

He laughed, a drunkard's laugh, reckless and causeless.
"Looking at you, Tom, dear Tom, I would say the devil is
already amongst us. You have a look as black as any I have
seen this side of hell."

Thomas hurled his hat to the floor and with an oath

reached for Kit. He pushed up his face and kissed him with a roughness that left them both breathless. Then they fell together to the cot in a violent tangle of limbs, oaths mingling with words of desire as their clothes fell to the floor and the white bodies twisted and turned, above and beneath, in the lustful sharing that brought them to the furthest edge of pleasure. And when it was over, Thomas felt purged of rage by the acts of love, and Kit, still drunk, lay on his back, one hand over his eyes, and murmured further lines from his *Faustus*.

Chapter Twenty-one

SIR FRANCIS SENT for Rosamund the following morning when she was at breakfast with Ursula. She set down her tankard of small beer and rose. "If you'll give me leave, madam?"

"Yes, of course, my dear. You had better go directly."

Rosamund made her way to the business side of the house and knocked at the secretary's door. He bade her enter and she went in, trying to conceal her trepidation. "You wished to see me, sir." She curtsied as she spoke.

"Yes." He didn't immediately look up from the papers he was reading, but waved towards an armless wooden chair across from the desk.

Rosamund sat and contemplated the floor at her feet. After some minutes, her cousin set his quill in the inkwell, clasped his hands together on the desk, and regarded Rosamund with drawn eyebrows. "You are well?"

"Yes, sir. Puzzled, though."

"Hmm." He frowned, pursing his lips. "By what?"

Rosamund had the unmistakable feeling she was hovering on the brink of something important, something that would have long-standing consequences. She knew she must answer honestly but with wisdom. A near impossible feat when she had no idea what the secretary had in mind.

She plunged straight in. "You told me yesterday that you had a use for my wit, Sir Francis. I am puzzled as to your meaning, and somewhat apprehensive that I may not fulfill your expectations."

He gave a grim smile. "With good cause. I would expect nothing else. Very well. Listen, do not interrupt. When I have finished, you will have the opportunity for questions."

Rosamund listened in stunned disbelief as he told her what he wanted of her. She, who had no skill at prevaricating even in the most minor matters, was to become someone else. A Catholic sympathizer, an ardently devoted follower of Scots Mary, so devoted that when she had been disgraced at court, she had begged the queen to permit her to share Queen Mary's imprisonment as her banishment. And the queen had been pleased to grant her that boon. She was to offer herself to Mary for any service, however menial. And she was to listen, to draw, to keep a journal of everything, however trivial, that was said and done in the Scots queen's prison at Chartley Hall.

"If it is a prison, how will my records reach you?" she asked when Sir Francis seemed to have concluded his recitation.

"If it's possible, you will utilize the same method that Mary uses to communicate with her own agents. Thomas will explain that to you later. Alternatively you may be contacted by one of my agents. There are many of them working in this affair at present. One or other of them will make themselves known to you. You may also trust Mary's jailer, or guardian as he is more properly known, Sir Amyas Paulet. He will know your identity, although he will not distinguish you with any kindness. You will be treated in the same manner as Mary and her other ladies. And I need not stress that any contact you have with him outside the Scots queen's quarters must be unknown to those on whom you report."

Rosamund's gaze found the floor again. She stared at the bare oak boards as if she could read some kind of an answer in them. But an answer to what question? She had to obey this order. It was not offered as a choice.

She raised her eyes. "What if I cannot accomplish this deception?"

"I do not admit failure in those who work for me. You will do this, and you will do it well." He spoke without emphasis, and his gaze was calm and steady across the desk.

"How . . . may I ask how long I must do this?" Her voice was tentative as she wondered if it was a permissible question. It could seem as if she was setting conditions of her own.

"Until I consider your task completed."

Enough said there. Rosamund nibbled her lip, frowning in thought. "Forgive me, sir, but will not Queen Mary be suspicious of someone bearing the name of Walsingham? She must know that you are her implacable enemy."

"Which is why you will take the name of Rosamund Fitzgerald. A good Catholic name. Your family is from the Catholic stronghold of the north, and while your family has made peace with the Protestant church and its queen, hence your service at court, you yourself find it impossible to forsake your faith. You prefer martyrdom with the true queen to a life of heresy." Sir Francis's lip curled slightly as he spoke, and there was derision in his tone. Elizabeth's secretary of state had no time for heretics, and no time at all for martyrs.

Rosamund on the other hand had never given heretics or martyrs a moment's serious thought. And she had not given the imprisoned Mary, Queen of Scots, much thought either. The lady had been a prisoner of her cousin Queen Elizabeth's for almost eighteen years and her situation barely impinged on the daily life of an ordinary citizen. Besides, Mary had resided in the north of England throughout her captivity, and Rosamund was a southerner, born and bred.

She tried to think now if she knew any Catholics, or at least any openly confessed Catholics. Anthony Babington, of course, but she was certain she had not knowingly met anyone of that faith during her years at Scadbury. Religious differences had never been a topic around the dinner table or even a subject of her sparse formal education.

It seemed, Rosamund thought somewhat guiltily, that she was a woman of no particular religious conviction at all. She went to church on Sundays, dutifully listened to the long and generally boring sermons, and for the rest of the week never gave the subject another thought.

So could she possibly do what was being asked of her? Could she be sufficiently convincing to be accepted? There would be no physical danger. Mary's discovery of her deception was the worst that could happen. In that event, once useless, she would be taken away, a failure true, and the consequences of failure would be dreary, of that she had no doubt, but there was no danger to life or limb.

"Do you have any other questions?" Sir Francis interrupted her reflections with sharp impatience, and she realized she had been silent for several minutes.

"When do I go?" The simple question was clearly her only acceptable response.

"Tomorrow. Thomas will escort you, together with one Frizer . . ." He caught her grimace. "Ah, you do not care for our man Frizer, I see. He is not much liked, but he has his uses. And he will keep you on a tight rein on the long ride north. He is Thomas's choice, a degree of fraternal vengeance, I imagine. But I do not interfere."

Master Secretary unclasped his hands. "In general my agents . . . my eyes . . . operate according to their own lights. I am interested only in results. You, Rosamund, will bring me results . . . but you will need some preparation."

He opened a drawer in his desk and took out a book and an ivory rosary, sliding both across the desk. "*Our Lady's Psalter*, and a rosary. Make sure you are familiar with both."

Rosamund took the book and the beads, saying doubtfully, "I am not sure how fluent I can pretend to be."

"That will be explained by the difficulties of practicing the *true* religion in the Protestant court," Francis said. "The more anxious you are for religious instruction, the more you will endear yourself to Mary." He gave her a nod of dismissal and, as she rose to her feet, said, "When your work is complete, then we shall discuss your future."

"I will do my best to serve you, Sir Francis." She curtsied and left, running up to her chamber, closing the door at her back, leaning against it, her heart racing. It was a nightmare, yet it was reality.

The next day Henny woke her before daybreak. "Master Walsingham is waiting downstairs, mistress. He says you're to make haste as he wants to be well away from the city by sunup. There's a bowl of bread and milk on the washstand."

Rosamund had hardly slept and staggered to her feet feeling groggy. She accepted Henny's help to dress and ate the bread and milk standing up while Henny brushed her hair and tied it back so that it would be well covered by the hood of her cloak, protected from the dust of the summer roads.

She went downstairs to where Thomas was waiting in the hall, pacing up and down, slashing at his boots with his riding whip. He turned as she came down. "Hurry. We've a long ride and I've no wish to linger on the road."

Rosamund had not expected a warm brotherly greeting, but this was curter than she'd expected. Thomas usually recovered his good humor fairly rapidly, but then her present offense had obviously caused him considerable inconvenience.

She had made her farewells to Ursula the previous evening, so there was nothing to stay for. Without saying anything, she followed Thomas from the house.

Their horses were in the street, pawing the cobbles in the darkness, Ingram Frizer at their heads. He was chewing a piece of stick between blackened teeth and tossed it to the ground as they came out. He gave Rosamund a laconic glance that nevertheless unnerved her, before handing the reins to Thomas and mounting his own horse.

Thomas lifted his sister into Jenny's saddle, still without speaking, and mounted himself. The little party set off northwards in the graying darkness.

They rode for three days, stopping each night to claim hospitality at the houses of acquaintances and family connections. It didn't matter how loose the connection, how bare the acquaintanceship, hospitality was never refused. Each evening, Rosamund was escorted to a bedchamber and Ingram Frizer spent the night outside the door, while her brother enjoyed the company of his hosts at dinner. Rosamund had no idea what Thomas told their hosts of his sister's disgrace, but it was sufficient to ensure that no one exchanged friendly words with her when Frizer escorted her to her horse in the morning.

On the third day Thomas thawed a little, and that evening she was not immediately banished to a solitary chamber. Frizer still spent the night outside her door, but she joined the company for dinner, and no word was said of the scandal. By midmorning of the following day she judged her brother sufficiently softened to ask him what he knew of her task for Sir Francis.

Everything, it seemed. More to the point, he would instruct her in great detail how she was to deliver her information, and he would remain at Chartley for several days after she had joined Mary's retinue in case of some unforeseen difficulty. Rosamund was somewhat reassured by this and was beginning to regard her task with more equanimity when they finally rode into the village of Chartley that evening.

Chartley Hall stood separate from the village surrounded by a moat. A pleasant timbered mansion, its mullioned windows glowed gold in the setting sun as the small party rode across the moat and up the gravel path to the main doors. The doors were opened before they had dismounted, and a man in severe black velvet stepped through the archway to greet them.

"Sir Amyas, I give you good even." Thomas drew off his glove, extending his hand. "This is my sister, Rosamund Walsingham. You know all you need to know about her circumstances, I trust."

"Sir Francis sent a courier with a full explanation of the situation, Master Walsingham." Sir Amyas gave Rosamund a short bow. "You are welcome, Mistress Walsingham."

"My man Frizer you know." Thomas gestured to the man, who merely nodded in response to Paulet's curt glance of acknowledgment.

"Come inside. You are sharp set, I'm sure. We will dine at once if it please you. Master Phelippes is here too. He manages the intercepts." Sir Amyas led the way into the cool, gloomy interior.

Rosamund glanced up and around at the heavily raftered ceiling and carved paneling of the central hall. A carved staircase rose from the rear to a galleried landing above with a small minstrel's balcony jutting from the back wall. Two huge fireplaces, large enough to roast oxen, stood at each end of the hall, but they were fireless in the warmth of midsummer. All in all, it was a gloomy place, despite the warm and cheerful evening outdoors.

"If you will go with my housekeeper, Mistress Walsingham, she will show you to a chamber where you will spend tonight. In the morning I will take you to the Lady Mary."

Lady Mary, not queen, Rosamund noted. It seemed that Paulet was as much the Scots queen's implacable enemy as was the secretary of state.

"You will wish to sup alone abovestairs, I am sure."

Rosamund was about to deny any such desire, having grown heartily sick of her own company in the last days, but caught her brother's eye and prudently acceded. She went off with the housekeeper, a Mistress Tunston, who had an uncanny resemblance to Sir Amyas, the same sandy hair and severe cast of countenance.

She was shown to a pleasant enough chamber at the rear of Chartley Hall, overlooking a cobbled yard and a group of outbuildings. "The Lady Mary is housed over yonder," Mistress Tunston said, indicating the outbuildings.

"Why is she not housed in the Hall?" Rosamund was shocked. The outbuildings looked ramshackle, more like ill-built stables than a habitation, let alone the living quarters of a queen.

"'Tis no business of mine." The housekeeper closed her lips in a thin line, clearly meaning to imply that it was no business of Rosamund's either. "I'll send supper up to you. There's fresh candles, flint, and tinder on the mantel. Water in the ewer on the dresser. Anything else you need, ring the bell." She glanced around the chamber as if satisfying herself that all was in order, then left.

Rosamund stood at the window for a long time looking at the royal prison that she was soon to be sharing. Smoke curled from a chimney, otherwise there was no sign of life. What were the women doing in there at the moment?

She turned back to the room as a servant entered with a laden tray. She set it down on a table, bobbed a curtsy, and disappeared. Rosamund examined the dishes on the tray. It was Friday and she expected the usual Friday offering of plain white fish, but was pleasantly surprised by a fish pudding and a dish of green peas. A flagon of wine, a thick slice of barley bread, and a strawberry tartlet, completed the feast.

She took the pudding and the horn spoon to the window seat and ate looking out as the setting sun cast long shadows over the fields beyond the outbuildings. If she wished to, she could walk in those fields this evening. But when would she next have that freedom?

"You believe that your sister will manage to maintain this deception?" Sir Amyas reached across the table for the flagon of wine, refilling his guest's cup.

"It matters little what I believe, Paulet," Thomas said, circling his hand around his cup. "Master Secretary has decreed that she will." He shrugged. "I'll say this for Rosamund, she does not lack for wit . . . if she keeps her somewhat wilder impulses in check," he muttered.

"She will need all the wit she has. Scots Mary is as wily as Reynard eluding the hounds. I've taken everything possible away from her, but still she won't break." Sir Amyas scowled into his wine cup.

"And this beer-keg post?"

"Working well." It was Phelippes who answered. "Two deliveries so far. One came in from Mary's agent in Scotland. It was extracted from the keg by the brewer, and I deciphered it before it was replaced in the neck of the keg and Mary's maid retrieved it from the buttery when the kegs were stored. Mary's reply was inserted by the maid, retrieved by the brewer outside the Hall, again deciphered by me, and then sent on its way."

Phelippes reached for a strawberry tartlet, saying through a mouthful of pastry crumbs, "It is a brilliant invention. So far nothing sufficiently incriminating has come or gone, but one day soon this post will yield the fruit that will loose the hangman."

"A finale devoutly to be hoped for." Thomas reached for a sweetmeat. "These are exceptionally good. Your cook is uncommonly skilled."

"Aye. A good table compensates for a somewhat dreary watch." Paulet tapped the table with his fingers. "Six years I have been her jailer and I'll be glad to be rid of the task, Walsingham."

Thomas could understand. Six years watching over the royal captive in various prisons in the north of England without so much as a visit to the court, with never a break for family or personal pleasure, would grow tedious. Mary was not an easy prisoner to watch. Over the eighteen years of her imprisonment, she had hatched countless plots, had had a finger in every plot against the queen and in every project for a foreign invasion from the Catholic monarchs of France and Spain. She had drawn many with her charm, her beauty, and her sorrowful tale into her devious schemes and had missed no opportunity to outwit her jailer. Now neither she nor her ladies were permitted to walk outside, except for one short walk a day in the orchard, and that only because the physician had said that without it the Scots queen's health would suffer irreparable harm, and her cousin Elizabeth could not have it said that she had caused her cousin's death by ill treatment.

"Well, matters move apace now. Master Secretary spins his web ever tighter, and if all play their part well, we shall see its finish before year's end."

Paulet raised his cup. "I will drink to that, Walsingham."

Thomas and Phelippes raised their cups and drank the silent toast.

Rosamund was awoken by the housekeeper the next morning, soon after cockcrow. Mistress Tunston set a jug of hot water on the dresser. "Master Walsingham and Sir Amyas ask that you break your fast with them downstairs."

Rosamund dressed with care, trying to ensure that she looked suitably modest and devout. She let her hair fall loose to her shoulders, confined only by a black ribbon at her forehead, and selected a modest black lace partlet for the neck of her apple green gown. As a final touch she fastened the ivory rosary at her waist.

She made her way downstairs and was shown into a paneled parlor where Thomas, Master Phelippes, and Sir Amyas were already at breakfast. Thomas looked her over with a faint glimmer of amusement. "A suitably virgin appearance, Sister." The irony in his voice was not lost on Rosamund, who merely curtsied demurely and took a seat at the table.

"There are one or two things Master Phelippes here needs to explain to you." Thomas cut a thick slice of ham from the joint in front of him. "Listen well."

Mary, Queen of Scots, stood close to the fire in her chamber, warming her chilled fingers. The damp again, rather than the cold, made her joints ache. Some days her fingers were so swollen with chilblain it was too painful to take up her needle. After a few minutes she went to the prie-dieu and knelt with her rosary, murmuring her prayers. Her ladies ceased their quiet conversation and continued with their sewing in silent respect for the queen's devotions.

The maid Barbara came in to clear away the breakfast dishes and add more fuel to the fire. Despite the bright sunshine outside, the room with its single window high in the wall was gloomy, candles providing the only illumination.

Mary looked up from her prayers, turning her head towards the girl. "You're quite certain there was nothing in the beer keg yesterday, Barbara?"

"Quite certain, madam. I checked most carefully." It was the fifth or sixth time Mary had asked the same question, and Barbara wished fervently that she could give a different answer.

Mary sighed and rose to her feet. She looked forward to Fridays with an obsessive longing, and when the beer delivery day passed without a message, her spirits were lowered for days after. She began to pace the chamber, running the beads of her rosary through her fingers, her lips moving in silent prayer. In past prisons she had been able to ride whenever she chose, and the exercise had invigorated her. She had gone hawking across Hanbury Hill when she'd been kept at Tutbury Castle, and at Sheffield Castle she had ridden to hounds. She couldn't remember when last she had been on the back of a horse, and for a woman who had always been energetic, had loved outdoor sport, this enforced inactivity was almost the hardest thing to bear.

She paused in her perambulation at the sound of voices from the outer chamber. The little terrier pricked his ears and looked at the door. Her jailer's familiar tones made her lip curl with distaste. What fresh humiliation was he about to deliver? She sat down by the fire and waited, her hands clasped lightly in her lap.

The door opened and Sir Amyas entered with a young woman. "Madam, I have brought you a new attendant," he announced without preamble. "The queen is pleased to send you Rosamund Fitzgerald, who was lately in her service. Her majesty thought you would find a fresh face and fresh companionship to your liking."

"I have no need of either, Sir Amyas," Mary stated quietly. "And most particularly no need of someone sent directly from my cousin's court. Surely you cannot imagine I would be such a fool?"

Rosamund stepped forward, dropping to her knees. "Madam, I do most earnestly beg you to reconsider. I have long wished to serve you, and to practice the true religion. My family have abandoned the true faith, and I have been forbidden to pray as I choose. I have been cast out by my family, banished from court by the queen. I begged the queen to send me to you, and because she has some kindness for me despite my beliefs, she agreed, on condition that you were willing to accept me."

Mary regarded the kneeling girl with a flicker of interest. It was not inconceivable that Elizabeth would agree to grant such a wish. She would remember well enough her own religious persecution by her own sister, Queen Mary, who sought to compel Elizabeth, as a girl, to take instruction in the Catholic religion. Mary herself knew that Elizabeth had more tolerance for differing styles of worship as long as they were not blatantly practiced.

"Rise," she said. "You are called Rosamund?"

"Yes, madam. Rosamund Fitzgerald."

"Our life here is dreary and uneventful." Mary cast Sir Amyas a derisive glance as she spoke. "It is hard for someone as young as yourself to live day by day with so little diversion."

"Madam, my dearest wish was to enter a convent as a novice and to take my vows, but my family would not permit it. I have no other desire but to spend my days in prayer and service to God, and if in so doing I can be of service to you, then it is all I ask."

Rosamund was astonished at herself as the lies tripped off her tongue. They sounded so convincing she almost believed them herself. She kept her head lowered, her hands clasped against her skirt, and waited.

Mary leaned forward and took her hand in both of hers, drawing her closer to her chair. "My child, I would be pleased to accept your service. We spend much of our time in prayer." She looked at Paulet. "Is there anything else, Sir Amyas?"

Paulet bowed. "No, madam. Nothing." He turned and left.

Outside, Thomas Walsingham waited for him. "Well, did she accept her?"

"Your sister is quite the actor," Amyas said. "Rarely have I seen a more accomplished performance. Sir Francis must have trained her well."

"To my knowledge he hasn't trained her at all. But our master has an uncanny ability for picking his tools. He has agents the length and breadth of Europe convincing Catholics that they are among friends, only to bring them down."

"Well, your sister convinced Mary in short order. Now she is in, we have to see what she can discover."

Chapter Twenty-two

KIT MARLOWE SLUMPED in a drinking booth of the Black Bull tavern at Barnard's Inn regarding his companion through narrowed eyes. John Savage was clearly nervous, twisting his fingers into knots as he talked.

"I wait only word from Father Ballard before I honor my pledge. I told Gifford as much. I do not mean to renege. I made a vow and I will honor it."

"How do you mean to do it?" Kit reached for his wine cup. "The queen is much guarded when she goes abroad."

Savage sucked in his lower lip. "A present of jeweled gloves. It is well-known how the queen loves to receive gifts, the richer the better. Her vanity and her avarice are thus both fed. These gloves, beautiful on the outside, will conceal a serpent's tooth, a particular venom that once it touches the skin works instantly and irrevocably."

"A method worthy of a Medici or a Borgia," Kit said, savoring the idea. It could serve well as a plot device in a play one day. "How do you lay hands on this venom?"

Savage shook his head. "I dare not say, not even to you. But I have it in my possession and I wait only Father Ballard's word to honor my pledge."

Kit drained his cup and stood up. "Well, that is good enough for me. Father Ballard is expected any day now. If he brings good tidings, you should get your word soon enough." He raised a hand in farewell and strode away, leaving John Savage to his own thoughts.

Kit stepped out into the muggy heat of a late-June day. The stench of a dead cat in the kennel made him want to retch for a moment, and he thrust his handkerchief to his nose as he untethered his horse from the hitching post outside the tavern. He did not like this work that he was doing for Master Secretary. It had something of the stench of the rotting cat about it. Urging men on to commit an act that would ensure them a traitor's death sat ill in his belly, and if he could have found a way out of the web, he would have taken it without a backward glance for the payments lost.

He mounted and rode towards the river. He needed to get out of the city for a spell, and the cool freshness of Scadbury beckoned. Thomas had given him carte blanche to use the house whenever it suited him, for work or play, and today he had need of such refreshment.

It was an easy ride to Scadbury once he had made the river crossing and he arrived in late afternoon. The first person he saw was Ingram Frizer, lounging against the trunk of an oak tree just inside the gates. Kit loathed Frizer and the feeling was clearly mutual. But there was some compensation. Wherever Frizer was, Thomas was not far away.

"So Master Marlowe, what brings you here?" Frizer's voice had a nasal whine and was as unpleasant to hear as his appearance was unsavory. "The prospect of a frolic in the hay?"

Kit controlled his temper with difficulty. He knew Thomas thought highly of Frizer, knew that Frizer managed details of Thomas's personal affairs that were better not asked about. As a result, on Thomas's ground Frizer must be permitted his insolence unmolested. He rode past the man, drawing his horse aside with a fastidious air, and cantered up the drive to the house, the man's sardonic chuckle grating in his wake.

He found Thomas on the terrace, whittling a piece of wood with apparent absorption. Thomas looked up as Kit rode to the bottom of the steps leading to the terrace and smiled a wide smile of greeting.

"You are well come, Kit." He stood up, tossing the piece of wood aside. "Indeed, I was thinking of you just a few minutes ago." He came down the steps as Kit dismounted. "It has been too long since you were last here." He linked an arm in Kit's. "Let us go in. Someone will see to your horse."

The two went inside and upstairs, and the sound of the slamming door to Thomas's bedchamber echoed through the quiet house. Ingram Frizer stood in the hall and heard the sound. His expression was hard to read as he turned on his heel and left the house.

An hour later Thomas rolled onto his back, dabbing at his damp chest with the crumpled sheet. "Ah, I have missed that."

"I too." Kit stood up, stretching his thin frame. "Where have you been these last two weeks?"

"In the north. I had to escort Rosamund to Chartley. She has joined Mary's ladies in imprisonment."

Kit stared at him. "Rosamund is dragged into Walsingham's net too?"

"Rather she swam into it." Thomas sat up on the bed. "The wretched girl lost her virginity at some point. Sir Francis says it was last summer at Scadbury, but I don't believe it. However, that is the story and must not be questioned. The queen discovered she was no longer virgin and banished her. Master Secretary put the situation to good use as is his wont."

"I am sorry for it," Kit said slowly, reaching for his shirt. "She is too young to be so corrupted by Walsingham's machinations."

Thomas shrugged. "We are all grist to his mill, beloved. And mayhap he will find her a husband, spoiled virgin or no, if she does his work well."

"Savage wants to know how soon he can expect the word from Ballard." Kit laced his trunk hose.

"Soon enough. A week ago we intercepted a letter to Mary from Morgan in Paris advising her to make contact with Anthony Babington. He grows more committed by the day according to Will Creighton. We hope he will write to her himself, telling her of the efforts being made on her behalf. If she commits herself in writing, then . . ." Thomas shrugged eloquently. "Why, then we shall see what we shall see."

"I like it not." Kit stood at the window, gazing out at the sun-bathed fields around Scadbury.

"Then keep it to yourself." Thomas came up behind him, running a lascivious hand over his buttocks.

Kit turned with a smile into his lover's embrace.

At Chartley the long summer days passed in a tedium broken only by the Friday high spot when the brewer exchanged the empty ale kegs for full ones. Mary's excitement was palpable as she waited to see if there was a letter in the keg, and her anxiety as she waited for the following Friday when she could send off her own response was pathetic.

One Friday morning she emerged from her bedchamber with a sealed parchment. "Rosamund, I have a letter for the empty beer keg before the brewer arrives with a new delivery. Will you take it for me?" She reached into the little netted purse at her waist and drew out the leather pouch, carefully inserting the letter into its drawstring neck.

"Of course, madam." Rosamund took the pouch and slipped it into her bodice. It had become her duty almost by default to act as postman, and the task facilitated her own need to pass on her own reports. Mary's secretary, Claude de Nau, had visited the previous evening, and Rosamund had faithfully recorded the conversation between them. De Nau had talked of a Father John Ballard, an outlawed priest who had secretly landed from France in a small fishing village in Cornwall. He was gathering together a group of passionate Catholic supporters. Two of them were law students at the Inns of Court. The names Gifford and Savage had been mentioned.

Rosamund had no idea whether this information was new to Sir Francis, but he would want to know what Mary knew of the plots being hatched on her behalf. She hurried to the buttery and removed the bung from the empty keg. She opened the pouch containing Mary's letter and slipped her own folded sheets inside together with Mary's, then inserted the pouch into the space below the bung. She pushed the bung in tightly and returned to Mary's side, taking up her rosary to murmur the now familiar prayers.

An hour later they heard the sounds of the brewer's dray on the cobbles outside, the rolling rattle of the full kegs on the cobbles. The empty kegs sounded light as they were rolled out to the dray. And the brewer's horse clopped on iron hooves out of the yard.

Phelippes or some other agent of Walsingham's would read Mary's letter and Rosamund's reports. Hers would go on to Sir Francis, and Mary's to its intended destination, its contents no longer a secret.

"Hurry and check the fresh keg, Rosamund." Mary was pacing her chamber, her eyes febrile with anticipation. "Don't forget it will be the one with a cross on the side. I am certain there will be something today. I feel it in my bones."

Rosamund took two jugs from the kitchen and crossed the yard to the buttery. It was deserted, as she had hoped. Four full kegs stood against the far wall. Rosamund examined them, looking for the cross with which the brewer marked Mary's keg for identification. She prized up the bung from the top and felt inside. Her fingers encountered a leather pouch identical to the one she had inserted earlier in the empty keg. She drew it out rapidly, slipping it inside her bodice, then she filled her jugs with ale and sauntered back across the yard to the outbuildings.

Mary was waiting for her, her impatience visible in every line of her tall, thin body. "Well?"

"There is something, madam." Rosamund handed her the leather pouch, then bent to stroke the terrier, who had greeted her return with a wet nose pressed against her leg.

Mary almost snatched the pouch from her, her fingers shaking as she opened the drawstring and took out the closely written sheet. She sat down, drawing the candle close, and began to read. "Oh, 'tis from Master Babington." Her eyes moved rapidly along the lines, and when she had finished, she leaned back in her chair, closing her eyes briefly. "It is to be done," she said quietly. "Finally, may God be praised, it is to be done."

"What is that, madam? What is to be done?" Charlotte leaned close as if to hear secrets.

"Why an invasion, Charlotte. My cousin the Duc de Guise, together with Philip of Spain, has prepared a joint invasion force." Mary smiled, a rare thing these days. "I knew I could rely on the Holy League in the end. For my mother's sake if not for mine."

Her mother had been a Guise, and her cousin Henri de Lorraine, the third Duc de Guise, had formed the alliance of the Holy League with Philip II of Spain, the pope, the Catholic nobility of France, and the powerful Parlement of Paris, which brought the full weight of the Catholic Church in France to bear. The league was a vital counter-weight to King Henry III of France should he renege on his promise to continue the persecution of the Huguenots. If the king stayed true, then he could count on the support, both military and diplomatic, of the immensely power-ful Guise family. Should he fail, he would find himself in armed conflict with the most powerful and influential families in France.

"How is it to be done, madam?" Rosamund asked the question when it seemed Mary's reverie would continue unbroken.

Mary seemed visibly to shake herself back to reality. "Master Babington says that he and his fellows are prepar-ing the ports to receive the invasion, supplying them with a strong cadre to join with the invaders when they land. After they land, I am to be delivered from this captivity." She fell silent, a shadow passing over her previously radiant countenance.

"And what then, madam?"

Mary sat up straighter and took up the letter again, reading aloud. "He writes of the dispatch of the usurping competitor, Elizabeth, by six noble gentlemen, all private friends of his, who for the zeal they bear to the Catholic cause and to my service will undertake . . ." She paused as if finding the words hard to form. Then she continued with resolution, "Will undertake that tragical execution."

She let the letter fall into her lap, from where it fluttered to the floor. "I would wish the last was not necessary." She closed her eyes again.

Rosamund bent to pick up the letter. Sir Francis's interest in Babington was now explained, as was Will Creighton's friendship with Anthony Babington. Will was presumably acting on Master Secretary's orders. Was there anyone she knew not playing on Sir Francis's stage?

She glanced down at the letter in her hand. It was addressed to *My dread Sovereign Lady and Queen, unto whom only I owe all fidelity and obedience.* Her eye skimmed the page, and two lines jumped out at her, lines that Mary had not read aloud. *Forasmuch as delay is extremely dangerous, it may please your most excellent Majesty to direct us, and by your princely authority to enable such as may advance us.*

Sir Francis would know the contents of this letter. It would have been read by Phelippes before the brewer inserted it into the keg. And they would be waiting now for Mary's response.

"What will you reply, madam?" Rosamund laid the letter carefully on the table beside Mary.

"I do not know as yet, Rosamund." Mary took up the letter again. "I must consider very carefully. It is not possible to overestimate how much is at stake."

Jaunty pennants flew from the colorful tents dotting the vast stretch of lawn leading to the river at Hampton Court. The queen sat on a dais, beneath the shade of an awning, her household around her. She was leaning forward slightly, her expression rapt as she watched the two jousting knights in the lists below the dais. It was all in play, of course, on this hot summer day, but the ferocity of competition was still in the charge as the knights rode at each other, lances poised. The clash of lance on shield seemed to make the air shiver, and the crowd roared its approval as they turned, took fresh lances from their squires, and prepared for a second sally.

Agathe fanned herself as she watched, aware of a tight knot in her breastbone. Arnaud, sitting his horse at the far end of the field, was measuring up his opponent. Nothing in his bearing indicated tension, indeed he appeared almost nonchalant as he weighed the lance in his hand and waited for the trumpet call that would start the charge. But she was troubled nevertheless. A suppressed tension had been about him ever since the banishment of the Walsingham girl. A pent-up energy belied by his customary languid grace, and she could only think that his feelings for the girl had run deeper than she had thought. He had given her the impression that he wanted a toy, a virgin to seduce, and she had gone along with it, not because she approved of his game, but because she had never yet refused him anything.

The trumpet sounded the challenge and Arnaud glanced once towards the stands. Agathe waved a scarlet ribbon in encouragement. He was too far away for her to see if he acknowledged her gesture, but then he dropped his visor and his horse leaped forwards. His opponent, young Lord Morganston, gave an exultant cry as he galloped, his lance held high. Arnaud's glossy black charger reared at the first clash of lances, then wheeled and charged again. Arnaud, his mouth twisted in a grimace of ferocious determination, drove his lance into the youth's shield, the full force of his body behind the thrust, his horse shivering beneath him with the power of the impact, and Lord Morganston fell from his saddle in an awkward tangle. His foot was caught in the stirrup, and as his horse pranced in distress, he bounced helplessly over the ground.

Men rushed onto the field, seizing the reins, calming the horse while they released the rider. Morganston lay in an armored heap on the dry ground, unmoving. Arnaud turned his horse back to the tent pavilion, his face impassive beneath his visor.

Agathe gazed in horror. She had been afraid of this, afraid that that suppressed energy would break loose and Arnaud would forget the essential fact that this tourney was a mock battle. No one was supposed to be hurt, it was all for show. The challengers were displaying their skill and grace, not their ability to unhorse or injure their opponents.

She looked at the queen and her heart sank. Elizabeth had risen from her chair and was leaving the dais with an expression of disgust on her rouged and powdered countenance. Her household were gathering themselves to follow her.

Roger Askew rode up the driveway of a half-timbered manor house in Barn Elms some miles to the south of London. It was a hot July afternoon and he was glad to be free of the stench and heat of the city for a few hours. He dismounted at the front door, handing his horse to a lad who came running from the stables at the side of the house, and banged the great brass knocker.

The servant who opened the door led him across the stone-flagged hallway and through a wainscoted parlor and out onto a terrace at the rear of the house. Sir Francis Walsingham was pruning rosebushes along the edge of the terrace. He looked up and a smile of pleasure creased his ordinarily severe countenance.

"Roger. You are well come indeed. Ursula will be pleased to see you. She and Frances are deciphering Philip's latest letter from Flushing. The man's script leaves much to be desired." He set aside his secateurs and shook his friend's hand vigorously. "Before we go to the ladies, I would have speech with you."

"Gladly." Roger looked around at the mellow stone and timber of the house, the sweep of lawn leading down to the gently ambling Thames, the vibrant rosebushes. "In truth, Francis, I have long envied you this patch of heaven. After Seething Lane it must bring sweet relief."

"It does. Unfortunately I have few opportunities to indulge these days. Her majesty's affairs keep me in Seething Lane. However, since the queen is disporting herself at Hampton Court, I thought to take a few days of peace myself . . . let us stroll to the river if you've a mind to."

"Gladly." The two men walked across the lawn and down to the riverbank. Walsingham's barge was moored at the water steps, and a stone bench beneath a weeping willow on the bank offered a haven from the hot sun.

"I am much troubled in my mind, my friend." Walsingham sat down, stretching his legs in front of him. Roger Askew was one of the very few people he trusted with more than the bare bones of his thoughts, his plans, his fears, and his hopes. "This conspiracy to liberate the Scots queen from captivity comes to a head. The plans are laid, and Mary has been informed of them and asked to give them her blessing. Once she has put her signature to the paper, then we will have her."

Walsingham sighed. "But my only fear is that her majesty will not . . ." He stood up abruptly, turning to his companion, his voice hard. "If the matter be well handled, it will break the neck of all dangerous practices during her majesty's reign. Once Mary is removed, there will be no figurehead for Catholic conspiracies. But I fear that the queen will not act with the necessary decision. And all my efforts will be for naught."

"You will use the Bond of Association to persuade her majesty?" Roger rose to his feet when it seemed that Francis was too restless to sit again.

"It exists for just that purpose. Burghley is as concerned as I that even when faced with irrefutable evidence of her cousin's treachery, the queen will continue to insist she cannot spill the blood of a kinswoman."

"Parliament may persuade her if Mary's guilt by association can be proved beyond a doubt."

"That may be so." Walsingham sighed again. "Ah, well, all is speculation until the Scots queen commits herself to an act of treachery. She will do so soon, I am convinced. Rosamund's reports are encouraging. They tell of Mary's despair that alternates with bouts of excitement and hope. According to Rosamund, Mary sets great store by the king of Scotland's filial loyalty. She believes that in the right circumstances he will bring an army across the border to support an English rebellion in her favor."

"And will he?" Roger bent and picked up a stone on the riverbank, sending it skimming across the undulating waters of the Thames.

"James is too careful of his throne and his own preservation to risk them in his mother's cause. Mary deludes herself in this as she has done throughout her life. She is no accurate reader of men," Walsingham observed drily.

Roger picked up another stone and sent it skimming. "Your cousin does her work well, I gather? Your confidence in her was justified?"

"Aye. She's not short on wit." Francis looked at him with a gleam of speculation. "Does your interest there remain steadfast, despite her . . ." He gestured with an open palm.

"Misstep?" Roger raised an eyebrow. "That is what you meant to say, I take it."

"Misstep, indiscretion . . ." Walsingham shrugged. "Call it what you will. She's young and has some of her brother's recklessness. But I do not see any harm in her . . . any deep-seated badness. Ursula would not have taken her to her heart so completely had there been."

Roger nodded, considering this. "Your lady wife has always been a sound judge of character, Francis. I see no reason to go back on our agreement." Roger smiled. "In all truth, I have never had much time for the saintly. It can be most dreadfully dull. A certain spirit on the other hand can be delightfully enlivening."

Francis looked relieved. "Ursula will be glad to hear you are still of the same mind, Roger. She is anxious that Rosamund should be comfortably and happily settled once her period of penance is over."

"Then we must hope that the young lady herself is of the same mind." With a wry smile, Roger followed Francis back up to the house. As they reached the terrace, Roger said thoughtfully, "Perhaps I should tend to my own garden, water the seeds myself. What think you, Francis?"

"Go to Chartley?" Francis raised an eyebrow in surprise.

"Why not? Perhaps you have some errand I can perform?"

"Oh, that, certainly, my friend. There are always errands. But let us ask Ursula. She will certainly have some trinkets or trifles that you could carry to Rosamund."

"A man bearing gifts is always well received," Roger murmured with another wry smile.

Chapter Twenty-three

WILL CREIGHTON TURNED his weary horse over to an ostler in the stable yard of the Devereux Arms in the village of Chartley and went into the taproom. He called for a tankard of ale and took it out to the ale bench to sit in the sun. Chartley Hall was visible across the village green, surrounded by its moat. Will had letters from Walsingham for Master Phelippes and for Sir Amyas Paulet, but he was in no hurry to deliver them. They would keep for an hour or so while he enjoyed the sunshine and rested his travel-weary bones. He had been instructed to make all speed on this courier's task and had ridden for two days from sunup to sundown.

The job of messenger, despite the arduous hard riding, had come as a welcome respite from his cultivation of Anthony Babington and the daily round at court, which was now ensconced at Greenwich for the rest of the summer. Hardly an hour passed without Will wondering where Rosamund was, and what she was doing. Once or twice he had been tempted to ask Thomas Walsingham for news of his sister, but had bitten his tongue in time. Such an inquiry would only raise questions.

He drank his ale and called for another pot. He could only assume that Rosamund had been sent back to Scadbury in disgrace, and he had struggled with the urge to ride over there, just on the off chance he might catch sight of her. He told himself he just needed to know that she was well, but he knew in his heart that his real need was much less selfless. That last passionate kiss in the privy garden the morning their own little world had fallen apart haunted his nights. He wanted her, almost to the point of obsession. And he knew that if he saw her, if they met again, he would not be able to resist this need.

When he got back to London, he would go in search of her. The scandal had died down now and was rarely mentioned; it would surely be safe enough, and if Rosamund no longer felt the same passionate desire for him, then maybe it would help put his own obsession to rest.

He finished his second ale pot, tossed a coin onto the ale bench, and strode off in the direction of Chartley Hall. He crossed the moat on the little stone bridge and made his way up the carriageway to the house.

"Creighton? What brings you here?"

Will turned at the voice. Master Phelippes stepped out from a shrubbery running alongside the driveway. He had a faraway look in his eye, as if his mind was elsewhere, and blinked myopically in the bright sunlight.

"I have letters for you and for Sir Amyas from Seething Lane." Will continued walking towards the house, Phelippes keeping pace. "And I am instructed to carry your correspondence back to Sir Francis."

"I have some intercepts, but as yet not the one we await most eagerly." Phelippes shook his head. "But it can only be a matter of time. The Scots queen cannot ignore Babington's letter. She must answer it. Tomorrow is Friday and we shall see if the beer-keg exchange bears fruit. You must stay until Saturday, Master Creighton, just in case we finally have what we need."

Will nodded. He had been at the meeting with Father Ballard, John Savage, and Anthony Babington when Ballard had brought the news from France that both France and Spain were preparing an invasion force to deliver the Scots queen from imprisonment. It was all the encouragement Babington and his cohorts needed to put the conspiracy in motion. Once freed, Mary would ascend Elizabeth's throne and return the country to Catholic hegemony.

Will had listened queasily as Thomas Walsingham and Robin Poley had encouraged Babington to write to Mary, asking for her support of the plan. They had done everything short of writing the letter for him. Will had held his tongue, trying to assuage his conscience with the reflection that Babington was a fool to be so easily led into self-betrayal. But he couldn't quite convince himself.

Sir Amyas Paulet greeted Will with an austere nod and took the packet of letters. "My housekeeper will find you a bed, Creighton. We will sup in an hour."

Will bowed his acknowledgment. The role of courier was lowly, but he would be paid for it. "If you have no objection, sir, I would stroll around the grounds before supper. I have ridden long and hard for two days and would welcome the chance to stretch my legs."

"By all means. Go where you please." Paulet turned back to his study, Phelippes accompanying him.

Will returned outside and began to stroll around the house in the direction of the orchard. He heard women's voices as he entered the orchard and hesitated, wondering whether he should leave. A small dog scampered ahead of a party of women who appeared at the end of the alley of pear trees. His heart seemed to stop for an instant. He knew it had to be the Queen of Scots, although he had never before seen her. But no other woman so richly dressed and with a party of attendants would be walking in the orchard of Chartley Hall. And then he saw the young woman standing just behind the queen.

Rosamund Walsingham, with a rosary at her waist, was reading aloud from a psalter.

Will ducked into the pear trees, trying to make sense of what he was seeing as the small group of women progressed along the tree-shaded alley. What was Rosamund doing in the Scots queen's company? The dog caught his scent when they were a few yards away and made little runs at Will's hiding place, yapping excitedly. Swiftly Will stepped out of concealment, then seemed to start with surprise at seeing them.

He bowed low, his hat at his breast. "Madam, forgive me for the intrusion. I didn't realize you were walking here."

Mary regarded him for a moment, then smiled. She was still as susceptible to handsome young men as she had ever been in her own stunningly beautiful youth. "There is no need for pardon, sir. The orchard does not belong to me, indeed I am only permitted to walk here for one brief half hour a day. You, however, are free to walk in it whenever you choose."

"William Creighton, at your service, madam." He bowed again, his eyes this time flickering to Rosamund, who was standing stock-still on the path, her psalter ignored in her hand. Her face had paled but her composure seemed unruffled.

"Master Creighton, we are delighted to make your acquaintance. But pray don't let us keep you from your walk. We are returning to the house for supper now." Mary moved forwards, her ladies falling in behind her. Will bowed as they passed. Rosamund dropped her handkerchief on the path as she continued in Mary's wake, and Will hastened to pick it up.

"I believe you dropped this, mistress." He gave it to her.

"Oh, my thanks." She took it, her fingers brushing his. Under her breath she murmured, "The buttery after supper." Then she hurried after the women.

Will was at sea, his mind tumbling in a confused jumble of questions and emotions. The sight of Rosamund had affected him as he had known it would. Sensual memories of their times together flooded him, and the remembered scent of her filled his nostrils, the remembered feel of her skin made his hands tingle. All the problems inherent in this desperate attraction ceased to exist in the knowledge that she was so close, in the thought that they could be together again.

Alone in the orchard, he indulged both memory and anticipation in such a glorious swirl of lust and desire that he suddenly realized that in his present state he could not decently show himself at the supper table. The realization made him laugh out loud and he set off at a brisk walk to cool himself down.

Rosamund tried not to appear too preoccupied during supper. Mary's secretary, Claude de Nau, was paying one of his frequent visits to Chartley and joined them for the frugal meal. Rosamund knew she should be listening to as much as she could hear of their discussion, but her mind was filled with thoughts of Will, with memories and the glorious thrill of anticipation. She wanted to feel his body against hers, to run her fingers through those carefully disheveled curls, to feel his mouth on hers. She had paid the price for pleasure already, so what was to stop her now?

With an effort she forced herself to concentrate on the conversation. Monsieur de Nau was in the Scots queen's confidence and worked tirelessly in her cause. He had perused Babington's letter many times over before supper, and now he and Mary talked in low voices at one end of the table, while her ladies spooned watery soup and fried beans and murmured among themselves at the other. The two spoke in such low voices that Rosamund could make out little of what was said, but it seemed obvious that they were discussing what response to make to Babington's letter. A response that must presumably be ready to go out with the beer-keg post on the morrow.

She gave up trying to hear and let her mind roam free again. After the first delicious shock at seeing Will, she felt no real surprise at his presence at Chartley. She knew he was working for her cousin, and it seemed somehow inevitable that he, like so many others, would find himself here, where all Master Secretary's efforts were presently concentrated. She smiled to herself as her blood began to dance.

At supper's end Mary conducted evening prayers, then she and her secretary retired to the queen's inner bedchamber to continue their discussion.

It was too early to slip away to the buttery, and Rosamund tried to distract herself by taking up her pen and beginning a sketch of one of the brewer's cart horses from memory while Mary's ladies talked softly as they sewed, and Charlotte read passages from the New Testament.

She couldn't concentrate, for once couldn't lose herself in the drawing, and after fifteen minutes Rosamund put down her pen and rose quietly. It would be easier to await Will in the buttery than sit here trying to contain her impatience. She slipped from the room, hoping that if her absence was remarked, it would be assumed she was paying a visit to the privy, abutting the kitchen wall.

No one said anything as she left. The kitchen was

deserted, the supper dishes cleared away, and the maids retired. She took up an ale jug as excuse for a trip to the buttery and slipped out into the yard. It was cool and dark in the buttery, fragrant with the aromas from the churns of butter, the great wheels of cheese, and the jugs of buttermilk and cream. The beer kegs stood as usual against the wall, and she went to fill her jug at the one marked with the cross.

"Rosamund?"

She whirled, spilling ale as she jerked the jug from the keg. "Will . . . oh, Will . . . couldn't you have coughed or something?" She laughed with the sheer joy of seeing him.

"I didn't mean to startle you." He crossed the stone-flagged floor in two strides and took her into his arms. He crushed her against him, burying his face in her hair. "Oh, God, Rosamund. I have missed you so." He groaned and held her even tighter as she put her arms around him, pressing herself against him as if she would become a part of him.

"I didn't realize how much I missed you until I saw you," she said against his mouth the instant before words were no longer possible. They kissed greedily, and it was almost as if somehow they would suck the lifeblood from each other, take the other into themselves.

They clung together, molded to each other, in the cool dimness, and when he bore her backwards against the cold wall, Rosamund braced herself, spreading her legs as he rummaged beneath her skirts, finding her core, fingering, delving, hearing her moan against his mouth. He fumbled with the laces of his britches and drove into her, and she cried out against his mouth, moving her hips to match his rhythm. And when it was over, she hung around his neck like a broken spar in a storm, until the wave receded.

Will leaned heavily against the wall, crushing her between his body and the cold stone until she pushed feebly at his chest and with a muttered apology he straightened, holding her waist between his hands as he gazed into her eyes. "Oh, my sweet Rosamund. What witchcraft do you make?"

"None," she said, leaning back against his hands. She reached up and touched a finger to his lips. "And do not speak of witchcraft. 'Tis a powerful evil that invokes."

"Aye, and we have no need of that, do we?" His smile was rueful as he traced the shape of her mouth with a fingertip. "You are *so* lovely." He lingered over the words, making of them a caress.

Rosamund smiled. "That makes two of us then." The cool air in the buttery was cold on her heated skin, and she realized her skirts were still hiked up around her waist, held there by his body. She must look the complete wanton. The reflection made her laugh again. She stepped away, and her skirts fell back into place. Will with a chuckle of his own as if he'd had the same thought swiftly laced his britches again.

"How long will you stay?" She combed her tangled hair with her fingers.

"I must leave on Saturday. I am just a courier, sweet, a mere message boy."

"Then we have tomorrow."

"Yes. We will have tomorrow." He raised a quizzical eyebrow. "What *are* you doing here?"

"Spying on the Scots queen," she said bluntly. "We are all actors, it seems, on my cousin's stage. He makes the play, we perform. This is my penance for my . . . indiscretion, shall we call it?"

His expression became grave. "Why didn't you tell

Walsingham of my part in that *indiscretion* if that's what you call it?"

She shook her head. "I was the one who was caught. What good would it have done either of us for you to suffer too?"

"That is so rational, Rosamund, but it makes me feel somehow unworthy . . . as if I have done something cowardly." He laid his hands on her shoulders, his eyes filled with remorse.

She shook her head again vigorously. "No . . . not so. You must never think that. I made the decision for both of us, because it was mine to make."

He drew her against him again, and this time the kiss was soft and gentle. He moved his mouth from hers and brushed a kiss across her closed eyelids, then slowly, reluctantly raised his head and let his hands fall from her.

"Let us not tempt providence a second time, Rosamund. You must go back before you're missed."

She nodded. "I imagine they're all abed, but you're right." She moved to the door, turned, and blew him a kiss, before slipping out into the darkened courtyard.

She fetched water from the rain barrel and washed herself in the kitchen, then crept to bed in the silent house. There was no candle beneath Mary's door, so Monsieur de Nau had presumably left.

Rosamund lay awake for a long time. The impediments to her liaison with Will were still there, as large as life. He was still a penniless courtier with a future to make, and she was a dowerless, disgraced maid of honor, ruined by scandal. And even if she was not, she knew her family would never permit an alliance with Will, her brother had said as much on that first theatre outing, which now seemed to have happened to someone else in another lifetime.

They might be short on fortune, but they were still Walsinghams, with a most powerful cousin and a connection however tenuous to the Boleyns.

But her spirit was too buoyant at present to dwell overlong on the difficulties. And they still had tomorrow to look forward to. If she had learned one thing in the last months, it was to take what was offered when it was offered. There was no telling in this troubled time when the offer would be rescinded. With a tiny smile she turned on her side and curled into sleep.

Chapter Twenty-four

PHELIPPES LOOKED UP from the paper in his hand and smiled the devil's own smile. Silently he handed it to the watching Paulet, who read it and gave a grunt of satisfaction. "Good. Where is Creighton? He must leave at once."

"He was strolling into the village when I saw him last."

Sir Amyas went to the door and opened it, bellowing for a servant, who came running from the back regions of the house. "Find Master Creighton. It is a matter of the utmost urgency. He may be in the village."

The servant tugged a forelock and ran off. He found Will on the ale bench outside the Devereux Arms nursing a cup of canary wine, tracing patterns in the dust with the toe of his boot. The exuberant joy of the previous evening had given way to despair as he racked his brain for a solution to an insoluble problem. He had toyed with the idea of an elopement, but that would make them both social pariahs and bring the queen's vengeance down on their heads. They would have nothing to live on and no way to make a living. He had no skills, apart from a certain fluency in the courtly arts. Rosamund could draw, but no living was to be earned from that. His own impoverished family had given him all they had to set him up at court, with the clear expectation that with his charm and good looks he would marry a woman with a decent dowry and provide for them in their declining years.

He looked up with a jaundiced eye at the sound of his name. The servant breathlessly delivered his message and Will sighed and got to his feet. He drained his cup, tossed a coin onto the bench, and strode back to the house.

Sir Amyas was waiting for him in the hall. "You must ride at once to London and take this to Sir Francis Walsingham." He held out a small leather satchel. "If you ride overnight, you should get there by late afternoon tomorrow."

Will took the satchel, frowning. "I understood I was to leave tomorrow, after the exchange of kegs this evening."

"The brewer was here earlier than usual. If you leave now, you will have another six hours of daylight. There must be no delay."

Will felt only a crushing disappointment as he stared down at the satchel in his hand. He would not see Rosamund tonight. She would go to the buttery and wait for him, and he would not come. And God only knew when or even if they would see each other again.

"*Hurry, man.* Your horse is saddled, there is food in the panniers, you wait for nothing." Paulet almost pushed Will to the door in his impatience.

There was nothing to be done about it and Will left at once, riding through the night. He exchanged his own horse for a fresh mount at dawn, instructing the groom at the inn to bring Sam in easy stages to Whitehall when the animal had rested, and set off again. It was early afternoon when he dismounted in Seething Lane, only to be informed that Master Secretary was at his house in Barn Elms. Wearily Will remounted his equally weary horse and took the road to Barn Elms.

Sir Francis was walking up from the river when he heard the sound of a horse galloping *ventre à terre* up the drive. He frowned, then strode towards the front of the house.

The dust-coated rider flung himself from a lathered horse. "A message, sir. From Master Phelippes."

"Catch your breath, Master Creighton," Sir Francis said calmly.

Will, his face scarlet in the heat, drew the satchel from inside his doublet. "It is of great urgency, Sir Francis. I was to ride night and day to bring it to you." He handed it over, suddenly conscious of his legs quivering beneath him.

Francis took the satchel. "You did well, Master Creighton. Take your horse to the stables and then go into the house for refreshment." Francis walked away to a wooden bench under a spreading copper beech on the lawn, unfastening the satchel as he did so.

He took out the single document it contained. It was sealed and he turned it over in his hands, knowing without opening it that this was what they had all been waiting for.

Phelippes, with a misplaced sense of ghoulish humor, had drawn a crude symbol of a gallows on the back. It was a triumphant and outrageously indiscreet declaration that the contents of the packet would lead its author to the gallows. Francis savored for a few moments the choice words he would deliver to his subordinate when next he saw him, then he slit the wafer and opened the sheet.

It was everything he could have hoped for. Mary had answered Babington's letter in minute detail, giving her permission for every detail of the conspiracy to go forward in her name. It was certainly enough to bring her to the headsman. Francis squinted at the last paragraph, where Mary asked Babington for the names of the six noble gentlemen who were to remove Elizabeth. Francis thought he could detect Phelippes's hand there, a postscript he had added to the original in the hope that it would elicit more information about the conspirators.

Walsingham folded the letter and tucked it into his doublet. Once it was copied, it would be resealed and sent on its way to Master Babington in his lodgings in Holborn. And then they could move. The conspirators would be arrested, confessions would be extracted, evidence that even Elizabeth could not deny. And they would die a traitor's death. And when the country was up in arms at the narrowly averted threat to their beloved queen, they would go to work on Scots Mary.

Mary fretted herself to a shadow. Once the die had been cast, she could only wait, and waiting was torment. She lived for Fridays, but for several weeks nothing further came from Anthony Babington. There were letters from her agents in Paris and from the French embassy in London, but nothing was said in them of Master Babington's conspiracy or of an impending invasion. It was as if she had dreamed it, and only Claude de Nau could confirm that the letter had been real and that she had answered it in full.

"Madam, perhaps Sir Amyas could be persuaded to permit you to walk a little more often in the grounds," Rosamund suggested, when she could no longer bear the queen's pacing. "Shall I send a message to ask him to wait upon you?"

"I will not plead with that man," Mary said. "It will merely give him pleasure, and I would not give him pleasure for my life's blood. Go again to the beer keg, Rosamund. Mayhap you missed something when you looked yesterday."

Rosamund knew she had not, but she welcomed the excuse to escape from the outbuilding, which increasingly oppressed her. She felt sometimes that she could no longer breathe and had to force herself to take deep breaths. When she had first arrived at Chartley, she had seen her exile in this northern outpost simply as something that had to be endured. She had had no feelings for the Queen of Scots, no particular opinion as to the rights or wrongs of Mary's captivity, but as the days passed and she saw Mary's graceful acceptance of the indignities and deprivations heaped upon her, her admiration for the deposed queen grew stronger with the stifling sense of her own captivity.

She took her time going to the buttery, walking slowly across the yard, savoring the air, even though it was hot and still and far from fresh on this early August afternoon. When Will had failed to appear for their rendezvous in the buttery, she had been deeply disappointed, but she was also certain that only something he could not control had kept him away. A few discreet questions to the maids, and she learned that the young man staying in the house had left in great haste to return to London.

It was not too hard to guess that Mary's letter to Babington had been the cause for his hasty departure, but her disappointment had been difficult to shake. That illicit passionate interlude in the buttery was burned into her soul, and she had spent the whole of the next day hugging their secret, dwelling with exquisite pleasure on the prospect of a repetition. When she had finally abandoned hope and had left the buttery, it felt as if her world had shattered, as if she could never feel pleasure again. She'd indulged her misery in full measure until she fell asleep, and when she awoke to the freshness of a new day, it seemed impossible to imagine that they would not meet again. They moved in the same world, their paths were bound to intersect. And she clung to that conviction like the proverbial drowning man to driftwood.

No one was around on this sultry, overcast afternoon. Rosamund hesitated at the entrance to the buttery. Even if she was seen going farther afield, would anyone from the house come after her? She could think of something to excuse a longer-than-expected absence on her return.

The temptation to walk a little was irresistible. Just for five minutes, she told herself, her feet taking her towards a path at the side of the house, away from the outbuildings.

At the end of the path she came to a charming knot garden, a sundial at its center. It was deserted and she walked slowly along the meandering redbrick paths bordered by low boxwood hedges, inhaling the delicate scents from the aromatic herbs and plants. At the center of the garden she sat down on a wooden bench and closed her eyes, absorbing the fragrant quiet around her.

"Mistress Rosamund?"

The voice startled her so that she jumped to her feet, wondering how she had not heard anyone approach. She looked blankly at the tall man regarding her gravely. He had a rather somber air, with serious gray eyes and an unsmiling mouth. His clothes were rich, although dark in hue, and the sword at his hip was sheathed in a plain silver scabbard. A businesslike weapon, she thought, in keeping with his soldierly posture.

For a moment she struggled with errant memory. Then it came to her. Sir Roger Askew, the man Thomas had told her Sir Francis intended her to marry. That was before her disgrace, of course. He certainly wouldn't be interested in her now . . . which was one less thing for her to worry about.

She dropped a hasty curtsy, murmuring, "I shouldn't be here. Excuse me." She moved away quickly down the walkway.

"Don't go, Mistress Rosamund. Not just yet."

She stopped, repeated, "I am not supposed to be here, sir. I need to get back to the queen."

"Then I will walk back with you." He came up beside her. "I am on business here for your cousin, and Lady Walsingham entrusted me with some trifles, ribbons and lace I think she said, that she wished you to have." He drew a slim packet out of the inner pocket of his doublet and handed it to her.

Rosamund took it with a sudden uplift of her spirits, slipping it into the pocket of her delicately embroidered apron. It meant a great deal that Lady Walsingham still thought of her with kindness. "I thank you, sir." She smiled somewhat distractedly and tried to increase her pace.

He laid a hand on her arm. "Is my presence distressing you, Rosamund?"

Her light laugh sounded unconvincing even to her. "Of course not. How should it? You are entitled to be wherever you wish, I'm sure. It is I who am in the wrong place."

"I don't believe anyone will object if we walk around the garden a little." He regarded her closely. "I was sorry not to see you again after that delightful evening in Seething Lane."

Rosamund met his gaze squarely. "I am sure you have heard why I am no longer at court, Sir Roger."

"Yes, I have." A slight smile lightened the gravity of his countenance. "And now we have established that fact, may we walk a little? Sir Amyas knows you are here, you were spied from the house."

"The queen will wonder where I am, however."

"I suspect you have sufficient wit to find an excuse to satisfy her." He frowned a little. "Is my company that distasteful, Rosamund?"

"No, no, of course not." And it was true. There was nothing distasteful about Sir Roger Askew. In fact she had no feelings about him one way or the other, except for the uncomfortable knowledge that something had been expected of her that she had not been prepared to give.

"Then we shall walk for a few minutes." Firmly he tucked her hand into the crook of his arm and began to walk again. "I met an acquaintance of yours the other day. A playmaker, one Christopher Marlowe. He was with your brother at the play and was good enough to let me read some of his *Tamburlaine*."

Rosamund was immediately diverted. "It is a fine play, I think. Did you not think so?"

"Unusual. The verse is resonant, the action bloody. I suspect it will go down well with the groundlings. Whether the queen will be pleased to have it played at court is another matter."

"The subject is the corruption of power," Rosamund said thoughtfully. "Do you think perhaps her majesty will see some insult?"

"It is the Earl of Leicester who must first be satisfied. As the master of the queen's revels, he will decide whether to grant Master Marlowe a license, and he knows better than any man what will please the queen and what will not."

"I hope he does grant a license. I would dearly like to see it performed." Rosamund found herself now quite at her ease as they strolled back through the knot garden. Sir Roger was an undemanding companion. He talked of his work in the Low Countries, of his Shropshire estates, of the house he was building along the river in London. Only when Sir Amyas Paulet came into the garden did Rosamund realize how much time had passed.

Sir Amyas came up to them. "You should tell the Lady Mary that you were detained by me, if she questions the length of your absence. It will be well to say that I questioned you in some detail about her health, that the queen is concerned for her welfare and wished for a report."

"And is she?" Rosamund asked directly.

Paulet frowned. "That is immaterial, Mistress Walsingham. I suggest you return without further delay."

Rosamund curtsied in ironic acceptance. "I give you good day, Sir Roger. Sir Amyas." She turned and walked away, her skirt swaying gently with the length of her stride.

Early on a morning two days later, Robin Poley awaited a visitor in the garden of a summer house in Bishopsgate. The man arrived, dressed in black, slipping through a gate at the bottom of the garden that gave access to a narrow alleyway. He greeted Robin with an unsmiling nod and took the tankard of ale he was offered.

"Where are the others?"

"They'll be here soon, Father Ballard." Robin drank from his own tankard and glanced once over his shoulder. His visitor caught the movement and seemed to stiffen. Then he saw the group of officers advancing across the lawn towards them and he looked at Robin with a harsh laugh.

"So, Robin, you have betrayed me . . . betrayed the one true religion. May your soul burn in hell's fires for all eternity." Ballard hurled the tankard and its contents to the grass and turned to face the approaching officers.

One man, the deputy alderman of the borough of Aldgate, stepped forward with a warrant, which he read in

a loud and careful voice. Poley listened closely. It was vital
that every part of this seizure be strictly according to the
law, and no suspicion must attach itself to the secretary
of state. The officers formed a guard around Ballard and
escorted him from the garden. He went without a word
of protest, or a move to escape, and Robin turned back to
the summer house, his task thus far completed. Now for
Babington, Gifford, Savage, and the rest.

It happened with shocking suddenness. The peaceful tedium of the prisoners' afternoon was shattered as Walsingham's men descended with brutal force upon Chartley.

Mary was conferring with her secretary, de Nau, and her
ladies were sitting over their sewing, Rosamund for once
busy with her needle as she sewed Lady Walsingham's lace
edging to the neckline of a gown. The outer door burst
open without ceremony, and the little terrier yowled and
wriggled beneath his mistress's skirts. The ring of booted
feet in the flagstone hall beyond sounded like an army.
Mary's hand went to her throat. Claude de Nau stood up.

The door to the inner chamber opened and Sir Amyas
Paulet marched in, accompanied by a phalanx of guards.
"Madam, I am come for your jewelry, your papers, and
whatever money is in your possession. Monsieur de Nau,
you are under arrest." Paulet gestured to the guards to take
hold of the trembling secretary. They grabbed his arms
with such violence they lifted him off his feet.

"What outrage is this?" Mary's face was paper white, but
she was a commanding presence, every inch a queen as she
stood ramrod straight in her rich black gown edged with
silver lace. "Release my secretary. I demand an explanation,
Sir Amyas."

"Madam, your conspiracy is discovered, its perpetrators

imprisoned." Paulet's voice was contemptuous as he extended an imperative hand. "The keys to your chests, if you please, madam."

Claude de Nau struggled, trying to move towards the queen, but the guards on either side wrenched his arms behind his back. "By what right do you arrest me?" he demanded, his voice quavering. "I am the servant of the queen regnant, Mary of Scots. I answer to no one but my queen."

"You will answer to her most sovereign majesty, Queen Elizabeth," Paulet stated. "You will be taken to London for questioning. . . . And now, madam, your keys."

De Nau was borne away, his feet dragging on the flagstones, his voice shrill with fear as he protested his innocence. After a moment's hesitation Mary opened her netted purse and took out a key ring. She dropped it onto a table and resumed her seat by the fire, quietly taking up her embroidery.

Paulet looked momentarily nonplussed, as if he'd expected a more satisfying resistance, then with a gesture to his men to accompany him he walked into Mary's inner chamber, where the chests containing her jewelry, money, and papers were kept.

Rosamund felt sick, clammy perspiration gathering on her forehead. She had known that this would happen in some form at some point, just as she knew the part she had played in it. But the abrupt violence of the last minutes shook her to her core. Mary's little dog had wriggled out from beneath her skirts and now jumped whimpering onto the queen's lap. Her ladies were gathered around her, their murmurs of fear and distress rising and falling as Rosamund stood immobile, not sure where to go or what to do. She could not bring herself to join the distressed women, to pretend to the same terrified dismay, such hypocrisy would make her feel even more despicable, and yet, until Sir Francis released her from her present servitude, she must continue to play her part.

"May I bring you wine, madam?" she asked softly, unable to think what else to do.

"If you please, Rosamund." Mary sounded almost composed as she comforted the dog with gentle strokes.

Rosamund poured a cup of wine and brought it to the queen. Mary was still pale, but her composure was untouched, as if the abrupt violence of the last hour had simply washed over her. It was the way she had reacted to each and every indignity as if such corporeal events could not affect her true self in any way. Rosamund knew that her strength came from religious conviction, a conviction that nothing could erode, and Rosamund was aware that mingling with her own admiration was a sense of envy for that astounding spiritual strength.

After close to an hour, Sir Amyas came out of the inner chamber with his men carrying sheaves of paper, jewel caskets, and money bags. "There will be guards set outside the building around the clock, madam, until I receive further instructions from London." He left with his men and the door clicked shut in the ensuing silence.

"Poor Master Babington," Mary said softly, sipping her wine. "I fear he and his noble gentlemen will suffer most grievously."

"And Monsieur de Nau, madam," Charlotte said. "They have taken him for questioning too."

"I trust my secretary will have the sense to save his skin if he can." Mary gently pulled on the terrier's ears. "He cannot in justice be accused of treachery simply because I conferred with him. He is a citizen of France."

An hour later the summons came for Rosamund.

"Mistress Fitzgerald, you are to come with me," the guard intoned.

Mary looked anxiously at Rosamund. "They will question you, my dear. They will question all my ladies. Tell them what you know. I would not have you suffer needlessly."

Rosamund's smile was wan as she went with the guard into the house. He escorted her to Paulet's office and left her at the door. She knocked. The door was opened instantly by her brother, and she couldn't prevent a little cry of pleasure at seeing him.

Thomas's warm embrace made it clear that all was now forgiven. "Come in, Rosamund." He put an arm around her shoulders, urging her in.

Sir Amyas came out from behind his desk. Rosamund disliked this man almost as much as did the Scots queen. His expression constantly expressed disapproval, and he had the hard, judgmental gaze of a passionate Puritan.

She curtsied, meeting his gaze without expression. "You have questions for me, sir?"

"I shall question all the Lady Mary's attendants in good time. It would look peculiar if you were absolved. But in fact not I but Sir Francis wishes to question you. You are to return now with your brother to London. If Sir Francis considers it necessary, you will return to the Lady Mary at some point. She will be told only that for reasons of our own we wished to examine you more extensively and you have been sent to London."

Mary would accept that, Rosamund knew. Now that the conspiracy was blown open, anyone who could have been touched by it was vulnerable, and the queen's inquisitors would spread the net as wide as they wished, pulling in innocent sprats with the plump trout. It was always the way.

She could think only that she was to be free of her present prison, even if but temporarily.

"We will dine now," Sir Amyas said, moving to the door. "You will sleep in the house tonight, Mistress Walsingham."

It seemed wrong to be eating and drinking in freedom when her erstwhile companions languished in their dreary imprisonment across the courtyard. Rosamund couldn't help the grim recollection that many folk were tonight suffering in dungeons and torture chambers for their loyalty to Mary Stuart. The reflection took away her appetite and she pushed her food around her plate, paying scant attention to the conversation around her.

It took her a moment to realize that her brother was addressing her. "We will leave soon after daybreak tomorrow, Rosamund. Sir Francis wishes to speak at some length with you. I don't know what plans he will have for you after that. He may send you back to Scadbury or keep you in Seething Lane. The one thing you may be sure of, you will not be returning to court."

"I have no particular wish to, Brother," she said with a spurt of annoyance. She was tired of playing the shamed and disgraced fallen woman. She'd paid the price. She pushed back her chair, her plate barely touched. "If you'll excuse me, I'll seek my bed."

"My housekeeper has prepared the bedchamber you used last time, Mistress Walsingham," Paulet informed her, rising with punctilious formality as she murmured a good-night and left the room.

Outside in the square hall Rosamund hesitated. She was not yet ready for bed, the sense of freedom was too heady. She went to the front door, which stood open to the warm night breeze. It was a brilliant starlit night and she could hear the croaking of bullfrogs from the duck pond. She stepped out onto the driveway and walked across the lawn to the pond.

What was to become of her now? If Sir Francis had a use for her, then he would use her, she had no illusions about that. She was a pawn in his game, as were they all. But if he didn't, what then? And where was Will right now? In London? Disporting himself at court? Or rushing around the countryside on some courier task for Master Secretary? He could even be somewhere across the English Channel, sent away for weeks on the secretary's business.

She turned to go back to the house. There was no point worrying away at that question or any other. Her own future seemed to fade into insignificance in the light of the dreadful events breaking around them. How many people were waiting in desperate terror for the sound of booted feet in the alley, the bang at the door, the hard-faced arresting officers?

How many were already in prison, shrieking in agony, their limbs stretched and dislocated on the rack as they told their interrogators what they wanted to hear, whether it was the truth or not? How many innocent people would suffer untold misery as a result of what she had told Master Secretary?

And how many men would go to their deaths? That most dreadful of deaths, to be hanged, drawn, and quartered, their hearts beating until the moment when they were cut from their still-living, sentient bodies.

Rosamund had no idea what pieces of the information she had supplied that Walsingham had considered valuable, but she knew she bore some responsibility for the disaster that had befallen Mary Stuart.

They all did, those who played upon Walsingham's stage.

Chapter Twenty-five

THE JUBILANT SOUND of church bells could be heard for miles as Thomas and Rosamund rode into London on a cloudy mid-August day three days after leaving Chartley. People thronged the streets, cheering, waving scarves and flags, drinking outside the taverns in riotous good humor.

"What's happened . . . what are they celebrating?" Rosamund asked as Jenny sidled past a mangy dog urinating against a wall.

Thomas drew rein outside a tavern. "Find out, Frizer."

The ubiquitous Frizer slid from his horse and vanished into the dark depths of the tavern. He reappeared in a few moments, remounted, and whispered to Thomas, leaving Rosamund impatiently awaiting enlightenment.

"They've run Babington and his fellows to earth," Thomas told her finally, when Frizer had stopped whispering. "They scattered immediately after Ballard was arrested, just before I rode to Chartley to fetch you, but they were discovered hiding in the country with a Catholic family. They brought them back to London, and the church bells are ringing in thanksgiving for the queen's safe deliverance."

"And what will happen to them now?"

"They are imprisoned in the Tower, where they'll be put to the question, tried, and executed," her brother said matter-of-factly. "The country will settle for nothing less."

"And Mary of Scots?"

"That is for the queen to decide."

Rosamund held her peace for the rest of the journey to Seething Lane. They were taken directly to Sir Francis's office, where Master Secretary awaited them. He greeted Rosamund with a brisk nod.

"You have done your work well, Rosamund. I may need you to return to Mary's side once it has been decided what is to be done with her, but for now, once you have answered my questions, it will be well for you to return to Scadbury for a while."

For several hours Rosamund answered his questions. Some of them seemed trivial and irrelevant, some of them merely repetitive. But when he started to question her about the women attendant on Mary, she forced her tired mind to focus. "How deeply are they in the queen's confidence? The Lady Charlotte, for instance. She was with the queen from her arrival on these shores, they must be unusually close."

Rosamund thought of the women whose lives she had shared so intimately. She thought of their loyalty and bravery. If Sir Francis wanted her to say something that would incriminate them along with their queen, he would not hear it. "They are devoted to Mary, Sir Francis, but I did not see or hear any discussion about the conspiracy or the conspirators. She shared one letter with us all, the letter from Anthony Babington, but other than that I was unaware of any open discussion about plots to rescue her."

"There must have been secret conversations, though. You may not have overheard them, but you surely saw them go apart together sometimes," he pressed, his eyes hard and searching fixed upon her.

"Obviously at times she is alone with one lady or another," Rosamund said coolly. "They are her personal attendants and take care of her most personal needs. But I did not see any whispering or feel a sense of shared secrets. We were all open with each other, sharing the same imprisonment. Just dealing with day-to-day hardships was enough to occupy us."

Francis's thin mouth was set in a tight line. His eyes raked her face, as if he would see everything that she had left out. Rosamund met his gaze in steadfast silence. "And what of Claude de Nau? He must have been closely in the queen's confidence."

She could not deny that, her reports had included every visit of the secretary's. Besides he was already under arrest and could well already have confessed. "He and the queen went apart quite often," she conceded. "We were not party to their conversations."

Silence fell again, then at last Walsingham nodded, although he did not look best pleased. "Well, no matter. The ladies themselves will be questioned in good time. You are tired and Lady Walsingham is waiting for you."

She rose with a curtsy and went to the door, feeling overwhelmingly exhausted. After three days in the saddle and two hours of interrogation it was hardly surprising. She found Ursula in her parlor and almost fell into her embrace.

"You poor girl, you're dead on your feet," Ursula exclaimed. "I don't know what Sir Francis was thinking of, keeping you answering questions before you've had a chance to rest from the journey." She poured wine. "Drink this, my dear. It will hearten you. I don't wish to hear anything about your time with Mary Stuart, so you need have no fear of further questions."

Rosamund felt the tension slide from her. After weeks of having to watch her every word in case she gave herself away, of having to listen attentively even when appearing not to, of hating the lie she was living, it was an immense relief to let go at last, to come home. This house and this parlor were home to her, almost as much as Scadbury. And Ursula was more of a mother to her than her own mother, Dorothy, had ever been.

The following morning she and Thomas rode to Scadbury, and despite her feelings for Seething Lane her heart lifted as the familiar house came into view through the trees. Jenny raised her head, sniffed the wind, and whinnied in glad recognition of her home stable.

Rosamund dismounted at the front door and, gathering up her skirts, ran into the house. It had been May when she'd left here and now it was August, almost an entire summer had passed. Wandering through the downstairs rooms felt like a voyage of rediscovery. Everywhere was as dusty and ill cared for as before, and after the orderly comfort of Seething Lane it seemed even more noticeable. The servants, as untidy and lackadaisical as ever, nevertheless greeted her with warmth, although a remarkable lack of surprise. Rosamund, walking through the house, checking the rooms to see what if anything had changed, or was missing, felt the sweet relief of being her own mistress once more, no longer a guest or a prisoner. This was her house and she was to all intents and purposes its mistress. She could go where she pleased, do what she pleased.

She unpacked her clothes in her own bedchamber, and the sound of voices on the terrace below brought her to the open window. Kit Marlowe was sitting on the low wall of the terrace. Thomas had not told her Kit would be here, and there had been no sign of him when she'd walked through the house earlier. Now he sat on the wall, a tankard in hand, idly swinging a crossed leg as he squinted up at her brother, who stood over him.

Rosamund moved sideways so that they wouldn't see her if by chance they looked up. Thomas had his hand on Kit's cheek, stroking with his forefinger, and Kit turned his face into the palm of the hand and nuzzled. She saw that Kit's free hand was caressing her brother through his trunk hose, and she stepped hastily back away from the window. They might not care if they had an observer, but she had no desire to be that observer.

She made her way to the kitchen, intending to discuss dinner with Mistress Riley. She was no longer the young girl, the youngest of the family with no responsibilities and no authority. She felt different and realized from Mistress Riley's expression of stunned amazement as Rosamund issued domestic instructions that she must in some indefinable way *be* different.

"Send Tabitha to dust the dining parlor, Mistress Riley, before we eat there this afternoon. And she should put fresh flowers in the grate in Master Walsingham's study when she's dusted it. Do we have any beeswax for the floors and the furniture?"

"Lord knows, miss." The housekeeper stared at her, clearly not best pleased by this change in the youngest Walsingham. "If we do, it'll be in the scullery. Your mother, God rest her soul, used to like it used in the old days, but then she began to ail and forgot about such things. And since she's gone, we've few enough helping hands," she grumbled irritably.

"Well, that must change." Rosamund went into the scullery, looking through the stone jars. "There's some beeswax here, I think. Tell Jethro and the girl who comes up from the village to help out, that they're to polish the wooden floors and the flagstones tomorrow."

"Aye, no doubt they'll have nothing better to do." Mistress Riley sniffed and returned to her pastry. "I'll be making a Great Pie for your dinner. We've fresh-killed venison to go with the beef and chicken, and they slaughtered a pig last month."

Scadbury had a thriving herd of deer, as well as the hogs and cattle on the home farm, and a Great Pie, which used every kind of meat and poultry available, was a much loved delicacy.

"That sounds wonderful, Mistress Riley," Rosamund said with an appreciative smile that she hoped might sweeten the housekeeper somewhat, then went off to see what else she could put right in the ramshackle house.

Kit Marlowe was in the study, writing, when she passed the open door. There was no sign of her brother. She put her head around the door. "Good afternoon, Master Marlowe."

He said absently, without looking up, "Ah, Thomas said you were back."

"Are you still working on your play?"

"No, a poem concerning Hero and Leander. My *Tamburlaine* is all but complete." He looked up then. "I imagine you have not had an easy time of it, Mistress Rosamund."

"No," she agreed, coming into the room. "But I am not alone in that."

"I don't suppose you are." He leaned back in his chair and took a deep draft from his wine cup. His eyes had a faint glimmer of mischievous amusement as he asked, "How is that young sprig with a fondness for deliciously rounded pages?"

Rosamund to her annoyance felt herself blush. "I have

not seen him in a while. And I would be grateful, Master Marlowe, if you would not mention that afternoon at the theatre to Thomas."

He laughed, but a lascivious gleam was now in his eye. "Have no fear, your lovers' tryst remains safe with me."

"It was no tryst."

Kit raised his eyebrows. "If you say so, but some swain was responsible for whatever little indiscretion sent you into exile." He raised a hand as she opened her mouth in protest. "Have no fear, Mistress Rosamund, I will keep my speculation to myself."

"Do you love my brother?" The question came out of nowhere and seemed to ask itself, but Rosamund wished the words unspoken the moment they came out of her mouth.

Marlowe's eyes narrowed. He took another gulp of wine. "What is love but a word for poets? Lust is what drives men. Did you, *do* you, love your Will, Rosamund? Or lust after him?"

Rosamund realized she should have expected nothing less from the man who had translated the scandalous and forbidden Ovid, but the question nevertheless interested her. "Both, I believe," she said after a minute. "But please, Kit, do not mention Will in Thomas's company."

"Be assured I will not." He picked up his quill again, dipping it into the inkstand.

Rosamund hesitated, then said, "Could you make love with a woman?"

At that he looked up again, his expression one of utter disgust.

Rosamund accepted the wordless answer and left him alone with his muse. She took her own thoughts up to the peace of her bedchamber, where she sat on the window seat beneath the open window. Below, her brother was walking with Frizer, conferring in a low voice. She watched them idly, certain that neither love nor lust was between *them*. The very thought made her shudder, although it occurred to her that it was possible that Frizer, in his own fashion, loved her brother. His loyalty was certainly unshakable, and he would do anything Thomas demanded of him. And it was abundantly clear that Frizer had no liking for Marlowe. She had seen him watching her brother's lover with an expression of vindictive malice . . . jealousy, even.

Did Thomas love Kit Marlowe? Or simply lust after him? Probably the latter, she decided. What would happen when Thomas took a wife? He would have to do that at some point. Edmund and his various doxies were unlikely to produce a legitimate Walsingham heir, so it would be up to the younger son to fulfill the family obligations.

She wondered if the idea of making love with a woman was as repugnant to Thomas as it was to Marlowe. But her brother was very different from Marlowe. Thomas's emotions were fickle and ran close to the surface. He was inclined to do what suited him best at any one time, and perhaps he could turn his attentions to either sex without difficulty as circumstances demanded. She felt compassion though for this putative wife. Thomas would never be a faithful husband, his eye would always rove, in one direction or another.

Arnaud paced his chamber in the Golden Cock Inn on the Strand as he waited for Agathe. After the disaster at the joust he had prudently left the court before any official notice to do so had come from the queen, and now he kicked his heels in ever-increasing impatience while the town and the court buzzed with the excitement of a fantastic conspiracy to assassinate the queen. He couldn't bear to be so far from the heart of events, from the center of talk. Agathe kept him informed as far as she could, but she had no nose for sniffing out the underlying meanings of remarks, or the ramifications of incidents, accidental or deliberate. He felt helpless, and it was as previously unknown a sensation as it was detestable.

When he heard her light step on the stair, he yanked open the door before she had reached the top step. "Well? What is happening now? What have you heard?" He bombarded her with questions as she entered the chamber.

"Arnaud . . . Arnaud, give me a moment to catch my breath," she exclaimed, fanning herself briskly. " 'Tis so hot on the street." She sat on the broad window seat. "May I have a cup of wine, *please*. I am parched."

He controlled his impatience with difficulty and poured wine into a pewter cup. He handed it to her, then perched on the corner of the table, one leg swinging carelessly as he sipped from his own cup. "So, tell me."

"Well, it is said that the prisoners are being put to the question and Walsingham and Burghley are trying to persuade the queen to bring charges against Mary of Scots. But it is said that she will not listen to them."

Arnaud nodded. "The queen is always excessively cautious." He regarded Agathe thoughtfully over the lip of his cup. "Is aught said of my departure from court?"

She shook her head, knowing that this was the question closest to his heart. "The queen has not issued a decree of banishment, so your departure is considered voluntary." She gave him a placatory smile, seeing the frown in his eyes. "It means, *mon amour,* that it is for you to decide when to return to court."

He grunted. "A dangerous choice. Too soon and I risk

permanent banishment, too late and I will appear ashamed and cowardly. The queen cares for neither."

"At least you did not kill Lord Morganston," Agathe pointed out. "He has a broken leg and will no doubt limp for the rest of his life, but he lives." She watched Arnaud to see what effect her cheerful tone was having. His expression did not lighten by much. She tried again. "So many matters of state now occupy her majesty that it's likely your situation has slipped from her mind. It is good that you left when you did, but I believe she no longer thinks of the joust."

A tight smile crossed his lips. "Maybe, *ma chère,* you have an entrée into her majesty's innermost thoughts, although I doubt it. However, I seem to have no choice but to continue to keep out of her majesty's sight and memory for a while longer." He set down his cup and reached for her hands, drawing her to her feet. "I have need of distraction. I trust you are willing to provide it."

Agathe's skin prickled as she went into his arms. "Always, *mon amour.*" She fell back on the bed looking up at him as he stood over her, his gaze dark and hungry.

Sir Francis Walsingham and Lord Burghley stood waiting as they had been for several hours in the antechamber to the queen's privy chamber in Greenwich Palace. They knew why she kept them cooling their heels, she didn't wish to hear what they had come to discuss, but they were accustomed to their sovereign's methods and waited patiently. As the senior members of her council they had to be granted an audience eventually.

Finally they were summoned to the royal presence and entered, bowing in unison. Elizabeth was standing in front of the windows, the midday sun setting her red wig alight so that it seemed to throw off a halo above her richly jeweled, open ruff.

"Well?" Her tone was haughty, her gaze cold.

"Madam, the conspirators appeared this day before the commissioners at Westminster, where they were charged with high treason," Burghley said.

"In what condition were they?"

"It was necessary to carry Ballard into court in a chair, his interrogation has been severe," Walsingham said. "For the rest, they were able to walk."

"And did they confess their guilt?"

"In interrogation, yes. In court they denied it. But we have all the necessary witness statements as well as the confessions under interrogation. A verdict of guilt is foregone, but the trial will, of course, follow precedent. It must be seen to be a clear and just rendering of English law." Burghley stroked the furred lapels of his black robe as he spoke.

"Inform me when sentence is passed." Elizabeth gestured in dismissal to the door, but her advisers didn't obey.

"Madam, there is one other most urgent matter we must discuss." Walsingham spoke hurriedly before she could interrupt him. "The matter of the Queen of Scots, madam, must be resolved. She must be tried."

"I have told you countless times, Master Secretary, that I will not spill the blood of a queen regnant. Such a thing has never happened in English law, and I will not be responsible for the precedent. Think of the political consequences. We would have Scotland in arms against us. James might be willing to turn a blind eye to his mother's strict confinement, but I cannot expect him to countenance her death. And what of France? Mary is queen dowager, they will not stand idly by while another nation executes a member of their royal family."

"Madam, at the very least she must be imprisoned more straitly," Burghley said. "Your council believes she should be held in the Tower."

"No. I will not have her in the Tower. Or any other prison you may have in mind."

Walsingham tried once more. "Madam, the people are uncertain and frightened. There are rumors of a French landing in Sussex under the Duc de Guise, and a Spanish force at Newcastle under the Duke of Palma. There is talk of civil war, and some even believe that your majesty is already assassinated. The unrest grows dangerous and we must do something to stop it. Strong action against Mary Stuart will do that."

Elizabeth turned away, back to the window, her hand upraised as if to silence them. "I will hear no more of this. If the people need to see that I am alive and very much their queen, then I will show myself in procession through the streets of London."

The two men looked at each other, then as one accord bowed to their queen's averted back and left the privy chamber. "Paulet writes that he is uneasy keeping Mary at Chartley," Walsingham said as they paused in the antechamber. "She must be moved somewhere more secure."

"Then send for Paulet. Let him put the case to her majesty. Mayhap she'll listen to him." Burghley shook his head. "Mary Stuart must be brought to trial, the council is of one mind on this. Parliament is of the same mind."

Walsingham pulled at his neat beard. "Let us wait until the trials of these others are completed and they have met their deaths. Then I will go before Parliament and ask them to petition the queen. She cannot hold fast against her council and her Parliament."

"I wish I shared your optimism." Burghley offered a small bow and strode off.

Walsingham made his way to Westminster, where the trial continued throughout the long afternoon. The defendants were permitted no defense counsel as there could be no defense for their crime and their guilt was already proven. The interrogations had brought to light fourteen conspirators in all, but Master Secretary had the most interest in the seven principals, led by Ballard, Babington, and Savage. They were his pigeons, carefully nurtured, educated, cosseted by his own people so that they would fly along the designated path and be the means by which England would once and for all be rid of the Catholic threat to the throne.

But if Elizabeth could not be persuaded to do her part, then all his elaborate scheming and these deaths would be for naught.

When the prisoners were removed from the dock to be returned to the Tower, Sir Francis went back to Seething Lane to pen a summons to Sir Amyas Paulet. Maybe Mary Stuart's jailer could be more persuasive than the members of the queen's council.

He was about to leave his study when there came a scratching on the door. "Who is it?"

The door opened a fraction and Ingram Frizer slid into the room like an unsavory wraith. "Information you wanted, sir." He leaned against the door, letting it shut with his weight, and surveyed his master.

"About what?" Francis sat down again. Frizer's information was always pertinent.

"You wanted me to take a look at that Chevalier de Vaugiras, sir." Frizer sniffed and wiped his nose on his sleeve. "Something interesting came up . . . concerning Master Thomas."

"Oh?" Francis sat up, leaning his forearms on his desk. "Pray tell, Frizer."

"Well, it seems that the chevalier and your honor's cousin had a quarrel, years ago it was, when Master Thomas was but a young lad out of the university. He was in Paris and it seems there was a youngster involved . . . one that the chevalier had an interest in. He took offense when Master Thomas had his own interest and there was a fight. Master Thomas wounded him and he's been sworn to avenge himself ever since."

"A youngster? Boy or girl?" Walsingham demanded. Such details were important to a man who collected other men's secrets.

"Boy, sir. Lad of about fifteen. Master Thomas took him away after the fight, when the chevalier was wounded and couldn't do nothing to stop him. 'Tis said on the street, sir, that the chevalier don't ever forget an insult or a grievance." Frizer sniffed again and scratched the side of his nose with the broken nail of a filthy finger. "A man not given to a fondness for Walsinghams, sir."

"I see." Francis nodded, reaching into the drawer of his desk for a golden noble. He flicked it across the room and Frizer caught it deftly. "You've a nose to rival a bloodhound's, my friend."

Frizer inclined his head in acknowledgment, pocketing the coin. "One other thing, I heard talk of a wife . . ."

Walsingham leaned forwards ever attentive as Frizer continued his tale. At the end of his exposition, as he took his leave, Frizer said over his shoulder, "Mistress Rosamund seemed to have a fondness for the chevalier's company."

"What?" Francis was finally startled out of his composure. Frizer often left the best for last, tossing it out as if it were a mere bagatelle. "Are you telling me he was responsible . . . ?"

"Don't know about that, sir. But, as I say, she seemed to have a fondness for his company." Frizer slipped away as discreetly as he had come.

Francis sat in frowning reverie for a long time. Had the chevalier used Rosamund as a means of revenge on Thomas? Had he debauched his enemy's sister? It was a perfect vengeance, well suited to a devious mind. A grim smile touched the secretary's thin mouth. The chevalier had not taken into account that in one Walsingham at least he would meet his match.

Francis opened the drawer in his desk and took out one of Rosamund's sketches. It had interested him, although he had not thought of an immediate use for it. Now, however, he could see exactly what he would do with it.

Rosamund had been sketching in the orchard on a green and gold September day when the messenger arrived from London. When she walked back up to the house for dinner, she found Thomas issuing orders to the stables for his horse and Master Marlowe's.

"What's happened, Thomas? Where are you going?"

He turned at her question. "Oh, there you are. We're going to London. The conspirators have been found guilty and sentence is pronounced. Their executions will be the occasion of much revelry and rejoicing throughout the city. Sir Francis writes that if you wish to come, since you have been in some part involved in this success, you will be welcome at Seething Lane."

A trip to London for whatever reason was not to be sneezed at. Life at Scadbury was pleasant, but Rosamund found that once she was used to its peaceful routine again, it quickly palled. The prospect of a little variety was appealing. "Are we to leave now?"

"No, we will dine first. You had better pack now, only a few things for a short visit."

Rosamund went up to her bedchamber, hauling out the small leather trunk from beneath her bed. She packed what she would need for a few days and went downstairs for dinner. Kit seemed oddly morose during the meal, drinking deeply as always, and eating sparingly. He spoke hardly at all, ignoring Thomas's various jocular comments, until finally Thomas demanded, "What in God's name is the matter, Kit? You are as sullen as a whipped schoolboy."

Kit refilled his wine cup. "I like it not, this rejoicing at the closing of the trap. We make merry while men hang at our behest. It sickens me." He drained the contents of his cup, then thrust it from him with such force that it bounced across the table and fell to the floor. A violent push sent his chair tumbling and he left the dining room, the door slamming behind him.

Thomas shrugged and refilled his own cup. "When Kit is in drink, he makes for poor company" was his only comment.

Rosamund pushed the suckling pig on her trencher to one side. She too had lost her appetite. "What time do we leave?"

"At five, time enough to reach London before nightfall." Her brother drank and with the tip of his dagger speared the apple from the mouth of the suckling pig on its carving board in front of him.

Rosamund got up with a word of excuse and left her brother to his dinner. She wasn't sure now that she wanted to go to London and join in this celebration. She was not proud of the work she had done. She found Kit in the study, scribbling on a tablet.

"Why go, then?" she asked.

"Because Thomas goes." He didn't raise his eyes from the paper. "Isn't that obvious?"

"But you do not always go where my brother goes."

"Not if my steps take me in a different direction. On this occasion they do not. Besides, I feel a certain moral obligation to see the conclusion. To see what I have wrought." He looked at her then. "Do you not?"

Rosamund shook her head. "No, no obligation. I will not attend the executions."

They rode in silence, even Thomas accepting that his companions were in no mood for cheerful discourse, and reached Seething Lane just as the sun was setting. "The executions are set for tomorrow morning." Thomas helped his sister dismount. "You will attend with Sir Francis and Lady Walsingham. It will be a great spectacle."

Rosamund made no comment. She glanced at Kit but he was steadfastly staring ahead. She wondered that a man considered an atheistical heretic by many should hold to such an unusual moral compass. Even his play *Tamburlaine,* so full of bloody carnage and violent tyranny though it was, made moral judgments. Not religious judgments, or not as such things were generally understood, but right and wrong was clearly delineated in those lines. It seemed so strange that a man who could describe with such seeming relish hideous scenes of bloody degradation found it hard to contemplate witnessing the public executions of would-be assassins of his queen. Strange that he should feel so strongly his own guilt in bringing about those executions, when men such as Thomas, Sir Francis, and she guessed all those others, including Will, involved in Master Secretary's elaborate machinations relished only the success of the enterprise.

She turned and went into the house. Ursula greeted

her with her usual warmth, plying her with a hot posset and questions about how she had spent the last weeks at Scadbury. Sir Francis came in later and greeted her amiably enough, bidding her welcome, and when she went to bed in the chamber now considered to be her own, Rosamund felt she was at home again, the street sounds of nighttime London as much music to her ear as the nightingale at Scadbury.

Chapter Twenty-six

"MADAM, I WOULD prefer to stay here this morning." Rosamund spoke quietly but definitely when Ursula, still in a nightgown, came to her bedchamber early the next morning.

Ursula, who had been examining the contents of the linen press, turned to the bed with a look of surprise. "Not go? Why ever not, child?"

"I doubt I have the stomach for it," she said frankly.

"Nonsense. It is a salutary lesson for all to see the queen's justice in action." Ursula took out a petticoat and laid it on the bed. "Men who seek to kill the queen must face the punishment decreed for treason. . . . This petticoat needs some attention, the lace is torn. I will tell Henny."

She turned to the armoire. "I have some ribbon that will refurbish the green gown, and I have an ell of a most delicate embroidered damask that will furnish you with a new gown. It shall be made up for you while you're here."

Rosamund murmured her thanks before repeating, "Indeed, madam, I would much prefer not to attend the executions."

Ursula tutted. "Sir Francis expects you to be there, you and your brother. The family as a whole must show its loyalty to her majesty. Your absence, now that you are returned to London, would be remarked, and given your present rather parlous position with the queen, you will not wish to imply any lack of respect."

Rosamund had rarely encountered the steel beneath Lady Walsingham's pleasantly amenable exterior, but she understood that in this matter she had no choice. She cursed her stupidity in leaving Scadbury. She had had the choice to stay, but it had not occurred to her that she would be compelled to witness the morning's barbarisms as quid pro quo for a change of scene.

"Very well, madam. If I must, I must."

Ursula nodded her approval. "You must, my dear. Henny is bringing up hot water and some food for you to break your fast. We must leave before the crowds become too thick and unruly. Once the prisoners on the hurdles have left the Tower, the streets will become impassable."

She hurried away to see to her own dressing, and Rosamund, heavyhearted, got out of bed and went to the window, opening the casement wide. It was a warm morning, but overcast, and she could already hear a low rumble from the streets, as if a crowd was gathering.

"Here's water, mistress." Henny bustled in, setting a filled ewer on the washstand. "And there's a manchet of bread and smoked eel. We've all been given leave to attend the spectacle, and everyone's anxious to get to St. Giles Fields for a good view. They've set up a special gallows there because 'tis more open than Tyburn and more folks will be able to see." She chattered on as she helped Rosamund dress and seemed not to notice the young woman's monosyllabic responses.

Rosamund nibbled at a little of the bread and fish and washed it down with half a mug of small beer, but she was already feeling queasy at the prospect that lay ahead.

Dressed in the tawny velvet, she threw a hooded cloak over her shoulders and went down to the hall.

Sir Francis came into the hall from the street as she reached the bottom stair. "Good, the carriage is outside. We must make haste, the streets are already filling and soon the carriage will not be able to pass."

He hurried her ahead of him with a hand between her shoulder blades. Ursula, already ensconced in the iron-wheeled carriage, patted the bench beside her as Rosamund climbed up. "Sit here, my dear."

Rosamund did so and Sir Francis took the bench opposite. The carriage was far from a luxury vehicle, the benches plain wood, the windows shielded with leather curtains, and it moved slowly across the cobbles with a bone-shaking rattle rough enough to loosen teeth. Rosamund moved the leather curtain aside and stared at the sea of humanity keeping pace with the vehicle. Children rode on parents' shoulders, youths and girls chattered and sang, hoisting ale mugs as they went. Crones and matrons, dressed in their Sunday bonnets, bustled along, holding tight to the hands of small children.

The stench of unwashed humanity reminded Rosamund vividly of the reeking audiences at the theatre and in the bear pit, and she fumbled for her pomander at her waist. Beside her, Lady Walsingham held a lavender-soaked handkerchief to her nose, and after a moment Sir Francis leaned across and twitched the curtain into place.

At last the carriage came to a halt outside a house in Holborn, and Sir Francis stepped out, leaning in to take his wife's hand as she descended. The crowd ebbed and flowed past the carriage, but the vehicle was drawn up close to a door opening directly onto the street, and they were protected from the stream of people by the body of the carriage.

Rosamund jumped down while Master Secretary was ushering his wife into the safety of the house. He turned to Rosamund and with a sweep of his arm moved her ahead of him into the building. "Follow my wife upstairs."

She climbed in Ursula's wake and found herself in a large, sparsely furnished chamber with mullioned casements overlooking the street. Ursula was standing at the open window. "It is a very good view," she pronounced over her shoulder. "Come, Rosamund, stand beside me."

Reluctantly Rosamund stepped up and looked out across the green expanse of St. Giles Fields. The gallows stood on a cart stark in the middle, with a ladder leading up to it. A huge cauldron was set over a merrily crackling fire, and she wondered what on earth it could be for. A hooded man stood beside the gallows, two boys beside him. The massed humanity swayed and shouted in the street below, spilling onto the field jostling for a place near the gallows.

"Ah, Sister. Good. You are here already." Thomas entered the chamber in the company of men unknown to Rosamund, except for Kit Marlowe, who looked as drunk this morning as he had probably done the previous night. The group crowded up to the window, forming a half circle, and Rosamund found herself pushed forward so that her knees pressed against the windowsill.

The roar of the crowd grew louder, and at last she could make out the procession threading its way between the lines of spectators. Seven hurdles pulled by seven horses, each hurdle bearing a trussed figure. Beside them and in front marched the pikemen, their pikes held in front of them. A herald at the head of the procession blew a trumpet to clear the path through the jeering crowds.

Rosamund, unable to move back into the room for the

press of people behind her, stared, as if paralyzed, at the scene unfolding below.

"They're taking Ballard first," she heard Thomas say as one of the figures, dressed only in a rough homespun shirt, was untrussed from the hurdle and hauled to the ladder, his legs dragging uselessly behind him. He was held up by the two hangman's assistants and forced around to face the crowd and a man in the collar and black robes of a Protestant minister, who approached carrying a Bible.

"Ah, they have appointed Dr. White to seek their conversion and repentance," Sir Francis said, sounding satisfied. "The good doctor is very sound of doctrine. The queen finds his sermons most enlightening."

"'Tis to be hoped those traitors will find it so also," one of the observers stated.

The Protestant minister began to harangue Father Ballard, his voice carrying over the crowd. The prisoner listened in silence, then when the doctor had fallen into an expectant silence, he made the sign of the cross. The crowd roared its disapproval and cheered as he was dragged up the ladder to the gallows, where the noose was fastened around his neck.

The cart was pushed from underneath and he swung twisting in the air for the barest instant before the hangman stepped forward, his knife raised.

Rosamund watched in a paralyzed horror as the executioner sliced off the hanging man's genitals. His scream rose on the muggy air, then became a crescendo as they cut open his belly and pulled out his entrails. Her gorge rose and she pressed a hand to her mouth. She wanted to look away but she couldn't. They cut the body down and butchered it, hacking it into quarters, and then she saw what the cauldron was for. They threw the pieces into the boiling water as they severed them. Beneath the window a man was selling hot pies from a tray around his neck, crying his wares above the shouts of the crowd. The smell of meat rose on the air.

She swayed and would have fallen if the man behind her hadn't held her up. "The lady is about to swoon. Give her air." It was Kit, his own countenance a ghastly green as he pushed his way forward through the half circle. Men fell back and let him grab Rosamund's arm, pulling her back into the room.

She slumped onto a stool, her fist still pressed against her mouth. The roars of the crowd still reached them, the screams as the other men were hanged and butchered, and she didn't need to see to visualize exactly what was happening.

"Tilney died well," someone said as they moved away from the window, the spectacle completed. "Babington swooned and could not speak as they hauled him up."

Rosamund saw Anthony Babington as he had been by the river at Whitehall. A courtier to his fingertips, handsome, debonair, elegant, charming. Now merely pieces of flesh boiling in a cauldron. Had Will watched him die? Will, who had pretended to be his friend in order to betray him.

"I didn't hear Tilney's words." Thomas poured wine from a flagon into cups set out on a board against the wall.

"After Dr. White had harangued him on a point of doctrine, he said only, 'I came hither to die, Doctor, not to argue.' There was dignity in it."

"Aye, but he'd have done better to repent." Sir Francis took a cup of wine from Thomas. "Give one to your sister. She is like to swoon at any moment."

Thomas regarded his sister in some puzzlement as he handed her a cup. "Are you unwell?"

"Such a spectacle, Thomas, is not for everyone," Ursula chided sternly as she came over to Rosamund. "Indeed, I found it hard to watch myself." She took Rosamund's hands, chafing them. "It was necessary for you to be here, my dear, but I should probably have encouraged you to keep to the back of the chamber away from the casement."

Rosamund could only shudder. She sipped the wine, and the nausea faded somewhat, but she knew that the scenes of that day would haunt her nightmares to her dying day. She glanced across at Kit, who was leaning his shoulders against the wall behind him, his eyes unfocused.

"I must go and make report to the queen." Sir Francis moved to the door. "Thomas, you will see Lady Walsingham and your sister home, once the crowds have thinned. The carriage awaits downstairs."

Thomas did not look entirely pleased with this instruction, but he bowed his acknowledgment, and one by one the men who had witnessed their part in Master Secretary's schemes come to fruition that morning left the house, except for Kit and Thomas.

"I think it will be safe enough to leave now, madam." Thomas turned from the window where he had been watching the street. "The crowd is merry enough, and dispersing quickly into the taverns. The streets should be passable."

"Good, I own I have had enough of this place." Ursula gathered her cloak around her. "Rosamund, my dear, you will be better for the peace and quiet of home. You will soon forget what you've seen."

Rosamund shook her head. "Never, madam." She rose to her feet, angry and resentful that Ursula had forced this horror upon her, but more that she could so lightly dismiss its effects. She wanted to go back to Scadbury to lick her wounds, as far from Seething Lane as she could get.

"Kit, do you come with us?" Thomas adjusted the clasp of his short cape at his throat. "There is room for four in the carriage . . . if you permit, Lady Walsingham."

"Certainly. I have not before made Master Marlowe's acquaintance, but I understand from my husband that you are something of a playmaker, sir." Ursula drew on her fine kid gloves.

Kit managed a courteous response, but all he wanted to do was find the nearest, darkest tavern and drink his way to oblivion. He bowed, said, "If you'll excuse me, madam, much as I appreciate the offer, I have business elsewhere." He gave Thomas a curt nod and brushed past him on his way out.

Thomas looked put out, but he could do nothing about it. He escorted the ladies to the carriage and climbed in after them.

Back in Seething Lane, Rosamund did the only thing she knew to exorcise the morning's horrors. Slowly and deliberately she committed them to paper, re-creating line by visual line every aspect of the scene, from the steaming cauldron, to the blood on the knives, to the rubbery entrails, and the man's face uplifted in agony. And when it was done, she lay down on her bed and fell asleep.

She was awoken by Ursula late in the afternoon. "Do you feel better, Rosamund? You have slept long."

Rosamund sat up, her head a little muzzy, her limbs still heavily lethargic. "Yes, thank you, madam. I don't know why I was so tired."

But Ursula wasn't listening to her. She was looking at the drawing, her face shocked. "You drew this . . . it's a horror. What possessed you, child?"

"I needed to make sense of the horror. Drawing it seemed the only way," Rosamund said simply, swinging her legs so that she sat on the edge of the bed. "I'm sorry if it disturbs you."

"It does disturb me. There's something indecent about such a drawing."

"Do you not think that there was something more than a little indecent about this morning's spectacle, madam?"

Ursula regarded her for a moment, frowning. "Your tone lacks respect, Rosamund, but I will excuse it. You suffered this morning, and had I known how strongly you would feel, I would have ensured you were protected in part."

Ursula smiled suddenly, an almost cajoling smile. "Now let us say no more about it. Soon it will fade. We have company for dinner, so wear the rose velvet gown and dress your hair with that lovely silver fillet of your mother's. I'll send Henny straight up."

She bent and kissed Rosamund's brow. "There now, my dear girl. An unpleasant business, I agree, but over and done with. . . . I will send Henny directly." She picked up the drawing again with a grimace of distaste. "We can't leave this lying around." Scrunching the paper in her hand, she left, taking it with her.

Rosamund would have liked to protest at this unilateral destruction of her work, but decided she'd upset Ursula enough for one day. She could summon little enthusiasm for the evening ahead, but she was a guest and could hardly refuse to join her hosts at the board.

Henny was rather pale when she came in to help Rosamund dress and said little for quite a while. But finally she asked, "Did you witness the executions, Mistress Rosamund?"

"A little at the beginning." Rosamund turned her back so that Henny could lace the rose velvet gown. "In truth I hadn't the stomach for it."

"Oh, no, neither did I, Mistress Rosamund." Henny shuddered. "I was sick and lost my breakfast. The others all laughed at me." She smoothed the folds of the gown over the farthingale with a practiced hand, before taking up the hairbrush.

Rosamund sat on a low stool, her rose skirts billowing around her, as Henny brushed her hair until it glowed like burnished copper, before fastening the silver fillet around her forehead. Looking at herself in the beaten-silver mirror, Rosamund was surprised that she looked the same as usual. Somehow she had expected the morning's horrors to be etched on her countenance. She turned as the door opened.

"My dear, I wish you to wear this." A broadly smiling Lady Walsingham fastened a pearl and silver pendant around Rosamund's neck. "And this girdle at your waist." She handed Henny a thin belt of twisted silver thread.

Rosamund rose from the stool and Henny fastened the belt. "You are too kind to me, madam." Rosamund, for all her low spirits, couldn't deny her pleasure as she fingered the pendant at her throat and the delicate girdle that accentuated her small waist. The pearl in the pendant matched the seed pearls embroidered on the gown.

"Nonsense, you must look your best." Ursula stood back to examine her. "Yes, you will do very nicely, my dear. A most pretty picture. Now, if you are quite ready, we will go down. Our guests are already assembled."

The first person Rosamund saw as she entered the parlor was Sir Roger Askew. He was an old friend, so it was not surprising to see him a guest at the Walsinghams' dinner table, but a little question niggled at the back of her mind. *Is there some connection with his presence and Ursula's instructions as to the rose velvet gown and the borrowed gems?*

She curtsied to the room at large. Besides Sir Roger, there were two other guests, one she recognized immediately: Thomas Watson. He bowed and greeted her with smiling informality. "It has been a long time, Mistress Walsingham, but I understand you have been in the north. Permit me to make you known to my wife, Mistress Ann."

Rosamund curtsied to a plump woman, rather older than herself, in fact rather older than Master Watson she thought. Beside the robust, larger-than-life presence of witty Tom Watson, Ann Watson seemed small and almost mousy. It must be hard to live in that shadow, Rosamund thought, smiling at the woman. Ann returned the smile with a shy one of her own and a murmured greeting.

"You remember Sir Roger, Rosamund," Ursula prompted.

"Yes, of course." Rosamund turned to him with a curtsy, lowering her eyes. "Sir Roger."

"Mistress Rosamund, it is a great pleasure to see you again," he said quietly, taking her hand and drawing her upright and slightly to one side. "I understand you have been in the country since your return from Chartley."

"At my brother's estate in Chiselhurst. I came to London with my brother only yesterday."

He nodded. "I understand you witnessed the executions this morning?"

Rosamund met his gaze. "I will regret doing so to my dying day, sir."

"An unedifying spectacle, I'm sure. I did not attend, but I understand no cruelty was spared."

"Well, the ones tomorrow will be luckier." Sir Francis had been listening to the conversation with half an ear. "I spoke with the queen this afternoon, and when she heard of the severity of the executions, she decreed that the rest will be permitted to hang until they are dead, before the drawing and quartering."

"Oh, Sir Francis, pray do not talk of it," Mistress Watson begged, her hand at her throat. "It is too dreadful."

"Dreadful, madam, yes. But intended to be so and rightly. These public deaths are to be a deterrent to anyone who might contemplate treason. It is necessary for the safety of the realm."

"You are rather pale, Mistress Rosamund," Sir Roger spoke softly. "The subject distresses you."

"It is a distressing subject."

"Yes." He looked at her averted countenance before saying, "So, shall we talk of pleasanter things? Tell me about your family home. Scadbury, is it?"

"Perhaps Sir Roger would care to walk in the garden, Rosamund," Ursula suggested, opening the door onto the garden. "We shall dine in fifteen minutes, but a little fresh air will do you good. The evening air is so soft."

Rosamund could only accede, but her earlier suspicion was becoming a certainty. Ursula was up to something, and she wasn't being too subtle about it. Rosamund offered Sir Roger a faint smile. "Do you care to stroll in the garden, sir?"

"In your company, Mistress Rosamund, I can think of nothing pleasanter." He bowed, smiling.

He had a good smile, Rosamund noticed. His teeth were strong and even, and the little crinkly lines at the corners of his eyes brought humor to his generally grave, rather sad countenance. "You flatter me, sir." She moved ahead of him into the garden. It was another knot garden, smaller than the one at Chartley, but exquisitely laid out, a statue of Cupid with bow flexed on a plinth in the center.

"Have you been to Sir Francis's country house at Barn

Elms?" Roger inquired, walking beside her along the narrow walkway that led to the statue.

"No, I didn't realize he had such a thing." Rosamund paused by the statue. She felt awkward, trying to avert something, but she wasn't sure what. She couldn't refuse an offer that she hadn't as yet received, and why would he make her one anyway? He would have his pick of available women eager to be Lady Askew. He was rich, personable, of good family and standing. He could not possibly be interested in a dowerless spoiled virgin.

She tried to find a neutral topic. "Are you returning to the Low Countries soon, Sir Roger?"

"No, I don't think so. I have matters to attend to here. The house I am building in London, my estates in Shropshire. They have been without a master for two years and are in need of a firm hand on the reins. My agents have not been as attentive as I could wish."

He sighed and looked suddenly careworn, before turning to her again. "When do you return to Scadbury?"

"Soon. I await my brother's escort." She began to walk around the statue. He didn't follow her, merely stood watching.

"I am in need of a wife," he said abruptly.

Rosamund stopped walking, said casually, "I daresay you miss your late wife."

After a minute he said, "Yes, I do." His voice was flat. "We should go back into the house." He walked ahead of her to the open parlor door.

Rosamund didn't know whether she had disappointed him or angered him. But he hadn't asked the question direct, so she couldn't be held responsible for not giving him a direct answer. He must have been given encouragement by her brother and the Walsinghams. Why would they imagine she would turn down such a splendid offer when she was in no position to turn down even a mediocre one? Sir Roger had probably assumed that she would give him a dutiful response. It wasn't that she found anything distasteful about him. He was a little old, but young women married men old enough to be their grandfathers if it suited their families. And he was handsome in a dignified, calm way.

But what would it be like to couple with him? Would there be passion? He didn't seem capable of passion. She thought of those hasty, scrambling, passion-filled moments with Will and a surge of energy jolted her belly.

Ursula called her from the open door and she pulled herself together, walking back up to the house.

Chapter Twenty-seven

Sir Amyas Paulet stepped onto the pier at the water steps of Hampton Court Palace. The queen's barge was moored along the bank, the royal standard flying in the crisp breeze. A redbrick path wound its way through massive oak and beech trees up from the river to the sprawling palace.

Paulet took the path, deer from the palace herds scattering in front of him. He was not looking forward to the coming audience but it had to be faced. The queen must be made to understand certain realities. He walked through a massive arch into the outer court. People scurried hither and thither, messengers, servants, palace guards. No one took any notice of the somberly clad Sir Amyas. He went through another arch and into the inner court. The clock high on the wall showed ten in the morning. He had been summoned for half past the hour and increased his pace, taking the wide flight of stone stairs that led up into the palace.

Hampton Court was familiar ground and he walked briskly past lines of petitioners outside the various antechambers of members of the queen's council, all of whom had favors in their pockets to grant to the lucky few, or to those who could offer sufficient incentive.

Heralds bawled names as they walked the window-lined

corridors, summoning courtiers and servants. At the end of the corridor Paulet turned left and entered a vast antechamber where courtiers milled in chattering groups. He walked to the double doors at the far end and spoke to the chamberlain, who instantly opened the door and stepped aside.

A second antechamber stretched ahead, and Paulet, reflecting that a man could walk twenty miles in a day going about his business in this place, crossed the chamber and spoke again to the chamberlain at the door, who this time went in on his own.

Lady Shrewsbury came back with him. "Her majesty will see you in her privy chamber, Sir Amyas." She escorted him to the door to the chamber and left him to enter unannounced.

Elizabeth sat at her desk with a pile of documents. She had been at work since five that morning, and her eyes were tired from so much close reading. "Sir Amyas, I bid you welcome."

"Madam." He knelt, hat clasped to his chest.

"Rise . . . rise." She waved a hand impatiently and rose to her own feet as he stood up. "How is it with my cousin?"

"The Queen of Scots is in indifferent health, madam, but she will admit to no knowledge of the conspiracy. She denies any correspondence with Babington. Even when presented with her secretary's affidavit that her letter to Babington is genuine, she insists that it is not authentic. She holds fast to the story that she is innocent of any evil thoughts towards your majesty."

Paulet paused for breath, before continuing strongly, "But her present imprisonment cannot continue. I cannot be responsible for her, madam, if she remains at Chartley. It is too open, too easily accessed. It is no real prison, a gentleman's residence, merely. If I am to remain her guardian, she must be removed to a place of strict confinement."

Elizabeth paced the long wall of windows looking over the parkland to the river without saying anything for close to five minutes. Paulet waited in observant silence.

Finally Elizabeth paused and stood with her back to her visitor. "I am beset on all sides in this matter. My council wish me to have my cousin tried for treason, the Parliament asks for it. Even the people demand it. But she is still a cousin of my blood, a queen regnant, and the political consequences will be incalculable."

She stared out at the river, before saying in a low voice that was nonetheless clear as a bell, "If she were removed, an accident of some kind, it would relieve queen and country of an intractable problem. Such an accident could be contrived, Sir Amyas, could it not? It would be the greatest favor a man could do his sovereign and his country."

Paulet could not for a moment believe he had heard aright. The queen was asking him to arrange the murder of Mary Stuart. "Madam, I am a man of God. I could not thus endanger my immortal soul." He spoke with stiff dignity. "I would give anything but that to assist my sovereign lady, but I cannot."

Elizabeth sighed. "Very well, Sir Amyas. Let it be as if this conversation never took place."

"Gladly, madam." He waited for a few moments, then said firmly, "Some thought *must* be given to a more secure prison, madam. Chartley cannot be adequately defended if the northern Catholics join with the Scots Catholics and bring an attack force down upon us. As I cannot guarantee to ensure her continued imprisonment if she is not moved from Chartley, I will be obliged to resign my post."

"You are uncommonly bold this morning, Amyas."

Elizabeth turned away from the window, her well-plucked eyebrows arched. "First you refuse your queen's request, and then you issue ultimatums."

"Throw me in the Tower if you wish, madam. But I speak only the truth."

She laughed without mirth. "Yes, you are a man given to straight talk, and it makes you a reliable and honest servant. I will give the matter some thought."

"I have made a list of possible prisons, madam. I know you have rejected the Tower, but one of these may serve. They are all easily defended." He drew a folded sheet from his doublet and laid it on her desk.

"I will consider it." Her nod was dismissal, and he bowed and backed out of the royal presence.

Elizabeth sat down at the desk and opened the sheet. She would have to accede to Paulet's demand. Despite the successful end to the conspiracy, the country remained anxious and insecure, filled with unrest, and unrest bred rebellion. Mary's escape would be disastrous, even if it didn't involve the assassination of Elizabeth herself. If Chartley was as vulnerable as Amyas said, then a raid from Scotland or from any of the strongly Catholic families in the north could achieve Mary's release.

Her finger ran down the list and stopped in the middle. Fotheringay. A royal castle in the remote wilds of Northamptonshire. She had visited it only once and remembered it as a lonely place, standing on a hill overlooking the river Nene, with expansive views from the ramparts across the countryside. No one could approach without being seen. Moated, turreted, it was easily defended. She reached for the bell and rang it vigorously.

A chamberlain answered it before she had replaced the bell. "Majesty?"

"Summon my council."

"Yes, your majesty."

Well, that would please Walsingham and Burghley, Elizabeth thought. She would be spared their hectoring speeches and reproachful glances for a while at least. But this one concession would not close the matter, she knew. They would press now for a trial. She didn't know how long she could hold out against a united front.

Mary Stuart huddled into a furred robe in her barren apartments at Chartley, stripped now of every possible creature comfort. The fire smoldered on damp coal and threw off almost no heat. The carpets had been removed and the floor was damp underfoot. It was late September but the weather was dismal, cold and gray. Wind whistled through every crack in the ill-fitting walls and set the candles guttering. Her ladies, pinched with cold, rubbed chilblained fingers and struggled to ply their needles.

Mary's little Skye terrier crept close to her skirts, and she reached down to pat his rough head. His ears pricked suddenly and he stood, facing the door. Mary could hear nothing, but she guessed that the little dog had heard or sensed someone approaching across the yard from the house. The bang of the outer door confirmed her guess.

Sir Amyas came in, with two guards at his back. He spoke without greeting or bow, his voice peremptory. "Madam, you are to prepare for a journey. Your ladies should pack your personal possessions at once. You will be moved in one hour."

"May I ask where we are to go?" Mary inquired with the customary composure that infuriated Paulet.

"Your destination is not to be revealed."

"May we know at least the length of our journey?"

"Those details are not to be revealed. You have one hour for your preparations, madam." Paulet left, the guards at his heels.

Mary stared into the sullenly burning fire. It seemed difficult to imagine conditions worse than those she endured at present, but she was under no illusions. She was not being moved for her own comfort. "Charlotte, you had better prepare."

"Yes, madam." Charlotte went into the inner bedchamber, the other ladies accompanying her.

An hour later to the minute Paulet returned with his guards. "The carriages await, madam." He gestured to the guards to pick up the leather trunks that contained what remained of Mary Stuart's personal possessions. "If you would come with me."

Two carriages stood in the yard, and Mary, carrying her little terrier, entered the first one with her ladies. The maids and the luggage rode in the second. Mary leaned her head wearily against the leather squabs, her fingers moving over her rosary beads. She was certain, for whatever reason, that this would be the last of the many moves that had punctuated her long imprisonment, and the longing filled her that it would all soon be over. She was ready to die, if die she must, a martyr to her faith.

It was nightfall when, after six hours of jolting over uneven roads, the carriages clattered over the drawbridge and into the medieval fortress of Fotheringay Castle. Mary and her ladies alighted stiffly in an inner courtyard and Mary shuddered, murmuring a prayer, as she looked around at the high stone walls, the ramparts above. The stone was green with age and damp, and the cracks in the cobbles beneath her feet were clogged with weeds. It was a miserable place, and impregnable. There would be no gallant rescue from these walls.

"Madam, if you will follow me." Paulet gestured to a narrow archway into the edifice, and Mary, still carrying her dog, followed him into a gloomy passage that opened into a great hall, hung with royal coats of arms. Guards stood at attention around the walls, and the stone-flagged floor threw up the cold as she walked the length of the hall to a staircase rising from the far end. Paulet led the way up the stairs and through a set of double doors.

Mary was pleasantly surprised. She had expected an icy prison cell, but this apartment was large, with a good fire burning, rugs on the flagged floor, and wax candles. But there were no windows. No natural light at all.

"What is this place, Sir Amyas?"

"Fotheringay Castle, where I trust you will be comfortable, madam." Paulet opened a door in the far wall to reveal another inner apartment, a bedchamber, where another fire burned merrily and the bed was shielded from draft with thick tapestry curtains. Servants were bringing in the possessions from the carriage while Charlotte directed their placement.

"Am I never to see the light of day, Sir Amyas?" Mary inquired, setting her dog on the floor.

"Once a day you will be permitted to walk for an hour alone with your ladies in the inner court." Paulet waited for the servants to finish their unloading and then went to the door in their wake. "I will leave you now, madam. We will talk again in the morning." The key turned in the lock.

"It is more comfortable than Chartley, madam." Charlotte hugged her arms as she emerged from the bedchamber and looked around.

"Yes, it would seem my jailers have lost interest in making me suffer unduly," Mary observed. "A consideration, Charlotte, that I fear bodes ill." She gestured to a table where a flagon of wine stood with a platter of cold meat and a loaf of bread. "There seems to be our supper, ladies." Drawing her cloak tightly around her, she took a seat beside the fire, leaning forward to warm her hands.

"Will you take wine, madam?"

"Thank you, Charlotte." She took the cup and sipped, feeling warmth slowly seep into her chilled body. After a few minutes she rose and went into the bedchamber, where her prie-dieu had been placed beneath the cross that Charlotte had hung on the wall above. She knelt, her lips moving in soundless prayer.

A few days later Sir Francis returned to Seething Lane after a meeting with the queen and the privy council. He acknowledged his wife with a distracted word of greeting as he took his seat at the dinner table and nodded briefly at Rosamund's polite curtsy. He said little throughout the meal, and the two women knew better than to engage in small talk when the master of the house was clearly preoccupied.

When he'd finished eating, Francis rose from the table. "Rosamund, would you attend me in my office when you're quite finished?" He didn't wait for an assent that was not asked for and left the dining room.

Ursula glanced quickly at Rosamund, then spooned syllabub onto her plate and began to talk about some trivial domestic matter. Rosamund, puzzled and apprehensive, toyed with her pudding and, after ten minutes, excused herself and went to Sir Francis.

He was as usual deeply immersed in papers when she entered his office. "I have work for you, Rosamund. Sit down." He waved her to a chair.

She sat, folding her hands in her lap, and waited.

"The queen has informed her council this afternoon that Mary Stuart is to be tried for treason at her prison, which is now Fotheringay Castle in Northamptonshire. You will return to Mary in your former capacity and report to me everything that is said, every thought the Scots queen expresses in the privacy of her chambers, during the trial. She will deny her guilt at the trial, I would hear what she says of it in private."

This was even worse than her previous betrayal of Mary. This time the Scots queen's life was at stake. Rosamund stared down at her linked fingers in her lap. A refusal was inconceivable.

"How am I to explain myself to Mary, sir? It's been many weeks since I was removed from her side."

"I would suggest that you use your religious convictions. You may feel free to imply unpleasant coercion during your imprisonment in London, it will be expected that you suffered to some degree. If you say you withstood that coercion as best you could, and in the end you were sent back to share Mary's imprisonment again, I think she will probably be persuaded."

Rosamund thought so too. Mary was, in so many ways, easily deceived. "How am I to deliver these reports?" Her voice was dull and expressionless.

"Sir Amyas will arrange for that. It will be easier than at Chartley. At Fotheringay Mary is served by Sir Amyas's own servants, her food delivered from the castle kitchens. What little independence her household enjoyed at Chartley is no longer hers. You will have plentiful opportunities to pass messages to the servants."

Rosamund said nothing. She could only agree, so what was there to say?

"I take it you do not like this work?" Sir Francis linked

his hands on the desk in front of him. "I will remind you that it is in the queen's service. You do this for your queen and the safety of the realm. You should have no other considerations. You are part of my service, Rosamund, and you must perform as all my people do."

She hadn't heard the flint in Master Secretary's voice for quite a while, but she knew better than to confront it. "When do I go, sir?"

"In the morning, just after dawn. You will be escorted by my own men. It must appear as if you are returned to Mary a prisoner under guard."

Rosamund stood up. "I will go and make my preparations, sir."

"Before you go, there is one other matter." He gestured that she should sit down again. Rosamund did so.

He regarded her in silence for an unnerving moment, his eyebrows pulled together in a fierce frown. "How familiar have you been with the Chevalier de Vaugiras?"

The abrupt question, fired at her with the speed of an arrow from a bow, took her aback. The color came and went in her cheeks as she stared at him, unable to think of what answer she should make.

"I see. Your face gives you away. Was the chevalier responsible for debauching you?"

Numbly she shook her head. "No, sir."

He looked at her closely. "Don't lie to me, Rosamund. It is never wise to lie to me."

She shook her head again. "No, sir. He was not."

Another long silence, then he said, "Very well. But you should know that I do not believe for one minute your tale of an itinerant jongleur. However, I will not press you for the name of the man, unless it suits my purposes to know it. But I will ask you about this." He slid a paper out from beneath the pile on his desk and pushed it across to her.

She leaned forward and took it, gazing at it in surprise. It was a rendering of Arnaud and Agathe together. She couldn't remember drawing it, which meant it had been an idle sketch, probably just filling an idle moment, yet it was full of information. They were talking, laughing, their heads so close together, their bodies almost blending. The intimacy came off the page with such power she couldn't understand how she had never noticed it before.

"I knew they were old friends . . . but they are lovers," she murmured, half to herself.

"Yes, that is the conclusion I came to." He held out his hand for the drawing. "I have it on good authority that the chevalier has a quarrel with your brother, indeed with the Walsingham family. Did you ever sense a threat in his attentions?"

She gazed at the drawing for a moment longer before handing it back to Walsingham. "Not exactly, sir," she said slowly. "There was a little dalliance, but nothing out of the ordinary." *Or had it been?* Did ordinary courtly dalliance always involve those secret kisses, the electrifying physical closeness? Or had that simply been a prelude?

"Not exactly?"

Agathe said such games were perfectly acceptable. But she had never seen Agathe play them. Not even with Arnaud, not openly. Then something came to her, something she had heard Agathe say on that dreadful day of discovery, when they had walked beneath the window of her prison. *I did what you asked. I encouraged her.* And there was something else. She frowned trying to remember the snippet. Agathe had said, *It is not my fault if she used the lessons on someone else.*

"Well?" Sir Francis was watching her cogitations,

his eyes sharp as knives. "What does *not exactly* mean, Rosamund?"

"It means, sir, that there could have been a threat, but I didn't recognize it as such." She met his gaze across the desk.

"Hmm. That's honest, at least. You were certainly a naive unsophisticate, ready prey for such a predator as this one." He flicked the picture of Arnaud with his thumb. "You may count yourself fortunate, Rosamund. I have learned that the chevalier's wife died an unquiet death."

Rosamund's eyes widened. "*How?*"

"Her body was discovered in a cow byre. The condition of the body seemed to indicate some unusually rough treatment at some point. It was, however, agreed officially that the lady had died in childbed." Sir Francis's eyes showed no emotion, and his tone as he related this horror was as indifferent as if he were talking of finding a dead cat in an alley.

Rosamund didn't trouble to ask how her cousin had discovered this information, any more than she considered it might not be true. "Does Thomas know any of this?"

"No. And you will not mention your acquaintance with de Vaugiras to your brother. I will take care of the chevalier myself. I do not want Thomas acting Sir Galahad as an excuse for settling an old quarrel. I have more important work for him at present. Is that understood?"

"Yes," she said simply. She was stunned by this revelation. She had been a fool, so eager for acceptance that she had run blindly into the trap. It would never happen again, but that certainty didn't sweeten the sour taste of manipulation. She would still, however, like to know what quarrel Thomas had with the chevalier. At some point she would get it out of him.

"Go now, and prepare for your journey."

Rosamund accepted the brusque dismissal with a brief curtsy and made herself scarce.

It was a long, cold three-day ride into Northamptonshire, and Rosamund had plenty of time for reflection. Had the chevalier truly meant to hurt her? Had Agathe really, in full knowledge, set out to prepare her, present her on a silver platter to her own lover? It seemed fanciful . . . extraordinary. And yet Rosamund could not ignore the feeling that she had been duped. A feeling that, the more she went over the details of those occasions she had spent with Arnaud and Agathe, soon became a sick certainty.

Her cousin had said he would deal with the chevalier in his own way, and Rosamund knew she or even Thomas could do nothing to avenge themselves that would begin to compare with Sir Francis's methods. So finally she let it slip from the forefront of her mind. The immediate future needed all her concentration.

They rested each night at the houses of Walsingham men, some of them humble, some of them wealthy. Rosamund was treated with respect, as if she was someone important, a sensation she found both novel and pleasant. On the afternoon of the fourth day, Fotheringay Castle appeared on the skyline, easily visible on its high hill. It was a forbidding structure, looking to Rosamund to be filled with the medieval shadows of a ferocious past.

As they rode in under the portcullis, she gave an involuntary shudder, before castigating herself for fanciful thoughts that would do her no good on this present mission. The inner courtyard was damp, gloomy with long shadows thrown from the high walls by the last faint rays of the sun.

Paulet came out to greet her as she dismounted. "We will talk for a few minutes before I take you to the Lady Mary." He led her into the castle and into a round chamber that she thought must have been a guard chamber in the days when the castle was fortified. A fire burned brightly, however, and he gave her a mug of honey-sweet mead that warmed her travel-chilled bones.

"I understand Sir Francis wishes you to keep a daily journal, noting everything significant or otherwise. I imagine you will find it easy to disguise the act of writing under cover of your drawing, which will cause no remark. Every morning, while Mary and her ladies are at breakfast, maids enter the chambers to empty the chamber pots and make the beds. If you leave any communication you have under your pillow, it will be collected at that time."

Rosamund sipped her mead. "Is the queen expecting me?"

"No. It was thought better to surprise her. She is less likely to think too much about it if she doesn't have any warning. You will have the offensive, so to speak, and it will be up to you to persuade her of your loyalty."

"I understand." Rosamund set down her mug. "Will you take me to her now, Sir Amyas."

"Certainly." He escorted her across the great hall, up the stairs, and to the door to Mary's chambers. He knocked sharply and unlocked the door without waiting for permission to enter. "Madam, I bring you a familiar face. Mistress Fitzgerald has been released from prison and has begged to rejoin you. Her majesty was pleased to accede to her request, in the hopes that her presence will add to your comfort." He stepped back into the corridor and Rosamund walked into the apartment.

Mary was sitting by the fire, her little dog nestled at her

feet. Charlotte set down the Bible from which she had been reading aloud, and every eye turned to Rosamund.

Rosamund stepped forward and curtsied deeply to the queen. "Madam, I am come back to you if you will have me."

"How did they treat you, Rosamund?"

It was not hard to imagine after what she had seen at St. Giles Fields. Rosamund spoke in a low voice, as if reluctant to say anything. "I was kept in the Tower, madam, for a few weeks. I tried not to say anything, but . . . but it was very hard. I . . . I . . ." She dropped to her knees in a convincingly penitential posture. "Forgive me, madam, if I have in any way contributed to your trouble."

Mary leaned forward, taking Rosamund's hands, drawing her to her feet. "My poor child, of course I forgive you. No one can withstand that kind of pressure, and I would not expect it. My own secretary could not withstand them." She sighed. De Nau's affidavits had damned her almost as convincingly as her letter to Anthony Babington. "Nothing you said would have made any difference, Rosamund. Come now, Charlotte will show you our fine apartments."

She laughed, a brave attempt at gaiety. "So warm and comfortable we are, you would not believe."

Mary was as composed as ever, Rosamund thought. But the toll taken on her physical strength was shocking. She was thinner than ever, her eyes dark hollows in her sunken cheeks, her shoulders, once so straight, stooped now like those of a very old woman. Yet she could still try to laugh at her situation, to comment on its improvements, when she must know she was facing imminent death. Once again, Rosamund marveled at the queen's powers of endurance, at her unbreakable spirit.

"Come, Rosamund." Charlotte stood up. "You will share a bed with Dorothy." She led her into a large bedchamber off the main room. "This is connected to my lady's bedchamber through that door. One of us sits up with her all night. She is a prey to insomnia and nightmares, and she likes to be read to or prayed with. It will relieve us all to have another one to share the task. That is Dorothy's bed." Charlotte indicated a large feather bed. "When it is your turn, you will sit up with the queen."

"Of course. It will be an honor." Only the queen had had a feather bed at Chartley, her ladies had had to make do with horsehair and straw. It seemed a strange paradox that in this grim fortress Mary's comfort should be so assiduously attended to.

Rosamund had been told that Mary knew nothing of her impending trial and would not know until the commissioners arrived. It was not going to be an easy secret to keep, but in light of all the others that burdened her, maybe it wouldn't be so hard after all.

Chapter Twenty-eight

"MADAM, IT IS my task to inform you that your trial will commence at eight o'clock tomorrow morning in the Great Hall. Your presence is required by the commissioners to answer the charges brought against you."

Mary didn't look up from her prayer book for several minutes, leaving Sir Amyas standing at the door. She had expected this from the moment of her removal to Fotheringay, even though she had denied herself the knowledge. At last she looked up and across at him. "I will defend myself of all charges, sir. Am I to be permitted counsel to speak in my defense?"

"No, madam. In treason trials no defense counsel is permitted."

"Then I must conduct my own defense." Mary was calm, composed, almost serene. She rose and went into her bedchamber, closing the door behind her. She knelt at the prie-dieu, praying to her God who would be her strength. If they would martyr her, it would be God's will. But they would hear no admission of guilt from her lips.

Rosamund, despite her relief that that burdensome secret was no longer hers to carry, knew that her real work was to begin now. Her mind was busy in search of a way to appear to do the work expected of her, while somehow circumventing it. They would execute Mary Stuart for treason, whether Rosamund's testimony added to her guilt or not. So, somehow she must find a way to relieve her conscience of a spy's burden while satisfying Master Secretary.

She wrote her journal for Sir Francis that night as she sat up beside the sleeping queen in the softly firelit bedchamber. Nothing she had to say of today's events would incriminate the Scots queen, so she could be open and honest, and save deception for when it was needed. She described Mary's calm demeanor as she had listened to Sir Amyas, and how she had prayed. How she had passed the rest of the evening in talk, prayer, and backgammon, and how she was now sleeping peacefully, seemingly untroubled by the prospect of her trial in the morning. When Rosamund had finished, she went into the bedchamber and slipped the sheet under her pillow, before returning to Mary's bedside.

The queen continued to sleep and Rosamund sat drowsily by the fire, her mind returning as it so often did these days to the chevalier and Agathe. She cringed when she thought of how easily she had been led. Would Arnaud have hurt her as an act of revenge against Thomas? On the one hand it seemed fanciful; on another, when she conjured his image, the flicker of his mouth, the strange light in his eyes, utterly believable. It was much pleasanter to think of Will, and there she allowed her mind and imagination free rein. She would see him again, it was impossible that she wouldn't. He would be working somewhere within her cousin's net, it would be easy for him to discover where she was, what she was doing, and he would seek her out when this nightmare was finished.

The queen awoke with a start and a cry of *"Grâce de Dieu."*

Rosamund jumped up and went to the bed. "Can I get you anything, madam?"

Mary struggled up against the pillows. "A little wine, Rosamund, please, and bring me my psalter."

Rosamund did both and returned to her low stool by the fire, while Mary read silently for an hour, before letting her head fall back on the pillows and sleeping again, the psalter lying open on the covers. Rosamund picked it up and put it on the table beside the bed. Her own eyes were drooping and she let herself drift in the warmth of the quiet room.

Mary awoke before dawn and Rosamund started awake at the sound of her name. "Oh, forgive me, madam, I must have slept a little."

Mary smiled. "And so you should, my dear. I feel guilty keeping my ladies awake all night, but indeed your presence is a comfort. Without it, I doubt I would sleep."

"Will I fetch your night-robe, madam?" Rosamund went to the armoire for the furred robe, bringing it to the bed.

Mary slipped to the floor in her thin linen shift and hastily wrapped herself in the warm robe. She went to her prie-dieu for her morning prayers and Rosamund went into the main apartment to summon a servant to bring water, and breakfast.

Just before eight o'clock, Sir Amyas came to escort Mary to the Great Hall. She was dressed as always in black, with a small silver lace ruff at her throat. A black French hood concealed her hair, and her rosary hung at her waist.

"I am ready, Sir Amyas. My ladies are permitted to accompany me, I trust?"

"Yes, madam. They will attend you."

And so the little party proceeded down the corridor,

down the stairs, and into the Great Hall, where on the dais at the far end the commissioners were ranged in two rows. A seat for Mary was set in front of them, a bench for her ladies to one side.

"Mary Stuart, you are brought before this court to answer charges of treason. How answer you?"

Mary rose to her feet. "My lords, I have suffered eighteen years of unjust imprisonment, and as a sovereign anointed prince and thus not subject to common law, I do not acknowledge the jurisdiction of this court." She sat down.

"Madam, your guilt is already well established. We have signed affidavits from your secretary, Monsieur Claude de Nau, we have the signed confessions of those with whom you planned the assassination of our most sovereign majesty, and we have a letter written in your own hand to the conspirator Anthony Babington, giving your consent and encouragement for the assassination of Queen Elizabeth. What say you?"

Mary stood still and straight, facing her accusers. She spoke quietly. "Sirs, I would never make shipwreck of my soul by compassing the death of my dearest sister. I deny all knowledge of any conspiracy, I have had no correspondence with one Anthony Babington, and I question the truth of confessions wrung from those on the rack."

Rosamund, sketching the scene for Sir Francis, was filled with admiration. Mary was every inch a queen as she faced her accusers. She must know that nothing she could say would alter the judgment, or the inevitable sentence, but she seemed so confident in the rightness of her cause. It was hard to imagine how much courage it took to maintain such composure and confidence, surrounded as she was by her enemies. Yet Mary seemed almost transfigured, as if lit from within by some spiritual light that gave her strength. It was hard to capture that on paper, but she tried. It seemed somehow important that Sir Francis should see Mary's inner strength, her calm dignity in the face of everything they did to break her.

The court ended its day without pronouncing judgment, and Mary and her ladies were escorted back to their apartments. Mary went immediately to her prie-dieu.

The next morning they were preparing to return to the Great Hall, when a servant brought Mary a message from Sir Amyas. Mary slit the wafer and opened the sheet. She read it, then handed it to Charlotte, who read aloud, "The commission has been prorogued by her majesty for ten days. They are returned to London."

"What does that mean?" Rosamund asked, puzzled.

"I think it means that my dear sister is reluctant to have judgment pronounced on a queen regnant," Mary said serenely. "It is a dangerous thing she contemplates, and my cousin Guise will not sit idly by, neither will my son. If France and Scotland rise up in arms against England in my defense, it will put my cousin in an invidious position."

Rosamund made due note of Mary's understanding of Elizabeth's difficulties. So far Rosamund felt she had not been obliged to conceal anything from her journal. On the contrary, Mary's behavior was so admirable, she wanted Sir Francis to realize it.

Mary was walking in the inner court, her furred cloak wrapped tightly around her against the October cold. The sky was leaden and made the cheerless court even more so. Rosamund walked briskly, swinging her arms. They would all prefer to be inside warm by the fire, but Mary insisted that they take the air for this one precious hour a day, and so they walked round and around the walls of the court, talking little. Mary prayed her rosary as she walked, her little dog trotting at her heels.

The unexpected arrival of Sir Amyas in the court sent a deeper chill through the prisoners. Nothing good could ever come from a visit from Paulet, and he had not made an appearance for two weeks. Mary paused in her prayers and waited for him to reach her. Her ladies gathered around her.

Paulet looked if possible even more stern and austere than usual in his severe black garments, relieved only by a modest white ruff. He held himself rigid as he declared, "Madam, it is my duty to inform you that the Star Chamber has found you guilty of treason. I am charged to say that if you confess your treason before sentencing, her majesty may see fit to commute a sentence of death to one of continued imprisonment."

"Sir Amyas, you may tell my dear queen-sister that since I have nothing to confess, I cannot in all conscience do so." Mary's smile was almost pitying. "Now, if you please, I believe my time for exercise is not yet over." She resumed her walking, her lips moving soundlessly in prayer as her gloved fingers moved over her rosary.

Paulet had no choice but to accept his dismissal. He turned on his heel and departed.

Rosamund felt a surge of savage satisfaction. He just didn't know how to react to his prisoner, and Mary knew exactly how to discompose her guardian. Small satisfaction in the circumstances, but to be treasured nevertheless.

The days inched by. October became November without any further proclamations from London. Mary had been allowed her personal confessor throughout her long imprisonment and began now to talk of celebrating a

Christmas mass in the castle chapel. As the days passed
without further dread proclamations, a sense of purpose,
of possibility, crept back into the lives of the imprisoned
women.

Sir Francis read Rosamund's journals and studied her
sketches as they arrived on his desk. He sensed Rosamund's
admiration for Mary, indeed it came through as clearly as
Sir Amyas's unadorned statements that Mary appeared to
have no fear of judgment, no apprehension of death. Sir
Amyas had decided that the Queen of Scots' fearless composure arose because she believed that her cousin would
not dare to order her execution. Rosamund, on the other
hand, believed that Mary was ready to die, was indeed
eager for a martyr's death. And Sir Francis concluded that
Rosamund had the right of it.

On a cold, clear December morning, Sir Amyas arrived in
Mary's apartments with a paper. "Madam, this has not yet
been published, but it has been ratified by Parliament and
you can expect its publication within days." He presented
the paper to her.

Mary read it without expression, then said calmly, "So
be it." She handed it back to her guardian, who took it
without a word and departed.

"What is it, madam?" Charlotte asked anxiously.

"Parliament is to publish a sentence of death. Come
now, ladies, let us see if we can finish this tapestry. I dislike
leaving things undone." She drew her chair closer to the
frame where the vast tapestry was stretched. She and her
ladies had been working on it for months and only a corner remained unfinished.

Christmas came and went. Sentence was proclaimed and

the country rejoiced. London was illuminated with myriad lamps in celebration, but Elizabeth could still not bring herself to sign the death warrant. Finally, pushed to it by rumors of a plot to assassinate her emanating from the French embassy and a second rumor that flew through the country like wildfire that the Spaniards had landed on the coast, she signed, but then would not part with the warrant, until her councilors took matters into their own hands.

It was the night of February 7 when Mary received her visitors. She embraced her old friend Shrewsbury. "Ah, it is so good to see you again, my friend. What brings you to this wretched place?"

Shrewsbury, tears running down his face, knelt before her. "Madam, you must prepare to die in the Great Hall at eight o'clock tomorrow morning."

"Don't weep, my friend." Mary took his hand, drawing him to his feet. "Indeed, I am so wearied I will be pleased to lay down the burdens of this earthly travail. I go to my death joyfully. You must not weep for me."

Rosamund turned aside, her own tears flowing freely.

Chapter Twenty-nine

TWO DAYS PASSED after Mary's death with no word from the outside. Within, the castle was held in a vise of silence, everyone carrying within himself the horrendous memories of her death. No one spoke of the queen's last moments, of the bloody ax, the indrawn gasp of horror from the spectators as the ax had missed its target on the first swing, the dreadful silence broken by the thud of the severed head falling to the straw.

The queen's body remained embalmed in a secluded chamber of the castle, awaiting disposition. Her women were no longer confined behind a locked door and were free to roam the castle, although not to go beyond its walls. Rosamund took to walking the ramparts with Mary's little dog trotting beside her. Indoors, he whined constantly, inconsolable at the disappearance of his beloved mistress, but outside, particularly in the freshness of the windy open air on the ramparts, he quietened.

On the second day, Rosamund was making her second circuit when she saw a sizable group of horsemen approaching across the river Nene, their breastplates gleaming in the thin rays of the chilly midmorning sun. She leaned on the ramparts, watching as they forded the river and cantered towards the castle. As they drew closer, she saw that three men rode in front of the phalanx of soldiers. She recognized her brother in the front line.

Her heart jumped, her breath stopped. Will Creighton rode beside him. She wanted to shout her delight to the clouds above, to hurl herself down the winding stone stairs to the court below, to run to him the moment they entered through the portcullis. The Rosamund of last year would probably have done just that. But Rosamund was no longer the giddy young woman who had cavorted with Will in a hayloft and against a buttery wall. She had witnessed death, too much of it. She accepted responsibility for some part in those deaths. She was no longer an innocent with an untrammeled future ahead of her.

She drew several steadying breaths and watched the party as they approached the drawbridge. The odious Ingram Frizer trotted a few paces behind her brother.

Will would know she was here, so he would not be surprised into indiscretion. Thank God she had seen them in sufficient time to master her own reaction. As far as Thomas was concerned, she and Will were mere casual acquaintances, who had met once at the theatre and would occasionally have bumped into each other at court.

Slowly Rosamund started to walk again, the dog prancing at her heels. Her head began to clear, her composure to return in full. She looked over the ramparts again. The party of horsemen were coming up the hill to the drawbridge. She gathered up the dog and climbed down the winding stone stairs that led all the way down to the outer bailey.

Sir Amyas was greeting her brother as she appeared around the final curve in the stairs. Thomas was alone in the courtyard, no sign of the others of his party, and for a moment Rosamund wondered if she had imagined Will, and the soldiers and Frizer.

Her brother, who had already dismounted, saw her immediately and strode over to her. "Well, Little Sister, you have done your work well. Master Secretary is well pleased, you should know." He kissed her heartily. "But why this air of melancholy? This woebegone look." He gestured to her black gown, the black ribbon in her hair. "We are come to take you home. Anyone would think you weren't pleased to see me."

"I am pleased to see you, Brother," she said with quiet restraint. "But it is a melancholy time."

"Not so. 'Tis a time for jubilation. A most dangerous threat to our realm has been removed."

"It is true that my lady is at rest with her God. It was something she wished for most devoutly. I believe her death came as a relief in the end."

Thomas frowned at her, then with a brisk gesture he dismissed the whole business. Rosamund began to wonder how she could ever have thought of her brother as such a god, such a golden creature. She loved him, but now she seemed to see him with different eyes. She could never forget that Thomas had not flinched at the sights of St. Giles Fields. It was strange that a man who so loved poetry, plays, beauty in all its forms, could embrace the crude and the cruel with equal enthusiasm. Did he truly think she had felt nothing for Mary? That the events of the last days had left her untouched?

"Where did that come from?" Thomas pointed at the terrier, who was watching him with bright eyes from the safety of Rosamund's arms.

"A dead queen," she said flatly. Sir Amyas drew in a sharp breath, but Thomas merely laughed.

"Poor pampered tyke. He won't stand a chance with the hounds at Scadbury."

"He won't be expected to try, Brother."

Sir Amyas coughed and said, "Pray come into the castle, Master Walsingham. You must be in need of refreshment after your journey." He turned to Rosamund. "Do you accompany us, Mistress Walsingham?"

His manner had changed dramatically too. Rosamund was no longer a prisoner, even a pretend one, and thus no longer subject to his jurisdiction. She was now her brother's charge.

"Thank you," she murmured, following the men into the castle's lamplit Great Hall. It had a vastly different aspect now from that bitter morning of execution. The platform was gone, the bloodied ax was gone, the block was gone. Only the headless corpse abovestairs remained as mute witness to that morning. Half a tree trunk burned in the vast hearth, and the long board was spread with platters of cold meats and baskets of bread. Flagons of wine and ale stood sentinel at either end.

"Where is the rest of your party, Thomas? I saw half an army accompanying you up the hill."

Thomas shook his head, taking a chicken leg from a platter. "Not so many . . . they are settling into the barracks here. My young friend Creighton has gone with Frizer into the town. Our cousin entrusted him with some messages for someone in the vicinity. I know no more than that." He shrugged. "I doubt he will be overlong."

"When do we leave here?" With a faint smile of thanks she accepted the cup of wine offered by Sir Amyas.

Thomas took a bite of chicken and said through his mouthful, "The day after tomorrow. The horses must rest. We are escorting the Lady Mary's attendants to London.

They will travel in litters, so it will be a tedious journey."

"I would ride," she said swiftly. "If a horse can be found for me."

"I daresay that can be achieved, Mistress Walsingham," Sir Amyas said. "There are several spare horses in the stables here."

Booted feet sounded in the antechamber and Rosamund's pulse beat fast in her throat. Will came in, pulling off his gauntlets, tucking them into his belt. His eyes went immediately to Rosamund, who instantly bent to put down the dog, who raced to the skirting, sniffing at the telltale scent of mice.

Rosamund straightened, tucking a loose strand of russet hair whipped loose by the wind outside on the ramparts back into the netted snood. If her cheeks were at all pink, it would be explained by bending down to release the terrier.

"Master Creighton, you are well come. I thought you too occupied at court to venture this far from the delights of London." Her voice was light, pleasantly bantering, and she congratulated herself on striking just the right note. Courtiers spoke thus in the corridors of Whitehall Palace. Thomas would think nothing of it.

Will chuckled and tossed his hat onto the long bench at the side of the hall. "If I'd known what a long, cold ride it would be, I'd have willingly stayed among the fleshpots, Mistress Walsingham. Unfortunately, my presence on the journey was required by one who may not be gainsaid." He pulled a comical face at that and poured himself a foaming tankard of ale.

"It is true that when Master Secretary makes a request, it is advisable to accede," Thomas agreed. "But you have been gone barely half an hour, Will. Did you deliver your messages so quickly?"

Will shook his head, his eyes once more darting to Rosamund, before turning back to her brother. "Master Ingram took the task upon himself. It was hardly work for two men, so I came hotfoot in search of fire, drink, and meat."

"Then you will find all three here, sir," Rosamund said. She knew that Will had come back so quickly because he could not put off this meeting for one more minute, and it was torment to be in the same room with him, to talk in this inconsequential fashion, to behave as if he meant no more to her than the casual acquaintance Thomas believed him to be.

She watched him covertly as he took up a place by the fire, one boot resting on the massive andirons. He chewed on a mutton chop and his eyes met hers. One eyelid dropped in a quick conspiratorial wink before he turned and threw the chop bone into the fire.

"I must return to the queen's ladies," she said quickly. "They must be told of our departure without delay. There is much to do before we leave."

"You would do well not to refer to the traitor Mary with such a title," Thomas said sharply, glancing at Paulet, whose expression was deeply disapproving.

"As you say, Brother." Her curtsy was ironic if her brother chose to see it, and she went up the great staircase, calling for the terrier, who ceased his mouse hunt and scampered up the stairs after her.

She joined the rest of Mary's attendants in their chamber, explaining that their time at Fotheringay was come to an end and they were to go to London.

"And what awaits us there?" Charlotte asked with a heavy sigh. "The Tower, or some other drear prison?"

"I don't know," Rosamund confessed. Her position now felt if possible even more invidious than before. These women would see that she was returned to her brother's charge, and they would inevitably wonder why she seemed in favor when so much had been made of her rejection by her family. But in the end it mattered little what they thought, guessed, believed. They would go their ways and she would go hers.

She went into the bedchamber to pack her few belongings, her thoughts fully occupied with planning a way to be alone with Will, even for a few minutes, before they began the journey.

Will, who had been given a small, sparsely furnished chamber under the eaves, was similarly occupied as he lay upon the lumpy pallet, looking up at the beams in the sloping ceiling. He had spent every available minute of the journey from London worrying that his sudden arrival would unnerve Rosamund and she would give them both away. He need not have worried, he now realized. She had behaved with the cool composure of an experienced conspirator. But what now? How in this grim, closely watched castle could they contrive a meeting?

His door opened with a creak that seemed as loud as a thunderclap, and he sat up so suddenly he crashed his head against the low beam above.

"Shhh." Rosamund slid into the chamber, a finger on her lips. She closed the door at her back and stood looking at him as he rubbed his head and gazed at her in amazement.

"I . . . I was thinking of you, and suddenly there you are," he whispered. "A spirit conjured out of my thoughts."

Her eyes danced as she tiptoed to the pallet. "I didn't dare ask where you were housed, but I asked my brother where *he's* sleeping, which seemed a perfectly reasonable inquiry. He told me he had a chamber to himself, next to

Paulet, so I guessed if you were to be given privacy, they
would have given you one of the small chambers up here.
If I was discovered and questioned, I would say I am in
search of Mary's dog. No one would question that, the
poor creature still mourns his mistress."

Will reached for her hands and pulled her down beside
him. He cupped her face and kissed her. "I was so sorry
about that night at Chartley . . . I had no choice, and I
could not get a message to you."

"No, I know. I realized what had happened." She smiled,
brushed his mouth with her own. "I do not hold it against
you, Will."

He lay back, moving her on top of him so that she lay
along his length. "Dare we?" His blue eyes had that sapphire glow to them again.

Rosamund glanced over her shoulder to the door.
"No one is looking for me. Everything is so confused
since . . . since . . . that no one really knows who's where
and where anyone is supposed to be. If there's a question, I
am still looking for the dog."

She kissed him.

An hour later she crept from the attic chamber and ran
soundlessly to the main floor below. Soldiers were everywhere, mingling with the sheriff's men, who were guard-
ing the corpse. People bustled as if some great city were
about to be evacuated. The lords and dignitaries who had
presided over Mary's death had all departed Fotheringay
immediately after the execution; only Sir Amyas and his
household had remained with Mary's attendants. Now they
too were to depart. No one remarked on Mistress Walsingham's presence in the corridor, she blended seamlessly into
the confused bustle.

The terrier was asleep in front of the fire in the chamber she shared with Dorothy, who was saying her rosary on the prie-dieu in the corner. She didn't look up as Rosamund entered. The peace was disturbed by the clanging of a great gong resounding throughout the castle, and Dorothy jumped up from her knees with a gasp of fright.

"What is it? Is the castle under attack?"

Rosamund didn't answer. She ran from the bedchamber, through the main chamber, and out into the corridor. Her brother was striding down the corridor towards her. "You do not look ready for dinner, Sister," he chided, running his eyes over her. "Do you not hear the summons?"

"That is the summons for dinner?" She looked at him in astonishment. "Sweet heaven, Thomas, in the last weeks we have been summoned to a trial and to an execution in this place, and now someone chooses such a peremptory summons to the dinner table? It beggars belief."

"There is no longer any need for a diversion from customary practice, Mistress Walsingham." Sir Amyas spoke behind her and she turned to see the queen's erstwhile jailer, dressed in black as usual, but a particularly luxuriant black velvet, and a fine collar of cobweb lace, similar to her brother's.

"I will sup with Lady Mary's attendants," she said, turning back.

"No." Her brother spoke sharply. "Your work here is done, Sister. From now on you will remain by my side until I can return you to Scadbury. I suggest you tidy yourself for dinner."

Rosamund said nothing. She returned to her bedchamber, washed, brushed her hair, retied the black velvet ribbon, and went down to the Great Hall.

There was no further opportunity to be alone with Will

either before they began the long journey south or during it. But they managed a delightful kind of courtship nevertheless. They would brush up against each other in passing, a contact that had them continuing on their separate ways both wearing a deeply satisfied smile. They would exchange surreptitious glances, and Will in particular would make funny little gestures that reminded Rosamund of something they had done together in their loving, and she would be convulsed with silent laughter even as she struggled to contain a hot surge of remembered sensation.

Neither of them noticed Ingram Frizer's watchful attention.

They reached London late on the fourth day after leaving Fotheringay. Thomas was irritable. His horse had thrown a shoe earlier that day and it had held them up for two hours. The ladies in the litters were gently complaining about fatigue as they ceaselessly prayed their rosaries in a low, reproachful chant. He wanted to be rid of the whole burdensome charge, including his sister, who, he was obliged to admit, gave him no trouble. But he wanted his own bed, and he wanted Kit in it.

Their first stop was at one of the queen's houses on the outskirts of London. Here he left Mary's ladies, handing them over to the Earl of Cumberland, who was to be their guardian and supervise their eventual return to their own families. In much better humor Thomas continued to Seething Lane, where he was to leave his sister.

"We will continue to Scadbury in two days' time, Rosamund. Sir Francis wishes to talk with you first. I'll escort you home the day after tomorrow. No doubt you will be glad to return to the peace and quiet of the country."

"Will you be staying at Scadbury, Brother?" she asked, handing the reins of her mount to a servant. It was a simple enough question, but it carried a burden of implications, and Will listened closely while seeming to examine a crack in the leather of his mount's harness.

"No, not above a day."

"Is Master Marlowe at Scadbury?" she asked, all innocence.

Thomas shot her a sharp look. "No, he is in London."

She smiled. "I see."

She saw annoyance flash across his face, but he could say nothing. Nothing could be read into the demure statement unless one knew certain things. And once in a while Rosamund felt like pushing her brother close to his limits.

But now she continued as if her statement had never been made. "You are right, Brother. I shall certainly be glad of the peace and quiet of Scadbury. I cannot wait to walk again in the orchard, 'tis quite my favorite spot." She turned to Will with a bland smile. "I bid you farewell, Master Creighton."

He bowed from the saddle. "Farewell, Mistress Walsingham."

With a tiny smile, Rosamund went into the house, Mary's little terrier curled into her cloak as he had been throughout the journey.

Thomas came for her as promised and Kit rode with him. Rosamund was overjoyed to find Jenny waiting for her in the stables at Seething Lane, and the feeling was mutual. Jenny whickered and nuzzled the crook of her elbow and pranced out of the yard, Rosamund reveling in the familiar feel of her own horse beneath her. Mary's little dog was left behind. The newly widowed Lady Sidney had been so taken with the animal that Rosamund had readily entrusted the Skye terrier to Frances, privately thankful that she would not have to protect him from the more ferocious variety of hound in residence at Scadbury.

Rosamund noticed immediately that Thomas sported a bruise on his temple and Kit held his right arm awkwardly. But they seemed perfectly in harmony with each other, Kit reciting verses, Thomas complimenting him, and the familiar spark flashed between them, but it no longer made her uncomfortable. She understood it all too well.

"Are you particularly acquainted with the Chevalier de Vaugiras, Thomas?" she asked as they remounted after the ferry ride to the far bank of the river. Nothing in her demeanor showed the tension she felt. She had been longing for the right moment to ask the question, and her hands were clammy in her kidskin gloves.

Thomas, from the back of his piebald gelding, swiveled to look at her, his gaze both startled and forbidding. "And what, pray, do you know of the chevalier, miss?"

She shrugged. "Nothing more than that he is a courtier. I danced with him once or twice. I found him amusing." She kept her eyes on the road ahead. "I just thought of him. I don't know why."

"Well, you'd do well not to think of him again," Thomas declared. "He offended her majesty in a joust by unhorsing his opponent and has been all but banished from court."

"Oh? Has he returned to France?"

"I neither know nor care." Thomas slashed his whip against the gelding's flanks and the animal leaped forward, passing Rosamund and Jenny. Kit, with one of his wild halloos, kicked his mount and he passed Rosamund in a mad gallop. She held Jenny to a canter, following their careening progress down the lane.

Had Arnaud's banishment from court been engineered in some way by Sir Francis? Master Secretary had said he

Chapter Thirty

FRANCIS WALSINGHAM KEPT to the rear of the hall at Hampton Court Palace. His queen was not in charity with any of her councilors after her cousin's execution, which she insisted had not received her blessing. She was sitting in state this afternoon, the train of her ermine-trimmed, turquoise velvet robe flowing at her feet. She wore a circlet of turquoise and diamonds in her red wig, its long side locks falling to her shoulders, and a wide cartwheel ruff on which her head seemed to rest like the head of John the Baptist on Salome's charger.

Francis turned his narrow-eyed gaze to where Lady Leinster stood in a group of courtiers close to the queen. She seemed less assured than usual, he reflected. Her lover's continued absence from court seemed to take something from her, some of the light that had made her such an attraction for men and women alike. But she too must be brought down, however inadvertent her part. No one interfered with a Walsingham.

The queen, if she had not already done so, would find the incriminating papers among the state papers he had delivered to her privy chamber that afternoon. Rosamund's sketch would arouse the queen's interest, and the neatly penned, anonymous accusation of a forbidden liaison between the two parties would as surely fan the fire as bellows to a blacksmith's forge. Walsingham knew his queen well, and he knew that in her present mood, out of charity with almost everyone surrounding her, looking for someone, anyone except herself, to blame for her cousin's execution, she would have no tolerance for a clandestine liaison between two of her favorites.

As he watched, he saw one of her gentlemen approach Lady Leinster. Agathe looked startled and then approached the dais, curtsying low before the queen in her chair of state. Elizabeth looked at her in frigid silence for what seemed a very long minute, then she spoke. "I am no longer pleased to have you at my court, Lady Leinster. You will leave by sundown. I suggest you go to your paramour. I'm sure he'll welcome you. I wish to see neither of you again." The queen then turned her shoulder to the frozen Agathe and began to talk with the Countess of Pembroke and Lord Leicester, who stood beside her chair.

Sir Francis, had he been a different man, could have felt compassion for the woman, so publicly disgraced. Agathe's countenance took on the gray hue of dead ashes. Her hand went to her throat, adorned with a magnificent pearl collar. For a moment it looked as if she were choking, then she swayed. A compassionate hand went to her elbow, steadying her as she walked down the steps to the main body of the hall. People fell away from her as she crossed the vast expanse of the Great Hall, to the double doors at the far end, and behind her the whispers started.

Walsingham edged his own way out of the hall in her wake. He found her sitting on a bench in the corridor outside, plying her fan, her lovely purple eyes shocked in her deathly pale countenance. "Lady Leinster." He bowed and, without waiting for permission, took a seat beside her. "You were not expecting such a decree."

She turned to look at him, a wildness now in her eyes. "How should I have been? How could the queen know . . . ? Who could have . . . ?" She buried her face in her hands.

"You are wondering how the queen could know of your liaison with the Chevalier de Vaugiras," Walsingham stated matter-of-factly. "I think, madam, that you probably relied too much on the discretion of your companions. It is never wise to believe one's secrets are honored."

She looked blankly at him, then rose from the bench and walked away.

Francis nodded to himself and left the palace, walking briskly to the water steps where his barge awaited. Ingram Frizer was sitting on the quay, idly whittling a piece of stick with his dagger. He got up as the secretary emerged from the alley of plane trees. Walsingham gave him his instructions and entered the barge, wrapping his cloak tightly around him against the wind as he settled in the stern and the bargemen began the long pole down the river.

Agathe left the palace by road, her carriage rattling over the rough dirt tracks through tiny villages and then across the uneven cobbles of the city itself. The carriage stopped outside the Golden Cock on the Strand and she hurried inside. It was a cold evening, with a bitter wind. Arnaud would surely be at home.

Arnaud was indeed within, working on a chess puzzle by the blazing fire in a warm and welcoming chamber. He looked up from the board in surprise as she stood in the doorway, white-faced and shivering.

"Agathe, *ma chère*. Whatever brings you here tonight? The court is at Hampton Court, is it not?"

"Yes, and *I* am not." She rubbed her gloved hands

together, her face pinched and cold. "We are discovered, Arnaud. We are both banished." Her voice was barely above a whisper.

He stared at her for a moment as if not sure he had heard her aright. "How did this happen?" He uncurled himself from his chair and poured wine into two cups on a table beneath the window. His voice was calm, but his eyes belied his tone. "When were you told this?"

"The queen herself . . . she was sitting in state . . . I was summoned and banished in front of the whole court." Tears started in Agathe's eyes and she gulped at the wine, her slender shoulders still shivering. "In front of everyone, Arnaud . . . so dreadful . . . so humiliating."

"And what of me?" The question was harshly spoken and he seemed unaware of her distress.

Agathe swallowed. "My paramour . . . the queen told me to go to my 'paramour' . . . that we would never be welcome at court again. Walsingham said—"

"Walsingham? What has he to do with any of this?" Arnaud's voice was as harsh as before, his eyes like hot coals.

Agathe looked frightened. "I . . . I do not know, Arnaud. But he sought me out . . . said I should never trust the discretion of those around me. He spoke your name . . . he knew . . ." Her voice trailed away.

The chevalier turned away from her, his expression unreadable.

Rosamund waved farewell to her brother and Kit as they rode away from Scadbury. She felt the emptiness of the house around her as a benediction. The servants were in residence, of course, but there was no one to watch her, to call for her, to ask her what she was doing, where she was going. She was truly her own mistress, mistress of her time.

And she had but one question: When would Will come?

She took her cloak and went out into the blustery morning, making her way to the orchard. The weather hardly lent itself to alfresco assignations. If . . . *when* Will came, she would have to contrive some more comfortable bower than a leafless apple orchard.

She walked beneath the bare trees, the grass damp underfoot, thinking. Will would not venture to Scadbury until he was certain Thomas was back in London, so she had a day or two to come up with a solution. It couldn't be in the house. She couldn't risk any of the servants discovering her secret. By the same token, the stables and domestic outbuildings were out of the question. Then she remembered. The charcoal burner's cottage at the edge of the deer park. The itinerant charcoal burner was an annual visitor in the early autumn when the trees were thinned in the woods around the estate. He stayed usually until after Christmas, then went on to the next estate. His cottage stood empty the rest of the year, but it was snug enough, and sufficient charcoal was always lying around to make a decent fire.

With a gleeful little half skip, Rosamund left the orchard and walked briskly to the clearing in the thick coppice. The little stone cottage, with its slate roof, stood in the middle of the clearing with a small pile of discarded charcoal by the door. Inside it was dusty, a tapestry of spiderwebs lacing the windows. A narrow cot with a pile of rags stood against one wall, and the charcoal brazier was in the center of the single room.

Blankets and pillows for the cot, a flagon of wine, bread and cheese, winter apples, and maybe some sweet delicacy from Mistress Riley's kitchen. Thus furnished it would be a perfect love nest.

She left the cottage, hurrying back to the house, intent on acquiring what was needed. Ingram Frizer hovered on the edge of the coppice. What was the lass up to? Unfortunately he couldn't at the moment hang around Scadbury to find out. He had work to do for Master Secretary that must take precedence over his own nosing out of secrets. None of his masters had expressed an interest in Mistress Rosamund, or indeed in Master Creighton, but then none of them had seen what he had.

Will came to the orchard two days later. He left his horse in the village and approached the walled estate on foot. Bare branches of apple trees scraped the top of the wall on the south side, and he looked for a foothold in the brickwork. A toehold offered, about halfway up, and he made a leap for it, grabbing the top of the wall as his boot scrabbled for purchase. He transferred his hold to the branch of the tree and hauled himself up until he was sitting on the wall looking down into the orchard and the neat rows of fruit trees.

Rosamund stood laughing a few feet away, one finger pressed to her lips. He grinned and swung himself down to the soft ground. She came into his arms, face uptilted for his kiss. "I guessed you would come today," she murmured when he raised his head for a moment. "Did you see Thomas in London?"

"I passed him in Seething Lane. Your cousin is sending him to Ghent, and judging by his expression the prospect was unpleasing."

"I daresay because he will be separated from Kit Marlowe," Rosamund mused. "They have not had overmuch time together in recent weeks."

Will looked at her curiously. "They are good friends then, your brother and the playmaker?"

Rosamund's eyes sparkled with mischief. "Friends and more. I'm surprised you didn't know it." ·

Will looked at her askance. "They have an unnatural relationship? Is that what you're saying?"

She shrugged, the mischief still sparking in her green eyes. "I don't know about unnatural. From what I have seen, the passion between them is entirely natural."

Will was for a moment shocked at this casual statement. "Rosamund, that is heresy. How could such a gently bred maid say such a thing?"

She went into a peal of laughter. "Will . . . Will . . . there is nothing gently bred about me, my dear. Thomas has never sheltered me from the less acceptable aspects of the world. Oh, admittedly, on occasion his conscience would trouble him and he'd tell me to forget whatever it was I had heard or deduced from some remark, and I would dutifully promise to do so."

Her laughter died and her suddenly intense gaze was fixed upon him. Her voice was low and seductive. "If I had done so, I would not have created a love nest for us. Come." She took his hand with an imperative tug.

Will laughed, caught her to him for another fierce kiss, before letting her lead him through the orchard. In the charcoal burner's clearing he looked at the cottage, then looked at Rosamund, eyebrows lifted. "What is this?"

"A love nest. I told you." She pulled him with her to the door. "We will light the brazier, everything is ready. If you wish to eat or drink, we can do that, or . . . ?" She let her sentence trail suggestively away. She unlatched the door and pushed it open.

Will stood on the threshold looking around the small, square room while Rosamund with flint and tinder lit an oil lamp and then the charcoal already set in the brazier.

Both ignited with a flare and the charcoal roared into a full burn.

"Will you drink?" she asked, lifting a flagon from the rickety table.

"Later," he said, his voice husky. He threw off his hat and his cloak, heedless where they fell, and lifted Rosamund off the floor, holding her high for a moment, looking up into her face. "Oh, you are so lovely."

She smiled with pure pleasure, warmed to her core by the oft-repeated words that never failed to delight her, to fill her with an engulfing desire. She wrapped her legs around his hips and kissed him, biting his lip with a savage need, tasting blood on her tongue. Will moaned softly and carried her to the cot, tossing her down, his own eyes filled with ferocious need. He bent over her, throwing up her skirts, baring her to her waist, and knelt over her, stroking her white belly, her flanks, the soft thighs, before he bent and kissed her, his mouth moving down between her thighs, finding her essence, the little nub of aroused flesh, in a caress that made her hips dance.

He hauled at the laces of his britches. His erect penis pushed against her thighs and she opened her legs, fastening them around his hips, lifting herself off the bed to take him deep inside. Her eyes fixed upon his as he moved and she moved with him, up and up to completion. He murmured to her and she whispered back, nonsense words as the pleasure grew ever deeper, ever more intense, until Rosamund thought she would split asunder, scatter in a million pieces to the four winds.

Afterwards they lay in a tangle of limbs, spent and breathless. Rosamund could feel her heart beating so fast she thought it might burst from her chest, but slowly it settled and the world righted itself.

With a protesting groan, Will rolled sideways onto his knees beside the narrow cot. He leaned forward, resting his forehead on her belly in an attitude of complete exhaustion. "I have never, ever, in my entire life experienced anything like that." His breath was a damp breeze across her heated skin. "You are miraculous, sweet Rosamund."

Feebly she reached down to twine her fingers into his unruly curls, tugging gently. "Would you like wine? I raided Thomas's cellars for one of his finer burgundies. And there are some of Mistress Riley's chicken patties if you're hungry."

He raised his head and smiled up her length. "What a domestic creature it has become," he teased. "You have set up house, it seems."

Rosamund pushed him away, but her eyes were still dreamily smiling. "Don't mock. I had only your comfort in mind."

He got to his feet in one smooth movement. "And I am truly grateful." He poured wine into the two cups and brought one over to her, then bit into a chicken patty. "Mmm, very good, so fluffy and delicate. Your Mistress Riley must be an accomplished cook."

"She is . . . may I have one?" Rosamund sat up, swinging her legs over the edge of the cot. Will sat beside her and they ate and drank, laughing suddenly for no apparent reason, snatching quick kisses between mouthfuls, until the charcoal in the brazier died and the air grew chill.

"We mustn't linger, my sweet." Will stood up, adjusting his disheveled garments. "It's dangerous enough as it is, without courting discovery. You will be missed, and I must reclaim my horse before anyone thinks it has been stabled overlong at the inn."

Rosamund acceded reluctantly, knowing that Will was

right. If they were to manage to maintain this glorious connection, they had to practice excessive caution. There were eyes and ears in the village and around the estate. One wrong word to Thomas and the ensuing fracas didn't bear contemplation.

Will made sure the brazier was properly extinguished and Rosamund left the flagons and wine cups on the table. Later she would wash them with water from the rain butt. Will opened the door onto the clearing and stood looking around. The shadows were lengthening as the winter afternoon drew in, and the wind was getting up, setting the treetops lashing against the graying sky.

Rosamund stepped up beside him, drawing the door shut behind her. She looked at him and he kissed her, a lingering stroke over her lips, and a quick little nip of the tip of her nose that made her laugh.

"Until next time, sweet Rosamund."

"Next time." She ran the pad of her thumb over his mouth. "I'll walk with you to the wall."

They were halfway across the clearing when a voice behind them said, "Well, this is an interesting development."

Rosamund inhaled sharply and she whirled to face Arnaud, Chevalier de Vaugiras. He had stepped from the trees on the far side of the clearing and stood about fifty feet from them. Will had turned and now looked at the man in puzzlement.

"What the devil do you do here, Chevalier?"

Arnaud laughed. "Oh, many things, Master Creighton. I wish for your sake that you had not been here too."

Rosamund stepped instinctively in front of Will. "What do you mean?"

"I mean, Mistress Walsingham, that Walsinghams are my business. *You* are my business at this moment. And since Master Creighton seems to be *your* business and you his, then I fear he too becomes my business."

Rosamund stared at Arnaud. "How is my family your business?"

He shrugged. "Past history, *ma chère*, but a festering history nevertheless."

Will's hand was on his sword now. The menace in the clearing was an almost palpable thing, but he couldn't begin to imagine why the chevalier was here, and why he was so clearly intent on doing harm. Will moved Rosamund aside rather briskly and approached the chevalier. He might be confronting a madman and it would be wise not to antagonize him further.

"Can you be a little clearer, Chevalier? You seem to be threatening both Mistress Walsingham and myself. There must be an explanation." He tried to keep his voice moderate, the fear well in check. Mad dogs smelled fear and were further enraged by it.

"Is this clear enough, Master Creighton?" Arnaud's sword was out of its sheath in one swift, deadly movement. The blade glittered in the darkening clearing.

Will drew one sharp breath of surprise and yanked his own weapon from its scabbard. Rosamund's mouth was opened on an involuntary scream of shocked protest, but no sound came out. The blades met, there were no niceties here, none of the formal courtesies of the dueling field.

Will realized in befuddlement that he was fighting for his life. He had no idea why, no reason to imagine that the Frenchman could bear him sufficient enmity to kill him. But he had no choice. He fought with every desperate bone and muscle in his body. Their blades slashed, smashed against each other, no room for the delicate maneuvers of the fencing schools.

Rosamund ran towards them. She had no clear thought, no clear purpose, except that somehow this had to be stopped. But before she could reach them, Will went down, his hand pressed to his chest. Blood, thick red blood, bubbled between his fingers. He looked down at his chest in bewilderment, then up at the chevalier, who had lowered his sword and stood over him. Will seemed to slide gracefully sideways until he lay curled upon the ground, the blood soaking into the dirt around him.

Rosamund dropped to her knees. This wasn't happening. Hadn't happened. It wasn't possible. She was asleep and in a moment she would awaken in her own bed as the birds burst into the dawn chorus. "Will . . . Will . . ." But he didn't answer. He seemed to be looking at her, but he wasn't . . . he wasn't seeing her. A strange film was creeping over that wonderful, intense blue.

She looked up and saw the chevalier. His sword was still drawn and he was looking at her with a cold, fixed attention. "You and I have a score to settle, *ma chère.*" He bent and hauled her to her feet, pushing up her chin. "A kiss."

She fought him, biting and scratching, kicking and screaming at the top of her lungs. He merely laughed and silenced her with a backhanded slap. Then he was gone. His hands no longer held her. His smell no longer poisoned the air around her. She stepped back. He was on his knees, staring at the ground.

Ingram Frizer withdrew the knife from the chevalier's back and wiped it on the grass. "All right, Mistress Walsingham?" His tone seemed to indicate that the question was of little interest.

"Why?" The word stuck in her throat, sounded thick and strange to her ears.

"Master's orders," Frizer said, tucking the knife into his

boot. "Get rid of the Frenchman, he told me. I got rid of the Frenchman." He gave Rosamund a laconic sideways glance. "Not a moment too soon, neither."

The horror could not settle. It buzzed around her like swarming bees. She knelt beside Will, cradling his head in her lap, gently drawing her hand over his eyes.

Frizer regarded her, frowning. "You'd best go back to the house," he said after several minutes. "I'll deal with this mess. Your brother won't want you answering a coroner's questions, and 'tis my job to keep all smooth for him." As she opened her mouth to protest, he said sharply, "Get back to the house, girl. Weep to yourself, but never open your mouth on this. If you never speak of it, I won't. 'Twill do no good for anyone to hear it." His gaze was hostile, but Rosamund knew that salvation lay in trusting him. And Frizer could be trusted as long as it suited his interests.

She lifted Will's head, bent, and kissed his mouth. It was still as warm and pliant as it had been such a short time ago. Gently she laid his head upon the ground and stood up. She would grieve in private as they had loved in private. There was no other option.

Frizer seemed to experience a rare moment of compassion. "He'll have a proper burial, lass. I'll leave him where he'll be found easy. It'll look like an attack by footpads. If he has family, the right things will be done."

Rosamund nodded, speechless now, the tears thick in her throat. She had to get to the house, get up to her chamber, lock the door. And then she could feel.

Epilogue

June 5, 1593

Sir Roger Askew stepped out of the barge at the water steps of his house in the little riverside village of Putney. He paused for a moment as he always did on his return home to look up at the handsome manor house that sat on a bluff just above the river. A long sweep of lawn flowed from the wide terrace down to the winding Thames, where osier beds lined its banks. The red roof of the house glowed and the diamond-paned window winked at him in the afternoon sun. It was as always a pleasing prospect, redolent of peace and prosperity. But this afternoon, his soul was burdened. The document tucked into his doublet felt heavy as he took the path up the hill to the house.

He heard the childish voice raised in laughter before he saw her. The little girl exploded from a shrubbery, hurling herself against his knees. "Dadda . . . Dadda . . . we saw the barge . . . what did you bring me?"

He bent and picked her up, holding her above him, smiling into her pinkly exuberant countenance. "Why would I bring you anything, Meghan? Have you been exceptionally good?"

She nodded vigorously. "Exc . . . ex . . . *very* good. And

you promised you would bring me something . . . something for me *and* for Charles."

"Well, we shall see about that." He set her down, taking her hot, sticky little hand. "Where is Mama?"

"In the roses." She pointed to the shrubbery.

Roger took the winding path through the shrubbery to where it opened into a rose garden. The soft air was perfumed with myriad scents and filled with the gentle buzzing of honeybees. His wife was deadheading the rosebushes. She straightened, tucking an errant lock of russet hair back into her hood as she turned to him. It was such a familiar gesture and his heart as always turned over.

When he had married her six years earlier, she had been crushed with grief, a grief that she would never speak of, and he, who understood grief so well, had never questioned her. Seven months after the wedding she had delivered Meghan, a child with a mass of unruly curls and eyes of the most intense blue. Again he had asked no questions and from the moment of her birth had adored the child.

"Meghan insisted on coming to find you as soon as she saw the barge." Rosamund came over to him, smiling her pleasure, lifting her face for his kiss. She regarded him with a quizzical gleam in her green eyes. Something in his manner puzzled her.

"Why so grave, Roger?" She knew him so well now, and the sadness that had been so much a part of him in their early days was gone now. He would always be a serious man, but she loved the way his eyes danced with amusement, loved the laughter that was so often heard in his voice, particularly where his daughter was concerned.

"I have some grave news . . . sad news," he began, then the high-pitched cry of a baby interrupted him.

"Meghan has woken him up," Rosamund said, knowing her daughter all too well. She hurried to the wicker basket that lay in the shade of a rosebush and lifted her son, whose cry instantly ceased, and carried him to his father. "Bid your father welcome, Charles."

Roger took the child, nuzzling the soft cheeks, inhaling the sweet baby scent. The child put his hand on his father's cheek, gazing intently up at him with round, brown eyes.

"Libby." Rosamund summoned the nursemaid, hovering in the background. "Take the children up to the house."

"I'll bring your present to the nursery, Meghan. But you must go with Libby at once." Roger silenced his daughter's incipient protest and she did no more than pout before allowing herself to be taken away.

"Sad news?" Rosamund prompted, seating herself on the stone bench, patting the space beside her.

Roger drew the parchment from his doublet. He sat beside her, tapping it against his knee. "The playmaker, Kit Marlowe . . . he was killed in Deptford six days ago. A drunken brawl, according to the coroner . . . some quarrel over the reckoning for dinner." He opened the parchment. "This is a copy of the coroner's report."

Rosamund took the parchment in silence. The first name that flew out at her was that of Ingram Frizer, and something cold touched her skin. She read that in an argument, Marlowe, *moved with anger,* seized Frizer's dagger and attacked him with it. *And so it befell, in that affray, that the said Ingram, in defense of his life, with the dagger aforesaid of the value of twelve pence, gave the said Christopher a mortal wound above his right eye.*

She raised her eyes from the parchment, the final words seared into her brain. *Christopher Marlowe then and there instantly died.*

"Frizer" was all she said for a moment. Where Frizer was involved, nothing was simple, nothing as easily explained as a drunken brawl. "What a dreadful, dreadful waste." She gazed unseeing at a bee sucking nectar from the flower beside her. "Poor Thomas . . . I suppose he must know by now."

"Marlowe was staying at Scadbury, working on a play. I don't know if your brother was there with him. But his death is common knowledge now." He laid a hand over hers. "I know you had a fondness for Marlowe."

She nodded. "And for his plays."

"The world is much diminished without him." He interlaced his fingers with hers, holding her hand tightly. "He was no more than twenty-eight . . . twenty-nine. Imagine what literary jewels he could have written as he grew older and wiser." He disentangled his fingers and moved his arm around her shoulders, drawing her against him, and she rested her head on his chest, listening to the steady rhythm of his heart against her ear, as always drawing strength and reassurance from this man, her husband.

"I visited St. Paul's Churchyard this morning," he said into her hair, before pressing his lips to her brow. "I bought you some of the newly licensed plays. They may divert you a little."

St. Paul's Churchyard was the venue for booksellers of every type of literature, pamphlets, plays, poetry, tracts, and treaties. They sold the dross with the gems, and Rosamund loved every word she could lay hands upon.

She lifted her head. "Where are they?" She couldn't keep the eagerness from her voice and he chuckled softly.

"Bart was carrying them to the house, together with Meghan's spinning top and a rattle for Charles."

"You spoil her," she said, kissing the corner of his mouth. "And you spoil me."

"That I could never do. You bring light into every moment of my life, sweetheart." He stood up, reaching down a hand to pull her to her feet. "Let us go up to the house, and you may review the plays."

They walked silently, hand in hand, up to the house. Rosamund saw Kit in her mind's eye, prancing down the street, singing his ribald songs. She saw him at work in Thomas's study, his eyes burning with the power of his creation. She saw him with Thomas, the volatile temper that could move from embrace to antagonism in the blink of an eye. It occurred to her that she had always somehow known that he was too large a character, inhabited too much space in the world, burned too hot and bright, to live for long.

In the house Roger went up to the nursery with his gifts, and Rosamund settled onto the window seat in the bedchamber, the breeze from the river lifting her hair, cooling her cheeks. She untied the red ribbon around the rolled-up parchment from St. Paul's Churchyard and unfolded the sheets.

She smoothed them out, leafing through them. Then her hand stilled, her eyes fixed upon the name at the top of a sheet. A play by one William Creighton, newly licensed by the queen's Master of the Revels. A play entitled *The Hero's Return* to be put on at the Rose Theatre by Richard Burbage's company.

She sat staring at the sheet, seeing not the words but the unruly curls, the mischievous twitch to his mouth, the stunning blue of his eyes, something she saw every day in their daughter. She heard his voice as clearly as if he stood in the chamber with her.

Time passed and she was unaware of its passing, until her husband spoke from the open doorway. "What is it, Rosamund? You have not moved this hour."

She looked up, then back down at the paper in her lap. "There is a play here by someone I used to know . . . he died, in much the same way it seems that Kit did. A stupid tragedy . . . a mistake . . . being in the wrong place at the wrong time." She looked up again and a sheen of tears glazed her green eyes. "And he died not knowing that his play would finally be performed."

"Ah, I am sorry." He came swiftly to her, kneeling beside her, laying a hand on her shoulder. "What can I do?"

She smiled through her tears and put her own hand over his. "Just be here. That is all."

"I will," he promised, taking her hand, turning it up and pressing his lips into her palm. "Always."

They remained like that for several minutes, then Rosamund gently took back her hand. She rolled up the sheets again and tied them carefully with the ribbon. "Let us go down for supper, love. It grows late." She stood up, holding out her hand to him. He took it, drawing her into him for a moment, before hand in hand they left.

READERS CLUB GUIDE FOR

All the Queen's Players

BY JANE FEATHER

SUMMARY

Rosamund Walsingham is not your average sixteenth-century lady. Plucked from her simple country home by her conniving cousin, the secretary of state Sir Francis Walsingham, Rosamund is sent to London to spy on Queen Elizabeth's court. Francis asks her to gather information by keeping a sketchbook and diary of everything she observes and overhears in the queen's private chambers. Her work at the court leads to an unexpected romance with a young playwright and courtier, Will Creighton.

In the throes of romance, Rosamund's affair is discovered, and she is banished from Elizabeth's court, but Francis believes Rosamund can be of use to his cause of entrapping Mary, Queen of Scots, who is suspected of planning a conspiracy to assassinate Elizabeth and overtake the throne. But distance cannot shake Rosamund's feelings for Will, and serving Queen Mary teaches Rosamund what it means to be loyal and selfless even in the face of ruthlessness.

QUESTIONS AND TOPICS FOR DISCUSSION

1. Christopher "Kit" Marlowe says, "The world is not a pretty place. Why should anyone, man or woman, have to pretend that it is?" (p. 12). Rosamund learns this lesson early on in the story as she is forced from her quiet country life into the tough world of courtly existence. Was there a singular event you see as the moment of Rosamund's realization that this world is not an easy place—even in the seemingly perfect world of the queen's court? Who do you feel is most responsible for Rosamund's worldly education, and why?

2. Discuss Rosamund's connection with the theatre. What does it represent for her? The theatre is the setting where Will and Rosamund first fall in love, but without the theatre Rosamund would not have been caught in her affair with Will. Do you see the theatre more as escape or as entrapment for Rosamund?

3. What significance can you glean from the title *All the Queen's Players*? Who, in your opinion, were the most prominent of the queen's players? Would the title *All the Secretary's Players* also work? Who do you think had more control of the court—Elizabeth or Francis?

4. Rosamund successfully escapes from the palace disguised as a page by faking a stomach illness. She muses, "It hadn't occurred to anyone that a maid of honor would willingly forgo the delight of a trip on the river to Greenwich" (p. 230). Do you consider Rosamund an anti–maid of honor? Do you think

Rosamund considers herself different from the other ladies at court? To what extent?

5. How do Thomas and Kit factor into the story? Do you view them as minor characters or necessary to the integrity of the story? How much or how little do you think Thomas and Kit aided in Rosamund's discovery of love? Of happiness? Of survival?

6. The story opens with the death of Mary, Queen of Scots. Knowing that Mary is to die all along, are you more sympathetic to her plight? Consider the structure of the novel in your response.

7. Is Agathe a mentor to Rosamund? To what extent is she a positive influence? To what extent is she a negative influence? Do you think Rosamund would have fallen for Arnaud without Agathe's persuasion?

8. The struggle for power is a central theme in the novel. On page 125, Sir Francis advises Rosamund that "this world . . . runs on favors given and received. Remember that." Sir Francis uses an elaborate system of favors and threats as the means of maintaining his own considerable sphere of influence at court and beyond. Kit's play is likewise about this very struggle for power, something he believes that every man desires. Think of other examples of power struggles in the novel. Consider Thomas, Kit, Sir Francis, Elizabeth, Mary, Agathe, Arnaud, Frizer, Will, and Rosamund in your response, and how each of them struggles for their own version of power.

9. After Mary's cohorts' executions, Rosamund tells Lady Walsingham she "needed to make sense of the horror" (p. 393) by drawing the scene. Consider the ways in which drawing helps Rosamund understand the meaning of life. Is drawing a means of freedom for Rosamund? Does drawing also hinder Rosamund's freedom?

10. Discuss the significance of Rosamund losing her virginity in boys' clothing (p. 241). Was her new "identity" as Pip responsible for her newfound freedom or not? Agathe tells Rosamund that independence is the secret to happiness (p. 175). Is Rosamund able to be free—and therefore happy—dressed as Pip?

11. In All the Queen's Players, as in the theatre, appearances are never what they seem. For example, when Queen Mary's wig falls off in the first scene of the book, Rosamund is stunned to see that Mary's hair is short and gray underneath her gorgeous red wig. Think of other examples where things are not what they seem in the story. How does Jane Feather use this idea throughout the novel? For what purpose do you think the author uses theatrical devices? Is she successful?

12. Do you think Rosamund grew to care for Queen Mary, even love her? What did Mary teach Rosamund? Turn to pages 365–67 and discuss.

ACTIVITIES TO ENHANCE YOUR BOOK CLUB

1. Christopher Marlowe was a famous playwright and poet. He is considered one of the most important writers of the sixteenth century. Have each member of your book club pick up a copy of Marlowe's complete plays (Penguin, 2003) or poems (Penguin, 2007). Choose a poem or part of a play featured in the book and discuss. Can you find traces of Kit's character in the play or poem?

2. Queen Elizabeth's England is a popular topic in contemporary film. Rent *Elizabeth—The Golden Age* (2008), *Elizabeth* (2007), or *Mary, Queen of Scots* (2007) with your group and discuss the costumes and period diction. How are these depictions of Elizabethan life different from or similar to the world portrayed in *All the Queen's Players*?

3. *All the Queen's Players* explores some of the most interesting and provocative aspects of courtly life. Host a luncheon that Rosamund and the other maids of honors might have enjoyed. Have each member of your group research and make a recipe popular in sixteenth-century England. Over lunch, discuss the best and worst aspects of life in the queen's court.

4. Will and Rosamund's love shares many similarities with *Romeo and Juliet*. Go to a production of this famous love story if one is being performed near your town, or pick up a copy of the play or movie. Revisit the famous scenes, and compare and contrast with Will and Rosamund's story.

A Conversation with Jane Feather

Q. **You've written many historical romance novels. How did your experience writing those books impact your writing process on *All the Queen's Players*?**

A. I've always enjoyed the historical research involved, and this book, with its emphasis more on the history than on pure romance, offered more opportunity for in-depth research. I've always liked to have actual historical figures on the periphery of my novels, but with this one it was possible to make them central to the action and plot development. It was a wonderfully rich experience.

Q. **Rosamund is quite a dynamic young lady. Was her character inspired by anyone in history? By anyone in real life?**

A. I've always enjoyed creating women characters who stand out against the conventional lives expected of them in any particular historical period. Throughout history there are always real-life examples of strong, dynamic, and unconventional women to be found, and of course, during this period, Queen Elizabeth herself was the perfect example: a highly educated woman who ruled men, kept her country safe through some of its most turbulent times, practiced the most devious diplomacy, and avoided marriage because it would reduce her to the role of a mere consort rather than a most powerful sovereign.

Q. **Describe the research you had to do in order to correctly represent real-life characters such as Queen**

Elizabeth and Christopher Marlowe. Were there any interesting stories you came across about your characters that did not make it into the novel?

A. I was initially surprised at the number of scholarly books available about Marlowe's life and work, as I had thought very little was known about him apart from his writing. But dedicated scholars have pieced together a wonderful picture using scraps of information, including something as esoteric as his buttery accounts at Corpus Christi to support the theory of his activities with Sir Francis Walsingham. There is, of course, copious material available on Queen Elizabeth. I would have loved to incorporate more of the devious world of Walsingham's secret service and the detailed speculation about Marlowe's part in it. It reads like a detective story, and his death remains one of the great historical mysteries. Was his murder ordered by Essex? Was it ordered by Sir Francis Drake? Was someone trying to protect his own secrets? All of these are theories offered in explanation, and of course, there's the other little story about how Marlowe's death was faked, and he went on to live and write Shakespeare's plays.

Q. Who is your favorite character in the story and why? Do you relate particularly to any of the characters?

A. Kit Marlowe is my favorite, without question: an Elizabethan "roaring boy" whose extraordinary genius somehow blossomed despite his reckless, hot-tempered character. He killed at least one man in his short career, spent some time in prison, was accused of counterfeiting coins in the Low Countries, and yet was the acknowledged friend and confidant of some of the greatest scientific and literary minds of the period. And he died at twenty-nine, leaving the world to wonder, *What if?* As far as relating to a character is concerned, I probably relate more to Rosamund than to any other, although I am a lamentable artist!

Q. **How did you get started in your writing career? What is your background and what authors are your influences?**

A. My educational background is in clinical social work, rather a far cry from writing historical romances. But my real loves have always been history and literature, and I've always enjoyed writing stories. I have very eclectic tastes in authors, but in the field of historical novels I cut my teeth on Alexandre Dumas, Baroness Orczy, Daphne du Maurier, Georgette Heyer, Thackeray, Robert Graves . . . the list goes on.

Q. **Is Elizabethan England your favorite period in history? What other eras do you find intriguing?**

A. It's certainly a period I find fascinating, but there are many others. I am particularly enthralled by the English civil war period, the Restoration, Georgian England, the Napoleonic Wars.

Q. **You were born in Egypt, grew up in the south of England, and now live in Maryland. Explain how the various places you have lived have helped shape you as a writer.**

A. I was born in Egypt because my parents were stationed there, but as I left when I was three years old, I doubt it had much influence on me. I had a very "proper" English childhood and education, with a heavy emphasis on reading and literature. But I probably wouldn't have started writing novels if my husband and I had not taken the plunge and moved our family to the States in 1978. Shaking up life in one aspect makes it seem much easier to contemplate taking quite different paths in another.

Q. Your novel depicts a part of Elizabethan court life that we don't often see. Was it important to you to present an alternative point of view? Do you think your readers need this alternative portrayal of life at the queen's court?

A. A lot of romance has been written about the early Elizabethan days; rather less about the latter part of her reign, when she was a vain, raddled old woman with a penchant for the flattery of young men and a greedy delight in riches. I liked the idea of exploring that woman's world. Despite her faults, one can only admire from a distance all the incredible achievements of her reign, not least the fact that she survived to die a queen, and sole sovereign of one of the most powerful countries in the known world.

Q. Who is your favorite author? Who are you reading now?

A. I have many favorite authors; it would be impossible to pick any one. At the moment I'm reading *The Elegance of the Hedgehog* by Muriel Barbery.

Q. What is next for you? Are you currently working on anything?

A. I'm just beginning a romantic trilogy set in Georgian England toward the end of the eighteenth century.

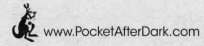